Streaker had been poking through a small gravitational tidepool, fifty thousand parsecs off the galactic plane, when she found the fleet.

Toshio sighed at the unfairness of it. One hundred and fifty dolphins, seven humans and a chimpanzee; how could we have known what we found?

Why did *we* have to find it?

Fifty thousand ships, each the size of a moon. That's what we found. The dolphins had been thrilled by their discovery—the biggest derelict fleet ever encountered, incredibly ancient. Captain Creideiki had psicast to Earth for instructions.

Dammit! *Why* did he call Earth? Couldn't the report have waited until we'd gone home? Why let the whole eavesdropping galaxy know you'd found a Sargasso of ancient hulks in the middle of nowhere?

The Terragens Council had answered in code:

"Go into hiding. Await orders. *Do not reply.*"

Creideiki obeyed, of course. But not before half the patron-lines in the galaxy had sent their warships to find them . . .

STARTIDE RISING
by
David Brin
author of *Sundiver*

STARTIDE RISING is an extraordinary achievement, a book so full of fascinating ideas that they would not have crowded each other at twice its considerable length."

—*Poul Anderson*

Bantam Books by David Brin
Ask your bookseller for the books you have missed

THE POSTMAN
THE PRACTICE EFFECT
STARTIDE RISING
SUNDIVER

STARTIDE RISING

David Brin

BANTAM BOOKS

TORONTO · NEW YORK · LONDON · SYDNEY · AUCKLAND

STARTIDE RISING
A Bantam Book / September 1983

Portions of this novel previously appeared in *Analog* (May 1981)
in a slightly different form under the title *The Tides of Kithrup*.

Poems by Yosa Buson from *Anthology of Japanese
Literature*, copyright 1955. Reprinted by permission
of Grove Press, Inc.

ISBN 0-553-23495-1

Published simultaneously in the United States and Canada

*Bantam Books are published by Bantam Books, Inc. Its trade-
mark, consisting of the words "Bantam Books" and the por-
trayal of a rooster, is Registered in U.S. Patent and Trademark
Office and in other countries. Marca Registrada. Bantam
Books, Inc., 666 Fifth Avenue, New York, New York 10103.*

PRINTED IN THE UNITED STATES OF AMERICA

O   098765

"To my own progenitors . . ."

Glossary
and
Cast of Characters

∞∞∞∞∞∞∞∞∞∞∞∞∞∞∞∞∞∞

Acceptor—A member of a Tandu client race. A psychic adept.

Akki (Ah-kee)—A dolphin midshipman from Calafia.

Beie Chohooan (Bay Choe-hoo-wan)—A Synthian spy.

Brookida (Broo-kee-dah)—A dolphin metallurgist.

Brothers of the Night—A Galactic patron race.

Gillian Baskin—A physician and agent for the Terragens Council. A product of human genetic engineering.

Calafia—A human/neo-dolphin colony world.

Client—A species that owes its full intelligence to genetic uplift by its patron race. An *indentured* client species is one which is still working off this debt.

Creideiki (Cry-dye-kee)—Captain of the exploration vessel *Streaker*.

Emerson D'Anite—A human engineer assigned to the *Streaker*.

Charles Dart—A neo-chimpanzee planetologist.

Derelict fleet—A drifting collection of giant starships, ancient and long undiscovered until found by the *Streaker*.

Episiarch—A member of a client race indentured to the Tandu. A psychic adept.

"Fin"—Vernacular for a neo-dolphin. ("Fen"—plural.)

"Fem"—Anglic term for a female human being.

Galactic—One of the senior starfaring species which comprise the community of the five galaxies. Many have become patron races, participating in the ancient tradition of uplift.

Gubru (Goo-broo)—A pseudo-avian Galactic race hostile to Earth.

Haoke (Ha-oh-kay)—A *Tursiops* neo-dolphin.

Herbie—The mummy of an ancient starfarer, of unknown origin.

Heurkea (Hee-urk-eeah)—A *Stenos* neo-dolphin.

Hikahi (Hee-kah-hee)—A female neo-dolphin, third in command of the *Streaker*.

Toshio Iwashika—A midshipman from the colony world Calafia.

Ifni—"Infinity" or Lady Luck.

Iki—An ancient island of death and destruction.

Kanten—One of a few Galactic species openly friendly to Earthmen.

Karrank% (Impossible for humans to pronounce properly)—A Galactic species so thoroughly modified during its indenture as a client race that it was driven insane.

Keeneenk—A hybrid school of discipline, combining logical, human-style thought with the heritage of the *Whale Dream*.

Keepiru (Kee-peer-ooh)—First pilot of the *Streaker*. A native of Atlast.

Kiqui (Kee-kwee)—Amphibious pre-sentient creatures native to the planet Kithrup.

K'tha-jon (K'thah-jon)—A special variant *Stenos* neo-dolphin. One of the *Streaker*'s petty officers.

Krat—Commander of the Soro forces.

Library—The information storehouse that holds Galactic society together; an archive of cross-referenced knowledge accumulated since the age of the Progenitors.

Makanee (Ma-kah-nay)—Ship's surgeon aboard the *Streaker*; a female neo-fin.

"Man"—Anglic term referring to both male and female human beings.

"Mel"—Anglic term referring specifically to a male human.

Ignacio Metz—An expert on uplift, assigned to the *Streaker*.

Moki (Moe-kee)—A *Stenos* neo-fin.

The Niss Machine—A pseudo-intelligent computer, lent to Thomas Orley by Tymbrimi agents.

Thomas Orley—An agent of the Terragens Council and a product of mild genetic engineering.

Pila—A Galactic patron race, part of the Soro clan and hostile to Earth.

Primal—The semi-language used by natural, unmodified dolphins on Earth.

Progenitors—The mythical first species, who established Galactic culture and the *Library* several billion years ago.

Sah'ot (Sah-ote)—A *Stenos* neo-dolphin. A civilian linguist onboard the *Streaker*.

Shallow Cluster—A seldom-visited, unpopulated globular cluster, where the derelict fleet was discovered.

Soro—A senior Galactic patron race hostile to Earth.

Stenos—A vernacular term for neo-fins whose genes include grafts from natural *Stenos bredanensis* dolphins.

Stenos bredanensis—A species of natural dolphins on Earth.

Dennie Sudman—A human exobiologist.

Hannes Suessi—A human engineer.

Synthian—A member of one of three Galactic races friendly to Earth.

Tandu—A militant Galactic species hostile to Earth.

Takkata-Jim (Tah-kah-tah-jim)—A *Stenos* neo-fin, Vice-Captain of the *Streaker*.

Thennanin (Thenn-an-in)—A militant Galactic species.

Tsh't (Tish-oot)—A female neo-fin, the *Streaker*'s fourth officer.

Tursiops—A vernacular word for neo-dolphins without *Stenos* gene grafts.

Tursiops amicus—A modern neo-dolphin. "Friendly bottlenose."

Tursiops truncatus—Natural bottlenose dolphins on Earth.

Tymbrimi (Tim-brye-me)—A Galactic race friendly to Earthmen, renowned for its cleverness.

Uplift—The process by which older spacefaring races bring
new species into Galactic culture, through breeding and
genetic engineering. The resulting client species serves
its patron for a period of indenture to pay for this
favor.

Wattaceti—A neo-fin non-commissioned officer.

STARTIDE RISING

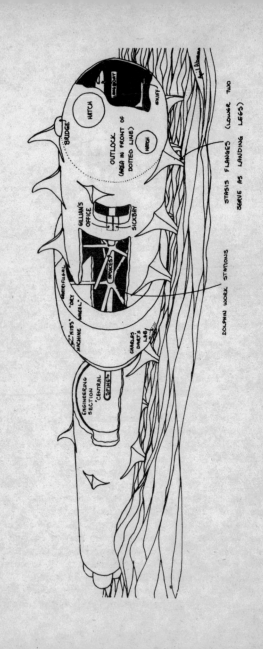

BRIDGE

HATCH

OUTLOCK
(AREA IN FRONT OF
DOTTED LINE)

SKIFF

HATCH

VILLIAM'S OFFICE

SICKBAY

SPOKES

'BESS' CENTRIFUGAL MACHINE 'DRY WHEEL'

CHARLIE'S D'ARCY'S LAB

ENGINEERING SECTION

'CENTRAL SPINE'

STASIS FLANGES (LOWER TWO
SERVE AS LANDING LEGS)

DOLPHIN WORK STATIONS

Prologue

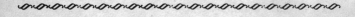

FROM THE JOURNAL OF GILLIAN BASKIN

Streaker is limping like a dog on three legs.

We took a chancy jump through overdrive yesterday, a step ahead of the Galactics who are chasing us. The one probability coil that had survived the Morgran battle groaned and complained, but finally delivered us here, to the shallow gravity well of a small population-II dwarf star named Kthsemenee.

The Library lists one habitable world in orbit, the planet Kithrup.

When I say "habitable," it's with charity. Tom, Hikahi, and I spent hours with the captain, looking for alternatives. In the end, Creideiki decided to bring us here.

As a physician, I dread landing on a planet as insidiously dangerous as this one, but Kithrup is a water world, and our mostly-dolphin crew needs water to be able to move about and repair the ship. Kithrup is rich in heavy metals, and should have the raw materials we need.

It also has the virtue of being seldom visited. The Library says it's been fallow for a very long time. Maybe the Galactics won't think to look for us here.

I said as much to Tom last night, as he and I held hands and watched the planet's disc grow larger in one of the lounge ports. It's a deceptively lovely blue globe, swathed in bands of white clouds. The night side was lit in patches by dimly glowing volcanoes and flickering lightning.

I told Tom that I was sure no one would follow us here—pronouncing the prediction confidently, and fooling

1

nobody. Tom smiled and said nothing, humoring my bout of wishful thinking.

They'll look here, of course. There were only a few interspatial paths Streaker could have taken without using a transfer point. The only question is, can we get our repairs finished in time, and get away from here before the Galactics come for us?

Tom and I had a few hours to ourselves, our first in days. We went back to our cabin and made love.

While he sleeps, I'm making this entry. I don't know when I'll have another chance.

Captain Creideiki just called. He wants both of us up on the bridge, I suppose so the fins can see us and know their human patrons are nearby. Even a competent dolphin spacer like Creideiki might feel the need from time to time.

If only we humans had that psychological refuge.

Time to put this down and awaken my tired fellow. But first, I want to jot down what Tom said to me last night, while we watched Kithrup's stormy seas.

He turned to me, smiled that funny way he does when he thinks of something ironic, and whistled a brief haiku in dolphin-Trinary.

> * *The stars shake with storms*
> > * *The waters below roll thunder—*
> > > * *Still, are we wet, love?* *

I had to laugh. Sometimes I think Tom is half dolphin.

PART ONE

Buoyancy

*"All your better deeds
shall be
in water writ ..."*

—Francis Beaumont
and John Fletcher

1

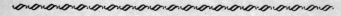

Toshio

Fins had been making wisecracks about human beings for thousands of years. They had *always* found men terribly funny. The fact that humanity had meddled with their genes and taught them engineering hadn't done much to change their attitude.

Fins were still smart-alecks.

Toshio watched the small instrument panel of his sea-sled, pretending to check the depth gauge. The sled thrummed along at a constant ten meters below the surface. There were no adjustments to be made, yet he concentrated on the panel as Keepiru swam up alongside—undoubtedly to start another round of teasing.

"Little Hands, whistle!" The sleek, gray cetacean did a barrel roll to Toshio's right, then drew nearer to eye the boy casually. "Whistle us a tune about shipsss and space and going home!"

Keepiru's voice, echoing from a complex set of chambers under his skull, rumbled like the groaning of a bassoon. He could just as well have imitated an oboe, or a tenor sax.

"Well, Little Hands? Where is your sssong?"

Keepiru was making sure the rest of the party could hear. The other fins swam quietly, but Toshio could tell they were listening. He was glad that Hikahi, the leader of the expedition, was far ahead, scouting. It would be far worse if she were here and ordered Keepiru to leave him alone. Nothing Keepiru said could match the shame of being protected like a helpless child.

5

Keepiru rolled lazily, belly up, next to the boy's sled, kicking slow fluke strokes to stay easily abreast of Toshio's machine. In the crystal-clear water of Kithrup, everything seemed strangely refracted. The coral-like peaks of the metal-mounds shimmered as though mountains seen through the haze of a long valley. Drifting yellow tendrils of dangle-weed hung from the surface.

Keepiru's gray skin had a phosphorescent sheen, and the needle-sharp teeth in his long, narrow, vee mouth shone with a teasing cruelty that *had* to be magnified . . . if not by the water, then by Toshio's own imagination.

How could a fin be so mean?

"Won't you sing for us, Little Hands? Sing us a song that will buy us all fish-brew when we finally get off this ssso-called planet and find a friendly port! Whistle to make the Dreamers dream of land!"

Above the tiny whine of his air-recycler, Toshio's ears buzzed with embarrassment. At any moment, he was sure, Keepiru would stop calling him Little Hands and start using the new nickname he had chosen: "Great Dreamer."

It was bad enough to be taunted for having made the mistake of whistling when accompanying an exploration crew of fins—they had greeted his absentminded melody with razzberries and chittering derision—but to be mockingly addressed by a title almost always reserved for great musicians or humpback whales . . . it was almost more than he could bear.

"I don't feel like singing right now, Keepiru. Why don't you go bother somebody else?" Toshio felt a small sense of victory in managing to keep a quaver out of his voice.

To Toshio's relief, Keepiru merely squeaked something high and fast in gutter Trinary, almost Primal Delphin—that in itself a form of insult. Then the dolphin arched and shot away to surface for air.

The water on all sides was bright and blue. Shimmering Kithrupan fish flicked past with scaled backs that faceted the light like drifting, frosted leaves. All around were the various colors and textures of metal. The morning sunshine penetrated the clear, steady sea to glimmer off the peculiar life forms of this strange and inevitably deadly world.

Toshio had no eye for the beauty of Kithrup's waters. Hating the planet, the crippled ship that had brought him here, and the fins who were his fellow castaways, he drifted

into a poignantly satisfying rehearsal of the scathing retorts he
should have said to Keepiru.

"If you're so good, Keepiru, why don't you whistle us up
some vanadium!" Or, "I see no point in wasting a *human* song
on a dolphin audience, Keepiru."

In his imagination the remarks were satisfyingly effective.
In the real world, Toshio knew, he could never say anything
like that.

First of all, it was the cetacean, not the anthropoid,
whose vocalizings were legal tender in a quarter of the
spaceports in the galaxy. And while it was the mournful
ballads of the larger cousins, the whales, that brought the real
prices, Keepiru's kin could buy intoxicants on any of a dozen
worlds merely by exercising their lungs.

Anyway, it would be a terrible mistake to try to pull
human rank on any of the crew of the *Streaker*. Old Hannes
Suessi, one of the other six humans aboard, had warned him
about that just after they had left Neptune, at the beginning
of the voyage.

"Try it and see what happens," the mechanic had suggested.
"They'll laugh so hard, and so will *I*, if I have the good luck to
be there when you do. Likely as not, one of them will take a
nip at you for good measure! If there's anything fins don't
respect, it's a human who never earned the right, putting on
patron airs."

"But the Protocols . . ." Toshio had started to protest.

"Protocols my left eye! Those rules were set up so
humans and chimps and fins will act in just the right way
when Galactics are around. If the *Streak* gets stopped by a
Soro patrol, or has to ask a Pilan Librarian for data somewhere,
then Dr. Metz or Mr. Orley—or even you or I—might have
to pretend we're in charge . . . because none of those stuffed-
shirt Eatees would give the time of day to a race as young as
fins are. But the rest of the time we take our orders from
Captain Creideiki.

"Hell, that'd be hard enough—taking brown from a Soro
and pretending you like it because the damned ET is nice
enough to admit that *humans*, at least, are a bit above the
level of fruit flies. Can you imagine how hard it would be if
we actually had to *run* this ship? What if we had tried to
make dolphins into a nice, well-behaved, slavey client race?
Would you have liked that?"

At the time Toshio had shaken his head vigorously. The

idea of treating fins as clients were usually treated in the galaxy was repulsive. His best friend, Akki, was a fin.

Yet, there were moments like the present, when Toshio wished there were compensations for being the only human boy on a starship crewed mostly by adult dolphins.

A starship which wasn't going anywhere at the moment, Toshio reminded himself. The acute resentment of Keepiru's goading was replaced by the more persistent, hollow worry that he might never leave the water world of Kithrup and see home.

* Slow your travel—boy sled-rider *
* Exploring pod—does gather hither *
* Hikahi comes—we wait here for her *

Toshio looked up. Brookida, the elderly dolphin metal-lurgist, had come up alongside on the left. Toshio whistled a reply in Trinary.

* Hikahi comes—my sled is stopping *

He eased the sled's throttle back.

On his sonar screen Toshio saw tiny echoes converging from the sides and far ahead. The scouts were returning. He looked up and saw Hist-t and Keepiru playing at the surface.

Brookida switched to Anglic. Though somewhat shrill and stuttered, it was still better than Toshio's Trinary. Dolphins, after all, had been modified by generations of genetic engineering to take up human styles, not the other way around.

"You've found no t-traces of the needed substances, Toshio?" Brookida asked.

Toshio glanced at the molecular sieve. "No, sir. Nothing so far. This water is almost unbelievably pure, considering the metal content of the planet's crust. There are hardly any heavy metal salts at all."

"And nothing on the long ssscan?"

"No resonance effects on any of the bands I've been checking, though the noise level is awfully high. I'm not sure I'd even be able to pick out monopole-saturated nickel, let alone the other stuff we're looking for. It's like trying to find that needle in a haystack."

It was a paradox. The planet had metals in superabundance. That was one reason Captain Creideiki had chosen this world as a refuge. Yet the water was relatively pure... pure enough to allow the dolphins to swim freely, although some complained of itching, and each would need chelating treatments when he got back to the ship.

The explanation lay all around them, in the plants and fishes.

Calcium did not make up the bones of Kithrupan life forms. Other metals did. The water was strained and sieved clean by biological filters. As a result, the sea shone all around with the bright colors of metal and oxides of metal. The gleaming dorsal spines of living fish—the silvery seed-pods of underwater plants—all contrasted with the more mundane green of chlorophyllic leaves and fronds.

Dominating the scenery were the metal-mounds, giant, spongy islands shaped by millions of generations of coral-like creatures, whose metallo-organic exoskeletons accumulated into huge, flat-topped mountains rising a few meters above the mean water mark.

Atop the islands the drill-trees grew, sending their metal-tipped roots through each mound to harvest organics and silicates from below. The trees laid a non-metallic layer on top and created a cavity underneath the metal mound. It was a strange pattern. *Streaker*'s onboard *Library* had offered no explanation.

Toshio's instruments had detected clumps of pure tin, mounds of chromium fish eggs, coral colonies built from a variety of bronze, but so far no convenient, easily gathered piles of vanadium. No lumps of the special variety of nickel they sought.

What they needed was a miracle—one which would enable a crew of dolphins, with the aid of seven humans and a chimpanzee, to repair their ship and get the hell out of this part of the galaxy before their pursuers caught up with them.

At best, they had a few weeks to get away. The alternative was capture by any of a dozen not-entirely-rational ET races. At worst it could mean interstellar war on a scale not seen in a million years.

It all made Toshio feel small, helpless, and very young.

Toshio could hear, faintly, the high-pitched sonar echoes of the returning scouts. Each distant squeak had its tiny, colored counterpoint on his scanner screen.

Then two gray forms appeared from the east, diving at

last into the gathering above, cavorting, playfully leaping and biting.

Finally one of the dolphins arched and dove straight down toward Toshio. "Hikahi's coming and wants the sssled topside," Keepiru chattered quickly, slurring the words almost into indecipherability. "Try not to get lost on the way up-p-p-p."

Toshio grimaced as he vented ballast. Keepiru didn't have to make his contempt so obvious. Even speaking Anglic normally, fins usually sounded as if they were giving the listener a long series of razzberries.

The sled rose in a cloud of tiny bubbles. When he reached the surface, water drained along the sides of the sled in long, gurgling rivulets. Toshio locked the throttle and rolled over to undo his faceplate.

The sudden silence was a relief. The whine of the sled, the pings of the sonar, and the squeaks of the fins all vanished. The fresh breeze swept past his damp, straight, black hair and cooled the hot feeling in his ears. It carried the scents of an alien planet—the pungence of secondary growth on an older island, the heavy, oily odor of a drill-tree in its peak of activity.

And overlying everything was the slight tang of metal.

It shouldn't harm them, they'd said back at the ship, least of all Toshio in his waterproof suit. Chelating would remove all of the heavy elements one might reasonably expect to absorb on a scouting trip . . . though no one knew for sure what other hazards this world might offer.

But if they were forced to stay for months? Years?

In that case the medical facilities of the *Streaker* would not be able to deal with the slow accumulation of metals. In time they would start to pray for the Jophur, or Thennanin, or Soro ships to come and take them away for interrogation or worse—simply to get off a beautiful planet that was slowly killing them.

It wasn't a pleasant thought to dwell on. Toshio was glad when Brookida drifted alongside the sled.

"Why did Hikahi have me come up to the surface?" he asked the elderly dolphin. "I thought I was to stay out of sight below in case there were already spy-sats overhead."

Brookida sighed. "I suppose she thinkss you need a break. Besides, who could spot as small a machine as the ssled, with so much metal around?"

Toshio shrugged. "Well, it was nice of Hikahi, anyway. I did need the rest."

Brookida rose up in the water, balancing upon a series of churning tail-strokes. "I hear Hikahi," he announced. "And here she isss."

Two dolphins came in fast from the north, one light gray in appearance, the other dark and mottled. Through his headphones Toshio could hear the voice of the party leader.

     * *Flame-fluked I—Hikahi call you* *
     * *Dorsal listening—ventral doing* *
     * *Laugh at my words—but first obey them* *
     * *Gather at the sled—and listen!* *

Hikahi and Ssattatta circled the rest of the party once, then came to rest in front of the assembled expedition.

Among mankind's gifts to the neo-dolphin had been an expanded repertoire of facial expression. A mere five hundred years of genetic engineering could not do for the porpoise what a million years of evolution had done for man. Fins still expressed most of their feelings in sound and motion. But they were no longer frozen in what humans had taken (in some degree of truth) to be a grin of perpetual amusement. Fins were capable now of *looking* worried. Toshio might have chosen Hikahi's present expression as a classic example of delphin chagrin.

"Phip-pit has disappeared," Hikahi announced.

"I heard him cry out, over to the south of me, then nothing. He was searching for Ssassia, who disappeared earlier in the same direction. We will forego mapping and metals search to go and find them. All will be issued weaponss."

There was a general sussuration of discontent. It meant the fins would have to put on the harnesses they had only just had the pleasure of removing, on leaving the ship. Still, even Keepiru recognized this was urgent business.

Toshio was briefly busy dropping harnesses into the water. They were supposed to spread naturally into a shape suitable for a dolphin to slip into easily, but inevitably one or two fins needed help fitting his harness to the small nerve amplifier socket each had just above his left eye.

Toshio finished the job quickly, with the unconscious ease of long practice. He was worried about Ssassia, a gentle fin who had always been kind and soft-spoken to him.

"Hikahi," he said as the leader swam past, "do you want me to call the ship?"

The small gray *Tursiops* female rose up to face Toshio. "Negative, Ladder-runner. We obey orders. Spy-sats may be high already. Set your speed sled to return on auto if we fail to survive what is in the sssoutheast."

"But no one's seen any big animals..."

"That-t is only one possibility. I want word to get back whatever our doom... should even rescue fever strike us all."

Toshio felt cold at the mention of "rescue fever." He had heard of it, of course. It was something he had no desire at all to witness.

They set out to the southeast in skirmish formation. The fins took turns gliding along the surface, then diving to swim alongside Toshio. The ocean bottom was like an endless series of snake tracks—pitted by strange pock-holes like deep craters, darkly ominous. In the valleys Toshio could usually see bottom, a hundred meters or so below, gloomy with dark blue tendrils.

The long ridges were topped at intervals by the shining metal-mounds, like hulking castles of shimmering, spongy armor. Many were covered with thick, ivy-like growths in which Kithrupan fishes nested and bred. One metal-mound appeared to be teetering on the edge of a precipice—the cavern dug by its own tall drill-tree, ready to swallow the entire fortress when the undermining was done.

The sled's engine hummed hypnotically. Keeping track of his instruments was too simple a task to keep Toshio's mind busy. Without really wishing to, he found himself thinking. Remembering.

A simple adventure, that's what it had seemed when they had asked him to come along on the space voyage. He had already taken the Jumpers' Oath, so they knew he was ready to leave his past behind. And they needed a midshipman to help with hand-eye work on the new dolphin ship.

Streaker was a small exploratory vessel of unique design. There weren't many finned, oxygen-breathing races flying ships in interstellar space. Those few used artificial gravity for convenience, and leased members of some client species to act as crafters and handmen.

But the first dolphin-crewed starship had to be different.

It was designed around a principle which had guided Earthlings for two centuries: "Whenever possible, keep it simple. Avoid using the science of the Galactics when you don't understand it."

Two hundred and fifty years after contact with Galactic civilization, mankind was still struggling to catch up. The Galactic species which had been using the aeons-old *Library* since before the first mammals appeared on Earth—adding to that universal compendium of knowledge with glacial slowness—had seemed almost god-like to the primitive Earthmen in their early, lumbering slowships. Earth had a branch *Library*, now, supposedly giving her access to all of the wisdom accumulated over Galactic history. But only in recent years had it proven to be much more a help than a confusing hindrance.

Streaker, with its complex arrangements of centrifugally held pools and weightless workshops, must have seemed incredibly archaic to the aliens who had looked it over just before launch. Still, to Earth's neo-dolphin communities, she was an object of great pride.

After her shakedown cruise, *Streaker* stopped at the small human-dolphin colony of Calafia to pick up a few of the best graduates of its tiny academy. It was to be Toshio's first, and possibly last, visit to old Earth.

"Old Earth" was still home to ninety percent of humanity, not to mention the other terrestrial sapient races. Galactic tourists still thronged in to gawk at the home of the *enfants terribles* who had caused such a stir in a few brief centuries. They were open in their wagering over how long Mankind would survive without the protection of a patron.

All species had patrons, of course. Nobody reached spacefaring intelligence without the intervention of another spacefaring race. Had not men done this for chimps and dolphins? All the way back to the time of the Progenitors, the mythical first race, every species that spoke and flew spaceships had been raised up by a predecessor. No species still survived from that distant era, but the civilization the Progenitors established, with its all-encompassing *Library,* went on.

Of the fate of the Progenitors themselves there were many legends and even violently contradicting religions.

Toshio wondered, as just about everyone had for three hundred years, what the patrons of Man might have been like. If they ever existed. Might they even be one of the species of fanatics that had ambushed the unsuspecting *Streaker*, and even now sought her out like hounds after a fox?

It wasn't a pleasant line of thought, considering what the *Streaker* had discovered.

The Terragens Council had sent her out to join a scattered fleet of exploration vessels, checking the veracity of the *Library*. So far only a few minor gaps had been found in its thoroughness. Here a star misplaced. There a species miscatalogued. It was like finding that someone had written a list describing every grain of sand on a beach. You could never check the complete list in a thousand lifetimes of a race, but you could take a random sampling.

Streaker had been poking through a small gravitational tide pool, fifty thousand parsecs off the galactic plane, when she found the Fleet.

Toshio sighed at the unfairness of it. One hundred and fifty dolphins, seven humans, and a chimpanzee; how could we have known what we found?

Why did *we* have to find it?

Fifty thousand ships, each the size of a moon. That's what they found. The dolphins had been thrilled by their discovery—the biggest Derelict Fleet ever encountered, apparently incredibly ancient. Captain Creideiki had psicast to Earth for instructions.

Dammit! *Why* did he call Earth? Couldn't the report have waited until we'd gone home? Why let the whole eavesdropping galaxy know you'd found a Sargasso of ancient hulks in the middle of nowhere?

The Terragens Council had answered in code.

"Go into hiding. Await orders. Do not reply."

Creideiki obeyed, of course. But not before half the patron-lines in the galaxy had sent out their warships to find *Streaker*.

Toshio blinked.

Something. A resonance echo at last? Yes, the magnetic ore detector showed a faint echo toward the south. He concentrated on the receiver, relieved at last to have something to do. Self-pity was becoming a bore.

Yes. It would have to be a pretty fair deposit. Should he tell Hikahi? Naturally, the search for the missing crewfen came first, but...

A shadow fell across him. The party was skirting the

edge of a massive metal-mound. The copper-colored mass was covered with thick tendrils of some green hanging growth.

"Don't go too close, Little Hands," Keepiru whistled from Toshio's left. Only Keepiru and the sled were this close to the mound. The other fins were giving it a wide berth.

"We know nothing of this flora," Keepiru continued. "And it'ss near here that Phip-pit was lost. You should stay safe within our convoy." Keepiru rolled lazily past Toshio, keeping up with languid fluke strokes. The neatly folded arms of his harness gleamed a coppery reflection from the metal-mound.

"Then it's all the more important to get samples, isn't it?" Toshio replied in irritation. "It's what we're out here for, anyway!" Without giving Keepiru time to react, Toshio banked the sled toward the shadowy mass of the mound.

Toshio dove into a region of darkness as the island blocked off the afternoon sunlight. A drifting school of silver-backed fish seemed to explode away from him as he drove at an angle along the thick, fibrous weed.

Keepiru squeaked in startlement behind him, an oath in Primal Delphin, which showed the fin's distress. Toshio smiled.

The sled hummed cooperatively as the mound loomed like a mountain on his right. Toshio banked and grabbed at the nearest flash of green. There was a satisfying snapping sensation as his sample came free in his hand. No fin could do that! He flexed his fingers appreciatively, then twisted about to stuff the clump into a collection sack.

Toshio looked up and saw that the green mass, instead of receding, was closer than ever. Keepiru's squawling was louder.

Crybaby! Toshio thought. *So I let the controls drift for a second. So what? I'll be back in your damned convoy before you finish making up a cuss-poem.*

He steepened his leftward bank and simultaneously set his bow planes to rise. In a moment he realized it was a tactical mistake. For it slowed him down just enough for the cluster of pursuing tendrils to reach his sled.

There must have been larger sea creatures on Kithrup than the party had seen so far, for the tentacles that fell about Toshio were obviously meant to catch big prey.

"Oh, Koino-Anti! Now I've done it!" He pushed the throttle over to maximum and braced for the expected surge of power.

Power came... but not acceleration. The sled groaned, stretching the long, ropy strands. But forward movement was lost. Then the engine died. Toshio felt a slithery presence across his legs, then another. The tendrils began to tighten and pull.

Gasping, he managed to twist around onto his back, and groped for the knife sheathed at his thigh. The tendrils were sinuous and knotty. The knots clung to whatever they touched, and when one brushed against the back of Toshio's exposed left hand the boy cried out from the searing pain of contact.

The fins were crying out to each other, and there were sounds of vigorous movement not far away. But other than a brief hope that nobody else was caught, Toshio had little time to think of anything but the fight at hand.

The knife came free, gleaming like hope. And hope brought hope as two small strands parted under his slashing attack. Another, larger, one, took several seconds to saw through. It was replaced almost instantly by two more.

Then he saw the place to which he was being drawn.

A deep gash split the side of the metal-mound. Inside, a writhing mass of filaments awaited. Deep within, a dozen meters farther up, something sleek and gray lay already enmeshed in a forest of deceptively languid foliage.

Toshio felt open-mouthed steam fill his facemask. The reflection of his own eyes, dilated and stricken, was superimposed on the motionless figure of Ssassia. Gentle as her life had been, though not her death, the tide rocked her.

With a cry, Toshio resumed hacking. He wanted to call out to Hikahi—to let the party leader know of Ssassia's fate—but all that came out was a roar of loathing of the Kithrupan creeper. Leaves and fronds flew off through the churning water as he sliced out his hatred, but to little good, as the tendrils fell more numerous about him to draw him toward the gash.

* Ladder climber—Sharp-eyed rhymer *
* Call a fix—for seeking finders *
* Trill sonar—through the leaf blinders *

Hikahi calling.

Above the churning of his struggle and the hoarseness of his breath, Toshio could hear the combat sounds of dolphin teamwork. Quick trills of Trinary, unslowed for human ears except for that one brief command, and the whining of their harnesses.

"Here! Here I am!" He slashed at a leafy vine that threatened his air hose, barely missing the hose itself. He licked his lips and tried to whistle in Trinary.

* Holding off—the sea-squid's beak *
* Suckers tight—and outlook bleak *
* Havoc done—on Ssassia wreaked! *

Lousy form and rhythm, but the fins would hear it better than they would a shout in Anglic. After only forty generations of sapience, they still thought better in an emergency when using whistle rhyme.

Toshio could hear the sounds of combat coming closer. But, as if hurried by the threat, the tentacles began drawing him back more rapidly, toward the gash. Suddenly a sucker-covered strand wrapped itself around his right arm. Before he could shift his grip, one of the burning knots reached his hand. He screamed and tore the tendril away, but the knife was lost into the darkness.

Other filaments were falling all about him. At that moment Toshio became distantly aware that someone was *talking* to him, slowly, and in Anglic!

". . . says there are ships out there! Vice-Captain Takkata-Jim wants to know why Hikahi hasn't sent a monopulse confirmation . . ."

It was *Akki's* voice, calling from the ship! Toshio couldn't answer his friend. The switch for the sled radio was out of reach, and he was a bit preoccupied.

"Don't respond to this message," Akki went on obligingly. Toshio moaned at the irony as he tried to pry a tendril off his facemask without doing further insult to his hands. "Just transmit a monopulse and come on back-k, all of you. We think there's a space battle going on over Kithrup. Probably those crazy ETs followed us here and are fighting over the right to capture us, just like at Morgran.

"Gotta c-close up, now. Radio silence. Get back as soon as you can. Akki out."

Toshio felt a tendril seize hold of his air hose. A solid grip, this time.

"Sure, Akki, old friend," he grunted as he pulled at it.

"I'll be going home just as soon as the universe lets me."

The air hose was crimped shut, and there was nothing he could do. Fog filled his facemask. As he felt himself blacking out, Toshio thought he saw the rescue party arrive, but he couldn't be sure if it was real or a hallucination. He wouldn't have expected *Keepiru* to lead the charge, for instance, or for that fin to have such a ferocious demeanor, heedless of the burning suckers.

In the end, he decided it was a dream. The laser flashes were too bright, the saser tones too clear. And the party came toward him with pennants waving in their wake like the cavalry that five centuries of Anglic-speaking man had come to associate with the image of rescue.

2

Galactics

On a ship in the center of a fleet of ships, a phase of denial was passing.

Giant cruisers spilled out of a rent in space, to fall toward the pinpoint brilliance of a non-descript reddish sun. One by one, they tumbled from the luminous tear. With them came diffracted starlight from their point of departure, hundreds of parsecs away.

There were rules that should have prevented it. The tunnel was an unnatural way to pass from place to place. It took a strong will to deny nature and call into being such an opening in space.

The Episiarch, in its outraged rejection of What Is, had created the passage for its Tandu masters. The opening was held by the adamant power of its ego—by its refusal to concede anything at all to Reality.

When the last ship was through, the Episiarch was purposely distracted, and the hole collapsed with soundless *violence. In moments, only instruments could tell that it had ever been. The affront to physics was erased.*

The Episiarch had brought the Tandu armada to the target star well ahead of the other fleets, those who would challenge the Tandu for the right to capture the Earth ship. The Tandu sent impulses of praise to the Episiarch's pleasure centers. It howled and waved its great furry head in gratitude.

To the Tandu, an obscure and dangerous form of travel had once again proved worth the risks. It was good to arrive on the battlefield before the enemy. The added moments would give them a tactical edge.

The Episiarch only wanted things to deny. Its task now finished, it was returned to its chamber of delusions, to alter an endless chain of surrogate realities until its outrage was needed by the Masters once again. Its shaggy, amorphous shape rolled free of the sensory web, and it shambled off, escorted by wary guardians.

When the way was clear, the Acceptor entered, and climbed on spindly legs to its place within the web.

For a long moment it appraised Reality, embracing it. The Acceptor probed and touched and caressed this new region of space with its farflung senses. It gave out a crooning cry of pleasure.

"Such leakage!" the Acceptor joyously announced. "I had heard the hunted were sloppy sophonts, but they leak even as they scan for danger! They have hidden on the second planet. Only slowly do the edges of their psychic shields congeal to hide from me their exact location. Who were their masters, to teach these dolphins so well to be prey?"

"Their masters are the humans, themselves unfinished," the Leading Stalker of the Tandu replied. Its voice was a rhythmic pattern of rapid clicks and pops from the ratchet joints of its mantis-legs. "The Earthlings are tainted by wrong belief, and by the shame of their own abandonment. The noise of three centuries shall be quieted when they are eaten. Then our hunter's joy will be as yours is, when you witness a new place or thing."

"Such joy," the Acceptor agreed.

"Now stir to get details," the Stalker commanded. "Soon we do battle with heretics. I must tell your fellow clients their tasks."

The Acceptor turned in the web as the Stalker left, and

opened its feelings to this new patch of reality. Everything was good. It passed on reports of what it saw, and the Masters moved the ships in response, but with the larger part of its mind it appreciated . . . it accepted . . . the tiny red sun, each of its small planets, the delicious expectancy of a place soon to become a battlefield.

Soon it felt the other war fleets enter the system, each in its own peculiar way. Each took a slightly inferior position, forced by the early arrival of the Tandu.

The Acceptor sensed the lusts of warrior clients and the cool calculations of calmer elders. It caressed the slickness of mind shields rigidly held against it, and wondered what went on within them. It appreciated the openness of other combatants, who disdainfully cast their thoughts outward, daring the listener to gather in their broadcast contempt.

It swept up savage contemplations of the Acceptor's own annihilation, as the great fleets plunged toward each other and bright explosions began to flash.

The Acceptor took it all in joyfully. How could anyone feel otherwise, when the universe held such wonders?

3

∽∾∽∾∽∾∽∾∽∾∽∾∽∾∽∾∽∾∽∾∽∾∽∾∽∾∽∾

Takkata-Jim

High in the port quarter of *Streaker*'s spherical control room, a psi operator thrashed in her harness. Her flukes made a turmoil of the water, and she cried out in Trinary.

  * *The inky, eight-armed, squid-heads find us!* *
  * *Ripping pods of them do battle!* *

The operator's report confirmed the discovery made by the neutrino detector only minutes before. It was a litany of bad news, related in trance-verse.

> * *They scream and lust—*
>   *To win and capture . . .* *

From another station came a calmer bulletin in dolphin-accented Anglic.

"We're getting heavy graviton traffic, Vice-Captain Takkata-Jim. Gravitational disturbances confirm a major battle is forming up not far from the planet-t."

The executive officer of the *Streaker* listened to the report quietly, letting himself drift sideways slightly in the circulating currents of the command center. A stream of bubbles emerged from his blowhole as he inhaled some of the special fluid that filled the ship's bridge.

"Acknowledged," he said at last. Underwater, his voice was a muted buzz. The consonants came out slurred. "How far away is the nearest contact?"

"Five AU, sssir. They couldn't get here for at leasst an hour, even if they came hell-bent."

"Hmmm. Very well, then. Remain in condition yellow. Continue your observationsss, Akeakemai."

The vice-captain was unusually large for a neo-fin, thick-bodied and muscular where most of the others were sleek and narrow. His uneven gray coloring and jagged teeth were marks of the *Stenos* sub-racial line, setting him and a number of others aboard apart from the *Tursiops* majority.

The human next to Takkata-Jim was impassive as the bad news came. It only confirmed what he had already feared.

"We had better inform the captain, then," Ignacio Metz said. The words were amplified by his facemask into the fizzing water. Bubbles floated away from the tall human's sparse gray hair.

"I warned Creideiki this would happen if we tried eluding the Galactics. I only hope he decides to be reasonable, now that escape's become impossible."

Takkata-Jim opened and closed his foodmouth diagonally, an emphatic nod.

"Yesss, Doctor Metz. Now even Creideiki must recognize that you were right. We're cornered now, and the captain will have no choice but to listen to you."

Metz nodded, gratified. "What about Hikahi's team? Have they been told?"

"I've already ordered the prospecting party back. Even the sled might be too much of a risssk. If the Eatees are already in orbit they might have means to detect it."

"Extraterrestrials . . ." Metz corrected, automatically professorial. "The term 'Eatee' is hardly polite."

Takkata-Jim kept an impassive face. He was in command of the ship and its crew while the captain was off watch. Yet the human treated him like a fresh-weaned pupil. It was quite irritating, but Takkata-Jim was careful never to let Metz know how much it bothered him. "Yes, Dr. Metz," he said.

The man went on. "Hikahi's party should never have left the ship. I warned Tom Orley that something like this might happen. Young Toshio's out there . . . and all those crewfen, out of contact with us for so long. It would be *terrible* if anything happened to them!"

Takkata-Jim felt he knew what was really on Metz's mind. The human was probably thinking about how terrible it would be if any of *Streaker*'s crew got themselves killed away from his sight . . . out where he was unable to judge how they behaved for his behavioral and genetic studies. "If only Creideiki had listened to you, sssir," he repeated. "You always have so much to say."

It was a little chancy, but if the human ever saw through Takkata-Jim's respectful mask to the core of sarcasm, he never gave it away.

"Well, it's nice of you to say so, Takkata-Jim. And very perceptive. I know you have many things to do now, so I'll find a free comm line and awaken Creideiki for you. I'll break the news gently that our pursuers have followed us to Kithrup."

Takkata-Jim gave the human a deferential nod from high body stance. "That-t is kind of you, Doctor Metz. You do me a favor."

Metz patted the lieutenant on his rough flank, as if to reassure him. Takkata-Jim bore the patronizing gesture with outward calm, and watched as the human turned to swim away.

The bridge was a fluid-filled sphere which bulged slightly from the bow of the cylindrical ship. The main ports of the command center looked out into a murky scene of ocean ridges, sediment, and drifting sea creatures.

The crew's web-lined work stations were illuminated by small spotlights. Most of the chamber lay in quiet shadows, as the elite bridge personnel carried out their tasks quickly and almost silently. The only sounds, other than the swish and fizz of recycling oxywater, were the intermittent click of sonar pulses and terse, professional comments from one operator to another.

Give Creideiki his due, Takkata-Jim told himself. He has crafted a finely tuned machine in this bridge crew.

Of course, dolphins were less consistent than humans. You couldn't tell in advance what might cause a neo-fin to start unraveling until you saw him perform under stress. This bridge crew performed as well as any he had ever seen, but would it be enough?

If they had overlooked a single radiation or psi leak, the ETs would be down on them quicker than orcas upon harbor seals.

The fins out there in the prospecting team were safer than their comrades aboard ship, Takkata-Jim thought somewhat bitterly. Metz was a fool to worry about them. They were probably having a wonderful time!

Takkata-Jim tried to recall swimming free in an ocean, without a harness, and breathing natural air. He tried to recall diving in deep water, the deep water of the *Stenos*, where the big-mouthed, smart-aleck, shore-hugging *Tursiops* were rare as dugongs.

"Akki," he called to the E.L.F. radio operator, the young dolphin midshipman from Calafia. "Have you received confirmation from Hikahi? Did she get the recall?"

The colonial was a small *Tursiops* variant of yellowish-gray coloration. Akki replied with some hesitation. He still wasn't used to breathing and speaking in oxywater. It required a very odd dialect of Underwater Anglic.

"I'm . . . sh-sorry, Vice-Captain, but there's no reply. I checked for a monopulse on all . . . ch-channels. There's been nothing."

Takkata-Jim tossed his head in irritation. Hikahi might have decided that even a monopulse reply would be too much risk. Still, confirmation would have taken from his back an unpleasant decision.

"Mm-m-m, sir?" Akki tipped his head down and lowered his tail in respect.

"Yess?"

"Ah . . . shouldn't we repeat the message? There's a chance they were distracted and missed it the firsh . . . first time . . ."

Like all dolphins from the colony planet Calafia, Akki was proud of his cultured Anglic. It apparently bothered him to have trouble with such simple sentences.

That suited the vice-captain fine. If there was one Anglic word that translated perfectly into Trinary, it was "smartass." Takkata-Jim didn't care for smartass midshipmen.

"No, comm-operator. We have our orders. If the captain wants to try again when he gets here, he's welcome. Meantime, attend your possst."

"Heth... er, aye aye, shir." The young dolphin spun about to return to his station, where he could breathe from an airdome instead of gulping water like a fish. There he could speak like a normal person while he awaited word from his closest friend, the human middie out in the wide, alien ocean.

Takkata-Jim wished the captain would come soon. The control room felt closed and dead. Breathing the fizzing, gas-charged oxywater always left him tired at the end of his shift. It never seemed to provide enough oxygen. His supplementary gill-lungs itched with the irritation of defied instinct, and the pills—the ones that forced extra oxygen into his system through his intestines—always gave him heartburn.

Once again he caught sight of Ignacio Metz. The white-haired scientist clutched a stanchion, with his head thrust under a comm airdome to call Creideiki. When he finished he would probably want to hang around. The man was always hovering nearby, watching... always making him feel he was being tested.

"I need a human ally," Takkata-Jim reminded himself. Dolphins were in command of *Streaker*, but the crew seemed to obey an officer more rapidly if he appeared to have the confidence of one of the patron race. Creideiki had Tom Orley. Hikahi had Gillian Baskin. Brookida's human companion was the engineer, Suessi.

Metz would have to be Takkata-Jim's human. Fortunately, the man could be manipulated.

The reports on the space battle were coming in faster on the data displays. It seemed to be turning into a real conflagration over the planet. At least five big fleets were involved.

Takkata-Jim resisted the sudden urge to turn and bite something, to lash out hard with his flukes. What he wanted was something to fight! Something palpable, instead of this hanging pall of dread!

After weeks of fleeing, *Streaker* was trapped at last.

What new trick would Creideiki and Orley come up with to get them away *this* time?

What if they failed to come up with a plan? Or worse, what if they contrived some squid-brained scheme that could only get them all killed? What would he do *then*?

Takkata-Jim mulled over the problem to keep his mind busy while he waited for the captain to come and relieve him.

4

∿∿∿∿∿∿∿∿∿∿∿∿∿∿∿∿∿∿∿∿∿∿∿∿

Creideiki

It had been his first really restful sleep in weeks. Naturally, it *had* to be interrupted.

Creideiki was used to taking his rest in zero gee, suspended in moist air. But as long as they were in hiding, anti-gravity beds were banned, and sleeping in liquid was the only other way for a dolphin.

He had tried for a week to breathe oxywater all through his rest period. The results had been nightmares and exhausting dreams of suffocation.

The ship's surgeon, Makanee, had suggested he try sleeping in the old-fashioned way, drifting at the surface of a pool of water.

Creideiki decided to try Makanee's alternative. He made sure that there was a big air-gap at the top of his state-room. Then he verified three times that the redundant oxygen alarms were all in perfect order. Finally, he shrugged out of his harness, turned off the lights, rose to the surface and expelled the oxywater in his gill-lung.

That part was a relief. Still, at first he just lay at the air-gap near the overhead, his mind racing and his skin itching for the touch of his tool harness. It was an irrational itch, he knew. Pre-spaceflight humans, in their primitive, neurotic societies, must have felt the same way about nudity.

Poor *Homo sapiens!* Mankind's histories showed such suffering during those awkward millennia of adolescence before Contact, when they were ignorant and cut off from Galactic society.

Meanwhile, Creideiki thought, dolphins had been in almost a state of grace, drifting in their corner of the Whale Dream. When men finally achieved a type of adulthood, and started lifting the higher creatures of Earth to join them, dolphins of the *amicus* strain moved fairly easily from one honorable condition to another.

We have our own problems, he reminded himself. He badly wanted to scratch the base of his amplifier socket, but there was no way to reach it without his harness.

He floated at the surface, in the dark, awaiting sleep. It *was* sort of restful, tiny wavelets lapping against the smooth skin above his eyes. And real air was definitely more relaxing to breathe than oxywater.

But he couldn't escape a vague unease over *sinking* . . . as if it would harm him any to sink in oxywater . . . as if millions of other dolphins hadn't slept this way all their lives.

Disconcerting was his spacer's habit of looking *up*. The ceiling bulkhead was inches away from the tip of his dorsal fin. Even when he closed his eyes, sonar told him of the nearness of enclosure. He could no more sleep without sending out echolocation clicks than a chimp could nap without scratching himself.

Creideiki snorted. *Beach himself* if he'd let a shipboard requirement give him insomnia! He blew emphatically and began to count sonar clicks. He started with a tenor rhythm, then slowly built a fugue as he added deeper elements to the sleep-song.

Echoes spread from his brow and diffracted about the small chamber. The notes drifted over one another, overlapping softly in faint whines and basso growls. They created a sonic structure, a template of *otherness*. The right combinations, he knew, would make the walls themselves seem to disappear.

Deliberately, he peeled away the duty-rigor of Keneenk— welcoming a small, trusted portion of the Whale Dream.

> * *When the patterns—*
> *In the cycloid*

> * *Call in whispers—*
>   *Soft remembered*
> * *Murmuring of—*
>   *Songs of dawning*
> * *And of the Moon—*
>   *The sea-tide's darling*
> * *Then the patterns—*
>   *In the cycloid*
> * *Call in whispers—*
>   *Soft remembered . . .* *

The desk, the cabinets, the walls, were covered under false sonic shadows. His chant began to open on its own accord, a rich and very physical poetry of crafted reflections.

Floating things seemed to drift past, tiny tail-flicks of schools of dream creatures. The echoes opened up space around him, as if the waters went on forever.

> * *And the Dream Sea,*
>   *Everlasting*
> * *Calls in whispers*
>   *Soft remembered . . .* *

Soon he felt a presence nearby, congealing gradually out of reflections of sound.

She formed slowly next to him as his engineer's consciousness let go . . . the shadow of a goddess. Then Nukapai floated beside him . . . a ghost of ripples, ribbed by motes of sound. The black sleekness of her body passed back into the darkness, unhindered by a bulkhead that seemed no longer there.

Vision faded. The waters darkened all around Creideiki, and Nukapai became more than just a shadow, a passive recipient of his song. Her needle teeth shone, and she sang his own sounds back to him.

> * *With the closeness—*
>   *Of the waters*
> * *In an endless—*
>   *Layer of Dreaming*
> * *As the humpback—*
>   *Older sibling*

> * *Sings songs to the—*
>   *Serious fishes*
> * *Here you find me—*
>   *Wandering brother*
> * *Even in this—*
>   *Human rhythm*
> * *Where the humans*
>   *And other walkers*
> * *Give mirth to—*
>   *The stars themselves . . .* *

A type of bliss settled over him as his heartbeat slowed. Creideiki slept next to the gentle dream-goddess. She chided him only teasingly for being an engineer, and for dreaming her in the rigid, focused verse of Trinary rather than the chaotic Primal of his ancestors.

She welcomed him to the Threshold Sea, where Trinary sufficed, where he felt only faintly the raging of the Whale Dream and the ancient gods who dwelt there. It was as much of that ocean as an engineer's mind could accept.

How rigid the Trinary verse sometimes seemed! The patterns of overlapping tones and symbols were almost human-precise . . . almost human-narrow.

He had been brought up to think those terms compliments. Parts of his own brain had been gene-designed along human lines. But now and then chaotic sound-images slipped in, teasing him with a hint of ancient singing.

Nukapai clicked sympathetically. She smiled . . .

No! She did no such land-ape thing! Of cetaceans, only the neo-dolphin "smiled" with their mouths.

Nukapai did something else. She stroked against his side, gentlest of goddesses, and told him,

> * *Be now at peace* *
> * *It is That is . . .* *
> * *And engineers* *
> * *Far from the ocean* *
> * *Can hear it still* *

The tension of several weeks at last broke, and he slept. Creideiki's breath gathered in glistening condensation on the ceiling bulkhead. The breeze from a nearby air duct brushed the droplets, which shuddered, then fell on the water like gentle rain.

When the image of Ignacio Metz formed a meter to his right, Creideiki was slow to become aware of it.

"Captain..." the image said. "I'm calling from the bridge. I am afraid the Galactics have found us here sooner than we expected..."

Creideiki ignored the little voice that tried to call him back to deeds and battles. He lingered in a waving forest of kelp fronds, listening to long night sounds. Finally, it was Nukapai herself who nudged him from his dream. Fading beside him, she gently reminded,

> \# *Duty, duty—honor is, is—*
> *Honor, Creideiki—alertly*
> \# *Shared, is—Honor* \#

Nukapai alone could speak Primal to Creideiki with impunity. He could no more ignore the dream-goddess than his own conscience. One eye at last focused on the hologram of the insistent human, and the words penetrated.

"Thank you, Doctor Metz," he sighed. "Tell Takkata-Jim I'll be right-t there. And please page Tom Orley. I'd like to see him on the bridge. Creideiki out."

He inhaled deeply for a few moments, letting the room come back into shape around him. Then he twisted and dove to retrieve his harness.

5

∾∾∾∾∾∾∾∾∾∾∾∾∾∾∾∾∾∾∾∾∾∾∾∾∾

Tom Orley

A tall, dark-haired man swung one-handed from the leg of a bed, a bed that was bolted to the floor in an upside-down room. The floor slanted over his head. His left foot rested precariously on the bottom of a drawer pulled from one of the inverted wall cabinets.

At the sudden yellow flash of the alert light, Tom Orley whirled and grabbed at his holster with his free hand. His needler was half-drawn before he recognized the source of the disturbance. He cursed slowly and reholstered the weapon. *Now* what was the emergency? He could think of a dozen possibilities, offhand, and here he was, hanging by one arm in the most awkward part of the ship!

"I initiate contact, Thomas Orley."

The voice seemed to come from above his right ear. Tom changed his grip on the bed leg to turn around. An abstract three-dimensional pattern swirled a meter away from his face, like multicolored motes caught in a dust devil.

"I suppose you would like to know of the cause of the alarm. Is this correct?"

"You're damned right I do!" he snapped. "Are we under attack?"

"No." The colored images shifted. "This ship is not yet assailed, but Vice-Captain Takkata-Jim has announced an alert. At least five intruder fleets are now in the neighborhood of Kithrup. These squadrons appear now to be in combat not far from the planet."

Orley sighed. "So much for quick repairs and a getaway." He hadn't thought it likely that their hunters would let them escape again. The damaged *Streaker* had left a noisy trail behind her when she slipped away from the confusion of the ambush at Morgran.

Tom had been helping the crew in the engine room repair *Streaker's* stasis generator. They had just finished the part calling for detailed hand-eye work, and the moment had come to steal away to the deserted section of the dry-wheel where the Niss computer had been hidden.

The dry-wheel was a band of workrooms and cabins that spun freely when the ship was in space, providing pseudo-gravity for the humans aboard. Now it was still. This section of upside-down corridors and cabins was abandoned in the inconvenient gravity of the planet.

The privacy suited Tom, though the topsy-turvy arrangement was irksome.

"You weren't to announce yourself unless I switched you on manually," he said. "You were to wait for my thumbprint and voice i.d. before letting on you were anything but a standard comm."

The swirling patterns took on a cubist style. The machine's voice sounded unperturbed. "Under the circumstances, I took the liberty. If I erred, I am prepared to accept discipline up to level three. Punishment of a higher order will be considered unjustified and be rejected with prejudice."

Tom allowed himself an ironic smile. The machine would run him in circles if he let it, and he would gain nothing by asserting his titular mastery over it. The Tymbrimi spy who had lent the Niss to him had made it clear that the machine's usefulness was partly based upon its flexibility and initiative, however irritating it became.

"I'll take the level of your error under advisement," he told the Niss. "Now, what can you tell me about the present situation?"

"A vague question. I can access the ship's battle computers for you. But that might entail an element of risk."

"No, you'd better not do that quite yet." If the Niss tried to inveigle the battle computer during an alert, Creideiki's bridge crew might notice. Tom assumed Creideiki knew about the presence of the Niss aboard his ship, just as the captain knew that Gillian Baskin had her own secret project. But the dolphin commander kept quiet about it, leaving the two of them to their work.

"All right, then. Can you patch me through to Gillian?"

The holo danced with blue specks. "She is alone in her office. I am placing the call."

The motes suddenly faded. They were replaced by the image of a blonde woman in her early thirties. She looked puzzled briefly, then her face brightened with a brilliant smile. She laughed.

"Ah, you're visiting your mechanical friend, I see. Tell me, Tom, what does a sarcastic alien machine have that I don't have? You've never gone head over heels so literally for me."

"Very funny." Still, her attitude relieved his anxiety over the alert. He had been afraid they would be in combat almost immediately. In a week or so, *Streaker* might be able to make a good accounting of herself before being destroyed or captured. Right now, she had all the punch of a drugged rabbit.

"I take it the Galactics aren't landing yet."

Gillian shook her head. "No, though Makanee and I are standing by in the infirmary just in case. Bridge crew says at least three fleets have popped into space nearby. They immediately started having it out, just like at Morgran. We can only hope they'll annihilate each other."

"Not much hope of that, I'm afraid."

"Well, you're the tactician of the family. Still, it might be weeks before there is a victor to come down after us. There will be deals and last-minute alliances. We'll have time to think of something."

Tom wished he could share her optimism. As the family tactician, it was *his* job to "think of something."

"Well, if the situation's not urgent..."

"I don't think it is. You can spend a little while longer with your roomie there—my electronic rival. I'll get even by getting intimate with Herbie."

Tom could only shake his head and let her have her joke. Herbie was a cadaver—their one tangible prize from the derelict fleet. Gillian had determined that the alien corpse was over two billion years old. The ship's mini-*Library* seemed to have seizures every time they asked what race it had once belonged to.

"All right, then. Tell Creideiki I'll be right down, okay?"

"Sure, Tom. They're waking him now. I'll tell him I last saw you hanging around somewhere." She gave him a wink and switched off.

Tom watched the place where her image had been, and

once again wondered what he had done to deserve a woman like her.

"Out of curiosity, Thomas Orley, I am interested in some of the undertones of this last conversation. Am I right in assuming that some of these mild insults Dr. Baskin conveyed fell into the category of affectionate teasing? My Tymbrimi builders are telempathic, of course, but they, also, seem to indulge in this pastime. Is it part of a mating process? Or is it a friendship test of some sort?"

"A little of both, I guess. Do the Tymbrimi really do the same sort of . . ." Tom shook himself. "Never mind about that! My arms are getting tired and I've got to get below quickly. Have you anything else to report?"

"Not of major significance to your survival or mission."

"I take it, then, that you haven't managed to coax the ship's mini-*Library* to deliver anything on Herbie or the derelict fleet."

The holo flowed into sharp geometries. "That is the main problem, isn't it? Dr. Baskin asked me the same question when she last checked in on me, thirteen hours ago."

"And did you give her any more direct an answer than you're giving me?"

"Finding ways to bypass the access programming on this ship's mini-*Library* is the reason I was put aboard in the first place. I would tell you if I had succeeded." The machine's disembodied voice was dry enough to dessicate melons. "The Tymbrimi have long suspected that the *Library Institute* is less than neutral—that the branch *Libraries* sold by them are programmed to be deficient in very subtle ways, to put troublesome races at a disadvantage.

"The Tymbrimi have been working on this problem since days when your ancestors wore animal skins, Thomas Orley. It was never expected we would achieve anything more on this trip than a gathering of a few shards of new data, and perhaps elimination of a few minor barriers."

Orley understood how the long-lived machine could take such a patient perspective. Still, he found he resented it. It would be nice to think *something* had come of all the grief *Streaker* and her crew had fallen into. "After all the surprises we've encountered, this voyage must have served up more than just a few new bits for you to crunch," he suggested.

"The propensity of Earthlings to get into trouble, and to learn thereby, was the reason my owners agreed to this mad venture in the first place—although no one ever expected such a chain of *unusual* calamities as have befallen this ship. Your talents were under-rated."

There was no way to answer that. Tom's arms had begun to hurt. "Well, I'd better get back. In an emergency I'll contact you via ship's comm."

"Of course."

Orley let go and landed in a crouch by the closed doorway, a rectangle high on one steeply sloping wall.

"Dr. Baskin has just passed on word to me that Takkata-Jim has ordered the survey party to return to the ship," the Niss spoke abruptly. "She thought you would want to know."

Orley cursed. Metz might have had a hand in that. How were they to repair the ship if the crew weren't allowed to go looking for the raw materials they needed? Creideiki's strongest reason for coming to Kithrup had been the abundance of pre-refined metals in an oceanic environment accessible to dolphins. If Hikahi's prospectors were called back the danger had to be severe . . . or someone was panicking.

Tom turned to go, but paused and looked up. "Niss, we *must* know what it is the Galactics think we found."

The sparkles were muted. "I have done a thorough search of the open files in this ship's onboard micro-branch *Library* for any record that might shed light on the mystery of the derelict fleet, Thomas Orley. Aside from a few vague similarities between the patterns we saw on those gigantic hulls and some ancient cult symbols, I can find no support for a hypothesis that the ships we found are in any way connected to the fabled Progenitors."

"But you found nothing to contradict it, either?"

"Correct. The derelicts might or might not be linked with the one legend which binds all oxygen-breathing races in the five galaxies."

"It could be we found huge bits of flotsam of almost no historical significance, then."

"True. At the other extreme, you may have made the biggest archaeological and religious find of the age. The mere possibility helps to explain the battle that is shaping up in this solar system. The refusal of the ship's mini-*Library* to give more details is indicative of how many of the Galactic cultures feel about events so long ago. So long as this ship is the sole repository of information about the derelict fleet, the survey vessel *Streaker* remains a great prize, valued by every brand of fanatic."

Orley had hoped the Niss would find evidence to make their discovery innocuous. Such proof might have been used to get the ETs to leave them alone. But if the derelict fleet was really as important as it seemed, *Streaker* would have to find a way to get the information to Earth, and let wiser heads figure out what to do with it.

"You just keep contemplating, then," he told the Niss. "Meanwhile I'll do my best to see that the Galactics stay off our backs. Now, can you tell me..."

"Of course I can," the Niss interrupted again. "The corridor outside is clear. Don't you think I would let you know if anyone were outside?"

Tom shook his head, certain the machine had been programmed to do this now and again. It would be typical of the Tymbrimi. Earth's greatest allies were also practical jokers. When a dozen other calamitous priorities had been settled, he intended taking a monkey wrench to the machine, and explaining the mess to his Tymbrimi friends as "an unfortunate accident."

As the door panel slipped aside, Tom grabbed the rim and swung out to drop onto the dim hallway ceiling below. The door hummed shut automatically. Red alert lights flashed at intervals down the gently curved corridor.

All right, he thought. Our hopes for a quick getaway are dashed, but I've already thought out some contingency plans.

A few he had discussed with the captain. One or two he had kept to himself.

I'll have to set a few into motion, he thought, knowing from experience that chance diverts all schemes. As likely as not, it will be something totally unexpected that turns up to offer us our last real hope.

6

Galactics

The first phase of the fight was a free-for-all. A score of warring factions scratched and probed at each other, exploring for weaknesses. Already a number of wrecks drifted in orbit, torn and twisted and ominously luminous. Glowing clouds of plasma spread along the path of battle, and jagged metal fragments sparkled as they tumbled.

In her flagship, a leathery queen looked upon viewscreens that showed her the battlefield. She lay on a broad, soft cushion and stroked the brown scales of her belly in contemplation.

The displays that rimmed Krat's settee showed many dangers. One panel was an overlay of curling lines, indicating zones of anomalous probability. Others pointed out where the slough from psychic weapons was still dangerous.

Clusters of lights were the other fleets, now regrouping as the first phase drew to a close. Fighting still raged on the fringes.

Krat lounged on a cushion of vletoor skin. She shifted her weight to ease the pressure in her third abdomen. Battle hormones always accelerated the quickening within her. It was an inconvenience which, in ancient days, had forced her female ancestors to stay in the nest, leaving to stupid males the fighting.

No longer, though.

A small, bird-like creature approached her side. Krat took a ling-plum from the tray it proffered. She bit it and savored the juices that ran over her tongue and down her whiskers. The little Forski put down the tray and began to sing a crooning ballad about the joys of battle.

36

The avian Forski had been uplifted to full sapiency, of course. It would have been against the Code of Uplift to do less with a client race. But while they could talk, and even fly spacecraft in a pinch, independent ambition had been bred out of them. They were too useful as domestics and entertainers to be fated anything but specialization. Adaptability might interfere with their graceful and intelligent performance of those functions.

One of her smaller screens suddenly went dark. A destroyer in the Soro rearguard had been destroyed. Krat hardly noticed. The consolidation had been inexpensive so far.

The command room was divided into pie sections. From the center, Krat could look into every baffled unit from her couch of command. Her crew bustled about, each a member of a Soro client race, each hurrying to do her will in its own sub-specialty.

From the sectors for navigation, combat, and detection, there was a quieting of the hectic battle pace at last. In planning, though, she saw increased activity as the staff evaluated developments, including the new alliance between the Abdicator and Transcendor forces.

A Paha sub-officer poked its head out of detection sector. Under hooded eyes, Krat watched it dash to a food station, snatch a steaming mug of amoklah, and hurry back to its post.

The Paha race had been allowed more racial diversity than the Forski, to enhance their value as ritual warriors. It left them less tractable than suited her, but it was a price one paid for good fighters. Krat decided to ignore the incident. She listened to the little Forski sing of the coming victory—of the glory that would be Krat's when she captured the Earthlings, and finally squeezed their secrets out of them.

Klaxons shrieked. The Forski leapt into the air in alarm and fled to its cubbyhole. Suddenly there were running Paha everywhere.

"Tandu raider!" the tactical officer shouted. "Ships two through twelve, it has appeared in your midst! Take evasive maneuvers! Quickly!"

The flagship bucked as it, too, went into a wild turn to avoid a spread of missiles. Krat's screens showed a pulsing, danger-blue dot—the daring Tandu cruiser that had popped into being within her fleet—which was even now pouring fire into the Soro ships!

Curse their damnable probability drives! *Krat knew that*

nobody else could move about as quickly as the Tandu, because no other species was willing to take such chances!

Krat's mating claw throbbed in irritation. Her Soro ships were so busy avoiding missiles, nobody was firing back!

"Fools!" Krat hissed into her communicator. "Ships six and ten, hold your ground and concentrate your fire on the obscenity!"

Then, before her words reached her sub-captains, before any Soro even fired back, the terrible Tandu ship began to dissolve on its own! One moment it was there, ferocious and deadly, ranging in on a numerous but helpless foe. The next instant the spindly destroyer was surrounded by a coruscating, discolored halo of sparks. Its shield folded, and the cruiser fell into itself like a collapsing tower of sticks.

With a brilliant flash, the Tandu vanished, leaving a cloud of ugly vapor behind. Through her own ship's shields, Krat could feel an awful psychic roar.

We were lucky, Krat realized as the psi-noise slowly faded. *It was not without reason that other races avoided the Tandus' methods. But if that ship had lasted a few moments longer . . .*

No harm was done, and Krat noted that her crew had all done their jobs. Some of them were slow, however, and these must be punished. . . .

She beckoned the chief tactician, a tall, burly Paha. The warrior stepped toward her. He tried to maintain a proud bearing, but his drooping cilia told that he knew what to expect. Krat rumbled deep in her throat.

She started to speak, but in the emotion of the moment, the Soro commander felt a churning pressure within. Krat grunted and writhed, and the Paha officer fled as she panted on the vletoor cushion. Finally she howled and found relief. After a moment, she bent forward to retrieve the egg she had laid.

She picked it up, punishments and battles temporarily banished from her mind. In an instinct that predated her species' uplift by the timid Hul, two million years before, she responded to the smell of pheromones and licked the birthing slime from the tiny air-cracks which seamed the leathery surface of the egg.

Krat licked it a few extra times for pleasure. She rocked the egg slowly in an ancient, untampered reflex of motherhood.

7

∽∿∽∿∽∿∽∿∽∿∽∿∽∿∽∿∽∿∽∿∽∿∽∿∽∿∽∿∽∿∽∿

Toshio

There was a ship involved, of course. All of his dreams since the age of nine had dealt with ships. Ships, at first, of plasteel and jubber, sailing the straits and archipelagos of Calafia, and later ships of space. Toshio had dreamt of ships of every variety, including those of the powerful Galactic patron races, which he had hoped one day to see.

Now he dreamt of a dinghy.

The tiny human-dolphin colony of his homeworld had sent him out with Akki riding on the outrigger, his Calafian Academy button shining brightly under Alph's sunshine. It started out a balmy day.

Only soon the weather darkened, and all around became the same color as the water. The sea grew bilious, then black, then changed to vacuum, and suddenly there were stars everywhere.

He worried about air. Neither he nor Akki had suits. It was *hard,* trying to breathe vacuum!

He was about to turn for home when he saw them chasing him. Galactics, with heads of every shape and color—long, sinuous arms, or tiny, grasping claws, or worse—were rowing toward him steadily. The sleek prows of their boats were as lambent as the starlight.

"What do you want?" he cried out as he paddled hard to get away. (Hadn't the boat started out with a motor?)

"Who is your master?!" They shouted in a thousand different tongues. "Is that He beside you?"

"Akki's a fin! Fins are *our* clients! We uplifted them and set them free!"

39

"Then they are free," the Galactics replied, drawing closer. "But who uplifted you? Who set *you* free?"

"I don't know!" he screamed. "Maybe we did it ourselves!" He stroked harder as the Galactics laughed. He struggled to breathe the hard vacuum. "Leave me alone! Let me go home!"

Suddenly the *Fleet* loomed ahead. The ships seemed bigger than moons—bigger than stars. They were dark and silent, and their aspect seemed to daunt even the Galactics.

Then the foremost of the ancient globes began to open. Toshio realized, then, that Akki was gone. His boat was gone. The ETs were gone.

He wanted to scream, but air was very dear.

A piercing whistle brought him around in a painful, disorienting instant. He sat up suddenly and felt the sled bounce unhappily with the motion. While his eyes made a blurred jumble of the horizon, a stiff breeze blew against his face. The tang of Kithrup greeted his nostrils.

"About time, Ladder-runner. You gave us quite a scare."

Toshio wavered, then saw Hikahi floating nearby, inspecting him with one eye.

"Are you okay, little Sharp-Eyes?"

"Um . . . yes. I think so."

"Then you had better get to work on your hose. We had to nip it to give you air."

Toshio felt the knife-edged cut. He noticed that both hands were neatly bandaged.

"Was anyone else hurt?" he asked as he felt through his thigh pocket for his repair kit.

"A few minor burns. We enjoyed the fight, after learning you were all right-t. Thank you for telling us about Ssassia. We'd never have looked there had you not been caught and then told us what you found.

"They are cutting her loose now."

Toshio knew he should be grateful to Hikahi for putting the misadventure in that light. By rights he should be getting a tongue-lashing for rashly leaving formation, and almost losing his life.

But Toshio felt too lost to allow himself even gratitude to the dolphin lieutenant. "I suppose they haven't found Phip-pit?"

"Of him there's been no sign."

The slow rotation of Kithrup had taken the sun past what

would look like four o'clock, Earth time. Low clouds were gathering on the eastern horizon. There was a choppiness to the water that had been absent before.

"There may be a small squall later," Hikahi said. "It may be unwise to use Earth instincts on another world, but I think we have nothing to fear...."

Toshio looked up. There was something to the south... He squinted.

There it was again, a flash, and then another. Two tiny bursts of light followed in quick succession, almost invisible against the sea glare.

"How long has that been going on?" he gestured toward the southern sky.

"What do you mean, Toshio?"

"That flashing. Is it lightning?"

The fin's eyes widened and her mouth curled slightly. Hikahi's flukes churned and she rose up in the water to turn first one eye, then the other, toward the south.

"I detect nothing, Sharp-Eyes. Tell me what you see."

"Multicolored flashes. Bursts of light. Lots of..." Toshio stopped wrapping his air hose. He stared for a moment, trying to remember.

"Hikahi," he said slowly. "I think Akkia called me during the fight with the weed. Did you get anything over your set?"

"No I didn't, Toshio. But remember, we fins aren't yet so good at abstract thought while fighting. T-try to recall what he said, please."

Toshio touched his forehead. The encounter with the weed wasn't something he wanted to think about, right now. It all blended in with his nightmare, a jumbling of colors and noises and confusion.

"I think... I think he said something about wanting us to keep radio silence and come home... something about a space battle going on?"

Hikahi let out a whistling moan and flipped out of the water in a backward dive. She was back immediately, tail churning.

* Close-up
  Lock-up
* Go the other way—than up! *

Sloppy Trinary. There were nuances in Primal Delphin which Toshio, of couse, couldn't understand. But they sent a thrill down his spine. Hikahi was the last fin he would ever have expected to slip into Primal. As he finished wrapping his air hose, he realized with chagrin what his failure to tell Hikahi earlier might have cost them all.

He slapped his faceplate shut and flopped over to press the buoyancy valve on the sled, checking simultaneously the telltales on his helmet rim. He ran through the pre-dive checklist with a rapidity only a fourth-generation Calafian colonist could have achieved.

The bow of the sled was sinking quickly as the sea erupted to his right. Seven dolphins breached in a spume of water and exhaled breath.

"S-s-sassia's tied to your stern, Toshio. Can you shake your leg?" Keepiru urged. "Now is no time to dawdle making up t-t-tunes!"

Toshio grimaced. How could Keepiru have fought so hard earlier to save the life of someone he ridiculed so?

He remembered the way Keepiru had torn into the weed, the desperate look in his eye, and the glow it had taken when he saw it. Yet now he was cruel and taunting as ever.

A sharp blast of light flashed in the east, searing the sky all around them. The fins squealed almost as one, and immediately dove—all except Keepiru, who stayed beside Toshio—as the eastern cloudline spat fire into the afternoon sky.

The sled finally sank, but in the last instant Toshio and Keepiru saw a hurtling battle of giants.

A huge, arrowhead-shaped space vessel plummeted down on them, pitted and fiery. Wind-swept trailers of purple smoke boiled out of great gashes in its sides, to be flung back into the needle-narrow shock front of its supersonic flight. The shock wave warped even the shimmer of the great ship's defensive shields, shells of gravity and plasma that sparkled with unhealthful overload.

Two grapnel-shaped destroyers dogged it no more than four ship lengths behind. Beams of accelerated anti-matter flashed from each of the trefoils, hitting their mark twice in terrible explosions.

Toshio was five meters below the surface when the sonic boom hit. It slammed the sled over, and kept it tumbling amid a roar that sounded like a house caving in. The water was a churning maelstrom of bubbles and bodies.

As he struggled with the sled, Toshio thanked Infinity he

hadn't been at the surface to hear the battle passing by. At Morgran they had seen ships die. But never this close.

The noise finally settled down to a long, loud growling. Toshio got the sled righted at last.

Ssassia's sad corpse still lay tied to the rear end of the sled. The other fins, too scared or prudent to go above, began taking turns at the small airdomes that lined the bottom rim of the sled. It was Toshio's job to keep the sled still. It wasn't easy in the churning water, but he did it without a thought.

They were near the sloping western edge of a huge, grayish metal-mound. Sea-plants grew at intervals along its side. They looked nothing like the strangle weed, but that was no guarantee.

More and more, Toshio was coming to dislike being here. He wished he was home, where the dangers were simple, and easily handled—kelp klingers and island turtles and the like—and where there were no ETs.

"Are you all right?" Hikahi asked as she came by. The dolphin lieutenant radiated calm.

"I'm fine," he grumped. "It's a good thing I didn't wait any longer to tell you about Akki's message, though. You have every reason to be mad at me."

"Don't be silly. Now we head back. Brookida is fatigued, so I've lashed him under an airdome. You will forge ahead with the scouts. We'll follow. Now t-take off!"

"Aye, sir." Toshio took his bearings and pushed the throttle. The thrusters hummed as the sled accelerated. Several of the stronger swimmers maintained pace alongside, as the mound slowly receded on the right.

It had taken them five minutes or so to get started. They were barely under way before the tsunami hit.

It was not a huge wave, merely the first of a series of ripples spreading from a point where a pebble had plunked into the sea. The pebble happened to be a space ship half a kilometer long. It had plunked, at supersonic speed, a mere fifty kilometers away.

The wave jerked the sled upward and sideways, almost shaking the boy off. A cloud of sea debris, torn-up plants, and dead and living fish whirled about him like clods in a cyclone. The roar was deafening.

Toshio clutched the controls desperately. Somehow, against incredible momentum, he managed slowly to drive the prow of the sled up and away from the wave front. Just in time, he thrust out of the curling, downward circulation and sent the tiny craft flying along the direction the current wanted to go. Eastward.

An ash-gray form speared past him on his left. In a flash he recognized Keepiru, struggling to keep control in the churning waters. The fin squeaked something indecipherable in Trinary, then was gone.

Some instinct guided Toshio, or perhaps it was the sonar screen, now a mess of jumbled snow, but still bearing the faint, fading traces of the terrain map it had shown only moments before. Toshio forced the sled to bear to the left as hard as possible.

The emergency-power roar of the engines changed to a scream as he suddenly slewed hard to port in desperation. The huge, dark bulk of a metal-mound loomed ahead! Already he could feel undertow as the wave began to form breakers to his right, curling as the cycloid rode up the sloping shore of the island.

Toshio wanted to cry out, but the struggle took all of his breath. He clenched his teeth and counted as the terrible seconds passed.

The sled drove past the cliff-like northern shore amid a cloud of bubbles. Though he was still underwater, he could look downward a dozen meters to his right, and see the lower beach plants of the island. He was riding in the center of a tall mound of water.

Then he was past! The sea opened up and one of the deep oceanic rills lay beneath him, dark and seemingly bottomless. Toshio slammed the bow planes forward and vented his tanks. The sled plummeted faster than he had ever dived before.

His stern pulled forward precariously. Toshio passed clouds of falling debris. The darkness and cold came up at him, and he sought the chill as a refuge.

The valley sloped below him as he brought the sled to a quiet depth. He could sense the tsunami rolling by above him. The sea plants all around waved in an obviously unaccustomed manner. A slow rain of falling rubbish drifted down on all sides, but at least the water wasn't trying to beat him to death anymore. Toshio flattened out his dive and headed toward the valley center, away from everything. Then he let himself sag in an agony of bruised muscles and adrenalin reaction.

He blessed the tiny, man-designed symbiotes that were right now scavenging his blood of excess nitrogen, preventing narcosis raptures at this depth.

Toshio cranked the engines down to one-quarter, and they sighed, sounding almost relieved. The lamps on the sled's display were mostly green, surprisingly, after the treatment the sled had received.

One of the telltales caught his eye—it indicated an airdome in operation. Suddenly Toshio noticed a faint, singing sound; it was a whistling of patience and reverence.

> * *The Ocean* is as is as is—
> the endless sigh of dreaming—
> * *Of other seas that* are that are—
> and others in them, dreaming— *

Toshio reached out and snapped on the hydrophones.

"Brookida! Are you okay! Is your air all right?"

There was a sigh, tremulous and tired.

"Fleet-t-t Fingers, hello. Thank you for saving my life. You flew as truly as any *Tursiops*."

"That ship we saw must have crashed! If that's what it was you can bet there will be aftershocks! Maybe we'd better stay down here a while. I'll turn on the sonar so others can find us and come for air while the waves pass." He flicked a switch, and immediately a low series of clicks emanated into the surrounding water. Brookida groaned.

"They will not come, Toshio. Can't you hear them? They won't answer your call."

Toshio frowned. "They *have* to! Hikahi will know about the aftershocks. They're probably looking for us right now! Maybe I'd better head back. . . ." He moved to turn the sled and blow ballast. Brookida had started him worrying.

"Don't go, Toshio! It will do no good for you to die as well! Wait until the waves pass-s-s! You must live to tell Creideiki!"

"What are you *talking* about?"

"Listen, Sharp-Eyes. Listen!"

Toshio shook his head, then swore and pulled back on the throttle until the engine died. He turned up the gain on the hydrophones.

"Do you hear?" Brookida asked.

Toshio cocked his head and listened. The sea was a mess

of intonation. The roar of the departing wave dopplered down
as he lay there. Schools of fish made panicky noises. All
around came the reports of rockslides and surf pounding on
the islands.

Then he heard it. The shrill repetitive squeals of Primal
Delphin. No modern dolphin spoke it when fully in command of his faculties.

That, in itself, was bad news.

One of the cries was clear. He could easily make out the
basic distress call. It was the earliest Delphin signal human
scientists had understood.

But the other noise… at least three voices were involved
in that one. It was a strange sound, very poignant and *very*
wrong!

"It isss rescue fever," Brookida groaned. "Hikahi is
beached and injured. *She* might have stopped this, but she is
delirious and now adds to the problem!"

"Hikahi…"

"Like Creideiki, she is an adept of Keneenk… the
study of logical discipline. She would have been able to force
the others to ignore the cries of those washed ashore, to make
them dive to safety for a t-time."

"Don't they realize there will be aftershocks?"

"Shockss hardly matter, Sharp-Eyes!" Brookida cried.
"They may beach themselves without assist! You are Calafian.
How can you not know this about usss? I thrash here to go
and die answering that call!"

Toshio groaned. Of course he knew about rescue fever,
in which panic and fear washed aside the veneer of civilization,
leaving a cetacean with only one thought—to save his comrades,
whatever the personal risk. Every few years the tragedy
struck even the highly advanced fins of Calafia. Akki had told
him, once, that sometimes the sea itself seemed to be calling
for help. Some humans claimed to have felt it, too—particularly
those who took dolphin RNA in the rites of the Dreamer
Cult.

Once upon a time the *Tursiops*, or bottlenose dolphin,
had been about the least likely cetacean to beach himself. But
genetic engineering had upset the balance somewhere. As
the genes of other species were spliced onto the basic *Tursiops*
model, a few things had been thrown out of kilter. For three
generations human geneticists had been working on the

problem. But for now the fins swam along a knife edge, where irrationality was a perpetual danger.

Toshio bit his lip. "They have their harnesses," he said uncertainly.

"One can hope. But is it likely they'll use them properly when they are even now speaking P-primal?"

Toshio struck the sled with his balled fist. Already his hand was growing numb from the chill. "I'm going up," he announced.

"No! You must not! You must guard your safet-ty!"

Toshio ground his teeth. *Always mothering me. Mothering or teasing. The fins treat me like a child, and I'm sick of it!*

He set the throttle to one-quarter and pulled up on the bow planes. "I'm going to unlash you, Brookida. Can you swim okay?"

"Yesss. But-t . . ."

Toshio looked at his sonar. A fuzzy line was forming in the west.

"Can you swim!" he demanded.

"Yesss. I can swim well enough. But don't cut me loose near the rescue fever! Don't you risk the aftershocksss!"

"I see one coming now. They'll be several minutes apart and weakening with time. I'll fix it so we rise just after this one passes. Then you've got to get going back to the ship! Tell them what's happened and get help."

"That's what *you* should do, Toshio."

"Never mind that! Will you do as I ask? Or do I have to leave you lashed up!"

There was an almost unnoticeable pause, but Brookida's voice changed. "I shall do exactly as you say, Toshio. I'll bring help."

Toshio checked his trim, then he slipped over the side, holding onto the rim stanchions with one hand. Brookida looked at him through the transparent shell of the airdome. The tough bubble membrane surrounded the dolphin's head. Toshio tore loose the lashings holding Brookida in place. "You're going to have to take a breather with you, you know."

Brookida sighed as Toshio pulled a lever by the airdome. A small hose descended, one end covering Brookida's blowhole. Like a snake, ten feet of hose wrapped around Brookida's torso. Breathers were uncomfortable, and hindered

speech. But by wearing one Brookida would not have to come
up for air. The breather would help the old metallurgist
ignore the cries in the water—a constant, uncomfortable
reminder of his membership in a technological culture.

Toshio left Brookida tied in place by a single lashing. He
pulled himself back onto the upper surface just as the first
aftershock rolled overhead.

The sled bucked, but he was prepared this time. They
were deep, and the wave passed with surprising quickness.

"Okay, here goes." He pushed the throttle forward to
max and blew ballast.

Soon the metal island appeared on his left. The screams
of his comrades became distinctly louder over the sonar set.
The distress call was now pre-eminent over the rescue fever
response.

Toshio steered past the mound to the north. He wanted
to give Brookida a big head start.

Just then, however, a sleek gray figure shot past Toshio,
just overhead. He recognized it at once, and where it was
headed.

He cut the last lashing. "Get moving, Brookida! If you
come back anywhere near this island again I'll rip off your
harness and bite your tail in half!"

He didn't bother looking back as Brookida dropped away
and the sled turned sharply. He kicked in emergency power
to try to catch up with Keepiru. The fastest swimmer in the
Streak's crew was heading directly for the western beach. His
cries were pure Primal Delphin.

"Damn you, Keepiru. Stop!"

The sled sped quickly, just under the water's surface.
The afternoon had aged, and there was a reddish tinge to the
clouds, but Toshio could clearly see Keepiru leaping from
wavelet to wavelet up ahead. He appeared indifferent to
Toshio's calls as he neared the island where his comrades lay
beached and delirious.

Toshio felt helpless. Another aftershock was due in three
minutes. If it didn't beach the dolphin, Keepiru's own efforts
probably would. Keepiru came from Atlast, a new and rather
rustic colony world. It was doubtful he had learned the tools
of mental discipline studied by Creideiki and Hikahi.

"Stop! If we time it right we can work as a team! We can
avoid the aftershocks! Will you let me catch *up*?" he screamed.

But it was no use. The fin had too much of a head start.

The futile chase frustrated Toshio. How could he have lived and worked with dolphins all his life and known them so poorly? To think the Terragens Council had chosen him for this tour because of his *experience* with fins! Hah!

Toshio had always taken a lot of kidding from fins. They kidded *all* human children, while protecting them ferociously. But on signing aboard *Streaker,* Toshio had expected to be treated as an adult and officer. Sure, there'd be a little repartée, as he'd seen between man and fin back home, but mutual respect, as well. It hadn't worked out that way.

Keepiru had been the worst, starting right off with heavy sarcasm and never letting up.

So why am I trying to save him?

He remembered the fierce courage Keepiru had shown in saving him from the weed. There was no rescue fever then. The fin had been in full control over his harness.

So, he thinks of me as a child, Toshio realized bitterly. No wonder he doesn't hear me now.

Still, it offered a way. Toshio bit his lip, wishing vainly for an alternative. To save Keepiru's life he would have to humiliate himself utterly. It wasn't an easy thing to decide to do, his pride had taken such a beating.

With a savage curse, he pulled back on the throttle and set the bow planes to descend. He turned up the hydrophones to maximum, swallowed, then cried out in pidgin Trinary.

> * Child drowning—child in danger! *
> * Child drowning—child's distress *
> * Human child—in need of savior *
> * Human child—come do your best! *

He repeated the call over and over, whistling through lips dry with shame. The nursery rhyme was taught to all the children of Calafia. Any kid past the age of nine who used it usually pleaded for transfer to another island to escape the subsequent razzing. There were more dignified ways an adult called for help.

None of which Keepiru had heard!

Ears burning, he repeated the call.

Not all Calafian kids did well with the fins, of course. Only a quarter of the planet's human population worked closely with the sea. But those adults were the ones who had learned the best ways to deal with dolphins. Toshio had always assumed he'd be one of them.

Now that was all over. If he got back to *Streaker* he'd have to hide in his cabin . . . for at least the few days or weeks it took for the victors of the battle over Kithrup to come down and claim them all.

On his sonar screen, another fuzzy line of static was approaching from the west. Toshio let the sled slip a little deeper. Not that he cared. He continued to whistle, but he felt like crying.

where—where—where child is—where child is? where #

Primal Delphin! Nearby! Almost, Toshio forgot his shame. He fingered a rope left over from Brookida's lashings, and kept whistling.

A streak of gray twilight flashed past him. Toshio gathered his knees under him and took the rope in both hands. He knew Keepiru would circle below and come up the other side. When he saw the first hint of gray hurtling upward, Toshio launched himself from the sled.

The bullet-like body of the dolphin twisted in an abrupt, panicky attempt to avoid collision. Toshio cried out as the cetacean's tail struck him in the chest. But it was a cry more of glee than pain. He had timed it right!

As Keepiru twisted around again, Toshio flung himself backward, allowing the fin to pass between himself and the rope. He clamped his feet around the dolphin's slick tail and pulled the rope with all the will of a garroter.

"Got you!" he cried.

At that instant the aftershock hit.

The cycloid clutched and pulled at him. Bits of flotsam struck him as the suction tossed his body about in apparent alliance with the mad, bucking dolphin.

This time Toshio felt no fear of the wave. He was filled with a fierce battle lust. Adrenalin seared through him like a hot flux. It pleased him to save Keepiru's life by physically punishing him for weeks of humiliation.

The dolphin writhed in panic. As the shock rolled past them, Keepiru cried out the basic call for air. Desperately, the fin drove for the surface.

They breached, and Toshio just missed getting blasted

by the spume from Keepiru's blowhole. Keepiru commenced a series of leaps, gyrating to shake loose of his unwelcome rider.

Each time they went underwater Toshio tried to call out.

"You're *sentient*," he gasped. "Damn you, Keepiru... you're... you're a *starship pilot!*"

He knew he should be doing his coaxing in Trinary, but it was no use even trying, when he could barely hold on for dear life.

"You pea-brained... phallic symbol!" he screamed as the water slammed against him. "You over-rated *fish!* You're *killing* me, you goddamed... The Eatees own Calafia by now because you fins can't hold your tongues! We never should have taken you along into space!"

The words were hateful. Contemptuous. At last Keepiru seemed to have heard. He reared out of the water like an enraged stallion. Toshio felt his grip tear loose, and he was flung away like a rag doll, to hit the sea with a splash.

Only eighteen cases were known, in the forty generations of dolphin uplift, in which a fin had attacked a human with murderous intent. In each case, every fin related to the perpetrator had been sterilized. Still, Toshio expected to be crushed at any instant. He didn't care. He had realized, at last, the cause of his depression. It had come to the surface when he was wrestling with Keepiru.

It hadn't been his ability to go home that had hurt, these last few weeks. It was another fact that he had not allowed himself to think of even once since the battle off Morgran.

The ETs... the extraterrestrials... the Galactics of every stripe and philosophy which were chasing *Streaker*...would not settle for hunting down the dolphin-crewed ship.

At least one ET race would have seen that the *Streak* might successfully go into hiding. Or they might imagine, erroneously, that her crew had succeeded in passing the secret of her discovery to Earth. Either way, the logical next step for one of the more amoral or vicious Galactic races would be coercion.

Earth might be able to defend herself. Probably Omnivarium and Hermes, as well. The Tymbrimi would defend the Caanan colonies.

But places like Calafia, or Atlast, must be captured by now. They were hostages, his family and everyone he had known. And Toshio realized that he blamed the fins.

Another aftershock was due any minute now. Toshio didn't care.

Pieces of floating debris drifted all about nearby. Not more than a kilometer away Toshio could see the metal-mound. At least it looked like the same one. He couldn't tell if there were dolphins stranded on the shore or not.

A large piece of flotsam drifted near him. It took him a moment to realize that it was Keepiru.

Toshio treaded water as he opened his faceplate.

"Well," he asked, "are you proud of yourself?"

Keepiru turned slightly to one side, and one dark eye looked up at Toshio. The bulge at the top of the cetacean's head, where human meddling had created a vocal apparatus from the former blowhole, gave out a long, soft, warbling sound.

Toshio couldn't be certain it was just a sigh. It might have been an apology in Primal Delphin. The possibility alone was enough to make him angry.

"Can that crap! I just want to know one thing. Do I have to send you back to the ship? Or do you think you can stay sentient long enough to help me? Answer in Anglic, and it had better be grammatically correct!"

Keepiru moaned in pure anguish. After a moment of heavy breathing he finally spoke, quite slowly.

"Don't sssend me back. They're still calling for help! I will do what you ask-k-k!"

Toshio hesitated. "All right. Go down after the sled. When you've found it, put on a breather. I don't want you hampered by need for air, and you need a constant reminder with you, too!

"Then bring the sled up near the island, *but not too close!*"

Keepiru flung his head up in a huge nodding motion. "Yesss!" he cried. Then he flipped and dove into the water. It was just as well Keepiru had left all the thinking to him.

The fin might have balked if he'd caught onto what Toshio had in mind to do next.

A kilometer to the island; there was only one way to get there fast and avoid a scramble up the slanting, abrasive, metal-coral surface. He checked his orientation one more time, then a drop in the water level told him that the wave was coming.

The fourth wave seemed the gentlest by far. He knew

the feeling was deceptive. He was in water deep enough so that the swell came at him as a gentle lump in the ocean, rather than a crested breaker. He dove down into the hump and swam against the direction of motion for a time before rising to the surface.

He had to gauge it just right. Swim back too far and he wouldn't reach the island before the following trough arrived and pulled him out to sea again. To remain at the front of the wave would be to body-surf a vicious breaker onto the beach, undertow and all.

It was all happening too fast. He swam hard, but couldn't tell if he had passed the peak of the wave or not. Then a glance told him that it was too late for remedial measures. He flipped around to face the looming, foliage-topped mound.

The breaker started a hundred yards ahead, but the slope rapidly ate away at the wave as bottom dragged the cycloid into a crested monster. The peak moved backward, toward Toshio, even as the wave hurtled upward onto the beach.

The boy braced himself as the crest reached him. He was prepared to look down on a precipice, and then see nothing more.

What he saw was a cataract of white foam as the wave began to die. Toshio cried out to keep his ear channels open, and started swimming furiously to stay atop the churning tide of spume and debris.

Suddenly, there was greenery all around. Trees and shrubs which had withstood the earlier assaults shook under this attack. Some tore loose of their moorings even as Toshio flew past them. Others stood and flailed at him as he hurtled through.

No sharp branch impaled him. No unbreaking vine garroted him as he passed. In a tumbling, tossing confusion he finally came to rest, somehow hugging the trunk of a huge tree, while the wave churned, and finally receded.

Miraculously, he was on his feet, the first man to stand on the soil of Kithrup. Toshio stared dazedly at his surroundings, briefly not believing his survival.

Then he hurriedly opened his faceplate, and became the first man to lose his breakfast on the soil of Kithrup.

8

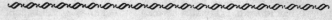

Galactics

"Slay them!" The Jophur high priest demanded. "Slay the isolated Thennanin battlecruisers on our sixth quadrant!"

The Jophur chief of staff bowed its twelve-ringed trunk before the high priest.

"The Thennanin are our allies-of-the-moment! How can we turn on them without first performing the secret rituals of betrayal? Their ancestors will not be appeased!"

The Jophur high priest expanded its six outer sap-rings. It rose high upon its dais at the rear of the command chamber.

"There is no time to perform the rites! Now, as our alliance finishes sweeping this sector, as our alliance has become the strongest! Now, while this phase of the battle still rages. Now, while the foolish Thennanin have opened up their flanks to us. Now may we harm them greatly!"

The chief of staff pulsed in agitation, its outer sap-rings discoloring with emotion.

"We may change alliances as it suits us, agreed. We may betray our allies, agreed. We may do anything to win the prize, agreed. But we may not do so without performing the rituals! The rituals are what make us the appropriate vessels for the will of the ancients! You would bring us down to the level of the heretics!"

The dais shook with the high priest's anger.

"My rings decide! My rings are those of priesthood! My rings . . ."

The oration-peak of the pyramidal high priest erupted in a geyser of hot, multi-hued sap. The explosion spewed sticky amber liquor across the bridge of the Jophur flagship.

"Continue fighting." The chief of staff waved the crew back to work with its sidearm. *"Call the Quartermaster of Religiosity. Have it send up rings to make up a new priest. Continue fighting while we prepare to perform the rituals of betrayal."*

The chief of staff bowed to the staring section chiefs. *"We shall appease the ancestors of the Thennanin before we turn on them.*

"But remember to make certain the Thennanin themselves do not sense our intentions!"

9

From The Journal of Gillian Baskin

It's been some time since I've been able to make an entry in this personal log. Since the Shallow Cluster it seems we've constantly been in frantic motion ... making the discovery of the millennia, getting ambushed at Morgran, and fighting for our lives from then on. I hardly ever see Tom any more. He's always down in the engine or weapons pods. I'm either here in the lab or helping out in sick bay.

Ship's surgeon Makanee has a mouthful of problems. Fen have always had a talent for hypochondria. A fifth of the crew shows up every sick call with psychosomatic complaints. You can't just tell them it's all in their heads, so we stroke them and tell them what brave fellows they are, and that everything's going to be all right.

I think if it weren't for the captain, half of this crew would be hysterical by now. To many of them he seems almost like a hero out of the Whale Dream. Creideiki moves about the ship, watching the repairs and giving little lessons in Keneenk logic. The fen seem to buck up whenever he's nearby.

Still, reports keep coming in about the space battle.

Instead of tapering off, it's only getting thicker and heavier!

And we're all getting more than a little worried about Hikahi's party.

Gillian put down her stylus. From the small circle of her desk lamp, the rest of the laboratory appeared dark and gloomy. The only other light came from the far end of the room. Silhouetted against the spots was a vaguely humanoid shape, a mysterious shadow, lying on a stasis table.

"Hikahi," she sighed. "Where in Ifni's name *are* you?"

That Hikahi's survey party hadn't even sent back a monopulse confirmation of the recall order was now of great concern. *Streaker* couldn't afford to lose those crewfen. For all of his frequent unreliability outside the bridge, Keepiru was their best pilot. Even Toshio Iwashika had a lot of promise.

But most of all, the loss of Hikahi would hurt. Without her, how could Creideiki manage?

Hikahi was Gillian's best dolphin friend, at least as close to her as Tom was to Creideiki or Tsh't. Gillian wondered why Takkata-Jim had been appointed vice-captain instead of Hikahi. It made no sense. She could only imagine that politics was behind it. Takkata-Jim was a *Stenos*. Perhaps Ignacio Metz had had a hand in choosing the complement for this mission. Metz was a passionate advocate of certain dolphin racial types back on Earth.

Gillian didn't write these thoughts down. They were idle speculations, and she didn't have time for speculation.

Anyway, it's time I got back to Herbie.

She closed her journal and got up to walk over to the stasis table, where a dry, dessicated figure floated in a heavily shielded field of suspended time.

The ancient cadaver grinned back at her through the glass.

It wasn't human. There hadn't even been multi-cellular creatures on Earth when this thing had lived and breathed and flown spaceships. Yet it looked eerily humanoid. It had straight arms and legs, and a very man-like head and neck. Its jaw and eye orbits were strange-looking, but its skull still had a very man-like grin.

How old are you, Herbie? she asked in her thoughts. *One billion years? Two?*

How is it your fleet of ancient hulks waited undiscovered

by Galactic civilization for so long, waited until we came
along...a bunch of wolfling humans and newly uplifted
dolphins? Why were we the ones to find you?

And why did one litle hologram of you, beamed home to
Earth, make half the patron-lines in the galaxy go crazy?

Streaker's micro-*Library* was no help. It refused to
recognize Herbie at all. Maybe it was holding back. Or
perhaps it was simply too small an archive to remember an
obscure race so long extinct.

Tom had asked the Niss machine look into it. So far the
sarcastic Tymbrimi artifact had been unable to cozen out an
answer.

Meanwhile, between sick bay and her other duties,
Gillian had to find a few hours a day to examine this relict
non-destructively, and maybe figure out what was stirring up
the Eatees so. If she didn't do it, no one would.

Somehow she would make it until tonight.

Poor Tom, Gillian thought, smiling. *He'll be coming
back from his engines, wiped out, and I'll be feeling amorous.
It's a damned good thing he's a sport.*

She picked up a pion microprobe.

*Okay Herbie, let's see if we can find out what kind of a
brain you had.*

10

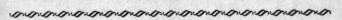

Metz

"I'm sorry, Dr. Metz. The captain is with Thomasss
Orley in the weapons section. If there's anything I can
do...?"

As usual, Vice-Captain Takkata-Jim was unfailingly polite.
His Anglic diction, even while breathing oxywater, was al-
most perfect. Ignacio Metz couldn't help smiling in approval.
He had a particular interest in Takkata-Jim.

"No, Vice-Captain. I just stopped by the bridge to see if the survey party had reported in."

"They haven't. We can only wait."

Metz tsked. He had already concluded that Hikahi's party was destroyed.

"Ah, well. I don't suppose there has been any offer of negotiations by the Galactics yet?"

Takkata-Jim shook his large, mottled-gray head left to right.

"Regrettably, no sir. They appear to be more interested in slaughtering each other. Every few hours, it seems, yet another battle fleet enters Kthsemenee's system to join in the free-for-all. It may be a while before anyone initiates diplomacy."

Dr. Metz frowned at the illogic of it. If the Galactics were rational, they'd let *Streaker* hand her discovery over to the *Library Institute* and have done with it! Then everyone would share equally!

But Galactic civilization was unified more in the breach than in fact. And too many angry species had big ships and guns.

Here we are, he thought, *in the middle, with something they all want.*

It can't just be that giant fleet of ancient ships. Something more must have set them off. Gillian Baskin and Tom Orley picked something up out there in the Shallow Cluster. I wonder what it was.

"Will you be wanting me to join you for dinner this evening, Dr. Metz?"

Metz blinked. What day was it? Ah, yes. Wednesday. "Of course, Vice-Captain. Your company and conversation would be appreciated, as usual. Shall we say sixish?"

"Perhapsss nineteen-hundred hours would be better, sir. I get off duty then."

"Very well. Until then."

Takkata-Jim nodded. He turned and swam back to his duty station.

Metz watched the fin appreciatively.

He's the best of my Stenos, Metz thought. *He doesn't know I'm his godfather . . . his gene-father. But I am proud nonetheless.*

All the dolphins aboard were of *Tursiops amicus* stock. But some had genetic grafts from *Stenos bredanensis,* the deep-water dolphin that had always been the closest to the bottlenose in intelligence.

Wild *bredanensis* had a reputation for insatiable curiosity and reckless disregard for danger. Metz had led the effort to have DNA from that species added to the neo-fin gene pool. On Earth many of the new *Stenos* had turned out very well, showing streaks of initiative and individual brilliance.

But a reputation for harsh temperament had lately caused some resentment in Earth's coastal communities. He had worked hard to convince the Council that it would be an important gesture to appoint a few *Stenos* to positions of responsibility on the first dolphin-crewed starship.

Takkata-Jim was his proof. Coldly logical, primly correct, the fin used Anglic almost to the exclusion of Trinary, and seemed impervious to the Whale Dream that so enthralled older models like Creideiki. Takkata-Jim was the most manlike dolphin Metz had ever met.

He watched the vice-captain manage the bridge crew, with none of the little Keneenk parables Creideiki was always inserting, but rather with Anglic precision and brevity. Never a word wasted.

Yes, he thought. This one is going to get a good report when we get home.

"*Doctor Metssss?*"

Metz turned, and recoiled at the size of the dolphin that had silently come up beside him. "Wha... ? Oh. K'tha-Jon. You startled me. What can I do for you?"

A truly large dolphin grinned at him. His blunt mouth, his counter-shaded body and bulging eyes, would have told Metz everything about him... if he hadn't already known.

Feresa attenuata, the human savored the thought. *So beautiful and savage. My most secret project, and nobody, not even you, K'tha-Jon, knows that you are more than just another* Stenos.

"Forgive the interruption, Dr. Metsss, but the chimp scientist Charlesss Dart-t has asked to speak with you. I think the little ape wantsss to bitch to somebody again."

Metz frowned. K'tha-Jon was only a bosun, and not expected to be as refined as Takkata-Jim. Still, there were limits, even considering the giant's hidden background.

I will have to talk to this fellow, he reminded himself. *This kind of attitude will never do.*

"Please inform *Dr.* Dart that I'm on my way," he told the
fin. "I'm finished here for now."

11

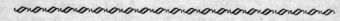

Creideiki & Orley

"So we're armed again," Creideiki sighed. "After a fash-
ion."

Thomas Orley looked up from the newly repaired missile
tubes and nodded. "It's about as good as we're going to get,
Creideiki. We weren't expecting any trouble when we popped
out into a battle at the Morgran transfer point. We were lucky
to get away with as little damage as we took."

Creideiki agreed.

"Just ssso," he sighed moodily. "If only I had reacted
faster."

Orley noticed his friend's mood. He pursed his lips and
whistled. His breather mask amplified a faint sound-shadow
picture. The little echo danced and hopped like a mad elf
from corner to corner in the oxywater-filled chamber. Workers
in the weapons pod lifted their narrow, sound-sensitive jaws
to follow the skipping sonar image as it scampered unseen,
chittering in mock sympathy.

> * *When one commands,*
> *One is envied by people—*
> *But, oh! the demands!* *

The sound-wraith vanished, but laughter remained. The
crew of the weapons pod spluttered and squawled.

Creideiki let the mirth settle. Then, from his brow came
a pattern of chamber-filling clicks that merged to mimic the
sounds of thunderclouds gathering. In the closed room those

present heard raindrops blown before the wind. Tom closed his eyes to let the sound-image of a sea squall close over him.

> * *They stand in my road,*
> *The mad, ancient, nasty things*
> *Tell them* "move, or else!" *

Orley bowed his head, acknowledging defeat. No one had ever beaten Creideiki at Trinary haiku. The admiring sighs of the fen only confirmed this.

Nothing had changed, of course. As Orley and Creideiki turned to leave the weapons pod, they knew that defiance alone would not get this crew through the crisis. There had to be hope, as well.

Hope was scarce. Tom knew that Creideiki was desperately worried about Hikahi, though he hid it well.

When they were out of earshot, the captain asked, "Has Gillian made any progressss studying that *thing* we found... the cause of all this trouble?"

Tom shook his head. "I haven't spent more than an hour with her in two days, so I don't know. Last I checked, the ship's micro-*Library* still claims nothing like Herbie ever existed."

Creideiki sighed. "It would have been nice to know what the Galacticsss *think* we found. Ah, well..."

They were stopped by a sudden whistle behind them. Tsh't, the ship's fourth officer, flew into the hallway in a cloud of bubbles.

"Creideiki! Tom! Sonar reports a dolphin at long range, far to the eassst, but apparently swimming this way at high speed!"

Creideiki and Orley looked at each other. Then Tom nodded at the captain's unspoken command.

"Can I take Tsh't and twenty fen?"

"Yesss. Get a team ready. But don't leave until we find out who this is. You may want to take more than twenty. Or it may be hopelesss to go at all."

Tom saw pain in the captain's eye. The next hour or so of waiting would be hard.

Orley motioned for Lieutenant Tsh't to follow him, then he turned to swim at top speed down the flooded corridor toward the outlock.

12

Galactics

Feeling the joy of patronhood and command, the Soro, Krat, watched the creatures, the Gello, the Paha, the Pila, her creatures, as they guided the Soro fleet toward battle once more.

"Mistress," the Gello detection officer announced. "We are approaching the water world at one-quarter of light-speed, per your instructions."

Krat acknowledged with a bare flick of her tongue, but secretly she was happy. Her egg was healthy. When they won here she would be due to go home and mate once more. And the crew of her flagship was working together like a finely tuned machine.

"The fleet is one paktaar ahead of timetable, mistress," the detection officer announced.

Of all the client species owing allegiance to the Soro, the Gello were special to Krat. They were her own species's first clients, uplifted by the Soro long ago. The Gello had in their turn become patrons as well, and brought two more client races into the clan. They had made the Soro proud. The chain of uplift went on.

Deep in the past had been the Progenitors, who began Galactic Law. Since then, race had aided race to sentience, taking indentured service as payment.

Many millions of years ago, the ancient Luber had uplifted the Puber, or so the Library said. The Luber were now long extinct. The Puber still existed, somewhere, though now degenerate and decadent.

Before their decadence, though, the Puber raised up the Hul, who in turn made clients of Krat's stone-chopping, Soro *ancestors. Shortly thereafter, the Hul retired to their homeworld to become philosophers.*

Now the Soro themselves had many clients. Their most successful upspring were the Gello, the Paha, and the Pila.

Krat could hear the high voice of the Pila tactician Cubber-cabub, haranguing its subordinates in planning section. It was insisting they strive harder to coax the information she had requested from the shipboard mini-Library. Cubber-cabub sounded frightened. Good. It would try harder if it feared her.

Alone of those aboard, the Pila were mammals, short bipeds from a high-gravity world. They had become a powerful race in many Galaxy-wide bureaucratic organizations, including the important Library Institute. The Pila had raised clients of their own, bringing credit to the clan.

Still, it was too bad the Pila were no longer indentured clients. It would have been nice to meddle with their genes again. The furry little sophonts shed, and had a bothersome odor.

No client race was perfect. Only two hundred years ago, the Pila had been thoroughly embarrassed by the humans of Earth. The affair had been difficult and expensive to cover up. Krat did not know all of the facts, but it had something to do with the Earthlings' sun. Since that time, the Pila had hated humans passionately.

Krat's mating claw throbbed as she thought of Earthlings. In only three hundred of their years they had become almost as great a nuisance as the sanctimonious Kanten, or the devil-trickster Tymbrimi!

The Soro race patiently awaited the right opportunity to erase the blot on their clan honor. Fortunately, the humans were almost pathetically ignorant and vulnerable. Perhaps the chance had already come!

How delicious it would be to have Homo sapiens assigned to the Soro as indentured foster clients. It could happen! Then what changes could be made! How humans could be molded!

Krat looked at her crew and wished she were free to meddle, to alter, to shape at will even these adult species. So much could be done with them! But that would require changing the rules.

If the upstart water-mammals from Earth had discovered what she thought they had, then the rules might be changed . . . if the Progenitors had, indeed, come back. How ironic that the newest spacefaring race should discover this derelict fleet! She almost forgave them for existing, for giving those humans the status of patrons.

"Mistress!" the tall Gello announced. "The Jophur-Thennanin alliance has broken up. They are fighting amongst themselves. This means they are no longer pre-eminent!"

"Maintain vigilance." Krat sighed. The Gello shouldn't make a big deal out of one little act of treachery. It was not unusual. Alliances would form and dissolve until one force emerged supreme. She intended that that force be Soro. When the battle was won she would collect the prize.

The dolphins must be here! When she won this battle, she would pry the handless ones out from their underwater sanctuary and make them tell all!

With a languid wave of her left paw, she summoned the Pil Librarian from his niche.

"Look into the data on these water creatures we pursue," she told it. "I want to know more about their habits, what they like and dislike. It is said their bonds to their human patrons are weak and corruptible. Give me a lever to pervert these . . . dolphins."

Cubber-cabub bowed and withdrew into the Library section, the sector with the rayed spiral glyph above its opening.

Krat felt destiny all around her. This place in space was a fulcrum of power. She didn't need instruments to tell her that.

"I will have them! The rules will be changed!"

13

Toshio

Toshio found Ssattatta by the bole of the giant drill-tree. The fin had been thrown against the monstrous plant and crushed. Her harness was a jumble of broken pieces.

Toshio stumbled through the ruined undergrowth, whistling a Trinary call when he felt able. Mostly he tried very hard to stay on his feet. He hadn't walked much since leaving Earth. Bruises and nausea didn't help much, either.

He found K'Hith lying on a soft bed of grass-like growth. His harness was intact, but the dolphin planetologist had already bled to death from three deep gashes in his belly. Toshio made a mental note of the spot and moved on.

Closer to the shore he found Satima. The little female was bleeding and hysterical, but alive. Toshio bound her wounds with fleshfoam and repair tape. Then he took the manipulator arms of her harness and used a large rock to pound them into the loam. It was the best he could do to bind her to the ground before the fifth wave hit.

It was more a flooding than a wave. Toshio clung to a tree as it flowed past, tugging at him and rising almost to his neck.

As soon as the wave began to recede, he let go and floundered over to Satima. He groped until he found the catch on her harness, then released her to float in the growing backtow. He pushed hard to join the flood and keep from being left behind.

He was struggling to shove her around a clump of shrubs, against the growing pull of the backwash, when a swift motion in a tree overhead caught his eye. The movement didn't fit into the overall pattern of swaying subsidence. He looked up, and met the gaze of a pair of small, black eyes.

There was little time for more than a startled double take before the tide pulled him and Satima straight through the obstruction and into a small, recently made marsh. Toshio was suddenly too busy to look anywhere but straight ahead.

He had to pull Satima down the last few yards of slippery sea-plant, taking care not to reopen her wounds. In the last few minutes it had seemed she was more lucid. Her Delphin squeakings were starting to take on form and sound like Trinary words.

A whistle brought Toshio's head up. Keepiru was only forty meters offshore, driving the sled toward him. The fin had on a breather, but he could still signal.

"Satima!" Toshio shouted to the wounded dolphin. "Go to the sled! Go to Keepiru!"

"Lash her to an airdome!" he called to Keepiru. "And keep your eye on that sonar screen! Get back out there when you see a wave coming!"

Keepiru tossed his head. As soon as Satima was a hundred feet out he used the sled to herd her toward deeper water.

Five accounted for. That left Hist-t and Hikahi.

Toshio climbed back up the sea-plant and stumbled into the undergrowth once again. The territory of his mind seemed as torn up and desolated as the island he trod upon. He had seen too many corpses for one day—too many dead friends.

He realized now that he had been unfair to the fins all along.

It had been unjust to blame them for teasing him. They couldn't help the way they were built. All of man's genetic meddling notwithstanding, dolphins had been dealing with humanity on a level of good-natured derision since the first person paddled a log canoe out to sea. That pathetic image had been enough to set a pattern that uplift could only alter, not eliminate.

And why eliminate it? Toshio now saw that those humans he had known on Calafia, who worked best with dolphins, had had a special type of personality, generally featuring a mixture of a thick skin, firmness, and a willing sense of humor. No one worked for long with fins who hadn't earned their respect.

He hurried over to a gray form that lay in the underbrush. But no. It was Ssattatta again. She had been moved by the last wave. Toshio stumbled on.

Dolphins were quite well aware of what Mankind had done for them. Uplift was a painful process. But none of them would go back to the Whale Dream if they could help it.

The fins knew, as well, that the loose codes that ruled behavior among the Galactic races, rules established in the *Library* for aeons, would have let humanity demand a hundred thousand years of servitude from its clients. Men had collectively shuddered at the thought. *Homo sapiens sapiens* himself was barely that age. If Mankind *did* have a patron out there—one strong enough to lay claim to the title—that species wasn't going to pick up *Tursiops amicus* as an added bonus.

There wasn't a fin alive who wasn't aware of Earth's attitude. There were dolphins on the Terragens Council, as well as chimpanzees.

Toshio knew at last how he had hurt Keepiru with his words during their struggle at sea. Most of all he regretted the remark about Calafia. Keepiru would willingly die a thousand times to save the humans of Toshio's homeworld.

Toshio's tongue would fall off before he said such things again. Ever.

He staggered into a clearing. There, in a shallow pool, lay a *Tursiops* dolphin.

"Hikahi!"

The fin was scratched and battered. Tiny bloody tracks lay along her sides. But she was awake. And as Toshio started forward she called out.

"Stay there, Sharp-Eyes! Don't-t move! We have company here!"

Toshio stopped in his tracks. Hikahi's command was specific. Yet the need to go to her was urgent. The dolphin's scratches did not look pleasant. If there were slivers of metal lodged under the skin they had to be removed soon, before blood poisoning set in. And it wasn't going to be easy getting Hikahi out to sea.

"Hikahi, there'll be another wave soon. It may reach this high. We've got to be ready for it!"

"Stay, Toshio. The wave will not reach here. Besides, look around. See how much more important this isss!"

For the first time, Toshio really noticed the clearing. The pool was set near one side, with scratch marks all around, indicating that it had been recently dug. Then he saw that the manipulator arms from Hikahi's harness were missing.

Then who...? Toshio's perception shifted. He saw twisted debris at the far end of the clearing, scattered through the undergrowth, and recognized the fragments of a ruined, shattered village.

In the chronic shimmering of a Kithrupan forest he saw the fragments of rude, torn, woven nets, scattered pieces of wrecked thatching, and bits of sharp metal crudely bound to wooden staves.

In the tree branches he saw fleet little movements. Then, one by one, small, splayed, web-fingered hands appeared—followed by slowly peeking, shining black eyes that peered back at him from under low, greenish brows.

"Abos!" he whispered. "I saw one earlier, then forgot completely! They look pre-sentient!"

"Yesss," Hikahi sighed. "And this makes secrecy even more vital than ever. Quickly, Sharp-Eyes! Tell me what has happened!"

Toshio related only what he had done since the first wave struck, leaving out only the details of his battle with Keepiru. It was hard to concentrate, with the eyes in the trees first staring down at him, then skittishly darting under cover whenever he glanced their way. He barely finished his story as the last wave arrived.

The breakers could be seen driving up the sloping shore with a loud roar and a white foaming. But clearly Hikahi was right. The water wouldn't rise this high.

"Toshio!" Hikahi whistled. "You've done very well. You may have saved these little people, as well as ourselves. Brookida will succeed. He will bring help.

"So saving me is not that important. You *must* do as I say! Have Keepiru dive at once! He must stay out of sight and remain quiet as possible as he searches for bodies and debris. You must bury Ssattatta and K'Hith and gather the fragments of their harnesses. When help comes we must be able to move quickly!"

"Are you sure you'll be all right? Your wounds..."

"I'll be fine! My friends keep me wet-t. The trees overhang to keep me hidden. Watch the skies, Sharp-Eyes! Don't be seen! When you're finished I hope to have coaxed our friends here into trusting you."

She sounded tired. Toshio was torn. Finally, he sighed and turned back to the forest. He forced himself to run through the broken foliage, following the receding waters to the shore.

Keepiru was just emerging as he arrived. The fin had removed his breather and wore an airdome instead. He reported finding the body of Phip-pit, the dolphin supposed lost earlier to the killer weed. The sucker-bruised body must have been torn loose during the tsunami.

"Any sign of Hist-t?" Toshio called.

Keepiru answered negative. Toshio passed on Hikahi's command and watched as the sled sank below again.

For a moment he stood there, then, looking out over the west.

Kithrup's reddish sun was setting. A few stars poked rays through the scattered clouds overhead. In the east the clouds were beginning to look ominous. There would be rain during the night. Toshio decided against taking off his drysuit, though he compromised by pulling the rubberized headpiece off. The breeze was chilling, but a huge relief.

He glanced to the south. If the battle in space continued, Toshio saw no sign of it. Kithrup's rotation had taken them past the shining globe of plasma and debris that must be drifting out there now.

Toshio lacked the will to shake his fist, but he grimaced toward the southern sky, hoping the Galactics had wiped each other out.

It wasn't likely. There would be victors. And someday soon they would be down here looking for dolphins and men.

Toshio pulled his shoulders back, in spite of his fatigue, and walked with deliberateness toward the forest, and the protecting, overhanging trees.

They found the young man and the dolphin shortly after landing. The two were huddled together under a crude shelter which dripped warm rain in long rivulets. Lightning flashes drowned out the muffled yellow light from the lamps the rescuers brought. In the first flash, Thomas Orley thought he saw a half-dozen small squat figures clustered around the Earthling and the Calafian. But by the time he and his partner had shoved through the undergrowth for a better view, the animals—or whatever they were—were gone.

His first fear that they had been carrion-eaters disappeared when he saw Toshio move. Still, he kept his right hand on the butt of his needler and held up the lantern to let Hannes Suessi pass underneath. He looked carefully around the clearing, taking in the smells and the sounds of the living surface of the metal-mound, memorizing details.

"Are they all right?" he asked after a few seconds.

"Shh, 't's okay, Toshio. It's just me, Hannes," he heard the engineer mutter. The fellow sounded downright maternal. "Yes, Mr. Orley." Suessi called back, "They're both awake, but not in much shape for talking."

Thomas Orley took in the clearing once more, then moved over to set the lamp down beside Suessi. "This lightning would cover anything," he said. "I'm going to call up the mechanicals so we can get these two out of here as quickly as possible." He touched a button on the rim of his faceplate and whistled quickly in perfect Trinary. The message lasted six seconds. It was said that Thomas Orley could actually speak Primal Delphin, though no human had ever witnessed it.

"They'll be here in a few minutes. They have to cover their tracks." He squatted down next to Toshio, who was sitting up now that Suessi had moved over to Hikahi.

"Hello, Mr. Orley," the boy said. "I'm sorry we dragged you away from your work."

"That's all right, son. I've been wanting to have a look around up here, anyway. This gave the captain a good excuse to send me. After we get you started back toward the ship, Hannes and Tsh't and I will be going on to look over that ship that crashed.

"Now, do you think you can lead us to Ssattatta and K'Hith? We want to comb this island clean before the storm passes."

Toshio nodded. "Yes, sir. I should be able to stumble around that long. I don't suppose anyone's found Hist-t?"

"No. We're worried about that, but nowhere near as worried as we were when Brookida got back. Keepiru's told us most of the story. That fin thinks rather highly of you, you know. You did quite a job here."

Toshio turned away, as if ashamed to receive the praise.

Orley looked at him curiously. He had never given much thought to the middie before. During the first part of the voyage, the youth had seemed bright, but a bit irresponsible. Later, after they found the derelict fleet, he had begun to turn morose, as their chances of ever going home diminished.

Now there was this new note. It was too soon to tell what the long-term effects would be, but this had obviously been a rite of passage for Toshio.

Humming sounds drifted up from the beach. Soon two spider-like mechanicals strode into view, a hammocked and harnessed dolphin piloting each of them.

Toshio sighed a little raggedly as Orley helped him up. Then the older man stooped to pick up an object from the ground. He hefted it in his left hand.

"A scraper, isn't it? Made from bits of metal fish spine glued to a wood handle..."

"I guess so."

"Do they have much of a language yet?"

"No, sir; well, the rudiments. They seem to be stabilized. Strict hunter-gatherers. Hikahi guesses they've been stuck for half a million years."

Orley nodded. This native species looked ripe, at first glance. A pre-sentient race at just the right stage for uplift. It was a miracle some Galactic patron line hadn't snapped them up already, for client status and an aeon of servitude.

Now the men and fen of *Streaker* had still another obligation, and secrecy was more important than ever.

He put the artifact in his pocket, then laid his hand on Toshio's shoulder.

"Well, you can tell us all about it back on the ship, son. In the meantime, you have some pondering to do."

"Sir?" Toshio looked up in confusion.

"Well, it isn't everybody who gets to name a future space-faring race. You know, the fen will be expecting you to make up a song about it."

Toshio looked at the older man, uncertain if he was joking. But Thomas Orley had on his usual enigmatic expression.

Orley glanced up at the rain clouds. As the mechanicals moved in to claim Hikahi, he stepped back and smiled at the curtain which, temporarily, hung across the theater of the sky.

PART TWO

Currents

"For the sky and the sea,
And the sea and the sky,
Lay like a load on my weary eye,
And the dead lay at my feet."

—S. T. COLERIDGE

14

Dennie

Charles Dart pulled away from the polarization micro-scope and growled an oath. In a habit he had spent half his life trying to break, he absently laid his forearms over his head and tugged on his hairy ears. It was a simian contortion no one else aboard ship could easily duplicate. Had he noticed he was doing it, he would have quit instantly.

Of a crew of one hundred and fifty, only eight aboard the *Streaker* even *had* arms . . . or external ears. One of these shared the drylab with him.

Commenting on Charles Dart's body behaviors did not occur to Dennie Sudman. She had long ceased to notice such things as his loose, rolling gait, his shrieking chimpanzee laughter, or the fur that nearly covered his body.

"What is it?" she asked. "Are you still having trouble with those core samples?"

Charlie nodded absently, staring at the screen. "Yeah."

His voice was low and scratchy. At his best, Charles Dart sounded like a man speaking with gravel in his throat. Sometimes, when he had something complicated to say, he unconsciously moved his hands in the sign language of his youth.

"I can't make any sense out of these isotope concentrations," he growled. "And there are minerals in all the wrong places . . . siderophiles without metals, complex crystals at a depth where there shouldn't be such complexity . . . Captain Creideiki's silly restrictions are crippling my work! I wish he'd let me do some seismic scans and deep radar." He swiveled about in his seat to look at Dennie earnestly, as if hoping she would concur.

Dennie's smile was broad under high cheekbones. Her almond eyes narrowed in amusement.

"Sure, Charlie. Why not? Here we are in a crippled ship, hidden under an ocean on a deadly world, with fleets from a dozen arrogant and powerful patron-lines fighting over the right to capture us, and you want to start setting off explosions and casting gravity beams around. Wonderful idea!

"Say! I've got an even better one! Why don't we just take out a large sign and wave it at the sky, something that says 'Yoohoo, beasties! Come and eat us!' Hmmm?"

Charlie cast a sidelong look at her, one of his rare, unhinged, lopsided grins. "Oh, they wouldn't have to be *big* gravity scans. And I'd only need a few teeny, tiny explosions for seismography. The ETs wouldn't notice those, you think?"

Dennie laughed. What Charlie wanted was to make the planet ring like a bell, so he could trace the patterns of seismic waves in the interior. Teeny tiny explosions, indeed! More likely detonations in the kiloton range! Sometimes Charlie seemed so single-minded a planetologist that it bothered Dennie. This time, however, he was obviously having some fun at his own expense.

He laughed as well, letting out brief whoops that echoed off the stark, white walls of the dry lab. He thumped the table beside him.

Grinning, Dennie filled a zip case with papers. "You know, Charlie, there are volcanoes going off all the time, a few degrees away from here. If you're lucky, one might start right near us."

Charlie looked hopeful. "Gee, you think so?"

"Sure. And if the ETs start bombing the planet to get at us, you'll have plenty of data from all the near misses. That is, if they don't bomb so hard as to make geophysical analyses of Kithrup moot. I envy you your potential silver lining. In the meantime, I intend to forget about it, and my own frustrating research, and go get some lunch. Coming?"

"Naw. Thanks, though. I brought my own. I think I'll stay and work for a while."

"Suit yourself. Still, you might try to see more of the ship, other than your quarters and this lab."

"I talk to Metz and Brookida all the time on screen. I

don't need to wander around gawking at this Rube Goldberg contraption that can't even fly any more."

"And besides..." she prompted.

Charlie grinned. "And besides, I hate getting wet. I *still* think you humans should have worked on dogs second, after casting your spells on us *Pan* types. Dolphins are all right— some of my best friends are fins. But they were a funny bunch to try to make into a space-traveling race!"

He shook his head with an expression of sad wisdom. Obviously he thought the whole uplift process on Earth would have been better handled had his people been in charge.

"Well, they're superb space pilots, for one thing," Dennie suggested. "Look at how hot a star-jockey Keepiru is."

"Yeah, and look at what a jerk-off that fin can be when he's *not* piloting. Honestly, Dennie, this trip has made me wonder if fins are really ready for spaceflight. Have you seen how some of 'em have been acting since we got into trouble? All the pressure is making some of 'em unravel, especially some of Metz's big *Stenos*."

"You're not being very charitable," Dennie chided. "Nobody ever expected this mission to be so stressful. I think most of the fen are doing marvelously. Look at how Creideiki slipped us away from that trap at Morgran."

Charlie shook his head. "I dunno. I still wish there were more men and chimps aboard."

One century, that's how much longer than dolphins chimps had been a recognized space-faring species. Dennie figured a million years from now they would still hold a patronizing attitude toward fins.

"Well, if you're not coming, I'm off," Dennie said. She took her notecase and touched the palm-plate by the door. "See you, Charlie."

The chimp called after her, before the door hissed shut behind her.

"Oh, by the way! If you run into Tkaat or Sah'ot, have em call me, eh? I'm thinking these subduction anomalies may be paleotechnic! An archaeologist may be interested!"

Dennie let the door close without answering. If she didn't acknowledge Charlie's request, she could feign ignorance later. There was no way she would go out of her way to speak to Sah'ot, whatever the significance of Charlie's find!

Avoiding that particular dolphin was already taking up too much of her time.

The dry sections of the starship *Streaker* were extensive, though they served only eight members of the crew. The one hundred and thirty dolphins—down by thirty-two since they had left Earth—could only visit the dry-wheel by riding a mechanical walker or "spider."

There were some rooms that should not be flooded with hyper-oxgenated water, nor be left to the gravity fluctuations of the cental shaft when the ship was in space. There were stores that had to be kept dry, and machine shops that performed hot processing under gravity. And there were the living quarters for men and chimp.

Dennie stopped at an intersection. She looked down the hallway where most of the humans had their cabins and thought about knocking on the door two cabins down. If Tom Orley were in, this could be the time to ask his advice about a problem that was growing daily more irksome, the way to handle Sah'ot's unusual... "attentions."

There were few people better qualified to advise her on non-human behavior than Thomas Orley. His official title was Alien Technologies Consultant, but it was clear he was also out here as a psychologist, to help Dr. Metz and Dr. Baskin evaluate the performance of an integrated dolphin crew. He knew cetaceans, and might be able to tell her what Sah'ot wanted from her.

Tom would know what to do, but...

Her habitual indecision reasserted itself. There were plenty of reasons not to bother Tom right now, like the fact that he was spending every waking moment trying to find a way to save all of their lives. Of course, the same could be said of most of the crew, but experience and reputation suggested that Orley just might be able to come up with a way to get *Streaker* and her crew away from Kithrup before the ETs captured her.

Dennie sighed. Another reason to put it off was pure embarrassment. It wasn't easy for a young fem to ask personal advice of a mel as worldly as Thomas Orley. Particularly when the subject was how to cope with the advances of an amorous porpoise.

However kind Tom would be, he would also be forced to laugh—or obviously bite back laughter. The situation, Dennie admitted, would *have* to seem funny, to anyone but the object of the seduction.

Dennie quickened her pace up the gently curved corridor toward the lift. *Why did I ever want to go into space, anyway?* she asked herself. *Sure, it was an opportunity to advance my career. And my personal life was in a shambles anyway, on Earth. But* now *where am I? My analysis of Kithrupan biology is getting nowhere. There are thousands of bug-eyed monsters circling over the planet slathering to come down and get me, and a horny dolphin's harassing me with suggestions that would make Catherine the Great blush.*

It wasn't fair, of course, but when had life ever been fair?

Streaker had been built from a modified *Snarkhunter*-class exploration vessel. Few Snarks were still in service. As Terrans became more comfortable with the refined technologies of the *Library,* they learned to combine the old and new—ancient Galactic designs and indigenous Terran technologies. This process had been in a particularly awkward phase when the Snarks were built.

The ship was a bulb-ended cylinder with jutting, crane-like reality flanges in five bands of five along her hull. In space the flanges anchored her to a protecting sphere of stasis. Now they served as landing legs as the wounded *Streaker* lay on her side in a muddy canyon, eighty meters below the surface of an alien sea.

Between the third and fourth rings of flanges, the hull bulged outward slightly for the dry-wheel. In free space the wheel rotated, providing a primitive form of artificial gravity. Humans and their clients had learned how to generate gravity fields, but almost every Earth ship still possessed a centrifugal wheel. Some saw it as a trademark, advertising what some friendly species had recommended Terrans keep quiet, that the three races of Sol were different from any others in space . . . the "orphans" of Earth.

Streaker's wheel held room for up to forty humans, though right now there were only seven and one chimpanzee. It also held recreation facilities for the dolphin crew, pools for leaping and splashing and sexual play during off-duty hours.

But on a planet's surface the wheel could not turn. Most of its rooms were tilted and inaccessible. And the great central bay of the ship was filled with water.

Dennie rode a lift up one of the spokes connecting the dry-wheel to the ship's rigid spine. The spine supported *Streaker's* open interior. Dennie stepped from the elevator into a hexagonal hallway with doors and access panels at all angles, until she reached the main bay lock, fifty meters forward of the wheel spokes.

In weightlessness she would have glided rather than walked down the long passage. Gravity made the corridor eerily unfamiliar.

In the bay-lock, a wall of transparent cabinets held spacesuits and diving gear. Dennie chose a bikini from her locker, and a facemask and flippers. Under "normal" circumstances she would have donned coveralls, a small jet belt, and possibly a pair of broad armwings. She could have leapt into the central bay and flown the humid air to any place she wanted, providing she was careful of the rotating spokes of the dry-wheel.

Now, of course, the spokes were still, and the central bay contained something more humid than air.

She quickly stripped and stepped into the swimsuit. Then she stopped in front of a mirror and tugged at the strings until the bikini was comfortable. Dennie knew she was attractively built. At least the mels she knew had told her so often enough. Still, slightly broad shoulders gave her an excuse for the self-reproach she always seemed to be looking for.

She tested the mirror with a smile. The image was instantly transformed. Strong white teeth brilliantly balanced her dark brown eyes.

She let it lapse. Dimples made her look younger, an effect to be avoided at all cost. She sighed and carefully pushed her jet black hair into a rubber diving cap.

Well, let's get this over with.

She checked the seals on her notecase and entered the lock. When she closed the inner hatch, fizzing saline water began flooding into the chamber from vents around the floor.

Dennie avoided looking down. She fumbled with her Batteau breather mask, making it snug over her face. The transparent membrane felt tough, but it passed air in and out freely as she took rapid, deep breaths. Numerous flexible plates around its rim would help pull enough air from supercharged oxywater. At the corners of her vision, the mask was equipped with small sonar displays, which were supposed to help make up for a human's substantial deafness underwater.

Warm bubbling wetness climbed her legs. Dennie readjusted her facemask several times. Her elbow pressed the notecase close against her side. When the fluid had almost reached her shoulders, she immersed her head and breathed hard with her eyes closed.

The mask worked. Of course, it always did. It felt like inhaling in a thick ocean mist, but there was enough air. A bit sheepish over her fearful little ritual, she stood up straight and waited for the water to rise over her head.

At last the door opened, and Dennie swam out into a large chamber where spiders, "walkers," and other dolphin gear lay neatly folded in recesses. Tucked into orderly shelves were racks of the small water-jetpacks that the dolphins used to move about in the ship in weightlessness. The jets made amazing acrobatics possible in free fall, but on a planet, with most of the ship flooded, they were useless.

Usually one or two fen were in this outer dressing room, wriggling into or out of equipment. Puzzled by the emptiness, Dennie swam to the opening at the far end of the chamber and looked out into the central bay.

The great cylinder was only twenty meters across. The vista wasn't as impressive as the view from the hub of one of the space cities of Sol's asteroid belts. Still, whenever she entered the central bay, her first impression was one of vast and busy space. Long radial shafts stretched out from spine to cylinder wall, holding the ship rigid and carrying power to the stasis flanges. Between these columns were dolphin work areas, arrayed on supports of resilient mesh.

Dolphins, even the *Tursiops amicus*, didn't like being cooped up any more than they had to be. In space, the crew worked in the weightless openness of the central bay, jetting about in humid air. But Creideiki had to land his damaged ship in an ocean. And this meant he had also had to flood the ship in order to enable his workers to reach their instruments.

The bay shimmered with a barely suppressed effervescence. Here and there tiny streams of bubbles rose toward the curving ceiling. The waters of Kithrup were carefully filtered, solvents added, and oxygen forced in to make oxywater. Neo-dolphins had been gene-crafted to be able to breathe it, though they didn't enjoy it much.

Dennie looked around, puzzled. Where was everyone?

Motion caught her eye. Above the five-meter span of the central spine, two dolphins and two humans swam rapidly toward the ship's bow. "Hey!" she shouted. "Wait for me!"

The facemask was supposed to focus and amplify the sound of her voice, but to Dennie it sounded as if the water swallowed her words.

The fen stopped at once. In unison they swooped about toward her. The two humans swam on for a few moments, then paused and looked about, moving their arms slowly. When they caught sight of Dennie, one of them waved.

"Hurry up, honored biologissst!" A large, charcoal-gray dolphin in heavy work harness swooped past Dennie. The other one circled about impatiently.

Dennie swam as hard as she could. "What's going on? Is the space battle over? Has someone found us?"

A stocky black man grinned as she approached. The other human, a tall, stately, blonde woman, impatiently turned to go as soon as Dennie had caught up.

"Now, wouldn't we have heard alarms, then, if there'd been ETs comin'?" The black man kidded her as they swam above the spine. Why Emerson D'Anite, with his dark coloration, chose at times to affect a burr was a secret which Dennie had yet to pry out of him.

She was relieved to hear they weren't under attack, but if the Galactics weren't coming to get them yet, what was all the fuss?

"The prospecting party!" The fate of the lost patrol had completely slipped her mind, so caught up had she been in her own problems. "Gillian, have they come back? Have Toshio and Hikahi returned?"

The older woman swam with a reaching, long-limbed grace that Dennie envied. Her low, alto voice somehow carried well through the water. Her expression was grim.

"Yes Dennie, they're back. But at least four of them are dead."

Dennie gasped. She had to make an effort to keep up. "Dead? How...? Who...?"

Gillian Baskin didn't slacken her pace. She answered over her shoulder. "We aren't sure how.... When Brookida made it back, he mentioned Phip-pit and Ssassia...and told the rescue party they'd probably find others beached or killed."

"Brookida...?"

Emerson jogged her with his elbow. "And where have *you* been? It was announced when he got in, hours ago. Mr. Orley took old Hannes and twenty crewfen to find Hikahi and the others."

"I . . . I must have been asleep at the time." Dennie contemplated slowly taking apart a certain chimpanzee. *Why didn't Charlie tell me when I came in for work? It probably slipped his mind entirely. One of these days that chimp's monomania will cause somebody to strangle him!*

Dr. Baskin had already pulled ahead with the two dolphins. She was almost as fast a swimmer as Tom Orley, and none of the other five humans aboard could keep up with her when she hurried.

Dennie turned to D'Anite. "Tell me about it!"

Emerson quickly summarized the story Brookida had told—of a killer weed, of a burning, falling star cruiser, and of the savage waves that followed its crash, setting off the desperate cycle of rescue fever.

Dennie was stunned by the story, especially young Toshio's role. That didn't sound like Toshio Iwashika at all. He had been the one person aboard *Streaker* who seemed younger and lonelier than she. She liked the middie, of course, and hoped he hadn't lost his life trying to be a hero.

Emerson then told her the most recent rumors—about an island rescue during a midnight storm, and aboriginal tool users.

This time Dennie stopped in midstroke. "*Abos?* You're sure? Native pre-sentients?" She tred water, staring at the black engineer.

They now were only ten meters from a great open hatch at the bow end of the central bay. Through it came a cacophony of high squeakings and chitterings.

Emerson shrugged. The action shook a coating of bubbles from his shoulders and the rim-plates of his facemask. "Dennie, why don't we go in and find out? So far all we have is gossip. They must be through decontamination by now."

From ahead there came a sudden, high-pitched whine of engines; then three white power sleds sped from the outlock hatch, single-file. They veered, one by one, around Dennie and D'Anite before either of them could move, leaving fizzing trails of supercritical bubbles in their wakes.

Strapped to the back of each, under a plastic shell, was an injured dolphin. Two of them had dreadful gashes in their flanks, crudely bandaged. Dennie blinked in surprise when she saw that one of them was Hikahi, *Streaker*'s third officer.

The ambulance sleds banked under the central spine and headed for an opening in the inner wall of the great cylinder. On the last sled, clutching a handrail, the dusky blonde who had accompanied them here allowed herself to be dragged along. With her free hand she pressed a diagnostic monitor to the flank of one of the wounded dolphins.

"No wonder Gillian was in such a hurry. It was stupid of me to slow her down."

"Oh, don't worry about it." Emerson held her arm. "The injuries didn't look like the kind you'd need a human surgeon for. Makanee and the autodocs can handle almost anything, you know."

"Still, there may be biochemical damage . . . poisons . . . I might be of use."

She turned to go, but the engineer's hand held her.

"You'll be called if it's anything Makanee or feMister Baskin can't handle. And I don't think you'll want to miss out on news that bears on your specialty."

Dennie looked after the ambulances, then nodded. Emerson was right. If she was needed, an intercom call would reach her anywhere, and a sled would arrive to fetch her faster than she could swim. They swam toward the buzzing of excited cetaceans in the outlook bay, and entered the forward chamber amid a swirl of swooping gray forms and a ferment of flying bubbles.

The forward outlook at *Streaker*'s bow was the ship's main link with the outside. The cylindrical wall was covered by storage cells, holding spiders, sleds, and other gear for crew who might leave the ship on errands. The bow had three great airlocks.

Port and starboard, the spacious chamber was taken up by the skiff and the longboat. The nose of each small spaceship almost touched the iris that would let it outside, into vacuum, air, or water, as needed.

The stern of the skiff stopped short of the rear bulkhead of the twenty-meter outlook, but the aft end of the larger longboat disappeared into a sleeve that extended into the maze of rooms and passages in *Streaker*'s thick cylindrical shell.

Overhead, a third berthing port lay empty. The captain's

gig had been lost to a strange accident weeks before, along with ten crew members, at the region Creideiki had named the Shallow Cluster. Its loss, in the course of investigating the derelict fleet, was a topic seldom brought up in conversation.

Dennie gripped D'Anite's arm as another sled passed by, more slowly than the white ambulances of sick bay. Sealed green bags were tied to its back. A bottle-like narrowness at one end of each, and a flat flaring at the other, revealed their contents.

There's no smaller bag, Dennie thought. Does that mean Toshio's alive then? Then she saw, by the decontamination lock, a young drysuited human in a crowd of dolphins.

"There's Toshio!" she cried, a little surprised at the intensity of her relief. She forced herself to speak in a calm tone. "Is that Keepiru next to him?" She pointed.

D'Anite nodded. "Yeah. They seem all right. By my count I guess that means Hist't hitched a sky-current. That's a rotten shame. We got along." Emerson's affected burr was completely gone as he mourned the loss of a friend.

He peered through the crowd. "Can you think of an official enough reason for us to shove in there? Most of the fen would get out of our way out of habit. But Creideiki's something else. He'll chew our asses off, patrons or no, if he thinks we're hanging around useless and getting in the way."

Dennie had been thinking about just that. "Leave it to me." She led him into the jostling crowd, touching flipper and fluke to pry a passage through the press. Most of the fen moved to one side on catching a glimpse of the two humans.

Dennie looked about the squeaking, clicking mob. Shouldn't Tom Orley be here? she thought. He and Hannes and Tsh't were in on the rescue, weren't they? So why don't I see him anywhere? I've *got* to talk to him sometime soon!

Toshio looked like a very tired young man. Just out of decon, he slowly peeled off his drysuit as he spoke with Creideiki. Soon he floated naked but for a facemask. Dabs of synthetic skin coated his hands and throat and face. Keepiru drifted nearby. The exhausted dolphin wore a breather, probably under physician's orders.

Suddenly the spectators blocking Dennie's view began to spin about and dart away in all directions.

> * ...*bands of idle gawkers—*
> *cease their vain eavesdropping!*
> * *Lest the nets of Iki find them—*
> *for their lack of work and purpose!*

The sudden cetacean dispersal buffetted Dennie and Emerson; in moments the crowd had thinned.

"Do not-t make me repeat myself!" Creideiki reiterated. His voice pursued the fleeing spacers. "All is done in here. Think clear thoughts and do your jobs!"

A dozen fen remained near the captain and Toshio: outlock personnel and the captain's aides. Creideiki turned to Toshio. "Go on then, little shark-biter, finish your story."

The boy blushed, nonplussed by the honorific. He forced his heavy eyelids open and tried to maintain a semblance of standard posture in the drifting current.

"Uh, I think that's about it, sir. I've told you everything Mr. Orley and Tsh't told me about their plans. If the ET wreck looks usable, they'll send a sled back with a report. If not, they'll return with whatever they've salvaged as quickly as possible."

Creideiki made small slow circles with his lower jaw. "A hazardousss gamble," he commented. "They'll not reach the hulk for a day, at least. More days, still, will pass without contact . . ."

Bubbles rose from his blowmouth.

"Very well, then. You shall rest, then join me for supper. I'm afraid your reward for saving Hikahi for us, and possibly all of our lives as well, shall be an interrogation the likes of which you might not even receive from our enemies."

Toshio smiled tiredly.

"I understand, sir. I'll happily let you wring me of information, just so long as I can eat first . . . and get *dry* for a while!"

"Done. Until then!" The captain nodded and turned to go.

Dennie was about to shout to Creideiki when someone else called out first.

"Captain, please! May I have a word?"

The voice was musical. The speaker was a large male dolphin with the mottled gray coloration of one of the *Stenos* sub-breeds. He wore a civilian harness, without the bulky racks or heavy manipulator arms carried by the regular crew.

Dennie felt a strong urge to hide behind Emerson D'Anite. She hadn't noticed Sah'ot in the crowd until he spoke.

"Before you go, sir," the dolphin fluted. His tone of voice was quite casual. "I must asssk you for permission to go to that island where Hikahi was stranded."

With a tail-flick Creideiki arched over bottom side up to regard the speaker. He addressed the fin skeptically. "Talker-to-races, this is not a fishbrew bar, this island, where poetry can buy back an error. Why venture now courage you never before displayed?"

Sah'ot lay still for a moment. In spite of her dislike of the civilian specialist, Dennie felt sympathy rise within her. Sah'ot's behavior at the derelict fleet, in refusing to go along with the doomed survey party, had not been admirable. He had acted like a prima donna.

But he had been proven right. The captain's gig and ten fine crew members had been lost, along with *Streaker*'s former second in command.

All the sacrifice had gained them was a three-meter-long tube of some strange metal, thoroughly pitted by ages of micrometeorite impacts. It had been recovered personally by Thomas Orley. Gillian Baskin had taken over the sealed relic, and to Dennie's knowledge nobody else had seen it since. It hardly seemed worth the loss they had suffered.

"Captain," Sah'ot addressed Creideiki, "I believe that there is a matter that even Thomas Orley could not have had time to cover in detail. He has gone on to investigate the wrecked warship, but the island still does concern us."

No fair! Dennie had been ready to do this! It was to be an act of professionalism—of *assertion*, to speak out and demand. . . .

"Honestly, Captain," Sah'ot went on, "after our duty to escape this trap, and to serve the clan of Earth species, what is the most important responsibility that has fallen upon uss?"

Creideiki looked torn. He obviously wanted to chew Sah'ot's dorsal fin for baiting him like this. Also, obviously, Sah'ot had hit him with a double harpoon . . . mentioning the word "duty," and lacing it into a riddle. The captain thrashed his tail, giving out a low series of broad-band sonar clicks, like a watch ticking. His eyes were recessed and dark.

Dennie couldn't wait for the captain to figure the puzzle, or slap Sah'ot into a cell.

"The abos!" she shouted.

Creideiki turned and regarded her. Dennie blushed as she felt his field of analytic sound sweep over her. She knew the waves penetrated her very viscera, telling everything down to what she had had for breakfast. Creideiki frightened her. She felt very far from being patron to the powerful and involute mind behind that broad forehead.

The captain suddenly whirled about and swam to Toshio. "You still have those artifactsss that Thomas Orley selected, young hunter?"

"Yes, sir, I . . ."

"You will please lend them to Biologist Sudman and Race Speaker Sah'ot before you retire. When you've rested, collect them again, along with the specialists' recommendations. I will examine them myself during supper."

Toshio nodded. The captain flipped to face Dennie.

"Before I give permission, you must have a plan. You'll get little material assistance from me, and you will be recalled at any sign of danger. Can you accept these conditions?"

"Y-yes . . . we'll need a monofilament cable to the ship, for a computer link, and . . ."

"Talk this over with Keepiru, before he rests. He must help you come up with something militarily acceptable."

"Keepiru? But I thought . . ." Dennie looked at the younger dolphin, and quickly bit back the tactlessness she had been about to utter. Silently wearing his breather, the pilot seemed unhappier than ever.

"I have my reasons, femsir. As a pilot, he is of little use while we are immobile. I can spare him from the work here, to be your field liaison . . . *if* I agree to your plan."

The captain's attention made Keepiru hunch slightly and look away. Toshio put a hand on Keepiru's sleek back. That, too, was a change. The two had never struck Dennie as fast friends before.

Creideiki's teeth shone in the bright lights of the bay.

"Is there more comment-t?"

Everyone was silent.

Creideiki thrashed his tail, then whistled the phrase of command termination. He arched and sped away with rapid, powerful strokes. His aides followed in his wake.

Keepiru watched until his captain passed out of sight. Then he addressed Dennie and Sah'ot.

> * At your service, you will find me—
>   In my quarters, floating, breathing—
> * After seeing Toshio resting....*

Toshio smiled when Dennie gave him a brief hug. Then he turned to swim away, arm over Keepiru's back, keeping to the fin's slow pace.

Just then one of the intrahull lift tubes opened, and a blue and yellow shape bulletted out of the tube. A joyful racket filled the chamber as the ship's other midshipman speared past Keepiru and the boy, then zoomed around them in ever-tightening circles, chattering excitedly.

"Do you really think Toshio's going to get any sleep?" Emerson asked.

"Not if Akki makes him tell the entire story before he has supper with the captain." Dennie envied Akki and Toshio their fellowship, as constant and intense as any star. She watched the boy laughing as he fended off his friend until they disappeared into the tube.

"Well, sister," Emerson D'Anite grinned at Dennie. "It appears you have a science command. My congratulations."

"Nothing's decided yet," she answered. "Besides, Keepiru will be in charge."

"Keepiru will have *military* command. That part confuses me a bit. I don't know where Creideiki's aiming, assigning Keepiru that job after the way I hear he behaved out there. My guess is it's his way of getting the poor dollie out of his hai... hide."

Dennie had to agree, though she thought it a bit cruel.

She suddenly felt a smooth, flat touch on the inner part of her left thigh. She yelped and whirled around with her hand at her throat, then sighed when she saw that it was the neo-dolphin anthropologist, Sah'ot, who had slipped in his left pectoral fin to goose her. The *Stenos* gave her an uneven grin. His rough teeth shone brightly.

Dennie's heart pounded. "Shark-breath! Doggerel-rhymer! Go make love to an unwashed specimen bottle!" Her voice cracked.

Sah'ot reared back, his eyes momentarily white-rimmed in surprise. Apparently he hadn't expected Dennie to be so high-strung.

"Aw, Dennie," Sah'ot sighed. "I was jussst trying to thank

you for interceding with Creideiki. Obviously your charms are more persuasive to him than any arguments *I* might raise. Sorry if I sstartled you."

Dennie sniffed at Sah'ot's double-edged apology. Still, her reaction might have been overdrawn. Her pulse slowly settled. "Oh... never mind. Just don't you sneak up on me like that!"

Without even turning around, she could *feel* Emerson D'Anite grinning behind his hand. *Males,* she thought. *Do they ever grow up?*

"Um, Dennie?" Sah'ot's voice crooned like a string trio. "There is one small matter we have to discuss, if we are going to be going on this expedition to the island together. Will you be churlish and let Creideiki choose the science commander on the basis of prejudice? Or will you give me a chance? Maybe we can *wrestle* for it-t-t?"

D'Anite started coughing. He turned the other way and cleared his throat.

Dennie blushed. "We'll let the captain decide what's best. Besides... I'm not sure both of us should go. Charlie told me his analysis of the planetary crust samples may be of interest to you... there are traces of paleotechnology in recent layers. You ought to go see him right away."

Sah'ot's eyelids narrowed. "That *isss* interesting. I'd thought this planet was fallow far longer than would allow paleotech-ch remnants."

But he dashed Dennie's hopes. "Alasss. Digging for long-toasted garbage of past Kithrupan civilizations cannot be half as important as making contact with pre-sentients and establishing a proper patron claim for you humans. We fins might have new client cousins before even neo-dogs are finished! Heaven help the poor creatures if the Tandu or Soro or similar ilk collect them!

"Besides," he soothed, "this is a chance for us to get to know each other better... and exchange professional information, of course."

Emerson D'Anite had to cough again.

"I've left the repairs for too long already, kids," he said. His burr was back in force. "I think I'll be gettin' on back to my engines, and let you two discuss your plans."

D'Anite's grin was barely suppressed. Dennie swore eventual revenge. "Emerson!" she hissed.

"Yes, lass?" He looked back at her innocently.

She glared, "Oh . . . I'll bet you haven't a drop of Celtic blood in your body!"

The dark engineer smiled at her. "Why, bairn, didn' ya know? All Scots are engineers, and all engineers are Scots." He waved and swam off before Dennie could think of a reply. *Trapped*, she cursed, by a cliche!

When D'Anite was out of earshot Sah'ot sidled close to Dennie. "Shall we start planning our expedition?" His blowmouth was near her ear.

Dennie started. Suddenly she noticed that everyone had gone. Dennie's heart beat faster, and her facemask seemed not to be giving her enough air.

"Not *here* we won't!" She spun away and began swimming. "Let's go to the wardroom. There are plotting boards . . . and airdomes! A man can breathe there!"

Sah'ot kept pace with her, uncomfortably close.

"Aw, Dennie . . ." he said, but he didn't press. Instead, he began to sing a low, atonal, hybrid melody in a complex and obscure dialect of Trinary.

Against her will, Dennie found herself drawn into the song. It was strange, and eerily beautiful, and it took her several minutes to realize that it was also dirty as hell.

15

Stenos

Moki, Sreekah-pol, and Hakukka-jo spent their latest off-duty period as they had spent every one for weeks, complaining.

"He was down in my section again, t-today," Sreekah-pol griped, "sticking his jaw into everybody's work-k. Thinks he's ssso-o-o discreet, but he fills the scound-scape with his Keneenk-k echoes!"

Moki nodded. There wasn't any doubt who "he" was.

> * *Crying—Crooning*
>   *Talk, talk rhythms*
> * *My group wags tails*
>   *To his Logic Logic!* *

Hakukka-jo winced. Moki seldom spoke Anglic anymore, and his Trinary had a little too much Primal in it to be decent.

But Sreekah-pol obviously thought Moki's point valid. "All the *Tursiopsss* worship Creideiki. They imitate him and try to act like Keneenk-k adeptsss! Even half of our *Stenos* seem just as swallowed by his spell!"

"Well, if he can get-t us out of here alive, I will forgive even his nosy inspections," Hakkuka-jo suggested.

Moki tossed his head.

> * *Alive! Alive!*
>   *To deep, rich waters!*
> * *Follow, Follow*
>   *A rough-toothed leader!* *

"Will you make quiet-t-t?" Hakukka-jo swung about quickly to listen to the echoes in the rest area. A few crewfen were gathered by the food machines. They gave no sign of having heard. "Heed your scatter! You're already in trouble without clicking mutiny talk! I hear Doctor Metz has gone to Takkata-Jim to ask about you!"

Moki smirked defiantly. Sreekah-pol agreed with Moki's unspoken comment. "Metz won't do nothing," Sreekah said. "It'sss common knowledge half the *Stenos* aboard were chosen by him. We're his babiesss," Sreekah-pol crooned. "With Orley and Tsh't gone, and Hikahi in sick bay, the only's we gotta watch out for is the chief smartass himself!"

Hakkuka-jo looked about wildly. "You too? Look-k, will you be quiet? There comes K'tha-Jon!"

The other two turned the way he indicated. They saw a huge neo-fin swim out of a hull lift and head their way. Dolphins half his size got out of the giant's way quickly.

"So what-t-t? He is of us!" Sreekah-pol said uncertainly.

"He's also a bosun!" Hakkuka-jo answered hotly.

"He hates *Tursiopsss* smartasses, too!" Moki cut in in Anglic.

"Maybe, but if so he keeps it to himself! He knows how humans feel about racism!"

Moki looked away. The dark mottled dolphin was like a lot of fins in holding the patron race in a sort of superstitious dread. He countered weakly in Trinary.

> * *Ask the black men—*
> *The brown and yellow men*
> * *Ask the whales—*
> *About human racism!* *

"That was a long time ago!" Hakkuka-jo snapped, somewhat shocked. "And humans had no patrons to guide them!"

"Jussst ssso..." Sreekah-pol said, but his agreement sounded unsure.

They all shut up as K'tha-Jon approached. Hakkuka-jo felt a recurring chill on contemplating the bosun.

K'tha-Jon was a giant, surpassing three meters in length with a girth that two men couldn't span with their arms. His bottle nose was blunt, and, unlike the other so-called *Stenos* aboard, his coloring was not mottled but deeply countershaded. Rumor had it K'tha-Jon was another of Dr. Metz's "special" cases.

The giant swam up nearby and exhaled a loud spurt of bubbles. His open jaws displayed a fearful array of rough teeth. The others almost unconsciously adapted a submissive posture, eyes averted, foodmouths closed.

"I hear there's been more fighting..." K'tha-Jon rumbled in deep Underwater Anglic. "Fortunately, I was able to bribe senior bosun S'thata with a rare sensie tape, and he agreed not to report it to the captain. I'll expect the cost of the tape to be covered by somebody, with interest-t...."

Moki seemed about to speak, but K'tha-Jon cut him off.

"No excuses! Your temper is a burden I can do without. S'thata would have been right to challenge you for biting him from behind like that-t!"

> * *Dare him! Dare him!*
> *Tursiops coward!*
> * *Dare him...*

Moki barely blatted out the beginning before being slammed amidships by a blow from K'tha-Jon's mighty flukes.

He slewed several meters through the water before coming to rest, whistling in pain. K'tha-Jon came close and murmured softly.

"YOU are *Tursiops*! That is the name of our entire, *Library*-registered species! *Tursiopsss amicusss* . . . 'friendly bottlenose'! Ask Dr. Metz if you don't believe me! Embarrass the rest of uss aboard who have *Stenos* grafts in our genes—Vice-Captain Takkata-Jim and myself, for instance—by acting like an animal, and I will show you *how* to be a friendly bottlenose! I'll use your gutssss for hawsers!"

Moki trembled and turned away, jaw closed tightly.

K'tha-Jon swept the cowering fin with a contemptuous spray of sonar, then turned to regard the others. Hakkuka-jo and Sreekah-pol looked idly at the bright, decorative garibaldi and angel fish which were allowed to swim unmolested throughout the central bay. Hakkuka-jo whistled softly.

"Break is almost over," the bosun snapped. "Back to work-k. And save your hatred for your private time!" K'tha-Jon turned about and sped away, the turbulence from his flukes almost toppling the others.

Hakukka-jo watched him go, then whistled a long, low sigh.

That should do it, K'tha-Jon thought as he hurried off to duties in the cargo section. *Moki, especially, would be quiet for a while. He had better be.*

If there was anything he and Takkata-Jim did not need, it was a spate of racist innuendo and suspicion. Nothing would unite the humans in alienation like that sort of thing.

And catch the attention of Creideiki, too. Takkata-Jim insists we give the captain one more chance to come up with a plan to get us home alive.

All right, then, I can wait.

But what if he doesn't? What if he keeps asking for sacrifice from a crew that never volunteered to be heroes?

In that case, someone would have to be able to present the crew with an alternative to follow. Takkata-Jim was still reluctant, but that might not last.

If the time did come, they would need human support, and Moki's kind of interracial bullying could wreck the chances of that. K'tha-Jon intended to ride close herd on that *Stenos*, to keep him nice and docile.

Even if it was nice, from time to time, to chew the tail of some bloody, shore-hugging, sanctimonious, smartass *Tursiops*!

16

Galactics

—Rejoice—*crooned the fourth Brother of the Ebony Shadows.* Rejoice that the fifth moon of the small dusty planet has been conquered!—

The Brothers of the Night had fought bitterly for this fulcrum of power, from which they would soon project irresistible might and sweep the skies of heretics and blasphemers. This moon would guarantee that the prize would be theirs, *and theirs alone!*

None of the other moons in the Kthsemenee system had the one attribute this one possessed: a core of almost one percent unobtainium. Already thirty of the Brothers' ships had landed, to begin construction of the Weapon.

The Library, *as always, had been the key. Many cycles ago the fourth Brother of the Ebony Shadows had come across an obscure reference to a device once used in a war between two races now long extinct. It had taken him half of his lifespan to hunt down the details, for the* Library *was a labyrinth. But now would come his payment!*

—Rejoice!—*The cry resounded. It was a paean of triumph meant to be heard, and indeed a few of the other combatants began to notice that something curious was going on over in a corner of Kthsemenee's system. While the fiercest battles raged around the strategic gas-giant world, and Kithrup itself, some enemies had begun to send scouts this way to see what the Brothers of the Night were up to.*

—Let them come and look! Can it matter?—

A ship of the Soro had been watching them for some time. Could it have divined their purpose?

—Never! *The citation was too obscure! Our new weapon has sat unnoticed too long in the dusty archives. They will first understand when this moon begins to vibrate on the fifteenth probability band, sending out waves of uncertainty that will tear their battle fleets apart! Then their shipboard Libraries will undoubtedly remember, but too late!*—

The Brother of the Ebony Shadows watched from space as the resonator neared completion, watched as the grounded ships fed their combined energies to the resonator. From a thousand units out he could feel the wave build....

—*What are they doing? What are the Progenitor-scorned Soro doing?*—

Instruments showed that the Brothers of the Night were not alone on the fifteenth band! From the Soro ship came a small tone, a variation of the beat emanating from the small moon. An echo.

The fifteenth band began to beat. It was impossible, but it resonated along with the Soro rhythm!

The Brothers on the ground tried to damp the runaway signal, but it was already too late! The small moon shook, and finally crumbled. Great shards of rock tumbled apart, crushing the little ships in their way.

—*How could they have known? How could they ...?*—

Then the Brother of the Ebony Shadows understood. Long ago, when he had begun his search for a new weapon, there had been a helpful Librarian ... a Pilan. The Pilan had always been there with the useful suggestion, with the helpful reference. The Brother had thought nothing of it. Librarians were supposed to be helpful, and neutral, whatever their backgrounds.

—*But the Pil are clients to the Soro*—*The Brother realized*—Krat knew all along—

He gave the order sending his remaining forces into hiding. —This is only a setback. We shall yet be the ones to capture the Earthlings!—

Behind the fleeing remnants, the small moon continued to dissolve.

17

Tom Orley

Hannes Suessi lay prone on the heavy work sled next to Thomas Orley. The gaunt, balding artificer gestured at the wreck before them.

"It's a Thennanin ship," the chief engineer said. "It's pretty badly crumpled, but there's no doubt. See? There are no objectivity anchors, only stasis projectors on the main flanges. The Thennanin are terrified of reality alteration. This ship was never designed to use a probability drive. Definitely, it's Thennanin, or a Thennanin client or ally."

The dolphins circled slowly nearby, taking turns at the airdomes underneath the sled, emitting excited sonar clicks as they eyed the gigantic crushed arrowhead below them.

"I think you're right, Hannes," Tom said. "It's a behemoth."

That the ship was still in one piece was amazing. In its Mach five meeting with the ocean, it had caromed off at least two small sub-surface islands—leaving substantial dents in them—and plowed a deep gouge in the ocean floor before finally catching up against a furrow of pelagic mud, just before it would have smashed into a sheer scarp. The cliff face looked crumbly and precarious. Another substantial jolt would surely cause a collapse, burying the wreck completely.

Orley knew that it was the quality of the Thennanin stasis shields that had made such a performance possible. Even in dying, a Thennanin ship was reputed to be not worth putting out of its misery. In battle they were slow, unmaneuverable—and as hard to disable permanently as a cockroach.

It was difficult to assess the damage yet. Down here the illumination from the surface was blue-tinged and dim. The fen wouldn't turn on the arc lights they had strung up until

Tsh't said it was safe. Fortunately, the wreck was in water shallow enough to visit, yet deep enough to shield them from spy eyes overhead.

A pink-bellied bottlenose dolphin swam up next to the sled. She worked her foodmouth in a thoughtful circular motion.

"It's really amazing, isn't it, Tom?" she asked. "It should be in a jillion piecesss."

This deep, there was an odd clarity to the fin's voice. Bursts of air from her blowmouth and sonar clicks joined in a complex manner to make speech an intricate juggling of bodily functions. To a landlubber human, a neo-dolphin speaking underwater sounded more like an avant-garde orchestra tuning up, than someone speaking a derivative of the English language.

"Do you think we can make any use of it-t?" The dolphin officer asked.

Orley looked again at the ship. There was a good chance that in the confusion of battle none of those contending over Kithrup had bothered to note where this sparrow had fallen. He already had a few tentative ideas, one or two of which might just be bold and unexpected—and idiotic—enough to work.

"Let's give it a look," he nodded. "I suggest we split into three teams. Team one heads for any center of emissions, particularly probability, psi, or neutrino radiation, and disables the source. They should also watch out for survivors, though that seems a bit unlikely."

Suessi snorted as he looked at the pounded wreck. Orley went on.

"Team two concentrates on harvesting. Hannes should lead that one, along with Ti-tcha. They'll look for monopoles and refined metals that *Streaker* might be able to use. With luck, they might find some replacements for those coils we need.

"With your permission, Tsh't, I'll take team three. I want to look over the structural integrity of that ship, and survey the topography of the surrounding area."

Tsh't did a jaw clap of agreement. "Your logic is good, Tom. That is what we'll do. I'll leave Lucky Kaa with the other sled, on alert. The ressst shall join their teams at once."

Orley grabbed Tsh't's dorsal fin as she was about to whistle the command. "Oh, we'd better go with breathers all around, hadn't we? Trinary may not be efficient, but I'd rather put off complex conversations in Anglic than have to risk everybody shuttling back and forth for air, and maybe someone getting hurt."

Tsh't grimaced, but gave the command. The party was composed of disciplined fen—the pick of *Streaker*'s crew—so the gathering at the sled was occasion merely for low-pitched grousing and indignant bubbles as each dolphin was fitted with his wraparound hose of air.

Tom had heard of prototype breathers that would give a fin a streamlined air suply without hindering his speechmouth. If ever he found the time, he might try to rig some up himself. Speaking Trinary posed no real difficulty for him, but he knew from experience that the fen would have problems conveying technical information in anything but Anglic.

Old Hannes was already grumbling. He helped pass out the breathers with ill-disguised reluctance. The chief artificer was conversant in Trinary, of course, but he found the three-level logic difficult. To cap things off, he was a lousy poet. He obviously didn't look forward to trying to discuss technical matters in whistle rhyme.

They had their work cut out for them. Several of the picked petty officers and crew that had accompanied them on the rescue effort had gone back to the ship, escorting Toshio and Hikahi and the other victims of the stranding waves. Only a short score of fen remained in the party. Should anything dangerous come up they would have to take care of it themselves. No help from *Streaker* could arrive in time to do any good.

It would have been nice to have Gillian here, Tom mused. Not that inspecting alien cruisers was her area of expertise, but she knew fins, and could handle herself if things got sticky.

But she had work of her own aboard *Streaker*, trying to solve the puzzle of a billion-year-old mummy that should never have existed in the first place. And in an emergency she was the only other person aboard *Streaker*, barring, possibly, Creideiki himself, who knew about the Niss machine, or its potential value if given access to the right data.

Tom smiled as he caught himself rationalizing again.

Okay, so there are good and logical reasons why the two of us can't be together right now. Take it for what it's worth. Do a good job here, and maybe you can be back to her in a few days.

There had never been any question, from the moment they had met as adolescents, that he and she would make a pair. He sometimes wondered if their planners had known in advance, in choosing gametes from selected married couples, that two of the growing zygotes would later fit together so perfectly—down to the simple telempathy they sometimes shared.

Probably it was a happy accident. Human genetic planning was very limited, by law and custom. Accident or no, Tom was grateful. In his missions for the Terragens Council he had learned that the universe was dangerous and filled with disillusionment. Too few sophonts—even those equipped for it—ever got enough love.

As soon as the breathers had been distributed Tom used the sled's speaker to amplify his voice. "Now remember, everybody; though all Galactic technologies are based on the *Library*, that collection of wisdom is so huge that almost any type of machine might be inside that hull. Treat everything like it's booby-trapped until you've identified it and rendered it harmless.

"The first goal of Team One, after silencing the wreck, is to find the main battle computers. There may be a record of the initial stages of the fight above. That information might be invaluable to the captain.

"And would you all keep an eye out for the *Library* glyph? If you find that symbol anywhere, please note its location and pass word to me. I'd like to see what kind of micro-branch they were carrying."

He nodded to Tsh't. "Is that all right with you, Lieutenant?"

Streaker's fourth officer clapped jaw and nodded. Orley's politeness was appreciated, but she was likelier to bite off her own tail than overrule any suggestion he made. *Streaker* was the first large expedition ever commanded and operated by dolphins. It had been clear from the beginning that certain humans were along whose advice bore the patina of patronomy.

She called out in Trinary.

> * *Team One, with me—*
>   *To diffract above, listening*
> * *Team Two, with Suessi—*
>   *To taste for treasure*

* *Team Three, with Orley—*
  To aid him scheming
* *Drop nothing of Earth here—*
  To betray our visit
* *Clean it up after—*
  If you must shit
* *Think before acting—*
  In tropic-clear logic
* *Now Streakers, with stillness—*
  Away! *

In precise order three formations peeled off, one group embellishing with a synchronized barrel roll as they passed Orley's sled. In obedience to Tsh't's orders, the only sound was the rapid clicking of cetacean sonar.

Orley rode the sled until he was within forty meters of the hulk. Then he patted Hannes on the back and rolled off to the side.

What a beautiful find the ship was! Orley used a hot-torch spectrograph to get a quick analysis of the metal at the edges of a gaping tear in the vessel's side. When he determined the ratios of various beta-decay products he whistled, causing the fen nearby to turn and look at him curiously. He had to make assumptions about the original alloy and the rate of exposure to neutrinos since the metal was forged, but reasonable guesses indicated that the ship had been fabricated at least thirty million years ago!

Tom shook his head. A fact like that made one realize how far Mankind had to go to catch up with the Galactics.

We like to think of the races using the *Library* as being in a rut, uncreative and unadaptable, Orley thought.

That appeared to be largely true. Very often the Galactic races seemed stodgy and unimaginative. But . . .

He looked at the dark, hulking battleship, and wondered.

Legend had it that the Progenitors had called for a perpetual search for knowledge before they departed for parts unknown, aeons ago. But, in practice, most species looked to the *Library* and only the *Library* for knowledge. Its store grew only slowly.

What was the point of researching what must have been discovered a thousand times over by those who came before?

It was simple, for instance, to choose advanced spaceship designs from *Library* archives and follow them blindly, understanding only a small fraction of what was built. Earth had a few such ships, and they were marvels.

The Terragens Council, which handled relations between the races of Earth and the Galactic community, once almost succumbed to that tempting logic. Many humans urged co-opting of Galactic models that older races had themselves co-opted from ancient designs. They cited the example of Japan, which in the nineteenth century had faced a similar problem—how to survive amongst nations immeasurably more powerful than itself. Meiji Japan had concentrated all its energy on learning to imitate its neighbors, and succeeded in becoming just like them, in the end.

The majority on the Terragens Council, including nearly all of the cetacean members, disagreed. They considered the *Library* a honey pot—tempting, and possibly nourishing, but also a terrible trap.

They feared the "Golden Age" syndrome . . . the temptation to "look backward"—to find wisdom in the oldest, dustiest texts, instead of the latest journal.

Except for a few races, such as the Kanten and Tymbrimi, the Galactic community as a whole seemed stuck in that kind of a mentality. The *Library* was their first and last recourse for every problem. The fact that the ancient records almost always contained something useful didn't make that approach any less repugnant to many of the wolflings of Earth, including Tom, Gillian, and their mentor, old Jacob Demwa.

Coming out of a tradition of bootstrap technology, Earth's leaders were convinced there were things to be gained from innovation, even this late in Galactic history. At least it *felt* better to believe that. To a wolfling race, pride was an important thing.

Orphans often have little else.

But *here* was evidence of the power of the Golden Age approach. Everything about this ship spoke silkily of refinement. Even in wreckage, it was beautifully simple in its construction, while indulgent and ornate in its embellishments. The eye saw no welds. Bracings and struts were always integral to some other purpose. Here one supported a stasis flange, while apparently also serving as a baffled radiator for excess probability. Orley thought he could detect other overlaps, subtleties that could only have come with aeons of slow improvement on an ancient design.

He was struck by a decadence in the pattern, an ostentation that he found arrogant and bizarre beyond mere alienness.

One of Tom's main assignments aboard *Streaker* had been evaluation of alien devices—particularly of the military variety. This wasn't the best the Galactics had, yet it made him feel like an ancient New Guinea headhunter, proud of his new muzzle-loading musket, but painfully aware of the fact of machine guns.

He looked up. His team was gathering. He chinned his hydrophone switch.

"Everybody about done? All right, then. Subteam two, head off and see if that canyon goes all the way through the ridge. It'd cut twenty klicks off the route from here to *Streaker*."

He heard a whistle of assent from Karacha-jeff, leader of subteam two. Good. That fin was reliable.

"Be careful," he added as they swam off. Then he motioned for the others to follow him into the wreck through the seared, curled rent in its hull.

They entered darkened corridors of eerily familiar design. Everywhere were signs of the commonality of Galactic culture, superimposed with the idiosyncracies of a peculiar alien race. The lighting panels were identical to those on ships of a hundred species, but the spaces in between were garishly decorated with Thennanin hieroglyphs.

Orley eidetically examined it all. But always he looked out for one thing, a symbol that could be found everywhere in the Five Linked Galaxies—a rayed spiral.

They'll tell me when they find it, he reminded himself. *The fins know I'm interested.*

I do hope, though, they don't suspect just how badly I want to see that glyph.

18

Gillian

"Aw, why should I? Huh? You aren't being very coopera-
tive with *me*! All I want is to talk to Brookida for just a
minute. It's not as if I was asking a lot!"

Gillian Baskin felt tired and irritable. The holo image of
the chimpanzee planetologist Charles Dart glared out at her.
It would be easy to become scathing and force Charlie to
retreat. But then he would probably complain to Ignacio
Metz, and Metz would lecture her about "bullying people
just because they are clients."

Crap. Gillian wouldn't take from a human being what
she had put up with from this self-important little neo-chimp!

She brushed aside a strand of dark blonde hair that had
fallen over her eyes. "Charlie, for the last time, Brookida is
sleeping. He has received your message, and will call you
when Makanee says he's had enough rest. In the meantime,
all I want from you is a listing of isotope abundances for the
trans-ferric elements here on Kithrup. We've just finished
more than four hours surgery on Satima, and we need that data
to design a chelating sequence for her. I want to get every
microgram of heavy metal out of her body as soon as possible.

"Now, if that's too much to ask, if you're too overworked
studying little geological puzzles, I'll just call the captain or
Takkata-Jim, and ask them to assign somebody to go down
and *help* you!"

The chimp scientist grimaced. His lips curled back to
display an array of large, yellowed, buck teeth. At the moment,
in spite of the enlarged globe of his cranium, his outthrust
jaw, and his opposable thumbs, he looked more like an angry
ape than a sapient scientist.

"Oh, all right!" His hands fluttered and emotion made him stammer. "B-But this is important! Understand? I think Kithrup was inhabited by technological sophonts as recently as thirty thousand years ago! Yet the Galactic Migration Institute's had this planet posted as fallow and untouchable for the last hundred million!"

Gillian suppressed an urge to say, "So what?" There had been more defunct and forgotten species in the history of the Five Galaxies than even the *Library* could count.

Charlie must have read her expression. "It's illegal!" he shouted. His coarse voice cracked. "If it's true, the Institute of M-migration should be told! They might even be grateful enough to help get those crazy religious n-n-nuts overhead to let us alone!"

Gillian lifted an eyebrow in surprise. What was this? Charles Dart pondering implications beyond his own work? Even he, then, must think from time to time about survival. His argument about the laws of migration were naive, considering how often the codes were twisted and perverted by the more powerful clans. But he deserved some credit.

"OK. That's a good point Charlie," she nodded. "I'm having dinner with the captain later. I'll mention it to him then. I'll also ask Makanee if she'll let Brookida out a little early. Good enough?"

Charlie looked at her with suspicion. Then, unable to maintain so subtle and intermediate an expression for long, he let a broad grin spread.

"Good enough!" he rumbled. "And you'll have that fax in your hands within four minutes! I leave you in good health."

"Health," Gillian replied softly, as the holo faded.

She spent a long moment staring at the blank comm screen. With her elbows on the desk, her face settled down upon the palms of her hands.

Ifni! I should have been able to handle an angry chimp better than that. What's the matter with me?

Gillian gently rubbed her eyes. *Well, I've been up for twenty-six hours, for one thing.*

A long and unproductive argument about semantics with Tom's damned, sarcastic Niss machine hadn't helped at all, when all she had wanted from the thing was its assistance on a few obscure *Library* references. It knew she needed help to crack the mystery of Herbie, the ancient cadaver that lay under glass in her private lab. But it kept changing the subject, asking her opinion on various irrelevant issues such as human sexual mores. By the time the session was through, Gillian was ready to disassemble the nasty thing with her bare hands.

But Tom would probably disapprove, so she deferred.

She had been about to go to bed when the emergency call came from the outlook. Soon she was busy helping Makanee and the autodocs treat the survivors of the survey party. Worry about Hikahi and Satima drove all thought of sleep from her mind until that was done.

Now that they seemed to be out of danger, Gillian could no longer use adrenalin reaction to hold off that empty feeling that seeped in around the edges of a very rough day.

It's not a time to enjoy being alone, she thought. She lifted her head and looked at her own reflection in the blank comm screen. Her eyes were reddened. From overwork, certainly, but also from worry.

Gillian knew well enough how to cope, but coping was a sterile solution. Instinct demanded warmth, someone to hold close and satisfy that physical longing.

She wondered if Tom felt the same way at this moment. Oh, of course he did; with the crude telempathic link they sometimes shared, Gillian felt she knew him pretty well. They were of a type, the two of them.

Only sometimes it seemed to Gillian that the planners had been more successful with him than they had been with her. Everyone seemed to think of her as superbly competent, but they were all just a little bit in awe of Thomas Orley.

And at times like the present, when eidetic recall seemed more a curse than a blessing, Gillian wondered if she really was as neurosis-free as the manufacturer's warranty promised.

The fax printer on her desk extruded a hardcopy message. It was the isotope distribution profile promised by Charlie—a minute ahead of schedule, she noted. Gillian scanned the columns. Good. There was little variation from the millennia-old *Library* report on Kithrup. Not that she had expected any, but one always checked.

A brief appendix at the bottom warned that these profiles were only valid in the surface crust and upper asthenosphere regions, and were invalid any more than two kilometers below the surface.

Gillian smiled. Someday Charlie's compulsiveness might save them all.

She stepped from her office onto a parapet above a large open chamber. Water filled the central part of the room up to two meters below the parapet. Bulky machines stuck out above the water. The upper half of the chamber, including Gillian's office, was inaccessible to dolphins unless they came riding a walker or spider.

Gillian didn't bother with the folded facemask at her belt. She looked below, then dove, plunging between two rows of dark autodocs. The large, oblong glassite containers were silent and empty.

All the waterways of sick bay were shallow to allow open breathing and dry surgery. She swam with long, strong strokes, gripped the corner of one machine to make a turn, and passed through a stripdoor into the trauma unit.

She surfaced, open-mouthed, for air, bobbed for a moment, then swam over to a wall of thick leaded glass. Two bandaged dolphins floated in a heavily shielded gravity tank.

One occupant, connected to a maze of tubing, had the dull-eyed look of heavy sedation. The other whistled cheerfully as Gillian approached.

"I greet you, Life-Cleaner! Your potions scour my veins, but it's this taste of weightlessness which liftsss my spacer's heart. Thank you!"

"You're welcome, Hikahi." Gillian treaded water easily, not bothering with the curb and rail near the gravity tank. "Just don't get too used to the comfort. I'm afraid Makanee and I are going to kick you out soon, as penalty for having such an iron constitution."

"As opposed to one of bismuth or c-c-cadmium?" Hikahi spluttered a razzberry-like chuckle.

Gillian laughed. "Indeed. And being healthy will be your tough luck. We'll have you out of here, breathing bubbles and standing on your tail for the captain in no time."

Hikahi gave her small neo-fin smile. "You're certain this isn't too risky, turning on thisss gravity tank? I wouldn't want Satima and me to be responsible for giving the show away."

"Relax, fem-fin," Gillian shook her head. "We triple-checked. The leak-detection buoys aren't picking up a thing. Enjoy it and don't worry.

"Oh, and I hear the captain may be sending a small team back to your island to examine those pre-sentients you found. I figured you'd be interested. It's a sign he's not worried about Galactics in the short term. The space battle may last a long time, and we might be able to hide indefinitely."

"An indefinite stay on Kithrup's not my idea of paradise!" Hikahi opened her mouth in a grin of irony. "If that's meant as cheery news, please warn me when your message is depressing!"

Gillian laughed. "I will. Now you get some sleep. Shall I turn down the light?"

"Yess, please. And Gillian, thanks for the news. I do think it's very important we do something about the abos. I hope the expedition is a success.

"Tell Creideiki I'll be back on duty before he can open a can of tuna."

"I will. Pleasant dreams, dear." Gillian touched the dimmer switch and the lights gradually faded. Hikahi blinked several times, apparently settling into a seaman's nap.

Gillian headed for the outer clinic, where Makanee would be dealing with a line of complaining crewfen at sick call. Gillian would show the physician Charlie's isotope profiles and then go back to her own lab to work for a while longer.

Sleep called to her, but she knew it would be a long time coming. In this mood that had come upon her she felt reluctant.

Logic was the blessing and the curse of her upbringing. She knew that Tom was where he was supposed to be—out pursuing ways to save them all. He knew it as well. His departure had been hasty and necessary, and there simply hadn't been time to seek her out to say good-bye.

Gillian was aware of all of these considerations. She repeated them to herself as she swam. But they only seemed to disconnect the larger from the smaller of her problems, and rob of poignant consolation the unattractiveness of her empty bed.

19

∿∿∿∿∿∿∿∿∿∿∿∿∿∿∿∿∿∿∿∿∿∿∿∿

Creideiki

"Keneenk is a study of *relationships*," he told his audience. "That part comes from our dolphin heritage. Keneenk is also a study of *strict comparisons*. This second part we learn from our human patrons. Keneenk is a synthesis of two world-views, much as we ourselves are."

About thirty neo-dolphins floated across from him, bubbles rising slowly from their blowmouths, intermittent unconscious sonar clicks their only sound.

Since there were no humans present, Creideiki did not have to use the crisp consonants and long vowels of standard Anglic. But, transcribed onto paper, his words would have pleased any English grammarian.

"Consider reflections from the surface of the ocean, where the air meets the water," he suggested to his pupils. "What do the reflections tell us?"

He saw puzzled expressions.

"Reflections from which side of the water, you wonder? Do I speak of the reflections felt from *below* the interface or from above?

"Moreover, do I mean reflections of *sound*, or of *light*?"

He turned to one of the attentive dolphins. "Wattaceti, imagine yourself one of our ancestors. Which combination would occur to you?"

The engine room tech blinked. "Sound images, Captain. A pre-sentient dolphin would have thought of sound reflections *in* the water, bouncing against the surface from below."

The tech sounded tired, but Wattaceti still attended these sessions, in a fervent desire for self-improvement. It was

for the morale of fen like Wattaceti that the busy captain
made time to continue them.

Creideiki nodded. "Quite right. Now, what would be the
first type of reflection thought of by a human?"

"The image of *light* from above," the mess chief, S'tat,
answered promptly.

"Most probably, though we all know that even some of
the 'big-ears' can eventually learn to hear."

There was a general skree of laughter at the harmless
little put-down of the patron race. The laughter was a measure of crew morale, and he weighed it as he might test the
mass of a fuel cell by hefting it between his jaws.

Creideiki noticed for the first time that Takkata-Jim and
K'tha-Jon had swum up to join the group. Creideiki quashed
a momentary concern. Takkata-Jim would have signaled if something had come up. He seemed to be here simply to listen.

If this was a sign the vice-captain was ending his long,
unexplained sulk, Creideiki was glad. He had kept Takkata-
Jim aboard, instead of sending him out to accompany Orley
and the rescue party, because he wanted to keep his exec
under his scrutiny. He had reluctantly begun to think that the
time might have come to make some changes in the chain of
command.

He waited for the snickering to die down. "Consider,
now. How are a human's thoughts about these reflections
from the surface of the water *similar* to our own?"

The students assumed expressions of concentration. This
would be the next-to-last problem. With so much repair work
to oversee, Creideiki had been tempted to cancel the sessions
altogether. But so many in the crew wanted desperately to
learn Keneenk.

At the beginning of the voyage almost all the fen had
participated in the lectures, games, and athletic competitions
that helped stave off spaceflight ennui. But since the frightening
episode at the Shallow Cluster, when a dozen crewfen had
been lost exploring the terrifying derelict fleet, some had
begun to detach themselves from the community of the ship,
to associate with their own little groups. Some even began
exhibiting a strange atavism—increasing difficulty with Anglic
and the sort of concentrated thought needed by a spacer.

Creideiki had been forced to juggle schedules to find
replacements. He had given Takkata-Jim the task of finding
jobs for the reverted ones. The task seemed to suit the

vice-captain. With the aid of bosun K'tha-Jon he seemed to have found useful work for even the worst stricken.

Creideiki carefully listened to the swish of flukes, the uncomfortable gurgling of gill-lungs, the rhythm of heartbeats. Takkata-Jim and K'tha-Jon floated quietly, apparently attentive. But Creideiki sensed in each of them an underlying tension.

Creideiki shivered. There had come a suddenly vivid mental image of the vice-captain's shrewd, sullen eye, and the bosun's great, sharp teeth. He suppressed it, chiding himself for having an overactive imagination. There was no logical reason to fear either of those two!

"We are contemplating reflections from an interface between air and water." He hurriedly resumed his lecture. "Both humans and dolphins envision a *barrier* when they consider such a surface. On the other side is a realm that is only faintly apparent until the barrier is crossed. Yet the modern human, with his tools, does not fear the water side, as he once did. The neo-fin, with *his* tools, can live and work in the air, and look down without discomfort.

"Consider how your own thoughts stretched out when I asked my original question. The idea of sound reflecting from below came to mind first. Our ancestors would have complacently stopped with that first generalization, but *you* did not stop there. You did not generalize without considering further alternatives. This is a common hallmark of *planning* creatures. For us it is a new thing."

The timer on Creideiki's harness chimed. It was growing late. Tired as he was, he still had a meeting to attend, and he wanted to stop at the bridge to find out if there had been any word from Orley.

"How does a cetacean, whose heritage, whose very *brain* is built on intuitive thinking, learn to *analyze* a complex problem, piece by piece? Sometimes the key to an *answer* is found in the way you formulate the *question*. I'll leave you all today with an exercise for your idle moments.

"Try to state the problem of reflections from the surface of water in *Trinary* . . . in a way that demands not a single answer, or a three-level opposition, but a plain listing of the reflections that are possible."

He saw several of the fen frown uncomfortably.

The captain smiled reassuringly. "I know it sounds difficult, and I will not ask you to recite today. But just to show you it can be done, accept the echo of this dream."

> * A layer divides
>   sky-star—Sea-star
> * What comes to us
>   At a narrow angle?
>
> * The huntsqueaking starcatching octopus
>   Reflects!
>
> * The night-calling, star-following tern
>   Reflects!
>
> * The star-twinkle in my lover's eye
>   Reflects!
>
> * The sun, *soundless, roaring showoff*—
>   Reflects! *

Creideiki was adequately rewarded by the wide-eyed appreciation of his audience. As he turned to go, he noticed that even Takkata-Jim was shaking his head slowly, as if considering a thought that had never occurred to him before.

After the meeting broke up, K'tha-Jon persisted in his argument.

"You sssaw? You heard him, Takkata-Jim?"

"I saw and heard, Bosun. And, as usual, I was impressed. Creideiki is a geniusss. So what is it you wanted to point out to me?"

K'tha-Jon clapped his jaw, not the most polite gesture to make before a superior officer.

"He sayss *nothing* about the Galacticss! Nothing about the siege! Nothing *at all* about plans to get us away from here! Or, barring that, to fight-t!

"And meanwhile he ignores the growing split amongst the crew!"

Takkata-Jim let out a line of bubbles. "A split you have busily been encouraging, K'tha-Jon. No, don't bother protesting your innocence. You've been subtle, and I know you've been doing it to build a power base for me. So I look away.

"But don't be sure Creideiki will always be too busy to notice! When he *does* notice, K'tha-Jon, watch your tail! For *I* won't have known a thing about your little tricks!"

K'tha-Jon blew quiet bubbles, not bothering to reply.

"As for Creideiki's plans, we'll see. We'll see if he's willing to listen to Dr. Metz and myself, or if he persisssts in this dream of carting his secrets back to Earth unopened."

Takkata-Jim saw the giant *Stenos* was about to interrupt.

"Yesss, I know you think we should consider a third option, don't you? You'd like to see us head out and take on all the Galactics single-handed, wouldn't you, K'tha-Jon?"

The huge dolphin didn't answer, but his eyes gleamed back at the vice-captain.

Are you my Boswell, my Seaton, my Igor, or my Iago? Takkata-Jim thought silently at the giant mutant. *You serve me now, but in the long run, am I using you, or are you using me?*

20

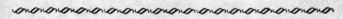

Galactics

Battle screamed all around the flotilla of tiny Xappish warships.

"We have just lost the X'ktau *and the* X'klennu! *That means almost a third of the Xappish armed might is gone!"*

The elder Xappish lieutenant sighed. "So? Young one, tell me news, not things I already know."

"Our Xatinni patrons spend their clients like reaction gas, and commit their own forces miserly. Notice how they hang back, ready to flee if the battle gets too furious! Yet we they send into danger!"

"That is ever their way," the other agreed.

"But if the Xappish fleet is destroyed here, in this futile fray, who will protect our three tiny worlds, and enforce our rights?"

"Is that not what we have patrons for?" The older lieutenant knew he was being ironic. He adjusted the screens *to resist a sudden psionic attack, without even changing his tone of voice.*

His junior did not dignify the reply with a comment. He grumbled instead. "What did these Earthlings ever do to us, anyway? In what way do they threaten our patrons?"

A searing blast from a Tandu battle-cruiser just missed the left wing of the small Xappish scout. The junior lieutenant sent the ship into a wild evasive maneuver. The senior lieutenant replied to the question as if nothing at all had happened.

"I take it you don't believe the story that the Progenitors have returned."

The other only snorted, while adjusting his torpedo sights.

"Aptly put. I, too, think this is merely part of a program to destroy the Earthlings. The senior patron races see the Terrans as a threat. They are wolflings, and therefore dangerous. They preach revolutionary uplift practices . . . more dangerous still. They are allies of the Tymbrimi, an insult beyond forbearance. And they proselytize—an unforgivable offense."

The scoutship shuddered as the torpedo leapt toward the Tandu destroyer. Their tiny craft accelerated mightily to get away.

"Well I think we should listen to the Earthlings," the junior lieutenant shouted. "If all the client races in the galaxy rebelled at once . . ."

"It has already happened," the elder interrupted. "Study the Library records. Six times in Galactic history. And twice successfully."

"No! What happened?"

"What do you think happened? The clients went on to become patrons of newer species, and treated them just the same as ever!"

"I do not believe it! I cannot believe it!"

The elder lieutenant sighed. "Look it up."

"I shall!"

But he never did. An undetected improbability mine lay across their path. The tiny scout departed the galaxy in a manner that was picturesque, if ultimately lethal.

21

Dennie and Toshio

Dennie checked the charges one more time. It was dark and crowded in the close passage of the drill-tree root. Her helmet's beam cast stark shadows through the thick maze of rootlets.

She called upward. "Are you almost finished, Toshio?"

He was planting his explosives in the upper section, near the surface of the metal-mound.

"Yeah, Dennie. If you're done, go back down now. I'll join you in a minute."

She couldn't even see his flippered feet above her. His voice was distorted in the narrow, water-filled thicket. It was a relief to be allowed to leave.

She picked her way downward carefully, fighting back waves of claustrophobia. This was no job Dennie would ever have chosen. But it had to be done, and the two dolphins were by nature unqualified.

Halfway down, she snagged herself on a strand of creeper. It didn't let go when she tugged. Thrashing only entangled her further, and she vividly recalled Toshio's story of the killer weed. Panic almost closed in, but she forced herself to stop kicking, to take a deep breath and study the snare.

It was just a dead vine wrapped around one leg. The strand parted easily under her knife. She continued her descent more cautiously and escaped at last into the grotto beneath the metal-mound.

Keepiru and Sah'ot waited below. Hose-like breathers covered their blowmouths and wrapped around their torsos. The headlights of the two sleds diffracted through thousands of tiny threads that seemed to fill the chamber in a drifting fog. A dim light filtered into the grotto from the cave mouth through which they had entered.

* *Echoes sounding, in this rock-cage*
  Will not be those of happy fishing *

Dennie looked at Sah'ot, unsure she had understood the poet's fancy Trinary.

"Oh! Yes. When Toshio sets the fuses, we'd better get outside. The explosion will reverberate in this chamber. I don't suppose that would be healthful."

Keepiru nodded in agreement. The expedition's military commander had been mostly silent all the way here from the ship.

Dennie looked around the underwater cavity. The coral-like, microscopic scavengers had built their castle on the rich silicate rocks of an ocean hillock. The structure had grown slowly, but when the mound finally breached the ocean surface toplife became possible. Among the vegetation which had sprouted was the drill-tree.

That plant somehow pierced the mound's metal core and penetrated to the organically useful layer beneath the island. Minerals were drawn up and deposited above. A cavity grew below, which would eventually accept the metal-mound into the crust again.

Something struck the ecologist in Dennie as odd about this arrangement. The tiny micro-branch *Library* aboard *Streaker* hadn't mentioned the metal-mounds at all, which was curious.

It was hard to believe the drill-tree could evolve into its niche in a gradual way, as most species did. For the tree to succeed was an all-or-nothing proposition, requiring great power and perseverance. How did it get that way? Dennie wondered.

And what happened to the mounds after they fell into the cavities the drill-trees prepared for them? She had seen some pits which had swallowed their mounds. Their depths were cloudy and obscure, and apparently far deeper than she would have expected.

She shone her beam on the bottom of the mound. The reflections were really quite startling. Dennie had expected something ragged and irregular, not a field of bright concave pits on the shining metal underside.

She swam to one of the larger depressions, bringing up her camera. Charlie Dart would like to get pictures and samples from this trip. She knew better than to expect thanks. More likely each tantalizing photo or rock would send him into exasperated sighs over her failure to follow up *obvious* leads.

Deep within one of the pits something moved, a twisting and slow turning. Dennie re-oriented her beam and peered closer. It was a *root* of some sort. She watched several of the tiny drifting threads fly within reach of the hanging tendril, to be caught and drawn within. She grabbed at a few for her sample bag.

"Let's go, Dennie!" She heard Toshio call. There was a thrumming sound as a sled moved just beneath her. "Come on! We've only got five minutes till they blow!"

"Okay, okay," she said. "Give me a minute." Professional curiosity momentarily overwhelmed other thoughts. Dennie could think of no reason why a living thing should burrow into the lightless underside of a mass of almost pure metal. She reached far into the pit and grabbed the twisting tendril root, then braced herself against the bulk of the mound and pulled hard.

At first the springy root was adamant, and seemed even to pull back. The possibility that she had trapped herself vividly occurred to Dennie.

The root tore free suddenly. Dennie glimpsed a shiny-hard tip as she stuffed the specimen into a sample bag. She flipped and kicked away from metal surface.

Keepiru looked at her reproachfully as she grabbed the sled. He gunned the machine toward the cave entrance and out into the daylight, where Toshio and Sah'ot waited. Moments later a loud concussion sent booming echoes through the shallows.

They waited an hour, then re-entered the grotto.

The charges had shattered the drill-tree trunk where it pierced the bottom side of the metal-mound. The severed shaft canted at an angle below, continuing down into murky depths. Bits of debris still fell from the opening in the mound's bottom. The chamber below the island was thick with swirling shreds of vegetation.

They approached the opening cautiously. "I'd better check it out with a robot first," Toshio said. "There may be unstable chunks left in the shaft."

* I will do this—ladder runner
* Robots heed my—close nerve socket *

Toshio nodded. "Yeah, you're right. You do it, Keepiru."
The pilot, with his direct machine-nerve interface, would be
able to control the probe better than Toshio could. Of the
humans aboard, only Emerson D'Anite and Thomas Orley
had such cyborg links. It would be a long time before most
humans could deal with the side effects of socket implantation
as well as dolphins, who had needed the interface far more
and had been bred for it.

Under Keepiru's direction, a small probe detached itself
from the rear of the sled. It jetted off toward the hole and
disappeared within.

Toshio had never expected to be sent right back out
again with Keepiru—to a site where, in his opinion, neither
of them had behaved particularly well. The importance of
their mission, to serve and protect two important scientists,
confused him even further. Why didn't Creideiki assign someone else? Someone more reliable?

Of course, the captain might have ordered all four of
them out of the ship to get them out of his way. But that
didn't seem to fit either.

Toshio decided not to try to pierce Creideiki's logic.
Inscrutability seemed to be at the heart of it. Perhaps that
was what it was to be a captain. Toshio only knew that he and
Keepiru were both determined to do a good job on this
mission.

As a midshipman he officially outranked Keepiru. But
tradition made warrant officers and pilots masters of middies
unless otherwise decided by higher authority. Toshio would
be assisting Dennie and Sah'ot in their studies. On security
matters, Keepiru was in charge.

Toshio was still surprised to find that others stopped and
listened when he made suggestions; his opinions had been
routinely solicited. That alone would take some getting used
to.

The screen showed a picture sent back by the robot—a
hollow cylindrical excavation through the foamy metal. Broken stumps were all that remained of the anchor bearings
that had held the drill-tree shaft in place. Bits of debris
drifted down past the camera as they watched.

As the robot rose, the light from above slowly grew brighter through a thin haze of bubbles.

"Think it's wide enough to pass a sled?" Toshio asked. Keepiru whistled that the passage looked navigable.

The robot surfaced into a pool several meters wide. Its camera panned the rim, transmitting images of blue sky and thick green foliage. The high trunk of the drill-tree had crashed into the forest. The slope of the pool made it hard to see the damage this had done, but Toshio was sure it hadn't fallen in the direction of the abo village.

They had worried that blasting a way to the interior of the island might panic the hunter-gatherers. They took the risk anyway, because routinely trying to scale the treacherous island walls in the open surf would have been dangerous, and a foolish exposure to Galactic spy satellites. The apparently random falling of a tree on an island would hardly be noted by anyone watching from above.

"Uh oh." Toshio pointed.

Dennie moved closer to look at the screen. "What is it, Tosh? Is there a problem?"

Keepiru stopped the camera as it was about to finish its scan. "There," Toshio said. "That jagged crop of coral is hanging over the pool. It looks about to fall."

"Well, can you have the robot wedge something under to prevent it?"

"I don't know. What do you think, Keepiru?"

> * *Some scheme may work—*
> *If fate buys it*
> * *We'll make a gamble—*
> *And simply try it* *

Keepiru eyed his twin screens and concentrated. Toshio knew the pilot was listening to a complex pattern of sound-images, transmitted over his neural link. Under Keepiru's command, the robot moved to the edge of the pool. Its claw arms grabbed the spongy metal of the rim to pull forward. There was a small rain of pebbles as it brought its treads to bear.

"Watch out!" Toshio called.

The jagged rock tipped forward. The camera showed it tottering ominously. Dennie cringed back from the screen.

Then the rock toppled over and crashed into the robot.

There followed a swirl of spinning images. Dennie continued watching the screen, but Toshio and Keepiru shifted their gaze to the bottom of the shaft. Suddenly a rain of objects fell from the gap, tumbling into the darkness below. The debris sparkled in the sled's beams as it dropped into the abyss.

After a long silence Keepiru spoke.

> * *The probe is down there—lungs unbreathing*
> * *I was spared—the cutoff false-death*
> * *It still whistles—stranded echoes* *

Keepiru meant that the probe still sent him messages from whatever murky ledge had finally stopped it. Its tiny brain and transmitter hadn't been destroyed, and Keepiru had not suffered the jolt that a sudden cutoff could send to a connected nervous system.

But the robot's flotation tanks had been ruined. It was down there for good.

> * *That must be—the last obstruction*
> * *I shall go then—*
>   *carefully,*
>   *testing—*
> * *Dennie, take the sled—and watch me!* *

Before Keepiru or Toshio could stop him, Sah'ot was off his sled and away. He fluked mightily and disappeared into the shaft. Keepiru and Toshio looked at each other, sharing a malign thought about crazy civilians.

At least, Toshio thought, he could have taken a camera with him! But then, if Sah'ot had waited, Toshio would have had a chance to insist on the dubious privilege of scouting the passage.

He looked at Dennie. She watched the robot probe screen, as if it might deliver some token about what was happening to Sah'ot. She had to be reminded, before she swam over and took control of the other sled.

Toshio had always thought of Dennie Sudman as one more adult scientist, friendly but enigmatic. Now he saw that she was not an awful lot more mature than he. And while she had the honor and status of a full professional, she lacked the eclecticism his officer training was giving him. She would never encounter the range of people, things, and situations he would, in the course of his career.

He looked again to the shaft entrance. Keepiru blew nervous bubbles. They would have to decide soon what to do if Sah'ot did not reappear.

Sah'ot was obviously a genetic experiment, in which the gene-crafters were pushing a set of traits toward a calculated optimum. If judged successful, the traits would be grafted back into the main pool of the neo-dolphin species. The process imitated, on a vastly quicker scale, the segregation and mixing that worked in nature.

Such experiments sometimes resulted in things not planned, though.

Toshio wasn't sure he trusted Sah'ot. The fin's obscurity wasn't like the inscrutability of Creideiki—deep and thoughtful. It grated, like the dissembling of some humans he had known.

Also, there was this sexual game between Sah'ot and Dennie. Not that he was a prude. Such hobbies weren't exactly forbidden, but they had been known to cause problems.

Apparently Dennie wasn't even aware of the subtle ways in which she was encouraging Sah'ot. Toshio wondered if he had the nerve to tell her—or if it was any of his business.

Another tense minute passed. Then, just as Toshio was about to go himself, Sah'ot shot down out of the shaft and swooped toward them.

> * *The way is clear—*
> *I'll lead you airward!* *

Keepiru jetted his sled over to the dolphin anthropologist, and squawked something pitched so high that Toshio couldn't quite catch it, even with his Calafian sensitivity.

Sah'ot's mouth twisted and closed into a reluctant attitude of submission. Still, there was something defiant in his eye. He cast a look at Dennie, even as he rolled over to offer one of his ventral fins to Keepiru's mouth.

The pilot took a token nip, then turned back to the others.

> * *The way is clear—*
> *I do believe him*

> * *Now let us go—*
>   *and drop these breathers*
> * *To talk like Earthmen—*
>   *about our work*
> * *And to meet our future—*
>   *pilot brothers* *

The sled moved under the drill-tree shaft, then rose in a cloud of bubbles. The others followed.

22

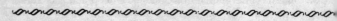

Creideiki

The briefing had gone on far too long.

Creideiki regretted ever letting Charles Dart attend via holoscreen. The chimp planetologist would certainly have been less long-winded if he were here in the fizzing oxywater of the central bay, wet and wearing a facemask.

Dart lounged in his own laboratory, projecting his image to the conference area in *Streaker*'s cylindrical bay. He seemed oblivious to the chafing of his listeners. Breathing oxywater in front of a console for two hours was highly uncomfortable to a neo-fin.

"Naturally, Captain," the chimp's scratchy baritone projected into the water. "When you chose to land us near a major tectonic boundary, I approved wholeheartedly. Nowhere else could I have had access to so much information in one spot. Still, I think I've made a convincing case for six or seven more sampling sites distributed about Kithrup, to verify some of the extremely interesting discoveries we've made here."

Creideiki was mildly surprised at the use of the first person plural. It was the first modest thing Charlie had said.

He glanced at Brookida, floating nearby. The metallurgist had been working with Charles Dart, his skills not currently required by the repair team. He had been largely silent for the last hour, letting the chimp pour out a tide of technical jargon which had left Creideiki dizzy.

What's the matter with Brookida? Does he think a captain under siege has nothing better to do?

Hikahi, recently released from sick bay, rolled over on her back, breathing the fizzing, oxygenated fluid and keeping one eye to the hologram of the chimpanzee.

She shouldn't do that, Creideiki thought. *I'm having enough trouble concentrating as it is.*

A lengthy, constricting meeting always did this to Creideiki. He felt a stirring of blood in and around his penile sheath. What he *wanted* to do was swim over to Hikahi and bite her softly in numerous places, up and down her flanks.

Kinky, yes, especially in public, but at least he was honest with himself.

"Planetologist Dart," he sighed. "I am trying very hard to understand what you claim to have discovered. The part about various crystalline and isotopic anomalies below the crust of Kithrup I think I follow. As for the subduction layer..."

"A subduction zone is a boundary of two crustal plates, where one slips below its neighbor," Charlie interrupted.

Creideiki wished he could let down his dignity to curse at the chimp. "I do know that much planetology, Dr. Dart." He spoke carefully. "And I'm glad our being near one of these plate boundaries has been useful to you. However, you mussst understand that our choice of a landing site was based on matters tactical. We want both the metals and the camouflage offered by the 'coral' mounds. We landed here in order to *hide*, and to repair our ship. With hostile cruisers overhead, I can't think of permitting expeditions to other parts of the globe. In fact, I must refuse your request for further drilling at this location. The risk is too great, now that the Galactics have arrived."

The chimp frowned. His hands began to flutter. Before he found the words, Creideiki cut him off.

"Besides, what does the ship's micro-branch say about Kithrup? Doesn't the *Library* contribute anything on these problems you face?"

"The *Library*!" Dart snorted. "That pack of lies! That friggin' morass of misinformation!" Charlie's voice dropped into a growl. "It has *nothin'* on the anomalies! It doesn't even mention the metal-mounds! The last survey was done over four *hundred* million years ago, when the planet was put on reserve status for the Karrank%...."

Charlie became so strangled around the extended glottal stop that he started to choke. He went bug-eyed and pounded himself on the chest, coughing.

Creideiki turned to Brookida. "Is this true? Is the *Library* so deficient in regard to this planet?"

"Yess-s," Brookida nodded slowly. "Four hundred epochs *is* a long time. When a planet is placed on reserve it's usually either to let it lie fallow while new species evolve to a level of pre-sentience ripe for uplift, or to provide a quiet place of decline for an ancient race that has entered senescence. Planets are placed off limits either to become nurseries or old age homes.

"Both seem to have occurred on Kithrup-p. We have discovered a ripe pre-sentient race which has apparently risen since the last *Library* update here. Also, the...Karrank-k%..." Brookida, too, had trouble with the name. "...were granted the planet as a peaceful place to die, which they apparently have done. There seem to be no Karrank%-%...anymore."

"But four hundred epochs without a re-survey?" It was difficult to imagine.

"Yes, a planet is usually re-licensed by the Institute of Migration long before that. Still, Kithrup is such a strange world...few species would choose to live here. Also, good access routes are scarce. This region of space is gravitationally very shallow. It'sss one reason we came here."

Charles Dart was still catching his breath. He drank from a tall glass of water. During the respite, Creideiki lay still, thinking. Despite Brookida's points, would Kithrup really have been left fallow for so long, in an overcrowded galaxy where every piece of real estate was desired?

The Institute of Migration was the only one of the loose Galactic bureaucracies whose power and influence rivaled even that of the *Library Institute*. By tradition, all patron-lines obeyed its codes of ecosphere management; to do otherwise courted galaxy-wide disaster. The potential of lesser species to one day become clients, then patrons in their own time, made for a powerful galaxy-wide ecological conservatism.

Most Galactics were willing to overlook humanity's pre-Contact record. The slaughter of the mammoth, the giant ground sloth, and the manatee were forgiven in light of Mankind's "orphan" status. The real blame was laid on *Homo sapiens*'s supposed patron—the mysterious undiscovered race that all said must have left man's uplift half-unfinished, thousands of years ago.

Dolphins knew how close the cetaceans themselves had come to extinction at the hands of human beings, but they never mentioned it outside Earth. For well or ill, their fate was now linked to Mankind's.

Earth was humanity's until the race moved on or died out. Man's ten colony worlds were licensed for smaller periods, based on complex eco-management plans. The shortest lease was a mere six thousand years. At the end of that time, the colonists of Atlast had to depart, leaving the planet fallow once again.

"Four hundred million years," Creideiki mulled. "That seems an unusually long time with no re-survey of this world."

"I agree!" Charlie Dart shouted, now fully recovered from his fit.

"And what if I told you there's signs Kithrup was occupied by a machine civilization as recently as thirty thousand years ago? Without any entry in the *Library* at all?"

Hikahi rolled over closer. "You think-k these crustal anomalies of yours may be the garbage of an interloper civilization, Dr. Dart?"

"Yes!" he cried. "Exactly! Good guess!

"You all know many eco-sensitive races will only build major facilities along a planet's plate boundaries. That way, when the planet is later declared fallow, *all* traces of habitation will be sucked down into the mantle and disappear. Some think that's why there are no signs of previous occupancy on Earth."

Hikahi nodded. "And if some species settled here illegally...?"

"They'd build at a plate boundary! The *Library* surveys planets at multi-epoch intervals. The evidence of the incursion would be sucked underground by then!" The chimp looked eagerly from the holo display.

Creideiki had trouble taking it all very seriously. Charlie made it sound like a whodunit! Only in this case the culprits were civilizations, the clues whole cities, and the rug under which the evidence was being swept was a planet's crust! It was the perfect crime! After all, the cop on the corner only swings by every few million years, and is late, at that.

Creideiki realized every metaphor he had just used was a human one. Well, that was to be expected. There were times, such as spacewarp-piloting, when cetacean analogies were more useful. But when thinking about the crazy politics of the Galactics, it helped to have watched a lot of old human movie thrillers, and read volumes of crazy human history.

Now Brookida and Dart were arguing some technical point... and all Creideiki could think of was the taste of the water near Hikahi. He badly wanted to ask her if the flavor meant what he thought it meant. Was it a perfume she had put on, or was it natural pheromone?

With some difficulty, he forced himself back to the subject at hand.

Charlie's and Brookida's discovery, under normal circumstances, would be exciting.

But this has no bearing on escape for my ship and crew, nor getting our data back to the Terragens Council. Even the mission I sent Keepiru and Toshio on, to help appraise the native pre-sentients, is more urgent than hunting arcane clues in ancient alien rocks.

"Excuse me, Captain. I'm sorry I'm late. I've been listening quietly for a while, though."

Creideiki turned to see Dr. Ignacio Metz drift up alongside. The gangling, gray-haired psychologist treaded water slowly, casually compensating for a small negative bouyancy. A slight pot belly distended the neat fit of his slick brown drysuit.

Brookida and Dart argued on, now about rates of heating by radioactives, gravity, and meteoritic impact. Hikahi, apparently, found it all fascinating.

"You're welcome even late, Dr. Metz. I'm glad you could make it."

Creideiki was amazed he hadn't heard the man approach. Metz normally made a racket you could hear halfway across the bay. He sometimes radiated a two kilohertz hum from his right ear. It was barely detectable now, but at times it was quite annoying. How could the man have worked with fins for so long and never had the problem corrected?

Now I'm beginning to sound like Charlie Dart! He chided himself. *Don't be peevish, Creideiki!*

He whistled a stanza which echoed only within his own skull.

> *   * Those who live
>   All vibrate,
>   * All,
>   * And aid the world's
>   Singing *

"Captain, I actually came out here for another reason, but Dart's and Brookida's discovery may bear on what I have to say. Can we talk in private?"

Creideiki became expressionless. He had to get some rest and exercise soon. Overwork was wearing him down, and *Streaker* could ill-afford that.

But this human had to be treated carefully. Metz could not command him, aboard *Streaker* or anywhere, but he had power, power of a particularly potent kind. Creideiki knew that his own right of reproduction was guaranteed, no matter how this mission ended. Still, Metz's evaluation would carry weight. Every dolphin aboard behaved as "sentiently" as he could around him. Even the captain.

Perhaps that's why I've put off a confrontation, Creideiki thought. Soon though, he would force Dr. Metz to answer some questions regarding certain members of *Streaker*'s crew.

"Very well, Doctor," he answered. "Allow me a moment. I think I'm finished here."

Hikahi swam close at a nod from Creideiki. She grinned and flicked her pectorals at Metz.

"Hikahi, please finish up here for me. Don't let them go more than another ten minutes before summing up their proposalsss. I'll meet you in an hour in recreation pool 3-A to hear your recommendations."

She answered as he had addressed her, in rapid, highly inflected Underwater Anglic. "Aye aye, Captain. Will there be anything else?"

Damn! Creideiki knew Hikahi's sonar showed her everything about his sexual agitation. It was easy to tell with a male. He would have to do an explicit sonic scan of her innards to gain the same information about her, and that would not be polite.

Things must have been so much simpler in the old times!

Well, he would find out her frame of mind in an hour. One of the privileges of captaincy was to order a recreation pool cleared. There had better not be an emergency between now and then!

"No, nothing else for now, Hikahi. Carry on."

She saluted snappily with an arm of her harness.

Brookida and Charlie were still arguing as Creideiki turned back to Metz. "Will it be private enough if we take the long way to the bridge, Doctor? I'd like to check with Takkata-Jim before going on to other duties."

"That'll be fine, Captain. What I have to say won't take long."

Creideiki kept his face impassive. Was Metz smiling at something in particular? Was the man amused at something he had seen or heard?

"I am ssstill confused by the pattern of volcanoes up and down the three-thousand-kilometer zone where these two plates meet," Brookida said. He spoke slowly, partly for Charlie's benefit and partly because it was hard to argue in oxywater. There never seemed to be enough air.

"If you look at the sssurvey charts we made from orbit, you see that vulcanism is dispersed sparsely elsewhere on the planet. But *here* the volcanoes are very frequent, and all about the same small size."

Charlie shrugged. "I don't see how that relates at all, old man. I think it's just a great big coincidence."

"But isn't this also the only area where the metal-mounds are found?" Hikahi suggested suddenly. "I'm no expert, but a spacer learns to be suspicious of twin coincidences."

Charlie opened and closed his mouth, as if he were about to speak, then thought better of it. At last he said, "That's very good. Yes! Brookida, you think these coral critters may need some nutrient that only this one type of volcano provides?"

"Possssibly. Our exobiology expert is Dennie Sudman. She's now at one of the islands, investigating the aboriginals."

"She must get samples for us!" Charlie rubbed his hands together. "Do you think it'd be too much to ask her to take a side trip to a volcano? Not too far away, of course, after what Creideiki just said. Just a little, teeny one."

Hikahi let out a short whistling laugh. The fellow had chutzpah! Still, his enthusiasm was infectious, a wonderful distraction from worry. If only she could afford to hide away from the dangerous universe in abstractions, like Charlie Dart did.

"And a temperature probe!" Charlie cried. "Surely Dennie'd do that much for me, after all I've done for her!"

Creideiki cruised in a wide spiral around the swimming human, stretching his muscles as he arched and twisted.

By neural command he flexed his harness's major manipulators, like a human stretching his arms. "Very well, Doctor. What can I do for you?"

Metz swam a slow kick-stroke. He regarded Creideiki amiably. "Captain, I believe it's time to re-think our strategy a bit. Matters have changed since we came to Kithrup. We need a new approach."

"Could you be specific?"

"Certainly. As you recall, we fled from the transfer point at Morgran because we didn't wish to be crushed in a seven-way ambush. You were quick to realize that even if we surrendered to one party, this would only result in all sides ganging up on our captors, inevitably leading to our destruction. I was slow to understand your logic at the time. Now I applaud it. Of course, your tactical maneuvers were brilliant."

"Thank you, Dr. Metz. Of course, you leave out another reason for our flight. We are under orders from the Terragens Council to bring our data directly to them, without leaks along the way. Our capture would certainly be a 'leak,' wouldn't you say?"

"Certainly!" Metz agreed. "And so the situation remained when we fled to Kithrup, a move which I now consider inspired. To my way of thinking, it was just bad luck this hiding place didn't work as planned."

Creideiki refrained from pointing out that they were still concealed on this hiding place. Surrounded, but not yet in anyone's net. "Go on," he suggested.

"Well, so long as there was the possibility we could avoid capture altogether, your strategy of flight was good. However things have changed. The chance of escape is now next to nil. Kithrup remains useful as a refuge from the chaos of battle, but it can't hide us for long once there is a final victor overhead."

"You're suggesting we can't hope to avoid eventual capture?"

"Exactly. I think we should consider our priorities, and plan for unpleasant contingencies."

"What priorities do you consider important?" Creideiki already knew the answer to expect.

"Why, the survival of this ship and crew, of course! And the data for evaluating the performance of both! After all, what was our main purpose out here. Hmm?" Metz stopped swimming and treaded water, regarding Creideiki like a teacher quizzing a pupil.

Creideiki could list a half-dozen tasks that had been set for *Streaker*, from *Library* veracity checks, to establishing contact with potential allies, to Thomas Orley's military intelligence work.

Those tasks were important. But the primary purpose of this mission was to evaluate the performance of a dolphin-crewed and dolphin-commanded spacecraft. *Streaker* and her complement were the experiment.

But everything had changed since they had found the derelict fleet! He couldn't operate under the priorities he had been given at the beginning of the cruise. How could he explain that to a man like Metz?

Judgment, Creideiki mused, *thou art fled to brutish beasts, and men have lost their reason....* Sometimes he thought that the Bard must have been half dolphin, himself.

"I understand your point, Dr. Metz. But I don't see how it calls for a change in strategy. We still face destruction should we poke our beaks above the Kithrup's sea."

"Only if we do so before there's a winner overhead! Certainly, we shouldn't expose ourselves until the crossfire is over.

"However, we *are* in a position to negotiate, once there is a victor! And if we negotiate cleverly we may win success for this mission!"

Creideiki resumed his slow spiral, forcing the geneticist to swim again toward the bridge lock.

"Can you suggest what we might have to offer in negotiation, Dr. Metz?"

Metz smiled. "For one thing, we have the information Brookida and Charles Dart have literally dug up. The Institutes reward those who report ecological crimes. Most of the factions fighting over us are traditionalist conservatives of one stripe or another and would appreciate our discovery."

Creideiki refrained from expressing in razzberries his contempt for the man's naiveté. "Go on, Doctor," he said levelly. "What-t else have we to offer?"

"Well, Captain, there's also the honor of our mission. Even if our captors decided to hold onto *Streaker* for a while, they'd certainly be sympathetic to our purpose. Teaching clients to use spaceships is one of the basic tasks of uplift. Surely they'd let us send a few men and fen home with our behavior-evaluation data, so progress toward future dolphin-crewed ships can continue. For them to do otherwise would be like a stranger interfering in the development of a child because of an argument with its parent!"

And how many human children were tortured and killed because of the sins of their parents, back in your own Dark Ages? Creideiki wanted to ask who would be the emissary to carry the uplift data back to Earth, while *Streaker* was held captive.

"Dr. Metz, I think you underestimate the fanaticism of those involved. But is there more?"

"Of course. I saved the most important for last." Metz touched Creideiki's flank for emphasis. "We must consider, Captain, giving the Galactics what they want."

Creideiki had expected it. "You think we should give them the location of the derelict fleet."

"Yes, and whatever souvenirs or data we picked up there."

Creideiki wore his poker face. *How much does he know about Gillian's "Herbie,"* he wondered. *Great Dreamer! But that cadaver's caused problems!*

"You'll recall, Captain, the one brief message we got from Earth ordered us to go into hiding and keep our data secret, *if possible*! They also said we should use our own best judgment!

"Will our silence really delay the rediscovery of that Sargasso of lost ships for long, now that it's known to exist? No doubt half the patron-lines in the Five Galaxies have swarms of scouts out now, trying to duplicate our discovery. They already know to look in a poorly linked, dim globular cluster. It's only a matter of time until they stumble across the right gravitational tide pool, in the right cluster."

Creideiki thought that debatable. Galactics didn't often think like the Earthborn, and wouldn't conduct a search in the same way. Witness how long the fleet had lain undiscovered. Still, Metz was probably right in the long run.

"In that case, Doctor, why don't we simply broadcast the location to the *Library*? It'll be public knowledge, and no longer our affair. Surely this important discovery should be investigated by a licensed team from the Institutesss?"

Creideiki was sarcastic, but he realized, as Metz smiled patronizingly, that the human took him seriously.

"You are being naive, Captain. The fanatics overhead care little about loose Galactic codes when they believe the millennium is at hand! If everyone knows where the derelict fleet is, the battleground will simply move out there! Those ancient ships will be destroyed in a crossfire, no matter how powerful that weird protective field that surrounds them. And the Galactics will *still* strive to capture us, in case we lied!"

They had arrived at the bridge lock. Creideiki paused there. "So it would be better if only one of the contesting groups got the data, and proceded to investigate the fleet alone?"

"Yes! After all, what is that bunch of floating hulks to us? Just a dangerous place where we lost a scoutboat and a dozen fine crewfen. We're not ancestor-worshipers like those ET fanatics fighting over us, and we don't give a damn except intellectually whether the derelict fleet is a remnant from the days of Progenitors, or even the returning Progenitors themselves! It sure isn't worth *dying* over. If we've learned one thing in the last two hundred years, it's that a little clan of newcomers like us Earthfolk has got to duck out of the way when big boys like the Soro and Gubru get something up their snoots!"

Dr. Metz's silvery hair waved as he bobbed his head for emphasis. A fizzing halo of effervescence collected amongst the strands.

Creideiki didn't want to go back to respecting Ignacio Metz, but when the man became passionate enough to drop his stuffy facade, he became almost likable.

Unfortunately, Metz was fundamentally wrong.

Creideiki's harness clock chimed. Creideiki realized with a start how late it had become.

"You make an interesting argument, Doctor Metz. I don't have time to go into it any further, right now. But nothing will be decided until a full staff review by the ship's council. Does that sound fair?"

"Yes, I think so, although . . ."

"And, speaking of the battle over Kithrup, I must go now and see what Takkata-Jim has to say." He hadn't intended to spend so much time with Metz. He did *not* plan to miss his long-delayed exercise period.

Metz seemed unwilling to let go. "Ah. Your mention of Takkata-Jim reminds me of something else I wanted to bring up, Captain. I'm concerned about feelings of social isolation expressed by some of the crewfen who happen to come from various experimental sub-breeds. They complain of ostracism, and seem to be under discipline a disproportionate amount of the time."

"You're referring to some of the *Stenos*, I assume."

Metz looked uncomfortable. "A colloquial term that seems to have caught on, although all neo-fen are taxonomically *Tursiops amicus*...."

"I have my jaws on the situation, Dr. Metz," Creideiki no longer cared if he interrupted the mel. "Subtle group dynamics are involved, and I am applying what I believe are effective techniques to maintain crew solidarity."

Only about a dozen of the *Stenos* showed disaffection. Creideiki suspected an infection of stress atavism, a decay of sapiency under fear and pressure. The supposed expert, Dr. Metz, seemed to think the majority of *Streaker*'s crew was practicing racial discrimination.

"Are you implying that Takkata-Jim is also having problems?" Creideiki asked.

"Certainly not! He's a most impressive officer. Mention of his name reminded me because..." Metz paused.

Because he's a Stenos, Creideiki finished for him silently. *Shall I tell Metz that I'm considering moving Hikahi into the vice-captaincy? For all of Takkata-Jim's skill, his moody isolation is becoming a drag on crew morale. I cannot have that in my pod-second.*

Creideiki sorely missed Lieutenant Yachapa-Jean, who had died back at the Shallow Cluster.

"Dr. Metz, since you bring up the subject, I have noticed discrepancies between the pre-launch psycho-biological profiles of certain members of the crew and their subsequent performance, even before we discovered the derelict fleet. I'm not a cetapsychologist, per se, but in certain cases I am convinced that the fen did not belong on this ship in the first place. Have you a comment?"

Metz's face was blank. "I'm not sure I know what you're talking about, Captain."

Creideiki's harness whirred as one arm snaked out to scratch an itch above his right eye. "I have little to go on, but soon I think I'll want to invoke command privilege and look over your notes. Strictly informally, of course. Please prepare them for . . ."

A chime interrupted Creideiki. It came from the comm link on his harness. "Yess, speak!" he commanded. He listened for a few moments to a buzzing voice on his neural tap.

"Hold everything," he replied. "I'll be right up. Creideiki out."

He focused a burst of sonar at the sensitive plate by the door lock. The hatch hummed open.

"That was the bridge," he told Metz. "A scout has returned with a report from Tsh't and Thomas Orley. I'm needed, but we will discuss these matters again, sssoon, Doctor."

With two powerful fluke strokes Creideiki was through the lock doors and on his way to the bridge.

Ignacio Metz watched the captain go.

Creideiki suspects, he thought. *He suspects my special studies. I'll have to do something. But what?*

These conditions of siege-pressure were providing fantastic data, especially on the dolphins Metz had inveigled into *Streaker*'s complement. But now things were starting to come apart. Some of his subjects were showing stress symptoms he had never expected.

Now, in addition to worry about ET fanatics, he had to handle Creideiki's suspicions. It wouldn't be easy to put him off track. Metz appreciated genius when he saw it, especially in an uplifted dolphin.

If only he were one of mine, he thought of Creideiki. *If only I could take credit for that one.*

23

∂∽∂∽∂∽∂∽∂∽∂∽∂∽∂∽∂∽∂∽∂∽∂∽∂∽∂∽∂∽

Gillian

The ships lay in space like serried rows of scattered beads, dimly reflecting the faint glow of the Milky Way. The nearest stars were the dim reddish oldsters of a small globular cluster, patient and barren remnants from the first epoch of star formation—devoid of planets or metals.

Gillian contemplated the photograph, one of six that *Streaker* had innocently transmitted home from what had seemed an obscure and uninteresting gravitational tide pool, far off the beaten path.

An eerie, silent armada, unresponsive to their every query; the Earthlings hadn't known what to make of it. The fleet of ghost ships had no place in the ordered structure of the Five Galaxies.

How long had they gone unnoticed?

Gillian put the holo aside and picked up another. It showed a closeup of one of the giant derelict ships. Huge as a moon, pitted and ancient, it shimmered inside a faint lambence—a preservative field of unguessable properties. The aura had defied analysis. They could only tell that it was an intense probability field of unusual nature.

In attempting to dock with one ghost ship, at the outer reaches of the field, the crew of *Streaker*'s gig somehow touched off a chain reaction. Brilliant lightning flashed between the ancient behemoth and the little scoutboat. Lieutenant Yachapa-Jean had reported that all the dolphins were experiencing intense visions and hallucinations. She tried to disengage, but in her disorientation she set off her stasis screens inside the strange field. The resultant explosion tore apart both the tiny Earthship and the giant derelict.

135

Gillian put down the photo and looked across the lab. Herbie still lay enmeshed in his web of stasis, a silhouette untold hundreds of million years—billions of years old.

After the disaster, Tom Orley had gone out all alone and brought the mysterious relic back in secret through one of *Streaker's* side locks.

A prize of great cost, Gillian thought as she contemplated the cadaver. *We paid well for you, Herb. If only I could figure out what we bought.*

Herb was an enigma worthy of concerted research by the great Institutes, not one solitary woman on a besieged starship far from home.

It was frustrating, but someone had to make this effort. Somebody had to try to understand why they had been turned into hunted animals. With Tom gone, and Creideiki busy keeping the ship and crew functioning, the task was hers. If she didn't do it, it wouldn't be done.

Slowly, she was learning a thing or two about Herbie... enough to confirm that the corpse was very old, that it had the skeletal structure of a planet-walker, and that the ship's micro-*Library* still claimed that nothing like it had ever existed.

She put her feet up onto the desk and pulled another photo from the stack. It clearly showed, through that shimmering probability field, a row of symbols etched into the side of a massive hull.

"Open *Library*," she pronounced. Of the four holo screens on her desk, the one at the far left—with the rayed spiral glyph above it—came alight.

"Sargasso file—symbols reference search. Open and display changes."

A terse column of text displayed in response against the wall to Gillian's left. The listing was dismayingly brief.

"Sub-persona: Reference Librarian—query mode," she said. The outline remained projected against the wall. Alongside it a swirling pattern coalesced into the rayed spiral design. A low, calm voice intoned, "Reference Librarian mode, may I help you?"

"Is this all you've been able to come up with, regarding those symbols on the side of that derelict ship?"

"Affirmative," the voice was cool. The inflections were correct, but no attempt had been made to disguise the fact that it came from a minimal persona, a small corner of the shipboard *Library* program.

"I have searched my records for correlates with these symbols. You are well aware, of course, that I am a very small micro-branch, and that symbols are endlessly mutable in time. The outline gives all possible references I have found within the parameters you set."

Gillian looked at the short list. It was hard to believe. Though incredibly small compared with planetary or sector branches, the ship's *Library* contained the equivalent of all the books published on Earth until the late twenty-first century. Surely there had to be more correlates than this!

"Ifni!" she sighed. "*Something* has got half the fanatics in the galaxy stirred up. Maybe it's that picture of Herbie we sent back. Maybe it's these symbols. Which was it?"

"I am not equipped to speculate," the program responded.

"The question was rhetorical, and not addressed to you anyway. I see you show a thirty percent correlation of five symbols with religious glyphs of the 'Abdicator' Alliance. Give me an overview of the Abdicators."

The voice shifted tone. "Cultural summary mode..."

"Abdicator is a term chosen from Anglic to represent one of the major philosophical groupings in Galactic society.

"The Abdicator belief dates from the fabled Tarseuh episode of the fifteenth aeon, approximately six hundred million years ago, a particularly violent time, when the Galactic Institutes barely survived the ambitions of three powerful patron lines (reference numbers 97AcF109t, 97AcG136t and 97AcG986s).

"Two of these species were amongst the most potent and aggressive military powers in the history of the five linked galaxies. The third species was responsible for the introduction of several new techniques of spacecraft design, including the now standard..."

The *Library* waxed into a highly technical discussion of hardware and manufacturing methods. Though interesting, it seemed hardly relevant. With her toe she touched the "skim" button on her console, and the narration leaped ahead...

"... The conquerors assumed an appellation which might be translated as 'the Lions.' They managed to seize most of the transfer points and centers of power,

and all the great *Libraries*. For twenty million years
their grip appeared unassailable. The Lions engaged in
unregulated population expansion and colonization,
resulting in extinction of eight out of ten pre-client races
in the Five Galaxies at the time.

"The Tarseuh helped bring about an end of this
tyranny by summoning intervention by six ancient species previously thought to be extinct. These six joined
forces with the Tarseuh in a successful counterattack by
Galactic culture. Afterward, when the Institutes were
re-established, the Tarseuh accompanied the mysterious
defenders to an obscure oblivion . . ."

Gillian interrupted the flow of words.
"Where did the six species that helped the rebels come
from? Did you say they had been extinct?"
The monitor voice returned. "According to records of the
time, they had been thought extinct. Do you want reference
numbers?"
"No. Proceed."

.   "Today most sophonts believe the six were racial
remnants not yet finished 'stepping off' into a later stage
of evolution. Thus the six might not have been extinct
per se, but merely grown almost unrecognizable. They
were still capable of taking an interest in mundane affairs
when matters became sufficiently severe. Do you wish
me to refer you to articles on the natural passing modes
of species?"

"No. Proceed. What do the Abdicators say took place?"

"Abdicators believe that there are certain ethereal
races which deign to take physical form, from time to
time, disguised in a seemingly normal pattern of uplift.
These 'Great Ghosts' are raised up as pre-clients, pass
through indenture, and go on to become leading seniors,
without ever revealing their true nature. In emergencies,
however, these super-species can quickly intervene directly in the affairs of mortals.
"The Progenitors are said to be the earliest, most
aloof, and most powerful of these Great Ghosts.

"Naturally, this is profoundly different from the common Progenitor legend, that the Eldest departed the Home Galaxy long ago, promising to return some day..."

"Stop!" The *Library* fell silent at once. Gillian frowned as she thought about the phrase "Naturally, this is profoundly different..."

Bull! The Abdicator belief was just a variant of the same basic dogma, differing only slightly from other millennial legends of the "return" of the Progenitors. The controversy reminded her of old-time religious conflicts on Earth, when adherents had performed frantic exegesis over the nature of trinity, or the number of angels that could dance on the head of a pin.

This particular frenzy over minor points of doctrine would be almost funny if the battle weren't going on right now, a few thousand kilometers overhead.

She jotted a reminder to try a cross-reference to the Hindu belief in the avatars of deities. The similarity to Abdicator tenets made her wonder why the *Library* hadn't made the connection, at least as an analogy.

Enough is enough.

"Niss!" she called.

The screen on the far right came alight. An abstract pattern of sparkling motes erupted into a sharply limited zone just above the screen.

"As you know, Gillian Baskin, it is preferable that the *Library* not know of my existence aboard this ship. I have taken the liberty of screening it so that it cannot observe our conversation. You wish to ask me something?"

"I certainly do. Were you listening to that report just now?"

"I listen to everything this ship's micro-branch does. It is my primary function here. Didn't Thomas Orley ever explain that to you?"

Gillian restrained herself. Her foot was too close to the offending screen. She put it on the floor to remove temptation. "Niss," she asked evenly, "why does the micro-branch *Library* talk gibberish?"

The Tymbrimi machine sighed anthropomorphically. "Dr. Baskin, virtually every oxygen-breathing race but Mankind has been weaned on a semantic which evolved down scores of patron-client links, all influenced by the *Library*. The languages of Earth are strange and chaotic by Galactic standards. The problems of converting Galactic archives into your unconventional syntax are enormous."

"I know all that! The ETs wanted us to all learn Galactic Seven at the time of Contact. We told them to take the idea and stick it."

"Graphically put. Instead, humanity applied immense resources to convert Earth's branch *Library* to use colloquial Anglic, hiring Kanten, Tymbrimi, and others as consultants. But still there are problems, are there not?"

Gillian rubbed her eyes. This was getting them nowhere. *Why* did Tom imagine this sarcastic machine was useful? Whenever she wanted to get a simple answer, it only asked questions.

"The language problem has been their excuse for over two centuries!" she said. "How much longer will they use it? Since Contact we've been studying *language* as it hasn't been studied in millions of years! We've tackled the intricacies of 'wolfling' tongues like Anglic, English, Japanese, and taught dolphins and chimps to speak. We've even made some progress communicating with those strange creatures, the Solarians of Earth's sun!

"Yet the *Library Institute* still tells us it's our language that's at fault for all of these lousy correlations, these clumsily translated records! Hell, Tom and I can each speak four or five Galactic tongues. It's not the language difference that's the trouble. There's something queer about the *data* we've been given!"

The Niss hummed silently for a time. The sparkling motes coalesced and separated like two immiscible fluids merging and falling apart into droplets.

"Dr. Baskin, haven't you just described the major reason for ships such as this one, which roam space hunting discrepancies in the *Library*'s records? And the very purpose of my existence, to attempt to catch the *Library* in a lie, to try to find out if the most powerful patron races, as you would say, 'stack the deck' against younger sophonts such as Men and Tymbrimi?"

"Then why don't you *help* me?" Gillian's heart raced. She gripped the edge of the desk, and she realized suddenly that the frustration had come close to overcoming her.

"Why am I so fascinated with the human way of looking at things, Dr. Baskin?" the Niss asked. Its voice turned almost sympathetic. "My Tymbrimi masters are unusually crafty. Their adaptability keeps them alive in a dangerous galaxy. Yet they, too, are trapped in the Galactic mode of thinking. You Earthlings, from a fresh perspective, may see what they do not.

"The range of behaviors and beliefs among oxygen-breathers is vast, yet the experience of Man is virtually unique. Carefully uplifted client races never suffer through the errors made by your pre-Contact human nations. These errors have made you different."

That was true enough, Gillian knew. Blatant idiocies had been tried by early men and women—foolishness that would never have been considered by species aware of the laws of nature. Desperate superstitions had bred during the savage centuries. Styles of government, intrigues, philosophies were tested with abandon. It was almost as if Orphan Earth had been a planetary laboratory, upon which a series of senseless and bizarre experiments were tried.

Illogical and shameful as they seemed in retrospect, those experiences enriched modern Man. Few races had made so many mistakes in so short a time, or tried so many tentative solutions to hopeless problems.

Earthling artists were sought out by many jaded ETs, and paid well to spin tales no Galactic would imagine. The Tymbrimi particularly liked human fantasy novels, with lots of dragons, ogres and magic—the more the better. They thought them terrifyingly grotesque and vivid.

"I am not discouraged when you grow frustrated with the *Library*," the Niss said. "I am *glad*. I learn from your frustration! You question things that all Galactic society takes for granted.

"Only secondarily am I here to help you, Mrs. Orley. Primarily, I am here to observe how you suffer."

Gillian blinked. The machine's use of an ancient honorific had to have had a purpose—as did its blatant attempt to make her angry. She sat still and monitored a flux of conflicting emotions.

"This is getting nowhere," she spat. "And it's making me crazy. I feel all cooped up."

The Niss sparkled without commenting. Gillian watched the motes spin and dance.

"You're suggesting we let it sit for a while, aren't you?" she said at last.

"Perhaps. Both Tymbrimi and Humans possess pre-conscious selves. Perhaps we should both let these matters lie in the dark for a time, and let our hidden parts mull things over."

Gillian nodded. "I'm going to ask Creideiki to send me to Hikahi's island. The abos are important. After escape itself, I'd guess they're the most important thing."

"A normal, moral view from the Galactic standpoint, and therefore of little interest to me." The Niss sounded bored already. The dazzling display coalesced into dark patterns of spinning lines. They whirled and converged, fell together into a tiny point, and disappeared.

Gillian imagined she heard a faint pop as the Niss departed.

When she reached Creideiki on the comm line the captain blinked at her.

"Gillian, is your psi working overtime? I was just calling you!"

She sat up. "Have you heard from Tom?"

"Yesss. He's fine. He's asked me to send you on an errand. Can you come down here right away?"

"I'm on my way, Creideiki."

She locked the door to her lab and hurried toward the bridge.

24

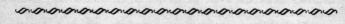

Galactics

Beie Chohooan could only rumble in amazement at the magnitude of the battle. How had the fanatics managed to gather such strength in so short a time?

Beie's little Synthian scout ship cruised down the ancient, rocky jet stream left by a long-dead comet. The Kthsemenee system was ablaze with bright flashes. Her screens showed the battle fleets as they merged into swirling knots all around her, scratching and killing and separating again. Alliances formed and dissolved whenever the parties seemed to sense an advantage. In violation of the codes of the Institute for Civilized Warfare, no quarter was being given.

Beie was an experienced spy for the Synthian Enclave, but she had never seen anything like this.

"I was an observer at Paklatuthl, when the clients of the J'81ek broke their indenture on the battlefield. I saw the Obeyor Alliance meet the Abdicators in ritual war. But never have I seen such mindless slaughter! Have they no pride? No appreciation of the art of war?"

Even as she watched, Beie saw the strongest of the alliances fall apart in a fiery betrayal, as one flank fell upon the other.

Beie snorted in disgust. "Faithless fanatics," she muttered.

There was a chitter from the shelf to her left. A row of small pink eyes looked down upon her.

"Which of you said that!" She glared at the little tarsier-like wazoon, each staring out the entrance hatch of its own little spy-globe. The eyes blinked back at her. The wazoon chittered in amusement, but none of them answered her directly.

Beie sniffed. "Well, you're right, of course. The fanatics have quick reactions on their side. They do not stop and consider, but dive right in, while we moderates must ponder before we act."

Especially the ever-cautious Synthians, she thought. Earthlings are supposed to be our allies, yet timidly we talk and consider, we protest to the impotent Institutes, and send expendable scouts to spy upon the fanatics.

The wazoon chattered a warning.

"I know!" she snapped. "Don't you think I know my business? So there's a watcher probe up ahead. One of you go take care of it and don't bother me! Can't you see I'm busy?"

The eyes blinked at her. One pair vanished as the wazoon scuttled into its tiny ship and closed the hatch. In a moment a small shudder passed through the scout as the probe departed.

Luck to you, small wazoon, faithful client, she thought.

Feigning nonchalance, she watched as the tiny probe danced up ahead amongst the planetoidal debris, sneaking toward the watcher probe that lay in Beie's path.

One expendable scout, she thought bitterly. The Tymbrimi are fighting for their lives. Earth is besieged, half her colonies taken, and still we Synthians wait and watch, watch and wait, sending only me and my team to observe.

A small flame burned suddenly, casting stark shadows through the asteroid field. The wazoon let out a low groan of mourning, stopping quickly when Beie looked their way.

"Do not hide your feelings from me, my brave wazoon," she murmured. *"You are clients and brave warriors, not slaves. Mourn your colleague, who died so well for us."*

She thought about her own cool, careful people, amongst whom she always felt a stranger.

"Feel!" she insisted, surprised by her own vehemence. "There is no shame in caring, my little wazoon. In this you may be greater than your patron race, when you are grown up and on your own!"

Beie piloted closer to the water world, where the battle raged, feeling more akin to her little client-comrades than to her own ever-cautious race.

25

Thomas Orley

Thomas Orley looked down upon his treasure: a thing he had sought for twelve years. It appeared to be intact, the first of its kind ever to fall into human hands.

Only twice had micro-branch *Libraries* designed for other races been captured by human crews, from ships defeated in skirmishes over the last two hundred years. In each case the repositories were damaged. Attempts to study them were informative, but one mistake or another always caused the semi-intelligent machines to self-destruct.

This was the first ever recovered intact from a warship of a powerful Galactic patron race. And it was the first taken since certain Tymbrimi had joined in this clandestine research.

The unit was a beige box, about three meters by two by one, with simple optical access ports. Halfway along one side was the rayed spiral symbol of the *Library*.

It was lashed to a cargo sled along with other booty, including three probability coils, undamaged and irreplaceable. Hannes Suessi would ride back to *Streaker*, protecting those as a mother hen her eggs. Only when he saw them safely in Emerson D'Anite's hands would he turn around to come back here.

Tom wrote routing instructions on a waxboard. With any luck, the crew back at *Streaker* would turn the micro-branch unit over to Creideiki or Gillian without undue attention. He adhered the shipping slip so that it covered the *Library* glyph.

Not that his interest in a captured micro-branch was particularly secret. The crew here had helped him pry it from the Thennanin ship. But the fewer who knew the details the better. Especially if they should ever be captured. If his instructions were followed, the unit would be plugged into the comm in his own cabin, to outward appearances a normal communications screen.

He imagined the Niss would be impressed. Tom wished he could be there when the Tymbrimi machine found out what it suddenly had access to. The smug thing would probably be speechless for half a day.

He hoped it wouldn't be *too* stunned. He wanted something from it right away.

Suessi was already asleep, tethered to his precious salvage. Tom made sure the instructions were well secured. Then he swam up toward the sheer outcrop of rock overlooking the wrecked alien starship.

Neo-fen swarmed over the hulk, making detailed measurements from without and within. At word from Creideiki charges would be set off, beginning a process that would leave the giant battleship's core a reamed and empty cavity.

By now the scout they had sent back should have reached *Streaker* with his initial report, and a sled should already be returning down the new shortcut they had found, bringing a monofilament intercom line from home. It ought to meet the salvage sled about halfway.

All this assumed "home" was still there. Tom guessed the battle still raged above Kithrup. Space war was a slow thing, especially as practiced by the long-viewed Galactics. They might still be at it in a year or two, though he doubted it. That much time would allow reinforcements to arrive and produce a war of attrition. It was unlikely the fanatic alliances would let things come to that pass.

In any event, *Streaker's* crew had to act as if the war were about to end any day now. So long as confusion reigned above, they still had a chance.

Tom went over his plan again, and came to the same conclusion. He had no other choice.

There were three conceivable ways they might escape the trap they were in—rescue, negotiation, and trickery.

Rescue was a nice image. But Earth herself didn't have the strength to come and deliver them. Together with her allies she could barely match *one* of the pseudo-religious factions in the battle over Kithrup.

The Galactic Institutes might intervene. What law there was demanded that *Streaker* report directly to them. Problem was, the Institutes had little power of their own. Like the feeble versions of world government Earth had almost died of in the Twentieth Century, they relied on mass opinion and volunteer levies. The majority "moderates" might finally decide that *Streaker's* discovery should be shared by all, but Tom figured it would take years for the necessary alliances to form.

Negotiation seemed as faint a hope as rescue. In any event, Creideiki had Gillian and Hikahi and Metz to help him if it ever came to negotiations with a victor in the space battle. They didn't need Tom for that.

That left clever schemes and subtle deceptions... finding a way to thwart the enemy when rescue and negotiation fail. *That's my job*, he thought.

The ocean was deeper and darker here than in the region only fifty kilometers to the east, where strings of metal-mounds grew in the hilly shallows along the edges of a thin crustal plate. In the area where Hikahi's party had been rescued, the water was metal-enriched by a chain of semi-active volcanoes.

There were no true metal-mounds in this area, and the long-dead volcanic islands were worn down to the water's surface.

When he looked away from the crumpled Thennanin wreck, and the trail of havoc it had left before coming to rest, Tom found the scenery restful, its beauty calming. Drifting, dark-yellow fronds of danglevine, waving like corn silk from the surface, reminded him of the color of Gillian's hair.

Orley hummed to himself a melody that few other human beings could attempt. Small gene-crafted sinuses reverberated under his skull, sending a low refrain into the water around him.

> * *In sleep, your caring*
> *Touches me,*
> * *Where, waking, I let it not*
>
> * *In distance, I will*
> *Call to you,*
> * *And touch you as you sleep* *

Of course Gillian couldn't actually hear his gift poem. His own psi powers were quite modest. Still, she might pick up a hint. Other things she had done had surprised him more.

The dolphin escort had gathered at the sled. Suessi had awakened and was checking his lashings with Lieutenant Tsh't.

Tom launched himself from his aerie toward the group. Tsh't saw him and took a quick breath from an airdome before swimming up to meet him halfway.

"I wish you would reconsider doing thisss," she implored when they met. "I'll be frank. Your presence is good for morale. If you were losssst it would be a blow."

Tom smiled and put a hand on her flank. He had already come to terms with his poor chances of returning.

"I don't see any other way, Tsh't. All the other parts of my plan can be handled by others, but I'm the only one who can bait the hook. You know that.

"Besides," he grinned, "Creideiki will have one more chance to call me back if he doesn't like the plan. I asked that he send Gillian to meet me at Hikahi's island, with the glider and the supplies I need. If she tells me his answer is no, I'll be back at the ship before you."

Tsh't looked away. "I doubt he'll sssay no," she whistled low and almost inaudibly.

"Hmm? What do you mean?"

Evasively, Tsh't answered in Trinary.

* Creideiki leads us—
      Is our master
* Yet we imagine—
      Secret orders *

Tom sighed. There it was again, the suspicion that Earth would never let the first dolphin-commanded vessel go out without disguised human supervision. Naturally, most of the rumors centered around himself. It was bothersome, because Creideiki was an excellent captain. Also, it detracted from one of the purposes of the mission, to make a demonstration that would boost neo-fin self-confidence for a generation.

* Then in my leaving—
      Learn a lesson,
* Aboard Streaker—
      Is your captain. *

Tsh't must have been running low on the breath she had taken at the sled's airdome. Bubbles leaked from her blowmouth. Still she looked back at him resignedly and spoke in Anglic.

"All right-t. After Suessi leaves, we'll get you on your way. We'll continue working here until we get ordersss from Creideiki."

"Good." Tom nodded. "And you still approve of the rest of the plan?"

Tsh't turned away, her eyes recessed.

* Keneenk and logic
      Join to sing
* Its tune

* The plan is all between
      Us and
* Our doom

* We'll all do our part *

Tom reached over and hugged her. "I know we can count on you, you sweet old fish-catcher. I'm not worried at all. Now let's say good-bye to Hannes, so I can be on my way. I don't want Jill to get to the island before me."

He dove toward the sled. But Tsh't remained behind for a moment. Although the air in her lungs was growing stale, she lay still, watching him swim away.

Her sonar clicks swept over him as he descended. She caressed him with her hearing, and sang a quiet requiem.

> * *They cast their nets to catch us—*
>   *Those of Iki,*
> * *Yet you are there—*
>   *To cut the nets.*

> * *Good Walker,*
>   *Always,*
> * *You cut the nets—*

> * *Though they'll take*
>   *In payment*
>   *Your life . . .* *

26

∽∾∽∾∽∾∽∾∽∾∽∾∽∾∽∾∽∾∽∾∽∾∽∾∽∾∽∾

Creideiki

The most formal Anglic, spoken carefully by a neo-dolphin, would be difficult for a human raised only in Man-English to understand. The syntax and many root words were the same. But a pre-spaceflight Londoner would have found the sounds as strange as the voices that spoke them.

The dolphin's modified blowhold provided whistles, squawks, vowels and a few consonants. Sonar clicks and many other sounds came from complex resonant cavities inside the skull.

In speech, these separate contributions were sometimes in phase and sometimes not. Even at the best of times, there were stretched sibilants, stuttered t's, and groaned vowels. Speech was an art.

Trinary was for relaxation, for imagery and personal matters. It replaced and greatly expanded on Primal Delphin. But *Anglic* linked the neo-dolphin to the world of cause and effect.

Anglic was a language of compromise between the vocal abilities of two races—between the hands-and-fire world of Men and the drifting legends of the Whale Dream. Speaking it, a dolphin could equal most humans in analytic thought, consider past and future, make schemes, use tools, and fight wars.

Some thoughtful humans wondered if giving the cetacean Anglic had really been much of a favor, after all.

Two neo-dolphins alone together might speak Anglic for concentration, but not care if the *sounds* resembled English words. They would drift into frequencies beyond human hearing, and consonants would virtually disappear.

Keneenk allowed this. It was the semantics that counted. If the grammar, the two-level logic, the time-orientation were Anglic, pragmatic results were all that mattered.

When Creideiki took Hikahi's report, he purposely spoke a very relaxed form of fin-Anglic. By example he wanted to say that what went on here was private.

He listened to her while he took the kinks out of his body, diving and racing back and forth across the exercise pool. Hikahi recited her report on the planetology meeting, enjoying the sweet smell of real air in her main lungs. Occasionally, she paused and sped alongside him for a stretch before continuing.

Right now her words sounded nothing like human speech, but a very good voicewriter could have translated them.

"... He feels very strongly about it, Captain. In fact, Charlie suggests that we should leave a small study team here with the longboat even if *Streaker* tries to escape. Even Brookida is tempted by the idea. I was a bit stunned."

Creideiki passed in front of her. He burst out a quick question.

"And what would they do if we left them behind, and we were then captured?" He dove back underwater and sped on toward the far wall.

"Charlie thinks he and a detached team could be declared noncombatants, and the Sudman-Sah'ot group out on the island, as well. He says there are precedents. That way, whether we get away or not, part of the mission is preserved."

The exercise room was in *Streaker's* centrifugal ring, ten degrees up the side of the wheel. The walls were canted and Creideiki had to watch out for shallows in the pool's port side. A cluster of balls, rings, and complex toys floated to starboard.

Creideiki swam quickly under a cluster of balls and shot out of the water. He spun as he sailed through the air and landed on his back with a splash. He did a flip underwater, then rose up above the surface on his churning tail. Breathing heavily, he regarded Hikahi with one eye.

"I've considered the idea already," he said. "We could leave Metz and his records, too. Getting him off our tails would be worth thirty herring and an anchovy dessert."

He settled back down into the water. "Too bad the solution is immoral and impractical."

Hikahi looked puzzled, trying to figure his meaning.

Creideiki felt much better. The frustration which had built to a peak when he listened to Tom Orley's message had now abated. He could put aside, for a while, the depression he felt when he agreed to the man's plan.

All that remained was to get the formal advice of the ship's council. He prayed they'd come up with a better idea, though he doubted they would.

"Think," he asked his lieutenant. "Declaring noncombatants might work if we are killed or captured, but what if we *escape*, and draw our ET friends chasing after us?"

Hikahi's jaw dropped open slightly—a borrowed human mannerism. "Of course. I hear it. Kthsemenee is so very isolated. There are only a few routes in and out. The longboat probably couldn't make it back to civilization all alone."

"Which would mean?"

"They would become castaways, on a deadly planet, with minimal medical facilities. Forgive my lack of foresight."

She turned slightly, presenting her left ventral fin. It was a civilized version of an ancient geture of submission, such as a human student's sheepish bowed head to his teacher.

With luck, Hikahi would someday command ships greater

than *Streaker,* by orders of magnitude. The captain and teacher within him was pleased with her combination of modesty and cleverness. But another part of him had more immediate goals for her.

"Well, we'll take their idea under advisement. In case we have to adopt the plan quickly, see to stocking the longboat.

"But put a guard on it, too."

They both knew that it was a bad sign, when security precautions had to be taken *within,* as well as without.

A brightly striped rubber ring floated past them. Creideiki felt an urge to chase it . . . as he wanted to push Hikahi into a corner and nuzzle her until . . . He shook himself.

"As for further tectonic research," he said. "That's out of the question. Gillian Baskin has left for your island, to take supplies to Thomas Orley and to help Dennie Sudman study the aboriginals. When she returns, she can bring back rock samples for Charlie. That'll have to satisfy him.

"The rest of us will be very busy as soon as Suessi gets back here with those spare parts."

"Suessi's sure he found what we need at the wreck?"

"Fairly certain."

"This new plan means we'll have to move *Streaker.* Turning on our engines may give us away. But I guess there's no choice. I'll get started on a plan to move the ship."

Creideiki realized that this was getting him nowhere. A few hours remained, at most, until Suessi arrived, and here he was talking to Hikahi in *Anglic* . . . forcing her by example to think rigidly and carefully! No wonder he was getting no hint, no body language, no suggestion that an advance might be welcomed or rejected.

He answered her in Trinary.

> * *We'll only move her—*
> *Below water*
> * *To the crashed ship—*
> *Empty, waiting*
> * *Soon, while battles—*
> *Still wrack the blackness*
> * *Filling space—*
> *With squid-like racket*
> * *At a time when—*
> *Orley, Net-bane,*

> * *Far away, does*
>   *Make*
>   *Distraction*
> * *Far away, does*
>   *Truth*
>   *Decipher*
> * *Drawing sharks—*
>   *To make us safer* *

Hikahi stared at him. This was the first time she had heard about that part of Orley's plan. Like many of the females aboard, Hikahi had a platonic passion for Thomas Orley.

I should have broken the news more gently, or, better yet, waited until later!

Her eyes blinked, once, twice, then closed. She sank slowly, and from her forehead melon came a faint keening.

Creideiki envied humans their enfolding arms. He dropped alongside her to touch her with the tip of his bottle-shaped rostrum.

> * *Do not grieve for—*
>   *Strong-eyed flyer*
> * *Orley's song shall—*
>   *By whales be sung*

Hikahi replied sadly.

> * *I, Hikahi—*
>   *Honor Orley*
> * *Honor captain—*
>   *Honor crewmates*
> * *Deeds are done, still—*
>   *For one I suffer—*
>
> * *For Jill Baskin—*
>   *Dear Life-Cleaner*
> * *For her loss—*
>   *And body sorrow* *

Shamed, Creideiki felt an enclosing shroud of melancholy fall around him. He shut his own eyes and the waters echoed back to him a shared sadness.

For a long time they lay side by side, rising to breathe, then settling once more below.

Creideiki's thoughts were far away when he finally felt Hikahi drift away. But then she was back, rubbing gently against his side, and then nibbling tenderly with sharp, small teeth.

Almost against his will, at first, Creideiki felt his enthusiasm begin to return. He rolled over to his side and let out a long sigh of bubbles as her nuzzling became more provocative.

The water began to taste happier then, as Hikahi crooned a familiar song, taken from one of the oldest of Primal signals. It seemed to say, amongst other things, "Life goes on."

27

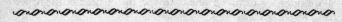

The Island

The night was quiet.

Kithrup's many small moons stirred low tides against the metal cliffs a hundred meters away. The ever-present winds, driven without brake across the planet ocean, tugged at the trees and ruffled the foliage.

Still, compared to what they had known for months, the silence was heavy. There were none of the ubiquitous machine sounds which had followed them everywhere from Earth, the unceasing whirrs and clicks of mechanical function, or the occasional smoking crackle of failure.

The squeaking, groaning drone of dolphin conversation was gone, too. Even Keepiru and Sah'ot were absent. At night the two dolphins accompanied the Kithrup aboriginals in their nocturnal sea hunt.

The surface of the metal-mound was almost too quiet. The few sounds seemed to carry forever. The sea, the distant rumble of a faraway volcano...

There was a gentle moan in the night, followed by a very quiet gasping cry.

"They're at it again," Dennie sighed, not particularly caring if Toshio heard her.

The sounds came from the clearing at the southern point of the island. The third and fourth humans on the island had tried to find their privacy as far from the abo village and the tunnel pool as possible. Dennie wished they could have gone even farther away.

There was laughter, faint but clear.

"I've never heard anything like it," she sighed.

Toshio blushed and fed another stick to the fire. The couple in the next clearing deserved their privacy. He considered pointing this out to Dennie.

"I swear, they're like minks!" Dennie said, intending to sound sardonic and mock-envious. But it came out just a little bitter.

Toshio noticed. Against his better judgment, he said, "Dennie, we all know that humans are among the sexual athletes of the galaxy, though some of our clients give us a run for it."

Toshio poked a stick into the fire. That had been a pretty brash thing to say. He felt a trifle emboldened by the night, and the desire to break the tension by the fire.

"What do you mean by that?" Dennie looked at him sharply.

Toshio played with the stick. "We-ell, there's a line in an old play . . . 'Why, your *dolphin* was not lustier!' Shakespeare wasn't the first to compare the two horniest of the brainy mammals y'know. I don't suppose anyone's come up with a scale to measure it, but I'd have to wonder if it weren't a prerequisite for intelligence.

"Of course, that's only one of the possibilities. If you take what the Galactics say about uplift into account . . ."

He rambled on, slowly drawing away from incitement, noticing how Dennie came *this* close to blowing her cool, before she turned and looked away.

He'd done it! He had played a round and won it! It was a minor victory in a game he had wondered if he would ever get to play.

The art of teasing had always been a one-sided affair to Toshio, and he'd always had the short end. To get the best of an attractive older woman by dint of clever conversation and character insight was a coup.

He didn't think he was being cruel, though a genteel cruelty did seem to be part of the game. All he knew for certain was that this was one way to get Dennie Sudman to treat him less like a child. If some of the easy mutual liking they'd had before had to suffer for it, that was too bad.

Much as he didn't care for Sah'ot, Toshio was glad the fin had provided the lever he needed to pry a chink in Dennie's armor.

He was about to try out another bon mot when Dennie cut in.

"I'm sorry, Tosh. I'd love to hear the rest, but I'm going to bed. We've a busy day tomorrow, launching Tom's glider, showing Gillian the Kiqui, and experimenting with that damned robot for Charlie. I suggest you get some sleep too."

She turned to wrap herself in her sleeping bag at the far end of the camp, near the watch-wards.

"Yeah," Toshio said, perhaps a bit too heartily. "I'll do that in a bit, Dennie. Good night. Pleasant dreams."

She was silent, with her back to the tiny glow from the fire. Toshio couldn't tell if she was asleep or awake.

I wish we humans were better at psi, he thought. *They say telepathy has its drawbacks, but it would sure be nice to know what's going on in another person's head sometimes.*

It'd take away a lot of the anxiety if I knew what she was thinking . . . even if I found out she just thought I was a nervy kid.

He looked up at the patchy sky overhead. Through long ragged openings in the clouds he could see stars.

In two places, there were nebiculae in the sky that hadn't been there the night before, signs of a battle still raging. The tiny false nebulae glowed in every visible color, and probably in other bands than light.

Toshio let a fistful of metallo-silicate dirt sift through his fingers onto the coals. Falling sparkles of metal winked at him like incandescent confetti, like winking stars.

He dusted off his hands and turned to crawl into his own sleeping roll. He lay there, eyes closed, reluctant to watch the stars, or to dissect the pros and cons of his behavior.

Instead, he listened to the wind-and-surf sounds of the

night. They were rhythmic and calming, like a lullaby, like the seas of home.

Except once in a while he thought he could pick up, on the edge of hearing, sighs and soft laughter coming from the south. They were sounds of complex happiness that filled him with a sad longing.

"They're at it again," he sighed to himself. "I swear, I've never heard of anything like it."

The humid air kept their perspiration slick upon them.

Gillian licked a moustache of tear-like salt off her upper lip. The same way, Tom cleaned some of the sheen off her breasts. The wetness of his mouth cooled on her aureoles and nipples when he took his mouth away.

She gasped and grabbed the wavy hair at the back of his head, where his slightly balding vanity feared no tugging. He responded with mock biting that sent shivers to her calves, thighs, and lower back.

Gillian locked her heel behind his knee and levered her pelvis up against his. Her breath whistled softly as he lifted his head and met her eyes.

"I thought what I was doing was afterplay," he whispered a little hoarsely. He made a show of wiping his forehead. "You should warn me when I cross over the line, and start promising what I can't deliver." He took her hand and kissed its palm and the inside of her wrist.

Gillian ran her fingers along his cheek, to touch, feather light, his jaw, throat and shoulder. She took sparse clumps of chest hair and pulled playfully.

She purred—not like a housecat, but with the feral rumble of a leopardess. "Whenever you're ready, love. I can wait. You may be the illegitimate son of a fecund test-tube, but I know you better than your planners ever did. You have resources they never imagined."

Tom was about to say that, planners or no planners, he was the quite legitimate son of May and Bruce Orley of Minnesota State, Confederacy of Earth . . . but then he noticed the slight liquid welling in her eyes. Her words were rough, light and teasing, but her grip on his chest hair only tightened as she looked up at his face, eyes roaming, as if she were memorizing every feature.

Tom felt suddenly confused. He wanted to be close to

Gillian on their last night together. How could they be any closer than they were right now? His body pressed against hers, and her warm breath filled his nostrils. He looked away, feeling somehow he was letting her down.

Then he felt it, a tender stroking that seemed to strive against a locked and heavy feeling inside his own head. It was a soft pressure that would not go away. He realized that the thing fighting it was himself.

I'm leaving tomorrow, he thought.

They had argued over who would be the one to go, and he had won. But it was bitter to have to go.

He closed his eyes. *I've cut her off from me! I may never come back, and I've cut myself off from the deepest part of me.*

Suddenly, Tom felt very strange and small, as if he were stranded in a dangerous place, the sole barrier between his loved ones and terrible foes, not a superhero but only a man, outnumbered and about to gamble all he had. As if he were himself.

He opened his eyes as he felt a touch on his face.

He pressed his cheek against her hand. There were still tears in her eyes, but also the beginnings of a smile.

"Silly boy," she said. "You can never leave me. Haven't you realized that by now? I'll be with you, and you'll come back to me."

He shook his head in wonder.

"Jill, I . . ." He started to speak, but his mouth was stopped as she pulled him down to kiss him hungrily. Her lips were hot and tender upon his, crosswise. The fingers of her right hand did inciteful things.

Still and all, it was the heady, sweet smell of her that made him realize that she had been right about him, once again.

PART THREE

Dissonance

"Animals are molded by natural forces
they do not comprehend.
To their minds there is no past and no future.
There is only the everlasting
present of a single generation,
its trails in the forest,
its hidden pathways in the air
and in the sea.

"There is nothing in the Universe more
alone than Man.
He has entered into the strange world of history . . ."

—LOREN EISELEY

28

Sah'ot

All night he had followed them. Toward morning, Sah'ot felt he was beginning to understand.

With the dawn, the Kiqui left their nocturnal hunting grounds and swam toward the safety of their island. They stowed their woven nets and traps in hidden coral clefts, took their crude spears, and hurried from the growing light. With daytime the killer vines would become active, and other dangers as well. By day, the Kiqui could forage in the forests atop the metal islands, seeking nuts and small animals in the thick foliage.

Underwater, the Kiqui looked like green puffer fish with short, web-handed arms and flippered legs. A pair of almost prehensile ventral fins helped them maneuver. Their strong, kicking legs left their hands free to carry burdens. Around each head a fin-like crest of wafer-thin flagellae waved, collecting dissolved oxygen to supplement each Kiqui's distended air-sac.

The hunter-gatherers pulled two nets full of bright, crab-like sea creatures, like multi-colored metal sculptures in the mesh. The Kiqui sang a song of flutters and squawks and yelps.

Sah'ot listened as they squeaked to one another, their tiny vocabulary hardly more than a series of vocalized signals coordinating their movements. Each time a few Kiqui rose to the surface for air, the act was accompanied by a chain of complex twitters.

The natives took little notice of the alien creatures that followed them. Sah'ot kept his distance, careful not to interfere. They knew he was here, of course. Now and then the younger Kiqui would cast suspicious sonar squirts his way. Strangely, the older hunters seemed to accept him completely.

Sah'ot looked up at the growing light with relief. In spite of the darkness, he had kept his own sonar down to a minimum all night to keep from intimidating the natives. He had felt almost blind, and a little panicky when he almost blundered into something... or "something" almost blundered into him.

Still, it had been worthwhile.

He felt he had a pretty good grasp of their language now. The signal structure, like Primal Delphin, was based on a hierarchical herd and the tempo of the breathing cycle. Its cause-and-effect logic was a bit more complicated than Primal, no doubt due to hands and tool use.

> :P: *Look, we well hunt*   *hunt*
>   *-hunted*   *-well*
> :P: *Careful, Careful,*
>
>   *Opportunistic*
>
> :P: *Eat, EAT well, will eat-*
>   *-not eaten*   *No!*
> :P: *Die above water, not in* ...

Based on semantic ability alone, these creatures seemed less ripe for uplift than fallow Earth-dolphins had been. Others, biased toward tool-using ability, might disagree.

Of course, the fact that they had hands probably meant the Kiqui would never be particularly good poets. Still, some of their current braggadocio had a certain charm.

The straps of Sah'ot's harness chafed as he rose for breath. In spite of its lightweight, streamlined design, he wished he could get rid of the damned thing.

Of course, these waters were dangerous, and he might need its protection. Also, Keepiru was out there somewhere, staying out of the way as requested, but listening, nonetheless. Keepiru would chew Sah'ot's dorsal fin down to the backbone if he caught him without his harness.

Unlike the ultra-technical fen of *Streaker's* crew, Sah'ot was uncomfortable with devices. He didn't mind computers, some of which could talk, and which helped him speak to other races. But implements for the moving, shaping, or killing of objects, these were unnatural things which he wished he could do without.

He hated the two nubby little "fin-gers" at the tips of each of his pectoral fins—which they said would someday lead to full hands for his species. They were unaesthetic. He also resented the changes made to the dolphin lungs, making them more resistant to land-based diseases, and adapting parts to breathing oxywater. Natural cetaceans needed no such mutations. Fallow *Stenos bredanensis* and *Tursiops truncatus* dolphins, left untouched by the gene-crafters, could outswim any of the "amicus" breed almost any time.

He was ambivalent to the expanded visual sense, bought at the cost of gray matter once dedicated to sound alone.

Sah'ot rose again to breathe, then submerged, keeping pace with the aboriginals.

His own line represented a drive to emphasize *language* ability, rather than tool use. It seemed to him a more natural extension of dolphin nature than all this crashing about in starships, pretending to be spacemen and engineers.

That was one reason he had refused to go along in the spaceboat, to help scout the derelict fleet back at the Shallow Cluster. Even had there been anything or anyone left to talk to—for which there'd been no evidence—he wasn't about to poke around supported only by a gang of inept clients! For *Streaker* to try to deal alone with the derelict fleet was like a group of children playing with a live bomb.

His actions had won contempt from the crew, even though he had been vindicated by the disastrous loss of the captain's gig.

Their contempt didn't matter Sah'ot reminded himself. He was a civilian. As long as he did his job he didn't have to explain himself.

Nor did disapproving clicks over his pursuit of Dennie Sudman bother him. Long before uplift, male dolphins had been fresh with woman researchers. *It's a long-standing tradition*, he rationalized. Whatever was good enough for horny old Flipper is good enough for his brainy descendant.

One of the things he hated about Anglic patterns of thought was this need to self-justify. Men were always asking "Why?" What did it *matter* why? There were other ways than the human way of looking at things. Any whale would tell you.

The Kiqui chittered excitedly as they swam toward the eastern end of their own island, preparing to hoist their catch up a crevice in the leeward seawall.

Sah'ot felt a sweep of sonar, like a passing searchlight. Keepiru approached from the north, to escort him back to the Earthling encampment.

Sah'ot flicked up to the surface. He tilted his head to look out on the new day. The sun rose behind a bank of haze in the east, and the wind carried a whisper of rain on the way.

A metal taint seemed to stain the air, reminding him of their deadly predicament on Kithrup.

No doubt Creideiki and his "engineers" were trying to jury-rig a scheme to get them out of this mess. Their plan would, no doubt, be frightfully bold and clever... and get them all killed.

Wasn't it obvious that neophytes at the game of making and conquering couldn't thwart the Galactics, who had been at it for aeons?

The humans had his loyalty, of course. But he knew them for what they were—clumsy wolflings, struggling to survive in a dangerously reactionary galaxy.

There was an old dolphin saying. "All humans are engineers, and all engineers are humans." It was cute, but patently a lie.

Keepiru broke the surface beside him. Sah'ot blew quietly, his breath condensing into spray. He lay watching the sunrise until Keepiru's patience wore thin.

"It'sss daylight, Sah'ot. We shouldn't be out here. We've got to report, and I want some food and rest!"

Sah'ot affected the role of an absent-minded scientist. He started, as if pulled from thoughts deeper than Keepiru might ever understand.

"What? Oh, yes. Of course, Pilot. By all means. I've very interesting data to report. You know, I think I've cracked their language?"

"How nice." Keepiru's reply was semantically Anglic, and phonemically a squawk. He dove and headed for the cave entrance.

Sah'ot winced at the pilot's sarcasm. But he was unrepentant.

Maybe I've time to finish a few suggestive limericks, to intersperse in my report to Dennie, he thought. *It's too bad she stays up on the bank of the pool and won't join me in the water. Maybe today she'll relent, though.*

He composed dirty poetry as he banked to follow Keepiru down into the night-like darkness below.

When they got to the bottom of the former drill-tree shaft, now lit by a small phosphor bulb, Sah'ot noticed that someone had taken both sleds out of the passage and moored them in the cavern below. But at least one sled was always supposed to be in the pool in case Dennie and Toshio had to escape quickly! He hurried after Keepiru, up the narrow vertical tunnel.

There were two more sleds in the pool at the top. Someone must have arrived from the ship during the night, he realized.

Toshio and Dennie were already down by the water, talking to Keepiru. Sah'ot eyed Dennie speculatively, but decided not to start in.

This evening I'll try to get her to join me in the water, he thought. *I'll think up a pretext, maybe something to do with the mechanics of the drill-tree root. It probably won't work, but the attempt should be fun.*

Sah'ot spy-hopped, churning his tail to rise up and look about the poolside clearing. He wondered who had come out from *Streaker*.

The thick brush parted to the south and two men, one female and one male, approached.

Gillian Baskin knelt by the poolside and whistled a Trinary welcome.

> * *Constant Keepiru*
> *Solid as surf rock*
> * *Orca-defier*
>
> * *Chameleon Sah'ot*
> *Ever adaptable*
> * *Ever so man-like*
>
> * *Under dark squalls I'd*
> *Recognize you two . . .*
> * *Study in opposites!*

Keepiru answered in Anglic, a pathetically unoriginal "Good to see you, Gillian. You too, T-Tom."

Sah'ot settled down, uncomfortably aware that he had a reputation to live up to. Unlike Keepiru, he would have to come up with a greeting that matched Gillian's.

He would rather have gone someplace to think about

Gillian's remark, especially that part about being "ever so man-like..." Was that a compliment, or was there a touch of pity in Gillian's upper register when she had whistled it?

Thomas Orley stood quietly next to Gillian. Sah'ot felt as if the man were seeing through him.

Sah'ot drew a breath.

> * *Look here!*
> *A monogamous*
> * *Miracle!*
>
> * *A pair of lovers!*
> *Silhouetted against*
> * *The wide sky.* *

Gillian clapped her hands and laughed.

Thomas Orley only smiled briefly. But apparently he had things on his mind.

"I'm glad you two fins are back," he said. "Gillian and I arrived here last night, she from *Streaker* and I from the site where Toshio's tsunami ship crashed. Jill brought you folks a monofilament cable, so you can stay in touch with the ship. She'll work with you for a few days on this vital matter of the Kiqui. Also, I understand there are some folks back at the ship who'd like to ask you to collect some data for them. That right, Gillian?"

The blonde woman nodded. Word of Charlie Dart's demands had not delighted Toshio and Dennie.

Orley continued.

"Jill's other purpose in coming here was to deliver some gear to me. I have to go away this morning. I'll be using a solar glider."

Keepiru sucked air. He started to object, but Orley raised a hand. "I know, it's risky. But there's an experiment I have to try in order to see if the escape plan we've put together will work. And since you people are the only ones available, I'm going to have to ask you for your help."

Sah'ot's tail thrashed under the water. He clamped down to hide his feelings, but it was hard. So hard!

So they were truly going to try to escape! He had hoped for better from Orley and Baskin. They were intelligent and experienced, almost-mythical agents of the Terragens Council. Survivors.

Now they were talking madness, and expected him to *help*! Didn't they realize what they were up against?

He swam up next to Keepiru, wearing the mask of a faithful, attentive client. But inside he felt a turmoil as he listened to the crazy "plan" that was supposed to save them from the bug-eyed monsters.

29

ᑐᑐᑐᑐᑐᑐᑐᑐᑐᑐᑐᑐᑐᑐᑐᑐᑐᑐᑐᑐᑐᑐ

Takkata-Jim

"The ship's council meeting was a disaster. It is worse than I thought," the vice-captain sighed.

> * They plan deception
>   To fool deceivers,
> * And veils
>   To cover whales!

K'tha-Jon tossed his great blunt head in agreement.

"I hear the codeword for thisss project is the 'Trojan Seahorse.' What does that mean?"

"It's a literary allusion," Takkata-Jim replied. He wondered where the bosun had gone to school. "I'll explain some other time. Right now I must think. There must be another way than this suicide plan Creideiki and Orley have devised.

"I had hoped Creideiki would see reason. But now, I just don't know."

"He didn't lisssten?"

"Oh he's *very* polite! Blowfish Metz swam in my wake point by point, and Creideiki listened so nicely to both of us. The meeting lasted four hours! But the captain decided to go with Orley's scheme anyway! The Baskin fem has already left with supplies for him."

The two *Stenos* drifted quietly for a long moment. K'tha-Jon waited for the vice-captain.

Takkata-Jim's tail slashed. "Why won't Creideiki even *consider* broadcasting the location of our find and have done with with it! Instead, he and Orley want to try to trick sophonts who have been trapping each other for millions of years! We'll be fried! Compared with this plan, even *your* idea of blasting forth with all guns blazing is better. At least we'd be able to maneuver!"

"I only offer a gloriousss alternative to his mad venture," K'tha-Jon said. "But I would go with your plan. Think, if *we* were the ones to find a way to save the ship and crew, would not the benefits go beyond simply preserving our livesss?"

Takkata-Jim shook his head. "If I were in command, perhapsss. But we are led by this mad, honor-bound genius, who'll only guide us to doom."

He turned away, deep in his thoughts, and swam silently down the corridor to his quarters.

K'tha-Jon's eyes narrowed as they followed the vice-captain. The bubbles from his blowmouth came out in tiny, rhythmic pops.

30

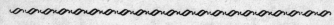

Akki

It wasn't fair! Almost everybody who counted had been allowed to go with Hikahi, to go join the crew working on the Thennanin wreck. The repairs to *Streaker* were nearly completed, and he was *still* stuck here, where nothing important was happening at all!

Akki drifted at his study-station, under an airdome near the top of the central bay. Bubbles from below passed unhindered through the pages of a holo-text displayed in front of him.

Of all the dumb ideas! Making him study astrogation while the ship was stuck at the bottom of an ocean!

He tried to concentrate on the subtleties of wormhole navigation, but his mind wandered. He got to thinking about Toshio. How long ago had it been since the two of them had had time to pull off a decent prank? It must have been over a month since they'd stolen Brookida's glasses and replaced them with Fresnel lenses.

I sure hope Toshio's okay. But at least he'd doing something. Why did Creideiki insist I stay here when they need every decent engineer out at the wreck?

Akki tried one more time to focus on the text, but was distracted by a sound. He looked down toward a noisy altercation at one of the food stations. Two fen were taking turns swatting at each other with their flukes while a circle of others watched.

Akki backed out of the airdome and dove toward the disturbance.

"Stop thisss!" he shouted. "Cut it out, now!" He struck out with his own flukes to knock Sth'ata and Sreekah-jo apart.

The observers backed away a little, but the combatants ignored him. They bit and flailed at each other. A kicking fluke struck Akki in the chest, sending him spinning.

Akki gulped to catch his breath. *How did they find the energy to fight in oxywater?*

He swam up to one of the observers. "Pk'Tow . . . Pk'Tow!" He bit the fin on his flank and assumed dominant stance as Pk'Tow whirled angrily. It wasn't easy to face him down; Akki felt very young. But Creideiki had taught him what to do. *When a fin reverts, make him focus!*

"Pk'Tow! Stop listening to them and use your *eyes*. *Look* at me! As a ship's *officer* I *order* you to help me break up this fight!"

The glazed expression faded from Pk'Tow's face. He nodded. "Aye, sssir." Akki was amazed by the fellow's dullness.

Drops of blood diffused into a pink stain as the combatants slowed down, trading blows, their gill-lungs gasping for breath. Akki collected three more crewfen, swatting and shouting at them to get them focused again, then he moved in. He got the *Stenos* and the cook separated at last, and led them under guard toward sick bay. Dr. Makanee could keep them isolated until he reported this to the captain.

Akki glanced up and noticed the bosun, K'tha-Jon, pass

by. The giant petty officer didn't even offer to help. He probably watched the whole thing, Akki thought bitterly. K'tha-Jon wouldn't have needed to cajole the onlookers. He could have intimidated the brawlers with a growl.

K'tha-Jon was headed swiftly for the outlock, his expression intent.

Akki sighed.

Okay, maybe Creideiki had his reasons for keeping me around, after all. Now that Hikahi has left with the engineers, he needs help taking care of the dregs that are still aboard Streaker.

He nosed Sreekah-jo to keep him moving. The *Stenos* squawked an almost Primal curse, but obeyed.

At least I've got an excuse not to study astrogation, Akki thought, sardonically.

31

∽∾∽∾∽∾∽∾∽∾∽∾∽∾∽∾∽∾∽∾∽∾∽∾∽∾∽∾

Suessi

"No! Stop it! Back off and try it again—this time more carefully!"

Hannes Suessi watched skeptically as the dolphin engineers reversed their heavy sleds and hauled the beam back out of the chamber.

It had been their third attempt to fit a supporting member into a gaping opening in the tail of the sunken Thennanin vessel. They had come closer to getting it right, but still the lead sled had hung back too long and almost let its end be driven into the inner wall of the battleship.

"There now, Olelo, here's how you avoid that beam." He addressed the pilot of the lead sled. His voice projected from the sled's hydrophones. "When you get to their hieroglyph thingie that looks like a two-headed jackal, lift your nose thusly!" He motioned with his arms.

The fin looked at him blankly, for a moment, then nodded vigorously.

* Roger—I'll dodge her! *

Suessi grimaced at the flippancy. They wouldn't be fins if they weren't sarcastic one-half the time and over-eager the other half. Besides, they really had been working hard.

Still, it was a royal bitch working underwater. In comparison, doing construction in weightlessness was a pure joy.

Since the Twenty-first Century, men had learned a lot about building things in space. They had found solutions to the problems of inertia and rotation that weren't even in the *Library*. Beings who'd had antigravity for a billion years had never needed to discover them.

There had been somewhat less experience, in the last three hundred years, doing heavy work underwater, even in Earth's dolphin communities, and none at all in repairing or looting spacecraft at the bottom of an ocean.

If weightless inertia caused problems in orbit, what about the almost unpredictable buoyancies of submerged materials? The force it took to move a massive object varied with the speed it was already traveling and with the cross-section it presented at any given moment. In space there were no such complications.

As the fen reoriented the beam, Suessi looked inside the battleship to see how the other work was progressing. Flashing laser saws, as bright as the heliarc lamps, illuminated the slow dismemberment of the central cavity of the Thennanin battleship. Gradually, a great cylindrical opening was being prepared.

Lieutenant Tsh't was supervising that end of the work. Her workers moved in that unique neo-fin pattern. Each dolphin used his eyes or instruments for close work. But when approaching an object, the worker's head would bob in a circular motion, spraying narrow beams of sound from the bulbous "melon" that gave the *Tursiops* porpoise its highbrow look. The sound-sensitive tip of his lower jaw waved to build a stereoscopic image.

The chamber was filled with creaking sounds. Suessi never ceased to marvel that they made anything out of the cacophony at all.

They were noisy fellows, and he wished he had more of them.

Suessi hoped Hikahi would get here with those extra crewfen. Hikahi was suposed to bring the longboat or skiff with her, giving Suessi a place to dry off, and the others a chance to rest with good air to breathe. If his own gang weren't relieved soon, there would be accidents.

It was a devil of a plan Orley had proposed. Suessi had hoped that Creideiki and the ship's council would come up with an alternative, but those objecting to the plan had failed to offer anything better. *Streaker* would be moved as soon as the signal came from Thomas Orley.

Apparently Creideiki had decided that they all had little to lose.

A "Ker-runch!" sound carried through the water. Suessi winced and looked around. One end of a Thennanin quantum-brake hung limply, broken at the join by the end of Olelo's bracing beam. The usually impassive fin looked at him in obvious distress.

"Now, boys and girls," Suessi moaned, "how are we going to make this shell look like it's survived a fight if we ourselves do more harm than the enemy ever did? Who'd believe it could fly with all these holes in it?"

Olelo's tail slashed at the water. He let out mournful chirps.

Suessi sighed. After three hundred years, one still wanted to tread lightly with dolphins. Criticism tended to break them up. Positive reinforcement worked much better.

"All right. Let's try it again, hmm? Carefully. You came a lot closer that time."

Suessi shook his head and wondered what kind of lunacy had ever driven him to become an engineer.

32

∽∾∽∾∽∾∽∾∽∾∽∾∽∾∽∾∽∾∽∾∽∾∽∾∽∾

Galactics

The battle had moved away from this region of space; the Tandu fleet had once again survived.

The Pthaca faction had joined with the Thennanin and Gubru, and the lot of the Soro remained dangerous. The Brothers of the Night had been almost destroyed.

The Acceptor perched in the center of its web and peeled back its shields in careful stages, as it had been trained to do. It had taken the Tandu masters millennia to teach its race to use mind shields at all, so loath were they to let anything pass unwitnessed.

As the barriers fell, the Acceptor eagerly probed nearby space, caressing clouds of vapor and drifting wreckage. It lightly skirted over untriggered psi-traps and fields of unresolved probability. Battles were lovely to look at, but they were also dangerous.

Recognition of danger was another thing the Tandu had force-fed them. In secret, the Acceptor's species didn't take it very seriously. Could something that actually happened *ever* be bad? The Episiarch felt that way, and look how crazy it was!

The Acceptor noticed something it would normally have overlooked. If it had been free to espertouch the ships, planets, and missiles, it would have been too distracted to detect such a subtle nuance—thoughts of a single, disciplined mind.

Delighted, the Acceptor realized the sender was a Synthian! There was a Synthian *here*, and it was trying to communicate with the Earthlings!

173

It was an anomaly, and therefore beautiful. The Acceptor had never witnessed a daring Synthian before.

Neither were Synthians famed for their psychic skill, but this one was doing a creditable job of threading through the myriad psi detectors all sides had spread through nearby space.

The feat was marvelous for its unexpectedness . . . one more proof of the superiority of objective reality over the subjective, in spite of the ravings of the Episiarch! Surprise was the essence of life.

The Acceptor knew it would be punished if it spent much longer marveling at this event instead of reporting it.

That, too, was a source of wonder, this "punishment" by which the Tandu were able to make the Acceptor's people choose one path over another. For 40,000 years it had amazed them. Someday they might do something about it. But there was no hurry. By that day they might be patrons themselves. Another mere sixty thousand years would be an easy wait.

The signal from the Synthian spy faded. Apparently the fury of the battle was driving her farther from Kthsemenee.

The Acceptor cast about, regretting the loss slightly. But now the glory of battle opened before it. Eager for the wealth of stimulus that awaited it, the Acceptor decided to report on the Synthian later . . . if it remembered.

33

Thomas Orley

Tom looked over his shoulder at the gathering clouds. It was too soon to tell if the storm would catch him. He had a long way to fly before finding out.

The solar plane hummed along at four thousand feet; the little aircraft wasn't designed for breaking records. It was little more than a narrow skeleton. The propeller was driven by sunlight falling on the wide, transluscent wing.

Kithrup's world-ocean was traced below by thin whitecaps. Tom flew to the northeast, letting the tradewinds do most of the work. The same winds would make the return trip—if there were one—slow and hazardous.

Higher, faster winds pushed the dark clouds eastward, chasing him.

He was flying almost by dead reckoning, using only Kithrup's orange sun for rough navigation. A compass would be useless, for metal-rich Kithrup was covered with twisty magnetic anomalies.

Wind whistled past the plane's small conical noseguard. Lying prone on the narrow platform, he hardly felt the breeze.

Tom wished he had just one more pillow. His elbows were getting chafed, and his neck was developing a crick. He had trimmed and retrimmed his list of supplies until he found himself choosing between one more psi-bomb to use at this destination and a water distiller to keep him alive when he got there. His compromise collection was taped to the platform beneath his cushion. The lumps made it almost impossible to find a comfortable position.

The journey was an unending monotony of sea and sky.

Twice he caught sight of swarms of flying creatures in the distance. It was his first inkling that any animals flew on Kithrup. Could they have evolved from jumping fish? He was a bit surprised to find flight on a world so barren of heights.

Of course, the creatures might have been molded by some ancient Galactic tenant of Kithrup, he thought. Where nature's variety fails, sophonts can meddle. I've seen weirder gene-crafted things than fliers on a water world.

Tom remembered a time when he and Gillian had accompanied old Jake Demwa to the Tymbrimi university-world of Cathrhennlin. Between meetings, he and Jill had toured a huge continental wilderness preserve, where they saw great herds of Clideu beasts grazing the grassy plains in precise and complex geometric patterns. The arrangements spontaneously changed, minute by minute, without any apparent communication among the individual animals—like the transient weavings of a moiré pattern. The Tymbrimi explained that an ancient Galactic race that had dwelt on Cathrhennlin ages ago had programmed the patterns into the Clideu as a form of puzzle. No one in all time since had ever managed to decipher the riddle, if there actually was one.

Gillian suggested that the patterns might have been adapted by the Clideu for their own benefit. The puzzle-loving Tymbrimi preferred to think otherwise.

Tom smiled as he recalled that trip, their first mission as a pair. Since then he and Gillian had seen more wonders than they could ever catalog.

He missed her already.

The local birds, or whatever, veered away from the growing bank of clouds. Orley watched them until they passed out of sight. There was no sign of land in the direction they flew.

The plane was making nearly two hundred knots. That should take him to the northeast chain of volcanic islands he sought in another two hours or so. Radio, satellite tracking, and radar were all forbidden luxuries. Tom had only the chart pinned to his windscreen to guide him.

He'd be able to do better on the return trip. Gillian insisted he take an inertial recorder. It could guide him blindfolded back to within a few meters of Hikahi's island.

Should the opportunity arise.

The pursuing clouds grew slowly above and behind him. Kithrup's jet stream was really cooking. Tom admitted that he wouldn't mind finding a landing site before the storm reached him.

As the afternoon wore on he saw another swarm of flying creatures, and twice he caught a glimpse of motion in the water below, something huge and sinuous. Both times the thing vanished before he could get a better look.

Scattered among the swells below floated sparse patches of seaweed. Some clusters came together to form isolated mounds of vegetation. Perhaps the flying things perched on those, he thought idly.

Tom fought the tedium and developed a profound hatred for whatever lumpy object lay directly under his left kidney.

The glowering cloudbank was only a couple of miles behind him when he saw something on the northern horizon, a faint smudge against the graying sky.

He applied more power and banked toward the plume. Soon he could make out a dusky funnel. Curling and twisting to the northeast, it hung like a sooty banner across the sky.

Tom strove for altitude, even as the threatening clouds

encroached on the late afternoon sun, casting shadow onto the solar collectors on his wing. Thunder grumbled, and flashes of lightning briefly illuminated the seascape.

When it began to rain, the ammeter swung far over to the red. The tiny engine began to labor.

Yes. There it was! An island! The mountain seemed a good way off yet. It was partly hidden by smoke.

He'd prefer to land on a companion isle, one that wasn't quite as active. Orley grinned at the presumption of anyone in his position making demands. He would land at sea, if need be. The small plane was equipped with pontoons.

The light was fading. In the growing dimness Tom noticed that the surface of the ocean had changed color. Something about its texture made him frown in puzzlement. It was hard to tell what the difference was.

Soon he had little time for speculation, as he fought his bucking craft, struggling for every foot of altitude.

Hoping it would remain light long enough to find a landing place, he drove his fragile ship through the pelting rain toward the smoldering volcano.

34

Creideiki

He hadn't realized the ship looked this bad.

Creideiki had checked the status of every damaged engine and instrument. As repairs were made, he or Takkata-Jim had discreetly triple-checked. Most of the damage that could be fixed, had been.

But as ship's master, he was the one who also had to deal with the intangibles. *Someone* had to pay attention to aesthetics, no matter how low their priority. And however successful the functional repairs were, *Streaker* was no longer beautiful.

This was his first trip outside in person. He wore a

breather and swam above the scarred hull, getting an over-view.

The stasis flanges and the main gravity drives would work. He had Takkata-Jim's and Emerson D'Anite's word on that, and had checked himself. One rocketry impeller had been destroyed by an antimatter beam at Morgran. The remaining tube was serviceable.

But though the hull was secure and strong, it was not the delight to the eye it had once been. The outer skin was seared in two places, where beams had penetrated the shields to blister the skin.

Brookida had told him that there was even one small area where the metal had been changed from one alloy to another. The structural integrity of the ship was intact, but it meant that someone had come awfully close to them with a probability distorter. It was disturbing to think that that piece of *Streaker* had been swapped with another similar but slightly different ship, containing similar but slightly different fugitives, in some hypothetical parallel universe.

According to *Library* records, no one had ever learned to control cross-universe distorters well enough to use them as anything but weapons, though it was rumored that some of the ancient species that "outgrew" Galactic civilization from time to time discovered the secret, and used it to leave this reality by a side door.

The concept of endless parallel universes was one known by dolphins since long before humans learned fire. It was integral to the Whale Dream. The great cetaceans moaned complacently of a world that was endlessly mutable. In becoming tool users, *amicus* dolphins lost this grand indifference. Now they understood the whales' philosophy little better than did men.

A tame version of the probability distorter was one of the dozen ways the Galactics knew to cheat the speed of light, but cautious species avoided it. Ships *disappeared* using probability drives.

Creideiki imagined coming out of FTL to find a convention of "*Streakers*"—all from different universes, all captained by slightly altered versions of himself. The whales might be able to be philosophically complacent about a situation like that. He wasn't so sure of himself.

Besides, the whales, for all their philosophical genius,

were imbeciles on levels dealing with spaceships and machines. They wouldn't recognize a fleet of ships any better than a dog knew its reflection in the water.

Less than two months ago, Creideiki had faced a derelict fleet of ships the size of moons, as old as middle-aged stars. He had lost a dozen good fen there, and had been fleeing fleets of ships ever since.

There were times when he wished he could be animal-blind to some things, as were the whales. Or as philosophical.

Creideiki swam up to a ridge overlooking the ship. Bright heliarc lamps cast long shadows in the clear euphotic water. The crews below were finished installing the booty Suessi had found at the Thennanin wreck. There remained only clearing the landing legs for movement.

Hikahi had left just hours ago, with a picked crew and the ship's skiff. Creideiki wished he could have spared more to go help Suessi, but *Streaker* was already well below minimum complement.

He still saw no alternative to Thomas Orley's plan. Metz and Takkata-Jim had been unable to come up with anything short of outright surrender to the winner of the battle overhead, and that was one thing Creideiki could never permit. Not while there was any chance at all.

Passive sensors showed the fight in space peaking in fury. Within days it might climax, and the last opportunity for an escape in confusion and disguise would be upon them.

I hope Tom arrived safely, and his experiment is successful.

The water echoed with the low grumbling of engines being tested. Creideiki had calculated the acceptable noise levels himself. There were so many forms of leakage—neutrinos from the power plant, gravitonics from the stasis screen, psi from everyone aboard. Sound was the least of his worries.

As he swam, Creideiki heard something above him. He turned his attention surfaceward.

A solitary neo-fin drifted near the detector buoys, working on them with harness manipulators. Creideiki moved closer.

> * Is there a problem—
> Here to bother
> * Duty's patterns? *

He recognized the giant *Stenos*, K'tha-Jon. The bosun started. His eyes widened, and momentarily Creideiki could see the whites around the flat, boat-like pupils.

K'tha-Jon recovered quickly. His mouth opened in a grin.

> * Noise buzz bothered—
> Neutrino listener
> * She could not hear—
> The battle raging

> * Now she tells me—
> Static has fled
> * I'll to my duty,—
> Now be leaving *

This was serious business. It was vital that *Streaker*'s bridge know what was going on in the sky and be able to hear news of Thomas Orley's mission.

Takkata-Jim should have detailed someone else to do the job. The buoys were the responsibility of the bridge crew. Still, with Hikahi and Tsh't gone, and most of the elite bridge crew with them, perhaps K'tha-Jon was the only petty officer who could be spared.

> * Good as jumping—
> Big wave rider
> * Now hurry back—
> To those who await you *

K'tha-Jon nodded. His harness arms folded back. Without another word, he blew a small cloud of bubbles and dove toward the bright opening of *Streaker*'s lock.

Creideiki watched the giant go.

Superficially, at least, K'tha-Jon appeared to have reacted more resiliently than many of the other fen to *Streaker*'s predicament. Indeed, he had seemed even to relish the fighting retreat from Morgran, and manned his gun battery with fierce enthusiasm. He was an efficient non-com.

Then why do my hackles rise whenever I'm near him? Is he another of Metz's sports?

I must insist Dr. Metz stop stalling, and show me his

*records! If necessary, I'll override the man's door-locks—
protocols be damned!*

K'tha-Jon had become Lieutenant Takkata-Jim's constant
companion. Together with Metz, the three were the chief
opponents to Tom Orley's plan. There was still bad bile
over it. Takkata-Jim had become more taciturn than ever.

The vice-captain was becoming a real problem. Creideiki
felt compassion for the lieutenant. It was not his fault this
test cruise had become a crucible. But pity would not prevent
Creideiki from promoting Hikahi over his head as soon as the
crew was reunited.

Takkata-Jim was likely aware of what was coming, and of
the report the captain had to write on each of his officers for
the Uplift Center. Takkata-Jim's right to have special, bonus
offspring might be in jeopardy.

Creideiki could imagine how the vice-captain felt. There
were times when even *he* felt oppressed by the towering
invasiveness of uplift, when he almost wanted to squawk in
Primal, *"Who gave you the right?"* And the sweet hypnosis of
the Whale Dream would call to him to return to the embrace
of the Old Gods.

The moment always passed, and he recalled that there
was nothing in the universe he wanted more than to command a starship, to collect tapes of the songs of space, and to
explore the currents between the stars.

A school of native fish swam past. They looked a little
like mullet, kitsch mullet, in garish, metal-flake scales.

He felt a sudden urge to give *chase*, to call his hard-
working crew out to join him in a hunt!

He envisioned his stolid engineers and techs dropping
their harnesses to join in the squealing pack, nimbly driving
the poor creatures, catching them in midair as panic drove
them leaping above the surface.

Even if a few fen got carried away and swallowed some
metal, it would be worth it for morale.

> * All the rains of Spring,
>   And then, one secret evening,
>   Riding waves, the Moon . . . *

It was a Haiku of regret.

There was no time for hunt-games, not while they
themselves were quarry.

His harness chime announced that he had only thirty minutes' air left. He shook himself. If his meditation had gone any deeper Nukapai might have come. The chimerical goddess would have teased him. Her gentle voice would have reminded him of Hikahi's absence.

The observation buoys bobbed nearby, tethered by slender strands to the seabed below. He swam closer to the smooth red and white ovoid K'tha-Jon had worked on, and noticed that the access plate had been left ajar.

Creideiki's head bobbed as he cast narrowly focused sound. The odd geometry of the buoy and guywires was mildly disturbing.

His sonar-speak receiver buzzed. An amplified voice came to him over the neural patchline.

"Captain, thisss is Takkata-Jim. We've just finished testing the impellers and the stasis generators. They're working up to your new specs. Also, Suessi called to say that the . . . the Trojan Seahorse *is coming along. Hikahi has arrived there and sends greetingsss."*

"Good." Creideiki sent the words directly along the neural link. "Has there been anything from Orley?"

"No, sir. And it's getting late. Are you sure you want to go with this plan of his? What if he can't get a psi-bomb message back to us?"

"We have already discussed the contingencies."

"And we're still going to move the ship? I do think that we ought to talk it over one more time."

Creideiki felt a wave of irritation. "We'll not discussss policy over an open channel, Pod-second. And it's already decided. I'll be back shortly. Meanwhile, seach for loose ends to bite off. We must be ready when Tom calls!"

"Aye, sir." Takkata-Jim didn't sound at all apologetic as he switched off.

Creideiki had lost count of the number of times he had been questioned about this plan. If they lacked faith because he was "only" a dolphin, they should have noted that the original idea was Thomas Orley's! Besides, he, Creideiki, *was* captain. He was the one saddled with saving their lives and honor.

When he had served aboard the survey vessel *James Cook*, he had never witnessed its human master, Captain Alvarez, questioned this way.

He slashed his tail through the water until his temper

cooled. He counted until the calming patterns of Keneenk settled over him.

Let it go, he decided. The majority of the crew did not question, and the rest obeyed their instructions. For an experimental crew, under immense pressure, that would have to do.

"Where there is mind, there is always solution," Keneenk taught. All problems contained the elements of their answer.

He commanded his manipulator arms to reach out and grab the access panel to the buoy.

If the buoy was in good order, he would find a way to praise Takkata-Jim. There would be a key to reach the lieutenant, to pull him back into the ship's community and break his vicious cycle of isolation. "Where there is mind . . ."

It would only take a few minutes to find out if it was in working order. Creideiki plugged an extension from his neural socket into the buoy's computer. He commanded the machine to report its status.

A brilliant arc of electric discharge flashed in front of him. Creideiki screamed as the shock blew out the motors of his harness and seared the skin around his neural tap.

A penetrator bolt! Creideiki realized in stunned rigidity. *How . . . ?*

He felt it all in slow motion. The current fought with the protective diodes of his nerve amplifier. The main circuit breaker threw, but the insulation almost immediately buckled under backlash.

Paralyzed, Creideiki seemed to hear a voice in the pulsing, battling fields, a voice taunting him.

> \# *Where there is mind—is mind,*
> *is—also deception*
> \# *Deception—is, there is* \#

In a body-arching squeal of agony, Creideiki screamed one undisciplined cry in Primal, the first of his adult life. Then he rolled belly-up, to drift in a blackness deeper than night.

PART FOUR

Leviathan

"Oh my father was the keeper of the Eddystone light,
He slept with a mermaid one fine night.
From this union there came three:
A porpoise, a porgy and me.

"Oh, for the life on the rolling sea."

—OLD CHANTY

35

Gillian

"Like most species derived from wholly carnivorous fore-bears, the Tandu were difficult clients. They had cannibalistic tendencies, and attacks on individuals of their patron race, the Nght6, weren't unheard of early in their uplift.

"The Tandu have remarkably low empathy for other sapient life-forms. They are members of a pseudo-religious alignment whose tenets propose the eventual extermination of species judged 'unworthy.' While they observe the codes of the Galactic Institutes, the Tandu make no secret of their desire for a less crowded universe, or their eagerness for the day when all laws are swept aside by a 'higher power.'

"According to followers of their 'Inheritor' alignment, this will happen when the Progenitors return to the Five Galaxies. The Tandu assume that they will be chosen, come that day, to hunt down the unworthy.

"While waiting for this millennium, the Tandu keep in practice by indulging in countless minor skirmishes and battles of honor. They join in any war of enforcement declared by the Galactic Institutes, whatever the cause, and are often cited for use of excess force. 'Accidental extinction' of at least three spacefaring species has been attributed to them.

"Although the race has little empathy for their patron-level peers, the Tandu are masters of the art of uplift. In their pre-sentient form, on their fallow homeworld, they had already tamed several local species for use as hunting animals: the equivalent of tracking dogs on Earth. Since release from indenture, the Tandu have acquired and adapted two of the

187

*most powerful psychic adepts of the recent crop of clients.
The Tandu are under long-term investigation for excessive
genetic manipulation in making the two (See references:
EPISIARCH-cl-82f49; ACCEPTOR-cl-82f50) totally dependent
instruments of their love of the hunt ..."*

Nice people, these Tandu, Gillian thought.

She put the flat reading plate down beside the tree
where she sat. She had allotted herself an hour for reading
this morning. It was almost over. She had covered another
two hundred thousand words or so.

This entry on the Tandu had come over the cable from
Streaker last night. Apparently the Niss machine was already
accomplishing things with the mini-*Library* Tom had re-
trieved from the Thennanin wreck. This report read too
clearly, and came to the point too directly to have come
straight from the English translation software of *Streaker's*
own pathetic little micro-branch.

Of course, Gillian already knew some things about the
Tandu. All Terragens agents were taught about these secretive,
brutal enemies of Mankind.

This report only reinforced her feeling that there was
something terribly wrong with a universe that had such
monsters in it. Gillian had once spent a summer reading
ancient space-romances from pre-Contact days. How open
and friendly those old-time fictional universes had seemed!
Even the rare "pessimistic" ones hadn't come close to the
closed, confined, dangerous reality.

Thinking about the Tandu put her in a melodramatic
mind to carry around a dirk, and to exercise a woman's
ancient last prerogative should those murderous creatures
ever capture her.

The thick, organic smell of humus overwhelmed the
metallic tang that permeated everywhere near the water. The
aroma was fresh after last night's storm. Green fronds waved
slowly under gentle buffeting from Kithrup's incessant
tradewinds.

Tom must have found his island crucible by now, she
thought, *and begun preparing his experiment.*

If he still lived.

This morning, for the first time, she felt uncertain about

that. She had been so sure she would know it, if he died, wherever or whenever it happened. Yet now she felt confused. Her mind was muddied, and all she could tell for certain was that terrible things had happened last night.

First, around sunset, had come a crawling premonition that something had happened to Tom. She couldn't pin the feeling down, but it disturbed her.

Then, late last night, she had had a series of dreams.

There had been faces. Galactic faces, leathern and feathered and scaled, toothed and mandibled. They yammered and howled, but she, in spite of all her expensive training, couldn't understand a single word or sense-glyph. A few of the jumbled faces she had recognized in her sleep—a pair of Xappish spacemen, dying as their ship was torn apart—a Jophur, howling through smoke at the bleeding stump of its arm—a Synthian, listening to whale songs while she waited impatiently behind a vacuum-cold lump of stone.

In her sleep Gillian had been helpless to keep them out.

She had awakened suddenly, in the middle of the night, to a tremor that plucked her spine like a bowstring. Breathing heavily in the darkness, she sensed a kindred consciousness writhe in agony at the limit of her range. In spite of the distance, Gillian caught a mixed flavor in the fleeting psychic glyph. It felt too human to have been only a fin, too cetacean to have been merely a man.

Then it ceased. The psychic onslaught was over.

She didn't know what to make of any of it. What use was psi, if its messages were too opaque to be deciphered? Her genetically enhanced intuition now seemed a cruel deception. Worse than useless.

She had a few moments left to her hour. She spent them with her eyes closed, listening to the rise and fall of sound, as the breakers fought their endless battle with the western shoreline. Tree limbs brushed and swayed with the wind.

Interleaved with the creakings of trunk and branch, Gillian could hear the high chittering squeaks of the aboriginal pre-sentients—the Kiqui. From time to time, she made out the voice of Dennie Sudman, speaking into a machine that translated her words into the high-frequency Kiqui dialect.

Though she was working twelve hours a day, helping Dennie with the Kiqui, Gillian couldn't help feeling guiltily that she was taking a vacation. She reminded herself that the little natives were extremely important, and that she had just been spinning her wheels back at the ship.

But one of the faces from her dream had stuck with her all morning. Only a half-hour ago she had realized that it was her own subconscious rendering of what Herbie, the ancient cadaver which had caused all this trouble, must have looked like when he was alive.

In her dream, shortly before she had begun feeling premonitions of disaster, the long, vaguely humanoid face of the ancient had smiled at her, and slowly winked.

"Gillian! Dr. Baskin? It's time!"

She opened her eyes. She lifted her arm and glanced at her watch. It might as well have been set by Toshio's voice. Trust a midshipman at his word, she remembered. Tell him to fetch you in one hour, and he'll time it down to the second. Early in the voyage she had had to threaten dire measures to get him to call her "sir"—or the anachronistic "ma'am"—only in every third sentence, rather than every other word.

"On my way, Toshio! Just a minute!" She rose to her feet and stretched. The rest break had been useful. Her mind had been in knots that only quiet could smooth.

She hoped to finish here and get back to *Streaker* within three days, about the time Creideiki had planned to move the ship. By then she and Dennie should have worked out the environmental needs of the Kiqui—how to take a small sample group with them back to the Center for Uplift on Earth. If *Streaker* got away, and if humanity first filed a client claim, it could save the Kiqui from a far worse fate.

On her way through the trees, Gillian caught a glimpse of the ocean through a northeast gap in the greenery.

Will I be able to feel it here, when Tom calls? The Niss said his signal should be detectable anywhere on the planet.

All the ETs will hear it, for sure.

She carefully kept all psychic energies low, as Tom had insisted she do. But she did form an old-fashioned prayer with her mouth, and cast it northward, over the waves.

"I'll bet this will please Dr. Dart," Toshio said. "Of course, the sensors might not be types he'd want. But the 'bot *is* still operational."

Gillian examined the small robot-link screen. She was no

expert on robotics or planetology. But she understood the principles.

"I think you're right, Toshio. The X-ray spectrometer works. So do the laser zapper and the magnetometer. Can the robot still move?"

"Like a little rock lobster! The only thing it can't do is float back up. Its buoyancy tanks were ruptured when the piece of coral crashed down on it."

"Where is the robot now?"

"It's on a ledge about ninety meters down." Toshio tapped the tiny keyboard and brought a holo schematic into space in front of the screen. "It's given me a sonar map that deep. I've held off going any lower until I talk to Dr. Dart. We can only go down, one ledge at a time. Once the robot leaves a spot there's no going back."

The schematic showed a slightly tapered cylindrical cavity, descending into the metal-rich silicate rock of Kithrup's thin crust. The walls were studded with outcrops and ledges, like the one the crippled probe now rested on.

A solid shaft ran up the great cavity, tilted at a slight angle. It was the great drill-root Toshio and Dennie had blown apart a few days earlier. The upper end rested against one rim of its own underwater excavation. The shaft disappeared into unknown territory below the mapped area.

"I think you're right, Toshio," Gillian grinned and squeezed the boy's shoulder. "Charlie will be glad about this. It may help get him off Creideiki's back. Do you want to ring him up with the news?"

Toshio was obviously pleased with the compliment, but taken aback by Gillian's offer. "Uh, no, thank you, sir. I mean, couldn't you just tuck this in when you report to the ship, today? I'm sure Dr. Dart will have questions I'm not qualified to handle..."

Gillian couldn't blame Toshio. Presenting good news to Charles Dart was barely more pleasant than delivering bad news. But Toshio would have to come to grips with the chimp planetologist sooner or later. It would be best if he learned to deal with the problem from the start.

"Sorry, Toshio. Dr. Dart is all yours. Don't forget that I'm leaving here in a few days. You're the one who's going to have to... *satisfy* Charlie, when he asks you to put in thirty-hour shifts."

Toshio nodded seriously, taking her advice soberly until

she managed to catch eye contact with him. She grinned until
he couldn't help but blush and smile.

36

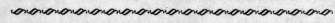

Akki

Hurrying to get to the bridge before watch change, Akki
took a shortcut through the outlock. In his haste he was
halfway across the wide chamber before he noticed anything
different.

He did an overhead flip to stop. His gill-lungs heaved,
and he cursed himself for an idiot, speeding and doing fancy
maneuvers when there just wasn't enough oxygen available!

Akki looked about. The outlock was as empty as he had
ever seen it.

The captain's gig had been lost at the Shallow Cluster.
Heavy sleds and a lot of equipment had been moved to the
Thennanin wreck, and Lieutenant Hikahi had taken the skiff
there only yesterday.

There was a cluster of activity around the longboat, the
last and largest of *Streaker*'s pinnaces. Several crewfen used
mechanical spiders to carry crates into the small spacecraft.
Akki forgot his haste to be early on duty, and kicked a lazy
spiral toward the activity.

He swam up behind one spider-riding dolphin. The fin's
spider carried a large box in its waldo-arms.

"Hey Sup-peh, v-what's going on here?" Akki kept his
sentences short and simple. He was getting better speaking
Anglic in oxywater, but if a *Calafian* couldn't speak properly,
what were the others to think?

The other dolphin looked up. "Oh, hello, Mr. Akki.
Change of orders is what-t. We're checking the longboat for
spaceworthiness. Also, we been told to load these cratesss."

"What are vey . . . er, what's in the boxes?"

"Dr. Metz's records, seemsss-s," the spider's third manipulator arm waved toward the pile of waterproof cartons. "Imagine, all our grandparents 'n' grandchildren here, listed on mag chips. It gives you a feeling of *continuity*, don't it-t-t?"

Sup-peh was from the South Atlantic community, a clan which took pride in quaint speech. Akki wondered if it were really eccentricity as much as plain dimness. "I thought you were on the supply run to the Thennanin ship?" he asked. Sup-peh was usually assigned tasks that required minimal finesse.

"That I were, Mr. Akki. But-t-t those runs have been stopped. The ship's closed down, didn't you hear? We're all swimming in circles t-til it's clearer about the captain'sss condition."

"*Wvhat?*" Akki choked. ". . . the *captain* . . . ?"

"Got hurt in an inspection outside the ship. 'Lectrocuted, I hear. Barely found him before his breather ran out-t. Been unconscious all this time. Takkata-Jim's in charge."

Akki lay there in shock. He was too stunned to notice Sup-peh turn suddenly and hurry back to work as a very large dark figure swam up.

"May I help you, *Mister* Akki?" The giant dolphin's tone sounded almost sarcastic.

"K'tha-Jon," Akki shook himself. "What's happened to the captain?"

Something in the bosun's attitude chilled Akki. And it wasn't just the minimal pretense of respect for Akki's rank. K'tha-Jon let out a quick squirt of Trinary.

> * Suggestions come
> to me,
> * How you can know more—*
>
> * Go and ask your
> leader,
> * Who awaits you on the shore—*

With an almost insolent wave of one harness arm, K'tha-Jon flipped about and swam off to rejoin his workcrew. The wake from his mighty flukes pushed Akki backward two meters. Akki knew better than to call him back. Something in K'tha-Jon's Trinary triple entendre told him it would be

useless. He decided to take it as a warning, and turned to
hurry toward the hull lift to the bridge.

He was suddenly aware of how many of the best fen in
Streaker's crew were absent. Tsh't, Hikahi, Karkaett, S'tat
and Lucky Kaa were all gone to the Thennanin wreck. That
left K'tha-Jon senior petty officer!

And Keepiru was away as well. Akki hadn't believed the
gossip he had heard about the pilot. He had always thought
Keepiru the bravest fin in the crew, besides the fastest
swimmer. He wished Keepiru, and Toshio, were here right
now. *They'd* help him find out what was going on!

Near the lift, Akki encountered a group of four *Tursiops*,
clustered in a corner of the outlock doing nothing in particular.
They wore morose expressions and lay in listless postures.

"Sus'ta, what's going on here?" he asked. "Don't you fen
have work to do?"

The messman looked up and twisted his tail in the
dolphin's equivalent of a shrug. "What'sss the point, Mr.
Akki?"

"The point ish . . . is we do our duty! Come on, what's
got you all in such a f-funk?"

"The c-captain . . ." one of the others began.

Akki cut him off. "The captain would be the first to say
you should p-p-persevere!" He switched to Trinary.

> * Focus on the far
>   Horizon—
> * On Earth!
>   Where we are needed—*

Sus'ta blinked, and tried to drop his forlorn stance. The
others followed suit.

"Yesssir, Mr. Akki. We'll t-try."

Akki nodded. "Very good, then. Carry on in the spirit of
K-k-keneenk."

He entered the lift and clicked out a code for the bridge.
As the doors slid shut, he saw the fen swim away, presumably
toward their work stations.

Ifni! It had been hard to posture and act reassuring,
when all he really wanted to do was squeeze the others for
information. But in order to *be* reassuring he had to seem to
know more than they!

Turtle-bites! Disfunctioning motors! How badly is the

captain hurt? How will we stand a *chance*, if Creideiki is taken from us?

He decided to be as innocuous and unnoticed as possible for a while... until he found out what was going on. He knew a middie was in the most exposed position of all, with an officer's duties and burdens and none of the protections.

And a middie was always the last to find out what was going on!

37

~~~~~~~~~~~~~~~~~~~~~~~~~~~~~~~~~~~~~~~

Suessi

The excavation was nearly ready. The Thennanin battleship had been reamed and braced. Soon they'd be able to fill the cylindrical cavity with its intended cargo and be off.

Hannes Suessi couldn't wait. He'd had it with working underwater. If the truth be told, he'd about had it with fins, too.

Gads, the stories he would be able to tell back home! He had bossed work gangs under the smog oceans of Titan. He had helped herd adenine comets through the Soup Nebula. He had even worked with those crazy Amerindians and Israelis who were trying to terraform Venus. But never had a job taught him the laws of perversity as this one had!

Almost all of the materials they'd had to work with were of alien manufacture, with weird ductility and even stranger quantum conductivities. He'd had to check the psionic impedance of almost every connection himself, and still their masked marvel would probably leak telekinetic static all over the sky when it took off!

Fins! They were the frosting! They'd flawlessly perform the most delicate operation, then swim about in circles squealing Primal nonsense when the opening of a hatchway set off a particular pattern of sonar reflections.

And every time a job was finished, they called for old Suessi. Check it for us, Hannes, they'd ask. Make sure we've done it right.

They tried so damned hard. They couldn't help feeling like half-finished clients of wolfling patrons in an impossibly hostile galaxy, especially when it was all true.

Suessi admitted he was bitching more to hear the echoes in his own skull than out of any real complaint. The *Streakers* had done the job; that was all that really mattered. He was proud of every one of them.

Anyway, it had been a lot better since Hikahi arrived. She provided an example for the rest, teasing with Keneenk parables, to help the fen concentrate.

Suessi rolled over onto one elbow. His narrow bunk was only a meter below the ceiling. Inches from his shoulder was the horizontal hatch to his coffin-like sleeper compartment.

I've rested enough, he thought, though his eyes were scratchy and his arms still ached. There was no sense in trying to go back to sleep. He would only stare at his eyelids now.

Suessi pushed the narrow hatch open. He shielded his eyes from the overhead lights of the companionway as he sat up and swung his legs over the side. They splashed.

Ugh. Water. Except for the top meter or so, up here near the ceiling, the skiff was full of water.

His body looked pale in the sharp hall light. I wonder when I'm scheduled to fade away, he thought, sliding into the water with his eyes closed. He swam over to the head and closed the door behind him.

Naturally, he had to wait until the room pumped out before he could use any of the fixtures.

A little later, he made his way to the control room of the tiny spacecraft. Hikahi was there with Tsh't, fussing over the comm set. They argued in a fast, squeaky version of Anglic he couldn't follow.

"Whoa!" he called. "If you want to keep me out, fine. But if I can help, you'd better change to thirty-three and a third. I'm not Tom Orley. I can't follow that jabber!"

The two dolphin officers lifted their heads clear of the water as Suessi took a grip on a nearby wall rail. Hikahi's eyes extended outward to refocus for above-water binocular vision.

"We aren't sure we have a problem, Hannesss, but we seem to have lost contact with the ship."

"With *Streaker*?" Suessi's bushy eyebrows went up. "Are they under attack?"

Tsh't rocked her upper body left to right slightly. "We don't think so. I was here, waiting for word that they'd heard from Orley, and would be moving the ship soon. I wasn't paying close attention, but heard the operator suddenly tell us to 'stand by'... then nothing!"

"When was this?"

"A few hours ago. I waited until shift change, hoping it was a technical glitch at the ship, then I called Hikahi."

"We've been tracing circuits since then," the senior officer finished.

Suessi swam over to look at the set. Of course, the thing to do was tear it apart and check it by hand. But the electronics were sealed away against the wetness.

If only we were in free fall so the fins could work without all this damned water everywhere.

"All right," he sighed. "With your permission, Hikahi, I'll kick you two officers and gentlefems out of the control room and look at the unit. Don't bother the fen resting in the hold."

Hikahi nodded. "I'll send a crew to follow the monofilament and see if it's intact."

"Good thinking. And don't worry. I'm sure nothing's really the matter. It's probably just gremlins at work."

38

Charles Dart

"I'm afraid they've only taken the damned robot down another eighty meters. That kid Toshio will only work on it for a few hours, then he's always got to be off helping Dennie and Gillian run their new clients through mazes, or having them knock down bananas with poles or something. I tell you it's frustrating! The rotten little half-wrecked probe's carrying mostly the wrong kinds of instruments for geological work. Can you imagine how bad it will be when we get it down to a decent depth?"

The holographic image of the metallurgist Brookida seemed to look past Charles Dart for a moment. Apparently, the dolphin scientist was referring to his own displays. Each eye was covered with a goggle lens to correct for astigmatism when reading. He turned back to look at his chimp colleague.

"Charlie. You talk so assuredly about sending thisss robot deeper into Kithrup's crust. You complain that it has gone down 'only' five hundred meters. Are you cognizant that that-t is half a kilometer?"

Charlie scratched his fuzzy jaw. "Yeah? So what? The excavation has got so little taper that it might easily drop down as much farther as it's already gone. It's a wonderful mineralogical lab! Already I'm finding out a lot about the subsurface zone!"

Brookida sighed. "Charlie, aren't you curious as to why the cavern under Toshio's island goes down even *one* hundred meterssss?"

"Hmmm? What do you mean?"

"I mean that the so-called 'drill-tree' that'ss responsible for this excavation cannot have dug so deep merely in search of carbon and silicate nutrients. It can't-t have..."

"How would you know? Are you an ecologist?" Charlie rapped out a sharp laugh. "Honestly, Brookida, what do you base these suppositions on? Sometimes you surprise me!"

Brookida waited patiently for the chimpanzee to finish laughing. "I base them on a well-informed layman's knowledge of basic lawsss of nature, and upon Occam's Razor. Think of the volume of material removed! Has it been scattered upon the watersss? Has it occurred to you that there are tens of thousands of these metal-mounds along this plate boundary, most with their own drill-trees... and that there may have been millions of such deep excavations dug in recent geologic time?"

Dart started to snigger, then he stopped. He stared for a moment at the image of his cetacean colleague, then laughed in earnest. He pounded the desk.

"Touché! All right, sir! We'll add 'Why these holes?' to our list of questions! Fortunately, I've been cultivating an ecologist lab-mate for the last few months. I've done her innumerable favors, and it happens she's at the site of our quandary! I'll ask Dennie to get to work on it right away! Rest assured, we'll know soon enough what these drill-trees are up to!"

Brookida didn't bother answering. He did let out a small sigh.

"Now that that's settled," Charlie went on, "let's get back to the really important stuff. Can you help persuade the captain to let me go out there in person and take a real deep-probe robot with me to replace that lousy little thing Toshio salvaged?"

Brookida's eyes widened. He hesitated.

"The c-captain remains unconscious," Brookida said at last. "Makanee has twice performed surgery. According to the latest reports, the outlook remains bleak-k."

The chimp stared for a long moment. "Oh, yeah. I forgot." Charlie looked away from the holo display. "Well, then maybe Takkata-Jim will be willing. After all, the longboat's not being used. I'll ask Metz to talk to him. Will you help?"

Brookida's eyes were sunken. "I'll study these mass spectrometer data," he answered evenly. "I will call you when I have results. Now I mussst sign off, Charles Dart."

The image dissolved. Charlie was alone again.

Brookida was awfully abrupt there, he thought. *Have I offended him somehow?*

Charlie knew he was offensive to people. He couldn't help it. Even other chimpanzees thought him abrasive and self-centered. They said neo-chimps like him gave the race a bad rep.

Well, I've tried, he thought. *And when a person's tried and failed so often, when his best attempts at gallantry turn to faux pas, and he constantly finds himself forgetting other people's names, well, then, maybe a guy should give up. Other people don't always win awards for kindness to me, either.*

Charles Dart shrugged. It didn't matter. What point was there in pursuing an ever-elusive popularity? There was always his personal world of rocks and molten cores, of magma and living planets.

Still, I thought Brookida, at least, was my friend....

He forced the thought aside.

I've got to call Metz. He'll get me what I need. I'll show 'em this planet is so unique they'll . . . they'll rename it after me! There are precedents. He chuckled as he tugged on his ear with one hand and punched out a code with the other.

An idle thought came to him, as he waited for the computer tracer to track down Ignacio Metz. *Wasn't everybody waiting to hear from Tom Orley? That was all anybody'd talk about, a while back.*

Then he remembered that Orley's report was supposed to come in yesterday, about the time Creideiki was hurt.

Ah! Then Tom was probably successful at whatever it was he was doing, and nobody bothered to tell me. Or maybe somebody did, and I wasn't listening again. Anyway, I'm sure he got everything squared away with the ETs. About time, too. Damned nuisance being hunted all over the galaxy, forced to fill the ship with water. . . .

Metz's number appeared on the intercom. The line was ringing.

It was a shame about Creideiki. He was awfully stiff and serious for a fin, and not always reasonable . . . but Charlie couldn't bring himself to feel happy to have him out of the way. In fact, it gave him a queer sensation in his stomach whenever he thought about the captain being removed from the picture.

Then don't think about it! Jeez! When has it ever paid to worry?

"Ah, Dr. Metz! Did I catch you as you were going out? I was wondering, could we have a talk together soon? Later this afternoon? Good! Yes, I do have a very, very small favor to ask . . ."

39

Makanee

A physician must be part intellectual and part alchemist, part sleuth and part shaman, Makanee thought.

But in medical school they never told her she might have to be a soldier and a politician, as well.

Makanee had trouble keeping a dignified demeanor. In fact, she felt on the verge of insubordination. Her tail crashed to the water's surface, sending spray over the canals of sick bay.

"I tell you I can't-t-t operate alone! My aides haven't the skill to assist me! I'm not sure I could do it even if they did! I must-t-t talk to Gillian Baskin!"

With one eye lazily lifted above the water line, one harness arm holding a channel stanchion, Takkata-Jim glanced at Ignacio Metz. The human returned an expression of great patience. They had expected this sort of reaction from the ship's surgeon.

"I'm sure you underrate your skill, Doctor," Takkata-Jim suggested.

"So you're a sssurgeon, now? I need your opinion? Let-t me talk to Gillian!"

Metz spoke placatingly. "Doctor, Lieutenant Takkata-Jim has just explained that there are military reasons for the partial communications blackout. Data from the detection buoys appear to indicate a psi leak somewhere within a hundred kilometers of this spot. Either the crew working under Hikahi and Suessi or the people at the island are responsible. Until we trace the leak..."

"You are acting on the basis of information from a buoy? It was a defective buoy that almost k-k-killed C-C-Creideiki!"

Metz frowned. He wasn't used to being interrupted by dolphins. He noted that Makanee was quite agitated. Too agitated, in fact, to speak with the Anglic diction a fin in her position should use. This was certainly data for his files... as was her belligerent attitude.

"That was a different buoy, Physician Makanee. Remember, we have three on station. Besides, we aren't claiming the leak is necessarily real, only that we must *treat* it as real until proven otherwise."

"But the blackout isn't total! I hear that chimpanzee is ssstill getting his Iki-damned robot-t data! So why won't you let me talk to Dr. Baskin?"

Metz wanted to curse. He had asked Charles Dart to keep quiet about that. Damn the necessity to keep the chimp placated!

"We are eliminating the possibilities one at a time," Takkata-Jim tried to soothe Makanee. At the same time he assumed a head-down forward stance, dominant assertive body language. "As soon as those in contact with Charles Dart—the young humans Iwashika and Sudman and the poet Sah'ot—have been eliminated as possible leaks, then we will contact Dr. Baskin. Surely you see that she is less likely to be the one carelessly leaking psi energy than these others, so we must check them first."

Metz's eyebrows rose slightly. Bravo! The excuse wouldn't hold up under close scrutiny, of course. But it had a *flavor* of reasonability! All they needed was a little time! If this kept Makanee quiet for just another couple of days, that should be enough.

Takkata-Jim apparently noticed something of Metz's approval. Encouraged, he grew more assertive. "Now, enough delaying, Doctor! We came down here to find out about the captain's condition. If he's unable to resume his duties, a new commanding officer mussst be selected. We're in a crisis and cannot put up with delays!"

If this was meant to intimidate, it had the opposite effect. Makanee's tail churned. Her head rose out of the water. She turned one narrowed eye to the male dolphin and chattered in sarcastic verse.

> * I'd thought that you
> —had misremembered
> —duty's orders

> * *How nice to note*
>   *—I had mistaken*
>   *—your behavior*
> * *You'll not claim, in*
>   *—hasty mischief*
>   *—captain's honors?*

Takkata-Jim's mouth opened, baring twin vee rows of rough white teeth. For a moment it seemed to Metz he would charge the small female.

But Makanee acted first, leaping up out of the water and landing with a splash that covered both Metz and Takkata-Jim. The human spluttered and slipped off the wall curb.

Makanee whirled and disappeared behind a row of dark life-support coffins. Takkata-Jim spun underwater, emitting rapid sonar clicks, seeking her out. Metz seized him by the dorsal fin before he could take off after her.

"Ah . . . ahem!" He grabbed a wall rail. "If we can put a stop to this foul temper, fin-people? Dr. Makanee? Will you please come back? It's bad enough half the known universe wants to hunt us down. We mustn't fight amongst ourselves!"

Takkata-Jim looked up and saw that Metz was earnest. The lieutenant continued to breathe heavily.

"Please, Makanee!" Metz called again. "Let's talk like civilized folk."

They waited, and a short time later Makanee's head emerged from between two autodocs. Her expression was no longer defiant, simply tired. Her physician's harness made tiny whirring sounds. The delicate instruments shook slightly, as if held in trembling hands.

She rose so only her blowmouth broke the surface.

"I apologize," she buzzed. "I know Takkata-Jim would not assume permanent captaincy without a vote by the ship's council."

"Of course he wouldn't! This is not a military vessel. The duties of the executive officer aboard a survey ship are mostly administrative, and his succession to command must be ratified by a ship's council as soon as one can be conveniently arranged. Takkata-Jim is fully aware of the rules involved, is that right, Lieutenant?"

"Yessss."

"But until then we must accept Takkata-Jim's authority or have chaos! And in the meantime, *Streaker* must have a chain of command. That will be ambiguous until you certify that Captain Creideiki can no longer function."

Makanee closed her eyes, breathing heavily. "Creideiki will probably not regain consciousness without further surgery. Even then it'sss chancy.

"The shock traveled along his neural connector socket into the brain. Most of the damaged areas are in the New Zones of the cortex . . . where basic *Tursiopsss* gray matter has been heavily uplift-modified. There are lesions in regions controlling both vision and speech-ch. The corpus callosum is seared . . ."

Makanee's eyes re-opened, but she did not appear to be looking at them.

Metz nodded. "Thank you, Doctor," he said. "You've told us what we need to know. I'm sorry we took so much of your time. I'm sure you're doing your best."

When she did not answer, the human slipped his oxymask over his face and slid into the water. He motioned to Takkata-Jim and turned to leave.

The male dolphin clicked at Makanee for a moment longer, but when she did not move he flipped about and followed Metz toward the exit.

A shudder passed through her as the two entered the lock. She lifted her head to call after them.

"Don't forget-t when you call a ship's council that *I'm* a member! And Hikahi and Gillian and T-Tom Orley!" The lock was hissing shut behind them as she called. She couldn't tell if they had heard.

Makanee settled back into the water with a sigh. *And Tom Orley,* she thought. *Don't forget him, you sneaky bastards! He'll not let you get away with this!*

Makanee shook her head, knowing she was thinking irrationally. Her suspicions weren't based on facts. And even if they were true, Thomas Orley couldn't stretch his hand across two thousand kilometers to save the day. There were rumors that he was already dead.

Metz and Takkata-Jim had her all confused. She had a gut feeling that they had told her a complex assortment of truths, half-truths, and outright lies, and she had no way of knowing which was which.

They think they can fool me, just because I'm female, and old, and two uplift generations cruder than any other fin aboard but Brookida. But I can guess why they're giving special favors to the one chimpanzee member on the ship's council. Here and now, they have a majority to back up any decision they make. No wonder they're not anxious to have Hikahi or Gillian back!

Maybe I should have lied to them . . . told them Creideiki would awaken any minute.

But then, who can tell how desperate they are? Or what they'd resort to? Was the accident with the buoy really an accident? They could be lying to cover up ignorance—or to cover up a conspiracy. Could I protect Creideiki, with only two female aides to help me?

Makanee let out a low moan. This sort of thing wasn't her department! She sometimes wished that being a dolphin physician, like in the old days, simply meant you lifted the one you were trying to save up on your brow, and held his head above the water until he recovered, or your strength failed you, or your own heart broke.

She turned back toward Intensive Care. The chamber was darkened except for a light that shone upon a large gray neo-dolphin, suspended in a shielded gravity tank. Makanee checked the life-maintenance readings and saw that they were stable.

Creideiki blinked unseeingly, and once a brief shudder passed down the length of his body.

Makanee sighed and turned away. She swam over to a nearby comm unit and considered.

Metz and Takkata-Jim can't be back on the bridge yet, she thought. She clicked a sonar code that activated the unit. Almost instantly the face of a young, blue-finned dolphin appeared before her.

"Communications. C-can I help you?"

"Akki? Yes, child, it's Dr. Makanee. Have you made any plans for lunch? You know, I do think I still have some of that candied octopus left. You're free? How sssweet. I'll see you soon, then. Oh, and let's keep our date our little secret. Okay? That'sss a good lad."

She departed Intensive Care, a scheme beginning to form in her mind.

40

~~~~~~

Creideiki

In the quiet grayness of the gravity tank, a faint moaning cry.

> * *Desperate, he swims*
>   *Tossed by gray storm winds, howling:*
>   *Drowning! Drowning!* *

41

~~~~~~

Tom Orley

A foul-tempered mountain growled in the middle of a scum-crusted sea.

It had stopped raining a while ago. The volcano grumbled and coughed fire at low overhanging clouds, casting orange on their undersides. Thin, twisting trails of ash blew into the sky. Where the hot cinders finally fell, it was not to a quenching by clean sea water. They landed in a muddy layer atop a carpet of dingy vines which seemed to go on forever.

Thomas Orley coughed in the dank, sooty air. He crawled up a small rise of slippery, jumbled weeds. The dead weight of his crude sledge dragged a tether wrapped around his left hand. With his right he clutched a thick tendril near the top of the weed-mound.

His legs kept sliding out from under him as he crawled. Even when he managed to wedge them into gaps in the slimy mass, his feet frequently sank into the mire between the vines. When he awkwardly pulled them out, the quagmire would let go reluctantly, giving off an awful sucking sound.

Sometimes "things" came out with his feet, squirming along his legs and dropping off to slither back into the noisome brine.

The tightly wrapped thong cut into his left hand as he pulled the sledge, a meager remnant of his solar plane and supplies. It was a miracle that he had been able to salvage even that much from the crash.

The volcano sent ochre flickers across the weedscape. Rainbow specks of metallic dust coated the vegetation in all directions. It was late afternoon, almost a full Kithrup day since he had banked his glider toward the island, searching for a safe place to land.

Tom raised his head to look blearily over the plain of weeds. All of his well-laid plans had been brought down by this plain of tough, ropy sea plants.

He had hoped to find shelter on an island upwind of the volcano, or, barring that, to land at sea and turn the glider into a broad and seaworthy raft from which to perform his experiment.

I should have considered this possibility. The crash, those dazed, frantic minutes diving after gear and piling together a crude sledge while the storm lashed at him, and then hours crawling among the fetid vines toward a solitary hump of vegetation—it all might have been avoided.

He tried to pull forward, but a tremor in his right arm threatened to turn into a full-scale cramp. It had been badly wrenched during the crash, when the plane's wing pontoons had come off and the fuselage went tumbling across the morass, splashing at last into an isolated pool of open water.

A gash across the left side of his face had almost sent him into shock during those first critical moments. It reached from his jaw almost to the neural socket above his left ear. The plastic cover that normally protected the delicate nerve interface had spun out into the night, hopelessly lost.

Infection was the least of his worries, now.

The tremor in his arm grew worse. Tom tried to ride it out, lying face down on the pungent, rubbery weeds. Gritty mud scraped his right cheek and forehead each time he coughed.

Somewhere he had to find the energy. He hadn't time for the subtleties of self-hypnosis, to coax his body back into working. By main force of will, he *commanded* the abused muscles to behave for one final effort. He could do little about what the universe threw at him, but *dammit*, after thirty hours of struggle, within meters of his goal, he would not accept a rebellion by his body!

Another coughing fit ripped at his raw throat. His body shook, and the hacking weakened his grip on the dry root. Just when he thought his lungs could take no more, the fit finally passed. Tom lay there in the mud, drained, eyes closed.

> * *Count the joys of movement?—*
> *First among advantages:*
> *Absence of Boredom—* *

He hadn't the breath to whistle the Trinary Haiku, but it blew through his mind, and he spared the energy for a brief smile through cracked, mud-crusted lips.

Somewhere, he found the reserves for one more effort. He clenched his teeth and pulled himself over the last stretch. The right arm almost buckled, but it held as his head rose over the top of the small hill.

Tom blinked cinders from his eyes and looked out at what lay beyond. More weeds. As far as the eye could see, more weeds.

A thick loop of neustonic vine stuck out at the summit of the modest hillock. Tom heaved the sledge high enough to wrap the slack line around the root.

Sensation flowed into his numbed left hand, leaving him open-mouthed in silent agony. He slumped back against the hillock, breathing rapidly and shallowly.

The cramps returned in force, and his body folded under them. He wanted to tear at the thousand teeth that bit at his arms and legs, but his hands were immobile claws. He lay curled around them.

Somehow, the logical part of Tom's mind remained disconnected from the agony. It still plotted and schemed and tried to set time limits. He'd come out here for a reason, after all.

There had to be a reason for going through all this. . . . If only he could remember why he was here in the stench and hurt and dust and grit . . .

The calming pattern he sought wouldn't form. He felt himself start to fade.

Suddenly, through pain-squinted eyes, he thought he saw Gillian's face before him.

Fronds of airy vegetation waved behind her. Her gray eyes looked his way, as if searching for something just out of range. They seemed to scan past him twice as he trembled, unable to move. Then, at last, they met his, and she smiled!

Pain-drenched static threatened to drown out the dream-words.

> *I send **** for good ****,*
> *though you *** skeptical, love.*
> **** though the whole **** might listen.*

He strained to focus on the message—more likely a hallucination. He didn't care which it was. It was an anchor. He clung to it as cramps made humming bowstrings of his tendons.

Her smile conveyed commiseration.

> *What a mess *** are! The *** I love*
> *is ****** and careless! Shall I *****
> *it better?*

Meta-Orley disapproved. If this was really a message from Gillian, she was taking a terrible chance. "I love you, too," he subvocalized. "But will you shut the hell up before the Eatees hear you?"

The psicast—or hallucination—wavered as a fit of coughing struck him. He hacked until his lungs felt like dry husks. Finally, he sank back with a sigh.

At last, Meta-Tom surrendered pride.

> *Yes!*

He cast into the murk before his eyes, calling after her dissolving image.

> *Yes, love. Please come back and make*
> *better . . .*

Gillian's face seemed to diffract in all directions, like a bundle of moonbeams, joining the shimmering volcanic dust in the sky. Whether a true message, or an illusion borne of delirium, it faded like a portrait done in smoke.

Still, he thought he heard a lingering trace of Gillian's inner voice...

> *** *** *is, that is, that is ...*
> *and healing comes, in dreaming ...*

He listened, unaware of time, and slowly, the tremors subsided. His fetal curl gradually unfolded.

The volcano rumbled and lit the sky. The "ground" beneath Tom undulated gently and rocked him into a shallow slumber.

42

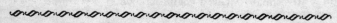

Toshio

"No, Dr. Dart. The enstatite inclusions are one part I'm not sure of. The static from the robot was really strong when I took that reading. If you'd like, I can double-check it right now."

Toshio's eyelids were heavy with ennui. He had lost track of time spent pushing buttons and reading data at Charles Dart's behest. The chimp planetologist would not be satisfied! No matter how well and quickly Toshio responded, it was never quite enough.

"No, no, we haven't got time," Charlie answered gruffly from the holoscreen at the edge of the drill-tree pool. "See if you can work it out on your own after I sign off, okay?

"It would make a nice project for you to pursue on the side you know, Toshio. Some of these rocks are totally unique! If you did a thorough study of the mineralogy of this shaft, I'd be happy to help you write it up. Imagine the feather in your cap! A major publication couldn't hurt your career, you know."

Toshio could well imagine. He was, indeed, learning a lot working for Dr. Dart. One thing he had learned, which would serve him well if he ever did go on to graduate school, was to be very careful in choosing his research advisor.

The question was moot, anyway, with aliens overhead getting ready to capture them. For the thousandth time, Toshio shied away from thinking about the battle in space. It only made him depressed.

"Thanks, Dr. Dart, but . . ."

"No problem!" Charlie barked in gruff condescension. "We'll discuss the details of your project later though, if you don't mind. Right now, let's have an update on where the drone is."

Toshio shook his head, amazed by the fellow's tenacious single-mindedness. He was afraid that if it got any worse he would lose his temper with the chimp, senior research associate or no.

"Um . . ." Toshio checked his gauges. "The 'bot's descended to a little over a kilometer, Dr. Dart. The shaft is narrower and smoother as we get down to more recent digging, so I'm anchoring the robot to the wall at each site."

Toshio looked over his shoulder to the northeast, wishing Dennie or Gillian would show up as a distraction. But Dennie was with her Kiqui, and he had last seen Gillian seated in lotus position in a clearing overlooking the ocean, oblivious to the world.

Gillian had been pretty upset earlier, when Takkata-Jim told her everyone at the ship was too busy getting *Streaker* ready for the move to talk to her. Even her questions about Tom Orley were brushed aside with abrupt politeness. They'd call her when they knew anything, Takkata-Jim had said before signing off.

Toshio had seen a frown settle over her face as every call she made was deflected. A new comm officer had replaced Akki. The fin told Gillian every person she wanted was unavailable. The one crew member she was able to talk to was Charles Dart, apparently because his skills weren't urgently needed at the moment. And the chimp refused to talk about anything but his work.

Immediately, she had begun getting ready to leave. Then

came orders from the ship, directly from Takkata-Jim. She
was to stay indefinitely and help Dennie Sudman prepare a
report on the Kiqui.

This time Gillian took the news impassively. Without
comment, she had gone off into the jungle to be alone.

". . . more of those tendrils of Dennie's." Charles Dart
had been talking as Toshio's mind drifted. Toshio made
himself sit up straight and pay attention to what the chimp
scientist was saying.

". . . The most exciting thing is the potassium and iodine
isotope profiles. They prove my hypothesis that within recent
geological time some sophont race has been burying garbage
in this subduction zone of the planet! This is colossally
important, Toshio. There's evidence in these rocks of multi-
ple generations of dumping of material from above, and rapid
recycling of stuff brought up by nearby volcanoes. It's almost
as if there's been a rhythm to it, an ebb and flow. Something
awfully suspicious has been going on here for a long time!
Kithrup's supposed to have been fallow since the ancient
Karrank% lived here. Yet somebody's been hiding highly
refined stuff in this planet's crust up until very recently!"

Toshio almost committed a rudeness. "Very recently"
indeed! Dart was sleuthing in geological time. Any day now,
the Eatees would be down on them, and he was treating the
alleged burying of industrial garbage thousands of years ago
as if it was the latest Scotland Yard mystery!

"Yes, sir. I'll get on it right away." Toshio wasn't even
sure what Dart had just asked him to do, but he covered his
ass.

"And don't worry, sir. The robot will be monitored day
and night. Keepiru and Sah'ot have orders from Takkata-Jim
to stay plugged into it at turns when I'm unavailable. They'll
call me or wake me if there's any change in its condition."

Wouldn't that satisfy the chimp? The fen hadn't taken
well at all to that order from *Streaker's* exec, but they would
obey, even if it slowed Sah'ot's work with the Kiqui.

Miracle of miracles, Charlie seemed to agree. "Yeah,
that's nice of them," he muttered. "Be sure to thank 'em for
me.

"And say! Maybe, while Keepiru's plugged in, can he
trace that intermittent static we keep getting from the robot?
I don't like it, and it's getting worse."

"Yes, sir. I'll ask him."

The chimpanzee rubbed his right eye with the back of a furry hand, and yawned.

"Listen, Toshio," he said. "I'm sorry, but I really need a break. Would you mind if we put off finishing this until just a little bit later? I'll ring you back after supper and answer all your questions then, hmmm? OK, bye, then, for now!" Charlie reached forward and the holo image disappeared.

Toshio stared at the empty space for a moment, slightly stunned. Mind? Would I mind? Why, no, sir, I don't believe I'd mind at all! I'll just wait here patiently, until either you call back or the sky falls down on my head!

He snorted. Would I mind.

Toshio stood up, his joints crackling from sitting cross-legged too long.

I thought I was too young for that. Ah, well. A midshipman is supposed to experience everything.

He looked toward the forest. Dennie was hard at work with the Kiqui. Should I bother Gillian, I wonder? She's probably worried about Tom, and who could blame her? We were supposed to have heard from him early yesterday.

But maybe she wants company.

Lately he had started having fantasies about Gillian. It was only natural, of course. She was a beautiful older woman—at least thirty—and by most standards quite a bit more alluring than Dennie Sudman.

Not that Dennie wasn't attractive in her own way, but Toshio didn't want to think about Dennie much any more. Her implicit rejection, by effectively overlooking him when the two of them were alone and so much alike, was painful.

Not that Dennie had said or done anything offensive, but she had become moody lately. Toshio suspected she sensed his attraction to her, and was overreacting by turning cold to him. He told himself that was an immature response on her part. But that didn't keep it from hurting.

Fantasizing about Gillian was another matter. He'd had shameful but very compelling daydreams about being there when she needed a man, helping her overcome her loss...

She probably knew how he felt, but didn't let it change her behavior toward him at all. It was a comforting forgiveness, and it made her a safe object of semi-secret adoration.

It could simply be that I'm very confused, of course,

Toshio thought. *I'm trying to be analytical in an area where I have almost no experience, and my own feelings keep getting in the way.*

I wish I wasn't just an awkward kid, and were more like Mr. Orley, instead.

An uneven electronic tone behind him interrupted his fantasy—the comm coming back to life.

"Oh, no!" Toshio groaned. "Not already!"

The unit spat static as the tuner sought to bring in an erratic carrier wave. Toshio had a wild desire to run over and kick the thing into the bottomless murk of the drill-tree shaft.

Suddenly, a crackling, noise-shrouded whistle broke out.

> * If (crackle) midshipmen
> >   Stuck together
> > >   Who could stop us?
> * And of midshipmen
> >   Who can fly
> > >   Like Calafians?

"Akki!" Toshio hurried over to kneel in front of the comm.

> * Right again,
> >   Diving partner—
> * Remember how we'd
> >   Once hunt lobster?

"Do I? Ifni! I wish we were home doing that now! What's happening? Are you having equipment trouble on the bridge? I'm getting no visual, and there's a lot of static. I thought you were taken off comm duty. And why the Trinary?"

> * Necessity
> >   Is someone's (crackle) mother—
> * I send this via
> >   Close nerve socket—
> * Anxious, I seek
> >   soft High Patron—
> * Urgently
> >   To pass (crackle) warning—

Toshio's lips pursed as he repeated the message to himself silently. ". . . soft High Patron." There were few humans given titles like that by fins. Only one candidate was here on the island right now.

"You want to talk to Gillian?"

> * Urgently
> To pass on warning—

Toshio blinked, then he said, "I'll get her right away, Akki! You hold on!"

He turned and ran into the forest, calling Gillian's name at the top of his lungs.

43

Akki

The monofilament cable was almost invisible against the rubble and ooze of the sea floor. Even in the light from Akki's harness lamp, it barely reflected a spiderweb's glimmer here and there amidst the rock and sediments atop this jagged ridgeline.

The cable had been *designed* to be hard to detect; it was the only certain way *Streaker* could communicate with her two outlying work parties without giving away her location. Akki had been forced to search for over an hour, using the best instruments at his disposal and knowing where to look, before finding the line to the island. By the time he had clipped his neural tap into the line, more than half of the oxygen in his breather was gone.

A lot of time had been spent just getting away from the ship. And Akki wasn't even sure his departure had gone unnoticed. The taciturn electrician's mate in charge of the equipment locker shouldn't have questioned orders when Akki asked for breathing gear. Another fin, an off-duty engine room rating, had followed him from a distance after he had left the equipment locker, and Akki had to dodge through the outlock to shake the *Stenos* off his tail.

In less than two days a subtle change had come over the crew of *Streaker*. A new alignment of power had been set up. Crew members who had formerly been of little influence now pushed their way to the front of the food lines and adopted dominant body postures, while others went about their duties with eyes downcast and flukes drooping.

Rank and official position had little to do with it. Such things had always been informal aboard *Streaker* anyway. Dolphins were more apt to pay attention to subtle shifts in dominance than to formal authority.

Now even racism seemed to be a factor. A disproportionate number of the new figures of authority were of the *Stenos* sub-breed.

It amounted to an informal coup. Officially, Takkata-Jim was acting on behalf of the unconscious Creideiki until a ship's council could be convened. But *Streaker*'s water had the taste of a herd with a new dominant male. Those close to the old bull were on the out, and the cronies of the new swam in the vanguard.

Akki found it all quite illogical and a bit disgusting. It brought home to him that even the highly selected fen of *Streaker*'s crew could submit to ancient patterns of behavior under stress. He now saw what the Galactics meant when they said that three hundred years of uplift was too short a time for a race to be ready for starships.

It was a rude realization. It made Akki feel more like a *client* than he ever had in the mixed, egalitarian colony of Calafia.

The discovery did help in one way, though. It gave him a primitive satisfaction in his act of mutiny. Legalistically, he was committing a serious crime, abandoning the ship to make contact with Gillian Baskin against specific orders from the acting captain.

But now Akki felt he knew the truth; he was a member of a crew of imitation spacemen. There was no way, short of Creideiki miraculously recovering, that they were going to get out of this mess without intervention by their patrons.

He discounted the value of Ignacio Metz—or Emerson

D'Anite or even Toshio, for that matter. He agreed with Makanee that their only hope lay in Dr. Baskin or Mr. Orley coming home.

By now he had come to accept that Orley was lost. The rest of the crew believed this, and it was one more reason morale had gone to hell since Creideiki's accident.

The comm line quietly sent a carrier tone directly to his stato-acoustic nerve, as Akki waited impatiently for Toshio to return with Gillian. The line was not being used for anything else, now that Charles Dart had signed off, but every second that passed increased the chance that the present comm operator aboard the ship would detect the resonance of his tap. Akki had set it up so they couldn't pick up his conversation with Toshio, but even a dullard CommSec fin couldn't miss the side effects, in time.

Where are they? he wondered. *Surely they know I only have so much air? And this metal-rich water makes my skin itch!*

Akki breathed slowly for calm. A teaching rhyme of Keneenk ran through his mind.

> * *"Past" is what once was—*
> *A remnant that's called memory . . .*
> * *In it lie the "causes"—*
> *Of what now is."*
>
> * *"Future" is what will be—*
> *Envisioned, seldom seen . . .*
> * *In it lie "results"—*
> *Of what now is.*
>
> * *"Present" is that narrowness—*
> *Passing, always flickering . . .*
> * *Proof of the "joke"—*
> *Of "what now is."*

Past, future and present were among the hardest ideas to express explicitly in Trinary. The rhyme was meant to teach causation as the human patrons, and most other sophonts, saw it, while keeping essential faith with the cetacean view of life.

It all seemed so simple to Akki. At times he wondered why some of these dolphins of Earth had so much trouble with such ideas. One thought, one imagined actions and their consequences, considered how the different results would taste and feel, then one acted! If the future was unclear, one did the best one could, and hoped.

It was how humans had muddled through during the ages of their horrible, orphaned ignorance. Akki saw no reason why it should be so hard for his people, especially when they were being shown the way.

"Akki? Toshio here. Gillian's coming. She had to break away from something important, so I ran ahead. Are you all right?"

Akki sighed.

> * In the depths—
>   With itching blowmouth
> * I tread in wait—
>   At duty's calling
>
> * As the cycloid—
>   Rolls in . . .

"Hang on," Toshio called, interrupting the rhyme. Akki grimaced. Toshio never would develop a sense of style.

"Here's Gillian," Toshio finished. *"Take care of yourself, Akki!"*

The line crackled with static.

> * You, too—
>   Diving/flying partner *

"Akki?"

It was the voice of Gillian Baskin, made tinny by the weak connection, but almost infinitely gratifying to hear.

"What is it, dear? Can you tell me what's going on on the ship? Why won't Creideiki talk to me?"

That wasn't what Akki had thought she would ask first. For some reason he had expected her main concern to be Tom Orley. Well, he wasn't about to bring the subject up if she didn't.

> * Makanee—
>   Patient healer
> * Sends me out—
>   With danger warning

  * Soundless, flukeless
      Lies Creideiki
  * Streaker's fortunes
      Strangely waning

    * And the taste—
  Of atavism
      * Fouls the waters—

There was silence at the other end. No doubt Gillian was
formulating her next question in a way that would let him
answer unambiguously in Trinary. It was a skill Toshio sometimes sadly lacked.

Akki brought his head up quickly. Was that a sound? It
hadn't come from the comm line, but from the dark waters
around him.

"Akki," Gillian began. "*I'm going to ask you questions
phrased to take three-level answers. Please spare artistry for
brevity in answering.*"

Gladly, if I can, Akki thought. He had often wondered
why it was so hard to hold direct conversations in Trinary
without beating around the bush in poetic allusion. It was his
native tongue as much as Anglic was, and still he was
frustrated by its resistance to shortcuts.

"*Akki, does Creideiki ignore the Fish-of-Dreaming, does
he chase them, or does he feed them?*"

Gillian was asking if Creideiki was still functioning as a
tool user, was he lost to injury, drifting in an unconscious
dream-hunt or, worse, was he dead. Somehow, Gillian had
immediately gone right to the heart of the matter. Akki was
able to answer with blessed brevity.

    * Chasing squid—
        In deepest water *

There was that sound again! A rapid clicking, coming
from not far away. Curse the necessity to keep his neural
socket linked to the static of this line! The sounds were close
enough to leave little doubt. Someone was hunting for him
out here.

"*All right, Akki. Next question. Does Hikahi calm all
with her Keneenk rhythms, does she echo herd obedience, or
does she sing an absent silence?*"

Dolphin sonar is a highly directional thing. He felt the edge of a lobe of a sonic beam pass just above him, without hitting him broadside. Akki got down as close to the ocean floor as he could, and made an effort to direct his own nervous clickings into the soft sand. He wanted to reach out with one of his harness arms and grab a rock or something for stability, but was afraid the tiny whirring of the motors would be heard.

> * *Absent silence—*
>   *Fades the memory—*
> * *Of Hikahi*
>
> * *Absent silence—*
>   *From Tsh't*
> * *And Suessi* *

He wished he, too, were absent this place and back in his quiet stateroom aboard *Streaker*.

"*Okay, is their silence that of netted capture? Is it of orca-fearful waiting? Or is it the silence of fishes feeding?*"

Akki was about to answer when, like one whose eyes were suddenly struck by a bright light, he was awash in a loud beam of pulsed sound, highly directional and from his left and above. There was no question a dolphin up there was instantly aware of him.

> * *Takkata-Jim—*
>   *Bites the cables*
>
> * *My own job—*
>   *Is mine no longer*
>
> * *His fen relay—*
>   *His lying songs* *

Akki was so agitated that some of that actually came out as sound rather than impulses sent to the monofilament. There was no use trying any longer for secrecy. He made ready to jettison the line and turned his melon toward the intruder. He fired off a sonar pulse strong enough, he hoped, to momentarily stun him.

The echoes of his burst returned giving him a vivid

image. There was a thrashing sound as a very large dolphin swung aside, out of his beam.

K'tha-Jon! Akki recognized the echo at once.

"Akki? What was that? Are you in fighting patterns? Break off if you have to. I'm coming home fast as I . . ."

Duty absolved, Akki popped the neural link free and rolled to one side.

He acted none too soon. A blue-green laser bolt sizzled through the spot where he had been seconds before.

So, that's the way of it, he thought as he dove into the canyon next to the ocean ridge. The hammerhead is out to get me, and no politeness about it.

He did a quick roll to his right and speared downward toward the shadows.

Dolphins were known for a reluctance to kill anything that breathed air, but they were not a limited race. Even before uplift, humans had witnessed cases of fin murdering fin. In enabling cetaceans to be starfarers, men also made them more efficient when they chose to kill.

A line-bright laser beam hissed a bare meter ahead of him. Akki clenched his jaw and dove through the streak of scalding bubbles in its wake. Another narrow, searing bolt sizzled between his pectoral fins. He whirled and dove for the long sonic shadow of a jagged outcrop of rock.

K'tha-Jon's laser rifle could kill at long range, while the welder/torch on Akki's harness was, like all sidearm-tools, of use only up close. Obviously, his only chances were in flight or in trickery.

It was very dark down here. All of the red colors were gone. Only blue and green could pass through from the day to illuminate a shadow-filled landscape. Akki took advantage of the rugged terrain and slipped between the sharp walls of a narrow rock cleft. There he stopped to wait and listen.

The echoes he picked up through passive listening only told him that K'tha-Jon was out there, somewhere, searching. Akki hoped his own rapid breathing wasn't as loud as it sounded to him.

He sent a neural query to his harness. The microcomputer in its frame told him he had less than half an hour's air left in his breather. That certainly put a limit on how long he could wait.

Akki's jaws ground together. He wanted K'tha-Jon's long

pectorals between his teeth, much as he knew he was no
match for the big *Stenos* in size or strength.

Akki had no way of knowing whether K'tha-Jon was out
here on his own or following orders from Takkata-Jim. But if
there were some cabal of *Stenos* at work, he wouldn't put it
past them to kill the helpless Creideiki if that were the way to
secure their plan. Unthinkable as it was, they could even get
it into their heads to harm *Gillian*, if she weren't careful how
she made her return to the ship. The mere thought of any fin
participating in such crimes made Akki feel sick.

*I've got to get back and help Makanee defend Creideiki
until Gillian arrives! That takes priority over everything else.*

He slipped out of the cleft and swam a series of floor-
hugging zigs and zags toward a small canyon to the southeast,
in a direction away from *Streaker*, and away from both Toshio's
island and the Thennanin wreck. It was the direction most
likely to be unwatched by K'tha-Jon.

He could hear the giant casting about for him. The
powerful beams of sound were missing for now. There was a
good chance he would get a head start before he was detected.

Still, it wasn't quite as *tasty* as the satisfaction he would
have felt in surprising K'tha-Jon with a snout-ramming in his
genitals!

Gillian turned from the comm set to see anxiety on
Toshio's face. It made him seem very young. Gone was the
role of a rough, tough, worldly mel. Toshio was an adolescent midshipman who had just found out his captain was
crippled. And now his best friend might well be fighting for
his life. He looked at her, hoping for reassurance that everything would be all right.

Gillian took the youth's hand and pulled him into a hug.
She held him, against his protests, until, at last, the tension
went out of his shoulders and he buried his face in her
shoulder, holding her tightly.

When he finally pulled away, Toshio didn't look at her,
but turned away and wiped at one eye with the heel of his
hand.

"I'm going to want to take Keepiru with me," Gillian
said to him. "Do you think you and Sah'ot and Dennie can
spare him?"

Toshio nodded. His voice was thick, but he soon had it
under control. "Yes, sir. Sah'ot may be a bit of a problem

when I start giving him some of Keepiru's duties. But I've been watching the way you handle him. I think I can manage."

"That's good. See if you can keep him off Dennie's back, too. You're going to be military commander now. I'm sure you'll manage fine."

Gillian turned to her small poolside campsite to gather her gear. Toshio went to the water's edge and switched on the hydrophone amplifier that would signal the two dolphins that they were wanted. Sah'ot and Keepiru had left an hour ago, to await the evening foray of the aborigines.

"I'll go back with you if you want, Gillian."

She shook her head as she gathered her notes and tools together. "No, Toshio. Dennie's work with the Kiqui is damned important. You're the one who's got to keep her from burning down the forest with a spent match while she's preoccupied. Besides, I need you to maintain a pretense that I haven't left. Do you think you can do that for me?" Gillian zipped shut her watertight satchel and started slipping out of her shirt and shorts. Toshio turned away, at first, and started to blush.

Then he noticed that Gillian didn't seem to care that he look. *I might never see her again*, he thought. *I wonder if she knows what she's doing for me?*

"Yes, sir," he said. Toshio's mouth felt very dry. "I'll act just as harassed and impatient as ever with Dr. Dart. And if Takkata-Jim asks for you I'll... I'll tell him you're off somewhere, er, sulking."

Gillian was holding her drysuit in front of her, preparing to step into it. She looked up at him, surprised by the wryness of his remark. Then she laughed.

In two long-legged strides she was over to him, seizing him into another hug. Without a thought Toshio put his arms around the smooth skin of her waist.

"You're a good man, Tosh," she said as she kissed him on the cheek. "And, you know, you've grown quite a bit taller than me? You lie to Takkata-Jim for me and I promise we'll make a *proper* mutineer of you in no time at all."

Toshio nodded and closed his eyes. "Yes, ma'am," he said as he held her tight.

44

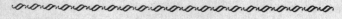

Creideiki

His skin itched. It had *always* itched, since that dim time when he rode alongside his mother in her slipstream—when he had first learned about touch from nursing and the gentle nuzzles she gave him to remind him to rise for air.

Soon he had learned that there were other kinds of touching. There were walls and plants and the sides of all the buildings of the settlement at Catalina-Under; there was the stroking, butting, and yes! biting play of his peers; there was the soft, oh, so deliciously varied touch of the mels and fems—the humans—who swam about like pinnipeds, like sea lions, laughing and playing catch with him underwater and above.

There was the feel of water. All the different kinds of feel there were to water.

The *splash* and *crash* of falling into it! The smooth laminar flow of it as you speared along faster than anyone *ever* could have gone before! The gentle lapping of it, just below your blowmouth as you rested, whispering a lullaby to yourself.

O, how he itched!

Long ago he had learned to rub against things, and he discovered what that could do to him. Ever since then, he had masturbated whenever he felt like it, just like any other healthy fin would . . .

Creideiki wanted to scratch himself. He wanted to masturbate.

Only there was no wall nearby to rub against. He seemed unable to move, or even to open his eyes to see what surrounded him.

He was floating in midair, his weight held up by

224

…othing . . . by a familiar magic . . . "anti-gravity." The word—like his memories of floating this way many times before—for some reason felt alien, almost meaningless.

He wondered at his lassitude. Why not open his eyes and see? Why not click out a soundbeam and hear the shape and texture of this place?

At intervals he felt a spray of moistness that kept his skin wet. It seemed to come from all directions.

He considered, and came to the conclusion that something must be very wrong with him. He must be sick.

An involuntary sigh made him realize he was still capable of some sound. He searched for the right mechanisms, experimented, then managed to repeat the sound.

They must be working to fix me, he thought. I must have been hurt. Though I don't feel any pain, I feel a vacancy. Something has been taken from me. A ball? A tool? A skill? Anyway, the people are probably trying to put it back.

I trust people, he thought happily. And the apex of his mouth curled into a slight smile.

* !!!! *

The apex of his mouth did what?
Oh. Yes. Smiling. That new thing.
New thing? I've done it all my life!
Why?
It's expressive! It adds subtlety to my features! It . . .
It is redundant.

Creideiki let out a weak, warbling cry of confusion.

* In the brightness*
*   Of the sunshine—*
* There are answers*
*   In schools, like fishes *

He remembered a little, now. He had been dreaming. Something terrible had happened, and he had been plunged into a nightmare of bewilderment. Shapes had darted toward and away from him, and he had felt ancient songs take new, eerie, forms.

He realized he must still be dreaming, with both hemi-

spheres at the same time. That explained why he couldn't
move. He tried to coax himself awake with a song.

> * *Levels there are—*
> *Known only to sperm whales*

> * *Physeter, who hunts*
> *In chasms of dreaming*

> * *To battle the squid*
> *Whose beaks are sea-mounts*

> * *And whose great arms*
> *Encompass oceans. . . .*

It was not a calming rhyme. It had overtones of darkness
that made him want to fly away in horror. Creideiki tried to
halt it, fearing what the chant might call up. But he could not
stop crafting the sound-glyphs.

> * *Go down to levels—*
> *In the darkness*

> * *Where your "cycloid"*
> *Never reaches*

> * *Where all music*
> *Finally settles*

> * *And it gathers*
> *Stacked in layers*

> * *Howling songs of*
> *Ancient storms,*

> * *And hurricanes*
> *That never died. . . .*

A presence grew alongside Creideiki. A great, broad
figure could be felt nearby, forming out of the fabric of his
song. Creideiki sensed its slow sonar pulses, filling the small
chamber he lay within . . . a small chamber that couldn't possibly hold the behemoth taking shape beside him.

Nukapai?

> * *Sounds of earthquakes—*
> *Stored for epochs*

> * *Sounds of molten*
> *Primeval rocks....*

The sound creature solidified with each passing verse. There was a muscular power in the presence forming beside him. The thing's slow, huge fluke strokes threatened to send him tumbling head over tail. When It blew, Its spume sounded like a storm breaking on a rocky shore.

Fear at last gave him the will to open his eyes. Moist mucus ran over his eyeballs as he labored to separate the lids. They were recessed to their deepest, and it took moments to make them switch to air-focus.

At first all he saw was a hospital suspension tank, small and confined. He was alone.

But sound told him he was in the open sea, and a leviathan rode next to him! He could *feel* its great power!

He blinked, and suddenly his vision shifted. Sight adopted the frame of reference of sound. The room vanished, and he *saw* It!

!!!!!!!

The thing beside him could never have lived in any of the oceans he had known. Creideiki almost choked in dread.

It moved with the power of tsunamis, the irresistibility of the tides.

It was a thing of darkness and depths.

It was a god.

> * *K-K-Kph-kree !!* *

It was a name Creideiki hadn't been aware he had known. It welled up from somewhere, like the dragons of a nightmare.

One dark eye regarded Creideiki with a look that seared him. He wanted to turn away—to hide or die.

Then it spoke to him.

It spurned Trinary, as he knew it would. It cast aside Primal, disdaining it a tongue for clever animals. It sang a song that brushed against him with physical force, enveloped him and filled him with a terrible undertanding.

:You Swam Away From Us Creideiki : You Were Starting To Learn : Then Your Mind Swam Away : But We Have Not Finished : Yet :

:We Have Waited Long For One Such As You : Now You Need Us As Much As We Need You : There Is No Going Back :

:As You Are : You Would Be A Hulk : Dead Meat : Emptiness Without A Song : Never Again A Dreamer *or* A Fire User :

:*Useless* Creideiki : Neither Captain : Nor Cetacean : Useless Meat :

:There Is One Path For You : Through The Belly Of The Whale Dream : There You May Find A Way : A Hard Way : But A Way To Do Your Duty : There You May Find A Way To Save Your Life... :

Creideiki moaned. He thrashed feebly and called out for Nukapai. But then he remembered. She was *one* of them. She waited, down below, with his other tormentors, some of them old gods he had heard of in the sagas, and some he had never heard mentioned even by the humpback whales....

K-K-Kph-kree had come to bring him back.

Though Anglic was lost to him, he conveyed a plea in a language he had not known he knew.

:I am damaged! : I am a hulk! I *should* be dead meat! : I have lost speech! I have lost words! : Let me die! :

It answered with a sonorous rumble that seemed born beneath the earth. Beneath the ooze.

:Through The Whale Dream You Go : Where Your Cousins Have Never Been : Even When They Played Like Animals And Barely Knew Men : Deeper Than The Humpbacks Go : In Their Idle Meditation : Deeper Than *Physeter* : In His Devil Hunt : Deeper Than The Darkness Itself.... :

:There You May Decide To Die, If Truth Cannot Be Borne.... :

The walls of the small chamber faded away as his tormentor began to take on a new reality. It had the great brow and bright teeth of a sperm whale, but Its eyes shone like beacons, and Its flanks were streaked with sparkling silver. All around It shimmered an aura like... like the glimmering fields around a starship....

The room disappeared entirely. Suddenly, all around him was a great, open sea of weightlessness. The old god began to swim forward with powerful fluke strokes. Creideiki, wailing a soft fluting cry, was powerless to prevent being swept along in the behemoth's pulling slipstream. They accelerated, faster ... faster ...

In spite of the absence of direction, he knew, somehow, they were going **DOWN**.

"Did you hear that-t-t?"

Makanee's assistant looked up at the tank in which the captain lay suspended. A dim spotlight within the gravity tank shone on the suture scars of repeated surgery. Every few seconds, recessed nozzles cast a fine mist over the unconscious dolphin.

Makanee followed the medic's gaze.

"Perhapsss. I thought I heard something a little while ago, like a sigh. What did you hear?"

The assistant shook her head from side to side. "I'm not sure. I thought it sounded like he was talking to somebody— only not in Anglic. It seemed like there was a snatch of Trinary, then ... then something else. It sounded weird!"

The assistant shivered. "Do you think maybe he's dreaming?"

Makanee looked up at Creideiki and sighed. "I don't know. I don't even know if, in his condition, dreaming is something to wish for him, or to pray devoutly he doesn't do."

45

Tom Orley

A chilly sea breeze swept over him out of the west. A bout of shivering shook him awake in the middle of the night. His eyes opened in the dark, staring into emptiness.

He couldn't remember where he was.

Give it a moment, he thought. *It'll come*.

He had been dreaming of the planet Garth, where the seas were small and the rivers many. There he had lived for a time among the human and chimp colonists, a mixed colony as rich and surprising as Calafia, where man and dolphin dwelt together.

Garth was a friendly world, though isolated far from other Earthling settlements.

In his dream, Garth was invaded. Giant warships hovered over her cities and spewed clouds of gas across her fertile valleys, sending colonists fleeing in panic. The sky had been filled with flashing lights.

He had trouble separating the trailing edges of the dream from reality. Tom stared at the crystal dome of Kithrup's night. His body was locked—legs pulled in, hands clutching opposite shoulders—as much from a rigor of exhaustion as from the cold. Slowly, he got the muscles to loosen. Tendons popped and joints groaned as he learned all over again how to move.

The volcano to the north had died down to only a feeble red glow. There were long, ragged openings in the clouds overhead. Tom watched the pinpoints of light in the sky.

He thought about stars. Astronomy was his mental focus.

Red means cool, he thought. That red one there might be a small, nearby ancient—or a distant giant already in its death throes. And that bright one over there could be a blue supergiant. Very rare. Was there one in this area of space?

He ought to remember.

Tom blinked. The blue "star" was moving.

He watched it drift across the starfield, until it intercepted another bright pinpoint, this one a brilliant green. There was a flash as the two tiny lights met. When the blue spark moved on, the green was gone.

Now what were the chances I'd witness that? How likely was it that I'd be looking at just the right place at the right time? The battle must still be pretty hot and heavy up there. It isn't over yet.

Tom tried to rise, but his body sagged back against the bed of vines.

Okay, try again.

He rolled over onto one elbow, paused to marshal his strength, then pushed upright.

Kithrup's small, dim moons were absent, but there was enough starlight to make out the eerie weedscape. Water sluiced through the shifting morass. There were croaking and slithering sounds. Once he heard a tiny scream that choked off—some small prey suddenly dying, he supposed.

He was thankful for the obstinacy that had brought him to this modest height. Even two meters made a difference. He couldn't have survived a night down in that loathsome mess.

He turned stiffly and began groping through his meager supplies on the crude sledge. First priority was to get warm. He pulled the top piece of his wetsuit from the jumbled pile, and gingerly slid into it.

Tom knew he should give some attention to his wounds, but they could wait just a little longer. So could a full meal—he had salvaged enough stores for a few of those.

Munching on a foodbar and taking sparing sips from a canteen, Tom appraised his small pile of equipment. At the moment what mattered were his three psi-bombs.

He looked up at the sky. Except for a faint purple haze near one bright star, there were no more signs of the battle. Yet that one glimpse had been enough. Tom already knew which bomb to set off.

Gillian had spent a few hours with the Niss machine before leaving *Streaker* to meet him at Toshio's island. She had connected the Tymbrimi device to the Thennanin micro-

branch *Library* he had salvaged. Then she and the Niss had
worked out the proper signals to load into the bombs.

The most important was the Thennanin distress call.
Ifni's fickle luck permitting, it would let Tom perform the
crucial experiment, to find out if the Plan would work.

All of the work Suessi and Tsh't and the others had put
into the "Trojan Seahorse" would come to naught if Thennanin
were not amongst those left in the war. What use would
it be for *Streaker* to slip inside a hollowed-out Thennanin
hulk, to rise into space in disguise, if all the combatants
would shoot anyway at a remnant of a faction which had
already lost?

Tom picked up one psi-bomb. It was spherical, and
rested in his hand like an orb. At the top was a safety switch
and timer. Gillian had carefully labeled each bomb on a strip
of tape. On this one she had added a flowing signature and a
small heart with an arrow through it.

Tom smiled and brought the bomb to his lips.

He had felt guilty of machismo, insisting on being the
one to come here while she remained behind. Now he knew
he had been right. Tough and competent as Gillian was, she
wasn't as good a pilot as he, and probably would have died in
the crash. She certainly wouldn't have had the physical
strength to haul the sledge this far.

Hell, he thought. *I'm glad because she's safe with friends
who'll protect her. That's reason enough. She may be able to
lick ten Blenchuq cave lizards with one hand tied, but she's
my lady, and I'll not let harm come near her if I can help
it.*

Tom washed down the last of the protein bar. He hefted
the bomb and considered strategy. His original plan had been
to land near the volcano, wait until the glider had recharged
for launching, then plant the bomb and take flight before it
went off. He could have ridden thermals from the volcano to
a good altitude and found another island from which to watch
the results of his experiment.

Lacking another island, he still could have gone far
enough, landed in the ocean, and used his telescope to watch
from there.

It was a nice plan, foiled by a raging storm and an
unexpected jungle of mad vines. His telescope had joined the
metal detritus at the bottom of Kithrup's world-sea, along
with most of the wreckage of his solar plane.

Tom rose carefully to his feet. Food and warmth made it merely an exercise in controlled agony.

Rummaging through his few belongings, he tore a long, narrow strip of cloth from the tattered ruins of his sleeping bag. The swatch of tough insu-silk seemed adequate.

The psi-bomb felt heavy and substantial in his hand. It was hard to imagine that the globe was stuffed with powerful illusions—a super-potent conterfeit, ready to burst free on command.

He set the timer for two hours and thumbed the safety release, arming the thing.

He laid it carefully into his makeshift sling. Tom knew he was being dramatic. Distance wouldn't help him much. Sensors all over the Kithrup system would light up when it went off. He might as well set it off at his feet.

Still, one never knew. He'd toss it as far away as he could.

He let the sling sway a few times to get the feel of it, then he began swinging it. Slowly, at first, he built up momentum, while a strange feeling of well-being spread outward from his chest into his arms and legs. Fatigue seemed to fall away. He started to sing.

> Oh, Daddy was a caveman,
> He played ball in skins, with shirts.
> He dreamed of lights up in the sky,
> While scratching in the dirt.
>
> You ETs and your stars....
>
> Oh, Daddy was a fighter,
> He killed his cousins, fourth and third.
> He dreamed of peace eternally,
> And died speared to the earth.
>
> You ETs and your stars...
>
> Oh, Daddy was a lover,
> And yet he beat his wife.
> He dreamed, longing for sanity
> Regretting all his life.
>
> You ETs and your stars...

Oh, Daddy was a leader,
He dreamed, yet still told lies.
He got the frightened masses,
To put missiles in the skies.

You ETs and your stars...

Oh, Daddy was unlearned,
But ever on he tried.
He hated his damned ignorance,
And struggled with his pride...

He stepped up on a bootstrap, then
And, up on nothing, cried.
That tragic orphan willed to me,
A mind and heart, then died.

So scorn me as a wolfling,
Sneer at my orphan's scars!
But tell me, boys, "WHAT'S *YOUR* EXCUSE?"
You ETs, and your stars?

You Eatees and your stars!

Tom's shoulders flexed as he took a step. His arm snapped straight, and he released the sling. The bomb sailed high into the night, whirling like a top. The spinning sphere shone briefly, still climbing, sparkling until it disappeared from sight. He listened, but never heard it land.

Tom stood still for a while, breathing deeply.

Well, he thought at last. That *built an appetite. I have two hours in which to eat, tend my wounds, and prepare a shelter. Any time I get after that, O Lord, will be accepted with humble gratitude.*

He laid the ragged strip of cloth over his shoulder and turned to prepare himself a meal by starlight.

PART FIVE

Concussion

"*In a world older and more complex than ours, they move finished and complete, gifted with extensions of the senses we have lost or never attained, living by voices we shall never hear . . . they are other nations, caught with ourselves in the net of life and time . . .*"

—HENRY BATESON

PART FIVE

Conclusion

46

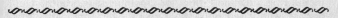

Sah'ot

It was evening, and the Kiqui were leaving for their hunting grounds. Sah'ot heard them squeaking excitedly as they gathered in a clearing west of the toppled drill-tree. The hunters passed not far from the pool on their way to a rock chimney on the southern slope of the island, chittering and puffing their lung sacks in pomp.

Sah'ot listened until the abos were gone. Then he sank a meter below the surface and blew depressed bubbles. Nothing was going right.

Dennie had changed, and he didn't like it. Instead of her usual delightful skittishness, she virtually ignored him. She had listened to two of his best limericks and answered seriously, completely missing the delicious double entendres.

In spite of the importance of her studies of the Kiqui, Takkata-Jim had ordered her also to analyze the drill-tree system for Charles Dart. Twice she had gone into the water to collect samples from below the metal-mound. She had ignored Sah'ot's nuzzling advances or, even more disturbing, petted him absently in return.

Sah'ot realized that, for all of his previous efforts to break her down, he hadn't really wanted her to change. At least, not *this* way.

He drifted unhappily until a tether attached to one of the sleds brought him up short. His new assignment kept him linked to this electrical obscenity, chafed and cramped in a tiny pool while his real work was out in the open sea with the pre-sentients!

When Gillian and Keepiru left, he had assumed their absence would free him to do pretty much what he wanted. Hah! No sooner had the pilot and the human physician left, than did Toshio—*Toshio*, of all persons—step in and assume command.

I should have been able to talk rings around him. How in the Five Galaxies did the boy manage to get the upper hand?

It was hard to remember how. But here he was, stuck monitoring a damned robot for a pompous, egocentric chimpanzee who cared only about rocks! The dumb little robot didn't even have a brain one could TALK to! You don't have conversations with microprocessors. You tell them what to do, then helplessly watch the disaster when they take you literally!

His harness gave off a chime. It was time to check on the probe. Sah'ot clucked a sarcastic response.

> * *Yes indoody,*
>   *Lord and master!*
> * *Metal moron,*
>   *And disaster!*
> * *Beep again,*
>   *I'll work faster!*

Sah'ot brought his left eye even with the sled's screen. He sent a pulse-code to the robot, and a stream of data returned.

The 'bot had finally digested the most recent rock sample. He ordered the probe's small memory emptied into the sled's data banks. Toshio had run him through the drill until Sah'ot could control the 'bot almost unconsciously.

He made it anchor one end of a monofilament line to the rough rock, then lower itself another fifty meters.

The old explanation for the hole beneath the metal-mound had been discarded. The drill-tree couldn't have needed to dig a tunnel a kilometer deep in search of nutrients. It shouldn't have been *able* to pierce the crust that far. The mass of the drill root was clearly too great to have been rotated by the modest tree that once stood atop the mound.

The amount of material excavated wouldn't fit atop ten metal-mounds. It was found as sediment all around the high ridge on which the mound sat.

To Sah'ot these mysteries weren't enticing. They only proved once again that the universe was weird, and that maybe humans and dolphins and chimps ought to wait a while before challenging its deeper puzzles.

The robot finished its descent. Sah'ot made it reach out and seize the cavity wall with diamond-tipped claws, then retract its tether from above.

Down in stages it would go. For this little machine there would be no rising. Sah'ot felt that way himself, sometimes, especially since coming to Kithrup. He didn't really expect ever to leave this deadly world.

Fortunately, the probe's sampling routine was fairly automatic once triggered. Even Charles Dart should have little excuse to complain. Unless...

Sah'ot cursed. There it was again—the static that had plagued the probe since it had passed the half-kilometer mark. Toshio and Keepiru had worked on it, and couldn't find the problem.

The crackling was unlike any static Sah'ot had ever heard...not that he was an expert on static. It had a syncopation of sorts, not all that unpleasant to listen to, actually. Sah'ot had heard that some people liked to listen to white noise. Certainly nothing was more undemanding.

The clock on his harness ticked away. Sah'ot listened to the static, and thought about perversities, about love and loneliness.

> ** I swim—*
> *circles—*   *like the others*
> *And learn *—*
> *sadly—*   *I am*
> *Sightlessly *—*
> *Sighing—*   *alone*

Slowly Sah'ot realized he had adopted the rhythm of the "noise" below. He shook his head. But when he listened again it was still there.

A song. It was a song!

Sah'ot concentrated. It was like trying to follow all parts of a six-part fugue at the same time. The patterns interleaved with an incredible complexity.

No wonder they had all thought it noise! Even *he* had barely caught on!

His harness timer chimed, but Sah'ot didn't notice. He was too busy listening to the planet sing to him.

47

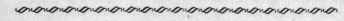

Streaker

Moki and Haoke had both volunteered for guard duty, but for different reasons.

Both enjoyed getting out of the ship for a change. And neither dolphin particularly minded having to stay plugged in to a sled for hours at a stretch in the dark, silent waters outside the ship.

But beyond that they differed. Haoke was there because he felt it was a necessary job. Moki, on the other hand, hoped guard duty would give him a chance to kill something.

"I wissshh Takkata-Jim sent me after Akki, instead of K'tha-Jon," Moki rasped. "I could've tracked the smartasss just as well."

Moki's sled rested about twenty yards from Haoke's, on the high underwater bluff overlooking the ship. Arc lamps still shone on *Streaker's* hull, but the area was deserted now, off-limits to all but those few cleared by the vice-captain.

Moki looked at Haoke through the flexible bubble-dome of his sled. Haoke was silent, as usual. He had ignored Moki's comment completely.

Arrogant spawn of a stink-squid! Haoke was another *Tursiops* smart-aleck, like Creideiki and that stuck up little midshipfin, Akki.

Moki made a small sound-sculpture in his mind. It was an image of ramming and tearing. Once, he had put Creideiki in the role of the victim. The captain who had so often caught him goldbricking, and embarrassed him by correcting his Anglic grammar, had finally got his just deserts. Moki was glad, but

ow he needed another fantasy target. It was no fun to
magine ripping into nobody in particular.

The Calafian, Akki, served well when it was discovered
hat the young middie had betrayed the vice-captain. Moki
ad hoped to be the one sent after Akki, but Takkata-Jim had
rdered K'tha-Jon out instead, explaining that the purpose
vas to bring Akki back for discipline, not to commit murder.

The giant had seemed oblivious to such nice distinc-
ions when he departed equipped with a powerful laser rifle.
'erhaps Takkata-Jim had less than perfect control over K'tha-
on, and had sent him away for his own safety. From the
leam in K'tha-Jon's eye, Moki did not envy the Calafian
rhen the youth was found.

Let K'tha-Jon *have* Akki! One small pleasure lost didn't
ake away much from Moki's overall joy.

It was good to be BIG, for a change! On his off-duty
ime, everybody got out of Moki's way, as if he was a pod
eader! Already he had his eye on one or two of those sexy
ttle females in Makanee's sick bay. Some of the younger
nales looked good, too... Moki wasn't particular.

They would all come around soon enough, when they
aw the way the current pulled. He briefly resisted an urge,
ut couldn't help himself. He let out a short skirr of triumph
1 a forbidden form.

> \# *Glory!* is, is,
>> *Glory!*
> \# *Biting* is   *and Glory!*
>> *Females submit!*
> \# *A new bull is!*   is! \#

He saw Haoke react at last. The other guard jerked
lightly and raised his head to regard Moki. He was silent,
hough, as Moki met his eye defiantly. Moki sent a focused
eam of sonar directly at Haoke, to show he was listening to
im, too!

Arrogant stink-squid! Haoke would get his, too, after
akkata-Jim had locked his jaws on the situation. And the
nen of Earth would never disapprove, because Big-Human
Aetz was at Takkata-Jim's side, agreeing with everything!

Moki let out another squeal of Primal, tasting the forbid-
len primitiveness with delight. It pulled at something deep
nside him. Each taste brought on further hunger for it.

Let Haoke click in disgust! Moki dared even the *Galactic*
to come and try to interfere with him and his new captain!

Haoke bore Moki's bestial squawking stoically. But i
reminded him that he had joined up with a gang of cretin
and misfits.

Unfortunately, the cretins and misfits were *right*, and th
brightest of *Streaker*'s crew were caught up in a disastrou
misadventure.

Haoke was desperately sad over the crippling of Creideiki
The captain had obviously been among the best the bree
could produce. But the accident had made possible a quie
and perfectly legal change in policy, and he couldn't regre
that. Takkata-Jim at least recognized the foolishness of pursu
ing the desperate Trojan Seahorse scheme.

Even if *Streaker could* be moved silently to the Thennanin
wreck, and *if* Tsh't's crew had miraculously set things up s
Streaker could wear the hulk as a gigantic disguise—an
actually take off under those conditions—what would that wi
them?

Even if Thomas Orley had reported that Thennanin wer
still in the battle in space, there remained the question c
fooling those Thennanin into coming to rescue a suppose
lost battleship, and escorting it to the rear. A dubious chance

The question was moot. Orley was obviously dead. Ther
had been no word for days, and now the gamble had turne
into a desperate wish.

Why not just give the thrice-damned Galactics what the
want! Why this romantic nonsense of saving the data for th
Terragens Council. What do *we* care about a bunch of danger
ous long-lost hulks, anyway? It's obviously no business of our
if the Galactics want to fight over the derelict fleet. Even th
Kithrup aboriginals weren't worth dying for.

It all seemed plain to Haoke. It was also apparent t
Takkata-Jim, whose intelligence Haoke respected.

But if it was so obvious, why did people like Creideik
and Orley and Hikahi disagree?

Quandaries like this were the sort of thing that had kep
Haoke a SubSec in the engine room instead of trying fo
non-com or officer, as his test scores had indicated.

Moki blatted another boast-phrase in Primal. It was eve
louder, this time. The *Stenos* was trying to get a rise out of him

Haoke sighed. Many of the crew had begun behaving that way, not quite as bad as Moki, but bad enough. And it wasn't just *Stenos*, either. Some of the *Stenos* were behaving better than some *Tursiops*. As morale dissolved, so did the motivation to maintain Keneenk, to keep up the daily fight against the animal side that always wanted out. One would hardly have been able to predict, weeks ago, who later turned out to be the most susceptible.

Of course, all the best crewfen were away, with Suessi and Hikahi.

Fortunately, Haoke thought. He dwelt on the irony of good going to bad, and right coming out of wrong. At least Takkata-Jim seemed to understand how he felt, and didn't hold it against him. The vice-captain had taken Haoke's support with gratitude.

He could hear Moki's tail thrash, but, before the angry little *Stenos* could voice another taunt, both of their sled speakers came to life.

"Haoke and Moki? CommSec Fin Heurka-pete calling . . . Ack-cknowledge!"

The call was from the ship's comm and detection operator. The fact that the jobs had been combined showed just how bad things were.

"Roger, Haoke here. Moki's indisposed at the moment. What'sss up?"

He heard Moki choke a protest. But it was clear the fin would be a while reformatting his mind for Anglic.

"We have a sonic bogey to the east-t, Haoke . . . sounds like a sled. If hostile, destroy. If it's someone from the island, they must be turned back-ck. If they refuse, shoot to disable the sled!"

"Understood. Haoke and Moki on our way."

"All right, gabby," he told the speech-tied Moki. Haoke gave his partner a long, narrow grin. "Let'sss check it out. And watch that trigger! We're only enforcing a quarantine. We don't shoot at crewmates unless we absolutely have to!"

With a neural impulse, he turned his sled motor on. Without looking back, he lifted off from the muddy rise, then accelerated slowly to the east.

Moki watched Haoke head out before turning his sled to follow.

> \# *Tempted, tempted . . . tempted, Moki, is, is*
> \# *Temptation, delicious is—is—is!* \#

The sleds dropped, one after another, into the gloom. On a passive sonar screen they were small, blurry dots that drifted slowly past the shadow of the seamount, then disappeared behind it.

Keepiru opened his harness's right claw and dropped the portable listening unit. It tumbled down to the soft ooze. He turned to Gillian.

> * *Done and gone—*
>   *They chase our shadows*
> * *They'll not like—*
>   *To catch false prey!* *

Gillian had expected guards. Several kilometers back they had left the sled on delayed automatic, and swam off to the north and west. By the time the sled started up again, they had circled to a few hundred yards west of the outlock.

Gillian touched Keepiru's flank. The sensitive hide trembled under her hand. "You remember the plan, Keepiru?"

> * *Need you ask?* *

Gillian raised an eyebrow in surprise. A triple upsweep trill and a wavering interrogative click? That was an unusually brief and straightforward reply for Trinary. Keepiru was capable of more subtlety than she had thought.

"Of course not, dear bow-wave rider. I apologize. I'll do my part, and I'll not worry for a moment about you doing yours."

Keepiru looked at her as if wishing he didn't have to wear a breather. As if he wanted to speak to her in *her* native language. Gillian felt some of this in a gentle telepathic touch.

She hugged his smooth gray torso. "You take care, Keepiru. Remember that you're admired and loved. Very much so."

The pilot tossed his head.

> * To swimming—or
>   Battle
> * To warning—or
>   Rescue
> * To earning—your
>   Trust *

They dropped over the edge of the bluff and swam quickly for the ship's outer lock.

48

Takkata-Jim

It was impossible to rest.

Takkata-Jim envied humans the total unconsciousness they called sleep. When a man lay down for the night, his awareness of the world disappeared, and the nerves to his muscles deactivated. If he *did* dream, he usually didn't have to participate *physically*.

Even a neo-dolphin couldn't just turn himself off that way. One or the other hemisphere of the brain was always on sentry duty to control his breathing. Sleep, for a fin, was both a milder and a far more serious thing.

He knocked about the captain's stateroom, wishing he could go back to his own, smaller cabin. But symbolism was important to the crew he had inherited. His followers needed more than the logic of legality to confirm his command. They needed to see him as the New Bull. And that meant living in the style of the former herd leader.

He took a long breath at the surface and emitted clicks to illuminate the room in sound-images.

Creideiki certainly had eclectic tastes. Ifni knew what sorts of things the former captain had owned which couldn't stand wetness, and had therefore been stowed away before *Streaker* landed on Kithrup. The collection that remained was striking.

Works by artists of a dozen sentient races lay sealed behind glass cases. Sound-stroke photos of strange worlds and weird, aberrant stars adorned the walls.

Creideiki's music system was impressive. He had recordings by the thousands, songs and eerie . . . *things* that made Takkata-Jim's spine crawl when he played them. The collection of whale ballads was valuable, and a large fraction appeared to have been collected personally.

By the desk comm, there was a photo of Creideiki with the officers of the *James Cook*. Captain Helene Alvarez herself had signed it. The famous explorer had her arm over her dolphin exec's broad, smooth back as she and Creideiki mugged for the camera.

Takkata-Jim had served on important ships—cargo vessels supplying the Atlast and Calafia colonies—but he had never been on missions like those of the legendary *Cook*. *He* had never seen such sights, nor heard such sounds.

Until the Shallow Cluster . . . until they found dead ships the size of moons. . . .

He thrashed his tail in frustration. His flukes struck the ceiling painfully. His breath came heavily.

It didn't matter. Nothing that he had done would matter if he succeeded! If he got *Streaker* away from Kithrup with her crew alive! If he did that, he would have a photo of his own. And the arm on his back would be that of the President of the Confederacy of Earth.

A shimmering collection of tiny motes began to collect to his right. The sparkles coalesced into a holographic image, a few inches from his eye.

"Yess, what is it!" he snapped.

An agitated dolphin, harness arms flexing and unflexing, nodded nervously. It was the ship's purser, Suppeh.

"Sssir! Sssomething strange has happened. We weren't sssure we should wake you, but-t-t . . ."

Takkata-Jim found the fin's Underwater Anglic almost indecipherable. Suppeh's upper register warbled uncontrollably.

"Calm down and talk slowly!" he commanded sharply. The fin flinched, but made an effort to obey.

"I . . . I was in the outlock-k. I heard someone say there

was an alert-t. Heurka-pete sent Haoke and Moki after sled-sounds . . ."

"Why wasn't I informed?"

Suppeh recoiled in dismay. For a moment he appeared too frightened to speak. Takkata-Jim sighed and kept his voice calm. "Never mind. Not your fault. Go on."

Visibly relieved, Suppeh continued. "A f-few minutes later, the light on the personnel outlock-k came on. Wattaceti went over, and I p-p-paid no heed. But when Life-Cleaner and Wormhole-Pilot entered . . ."

Takkata-Jim spumed. Only dire need to hear Suppeh's story without delay prevented him from crashing about the room in frustration!

". . . tried to stop them, as you ordered, but-t Wattaceti and Hiss-kaa were doing back flipsss of joy, and dashed about fetching for them both-th!"

"Where are they now?" Takkata-Jim demanded.

"Bassskin entered the main bay, with Wattaceti. Hiss-kaa is off, spreading rumorsss throughout the ship. Keepiru took a sled and breathers and is gone!"

"Gone where?"

"Back-k-k out-t-t!" Suppeh wailed. His command of Anglic was rapidly dissolving. Takkata-Jim took advantage of what composure the purser had left.

"Have Heurka-pete awaken Doctor Metz. Have Metz meet me at sick bay with three guards. *You* are to go to the dry-wheel dressing room, with Sawtoot, and let-t no one enter! Understood?"

Suppeh nodded vigorously, and his image vanished.

Takkata-Jim prayed that Heurka-pete would have the sense to recall Moki and Haoke and send them after Keepiru. Together, between Haoke's brains and Moki's feral ruthlessness, they might be able to cut the pilot off before he reached the Thennanin wreck.

Why isn't K'tha-Jon back yet? I chose him to go after that middie in order to get him out of the ship for a while. I was afraid he was becoming dangerous even to me. I wanted some time to organize without him around. But now the Baskin woman's returned sooner than I expected. Maybe I should have kept K'tha-Jon around. The giant's talents might be useful about now.

Takkata-Jim whistled the door open and swam out into

the hall. He faced a confrontation he had hoped to put off for
at least another forty hours, if not indefinitely.

*Should I have seen to Creideiki before this? It would
have been easy . . . a power failure in his gravity tank, a
switched catheter . . . Metz would not approve, but there was
already much of which Metz did not know. Much that Takkata-
Jim wished he didn't know.*

He swam hard for the intrahull lift.

*Maybe I won't need K'tha-Jon in order to deal with
Gillian Baskin,* he thought. *After all, what can one human
female do?*

49

The Psi-Bomb

The mound of partly dried weeds formed a dome on the
sea of vines. Tom had propped up a low roof using salvaged
bits of strutting from his sledge, making a rude cave. He sat
in the entrance, waiting in the pre-dawn dimness, and munched
on one of his scarce foodbars.

His wounds were cleaned as well as possible, and coated
with hardening dabs of medicinal foam. With food in his
stomach and some of the pain put down, he almost felt
human again.

He examined his small osmotic still. The upper part, a
clear bag with a filtered spout at one end, held a thick layer
of saltwater and sludge. Below the filter, one of his canteens
sat almost filled.

Tom looked at his watch. Only five minutes remained.
There was no time to dip for another load of scummy water to
feed the still. He wouldn't even be able to clean the filters
before the bomb went off.

He picked up the canteen, screwed its cap tight, and
slipped it into a thigh pouch. He popped the filter out of its

frame and shook most of the sludge out before folding it tightly and tucking it under his belt. The filter probably didn't take out all the dissolved metal salts in the water. It hadn't been designed with Kithrup in mind. Nonetheless, the little package was probably his most valuable possession.

Three minutes, the glowing numbers on his watch told him.

Tom looked up at the sky. There was a vague brightening in the east, and the stars were starting to fade. It would be a clear morning, and therefore bitterly cold. He shivered and zipped the wetsuit tight. He pulled in his knees.

One minute.

When it came it would be like the loudest sound he had ever heard. Like the brightest light. There would be no keeping it out.

He wanted to cover his ears and eyes, as if against a real explosion. Instead, he stared at a point on the horizon and counted, pacing each breath. Deliberately he let himself slide into a trance.

"... seven ... eight ... nine ... ten ..." A lightness filled his chest. The feeling spread outward, numbing and soothing.

Light from the few stars in the west diffracted spiderweb rays through his barely separated eyelashes as he awaited a soundless explosion.

"Sah'ot, I said I'm ready to take *over* now!"

Sah'ot squirmed and looked up at Toshio. "Just-t another few minutess, OK? I'm listening to ssssomething!"

Toshio frowned. This was *not* what he had expected from Sah'ot! He had come to relieve the dolphin linguist early because Sah'ot *hated* working with the robot probe!

"What's going on, Tosh?"

Dennie sat up in her sleeping bag, rubbing her eyes and peering in the pre-dawn dark.

"I don't know, Dennie. I offered to take over the robot, so Sah'ot wouldn't have to deal with Charlie when he calls. But he refuses to let go."

Dennie shrugged. "Then I'd say that's his business. What do you care, anyway?"

Toshio felt a sharp answer rise to his lips, but he kept them locked and turned away. He would ignore Dennie until she awakened fully and decided to behave civilly.

Dennie had surprised him after Gillian and Keepiru left,

by taking his new command without complaint. For the last two days, she hadn't seemed much interested in anything but her microscopes and samples, ignoring even Sah'ot's desultory sexual innuendo, and answering questions in monosyllables.

Toshio knelt by the comm unit attached by cable to Sah'ot's sled. He tapped out a query on the monitor and frowned at the result.

"Sah'ot!" he said severely. "Get over here!"

"In a ssssec..." The dolphin sounded distracted.

Toshio pursed his lips.

> * NOW, you will to HERE
>   Ingather
> * Or shortly cease ALL
>   Listening further! *

He heard Dennie gasp behind him. She probably didn't understand the Trinary burst in detail, but she got the basic idea. Toshio felt justified. This was a test. He wasn't able to be as subtle as Gillian Baskin, but he had to get obedience or he would be useless as an officer.

Sah'ot stared up at him, blinking dazedly. Then the fin sighed and moved over to the side of the pool.

"Sah'ot, you haven't taken any geological readings in four hours! Yet in that time you've dropped the probe two hundred meters! What's got into you!"

The *Stenos* rolled from side to side uncertainly. Finally, he spoke softly. "I'm get-tting a sssong..."

The last word faded before Toshio could be sure of it. He looked at the neo-fin civilian, unable to believe his ears. "You're getting a *what*?"

"A ssssong...?"

Toshio lifted his hands and dropped them to his sides. *He's finally cracked*, he thought. *First Dennie, now Sah'ot. I've been left in charge of two mental cases!*

He sensed Dennie approach the pool. "Listen, Sah'ot," Toshio said. "Dr. Dart will be calling soon. What do you think he's going to say when..."

"I'll take care of Charlie when he calls," Dennie said quietly.

"You?" Dennie had spent the last forty hours cursing over the drill-tree problem she had been assigned, at Takkata-Jim's order and Charles Dart's request. It had almost completely superseded her work with the Kiqui. Toshio couldn't imagine her *wanting* to talk with the chimpanzee.

"Yes, me. What I have to tell him may make him forget all about the robot, so you just lay off Sah'ot. If he says he heard singing, well, maybe he's heard singing."

Toshio stared at her, then shrugged. *Fine. My job is to protect these two, not to correct their scientific blunders. I just hope Gillian straightens things out back at the ship so I can report what's going on here.*

Dennie knelt down by the water to talk to Sah'ot. She spoke slowly and earnestly, patient with the Anglic slowness he suffered after his long seance with the robot.

Dennie wanted to dive to look at the core of the metal-mound. Sah'ot agreed to accompany her if she would wait until he had transcribed some more of his "music." Dennie assented, apparently completely unafraid of going into the water with Sah'ot.

Toshio sat down and waited for the inevitable buzz of the comm line from the ship. People were changing overnight, and he hadn't the slightest idea why!

His eyes felt scratchy. Toshio rubbed them, but that didn't seem to help.

He blinked and tried to look at Dennie and Sah'ot. The difficulty he was having focusing only seemed to be getting worse. A haziness began to spread between himself and the pool. Suddenly he felt a sense of dread expectancy. Pulsing, it seemed to migrate from the back of his head to a place between his shoulder blades.

He brought his hands to his ears. "Dennie? Sah'ot? Do you . . . ?" He shouted the last words, but could barely hear his own voice.

The others looked up at him. Dennie rose and took a step toward him, concern on her face.

Then her eyes opened in wide surprise. Toshio saw a blur of movement at the edges of his field of view. Then there were *Kiqui* in the forest, charging them through the bushes!

Toshio tried to draw his needler, knowing it was already too late. The aboriginals were already upon them, waving their short arms and screaming in tiny, high-pitched voices. Three plowed into him and two toppled Dennie. He struggled and fell beneath them, fighting to keep their slashing claws away from his face while the grating noise erupted in his brain.

Then, in an instant, the Kiqui were gone!

Amidst the grinding roar in his head, Toshio forced himself to turn over and look up.

Dennie tossed back and forth across the ground moaning, clutching at her ears. Toshio feared she had been wounded by Kiqui claws, but when she rolled his way he saw only shallow cuts.

With both shaking hands, he drew his needler. The few Kiqui in sight weren't heading this way, but squealing as they rushed the pool and dove in.

It's not their doing, he realized dimly.

He recognized the "sound" of a thousand fingernails scraping across a blackboard.

A psi attack! We have to hide! Water might cushion the assault. We should dive in, like the abos did!

His head roared as he crawled toward the pool. Then he stopped.

I can't drag Dennie in there, and we can't put on our breathing gear while shaking like this!

He reversed direction until he reached a pool-side tree. He sat up, with his back against the bole. He tried to concentrate, in spite of the crashing in his brain.

Remember what Mr. Orley taught you, middie! Think *about your mind, and go within. SEE the enemy's illusions . . . listen lightly to his lies . . . use the Yin and the Yang . . . the twin salvations . . . logic to pierce Mara's veil . . . and faith to sustain. . . .*

Dennie moaned and rolled in the dust a few meters away. Toshio laid the needler on his lap, to have it ready when the enemy came. He called to Dennie, shouting over the screaming noise.

"*Dennie!* Listen to your heartbeat! Listen to each breath! *They're* real sounds! This isn't!"

He saw her turn slightly toward his voice, agony in her eyes as she pressed white bloodless hands over her ears. The shrieking intensified.

"Count your heartbeats, Dennie! They're . . . they're like the *ocean,* like the surf! Dennie!" He shouted. "Have you ever heard any sound that can overcome the surf? Can . . . can anything or *anybody* scream loud enough to keep the tide from laughing *back?*"

She stared at him, trying. He could see her inhaling deeply, mouthing slowly as she counted.

"Yes! Count, Dennie! Breaths and heartbeats! Is there *any* sound the tide of your heartbeat can't laugh at?"

She locked onto his eyes, as he anchored himself to hers.

Slowly, as the howling within his head reached its crescendo, Toshio saw her nod faintly and give a faint grateful smile.

Sah'ot felt it too. And even as the psychic wave rolled over him, the pool was suddenly afroth with panicky Kiqui. Sah'ot was inundated by a babel of noise from all around and within. It was worse than being blinded by a searchlight.

He wanted to dive away from the cacophony. Biting back panic, he forced himself to lie still.

He tried to separate the noise into parts, the human contribution first. Dennie and Toshio seemed in worse shape than he. Perhaps they were more sensitive to the assault. There would be no help from them!

The Kiqui were in terror, squawling as they crashed into the pool.

> :?: *Flee!*   *Flight . . .*
>   *from the sad great things*
> :?: *Somebody*   *Help*
>   *the great sad hurt things!*

Out of the mouths of babes . . . When he concentrated on it, the "psi attack" *did* feel a bit like a call for help. It hurt like the hell of the deeps, but he faced it and tried to pin it down.

He thought he was making progress—certainly he was coping—when still *another* voice joined in, this one over his neural link! The song from below, that he had spent all night unable to decipher, had awakened. From the bowels of Kithrup it bellowed. Its simplicity *commanded* understanding.

> + *WHO*   *CALLS?* −
> − *WHO DARES BOTHER* +

Sah'ot moaned as he tore the robot link free. Three screaming noises, all at different levels of mind, were quite enough. Any more and he would go insane!

Buoult of the Thennanin was afraid, though an officer in the service of the Great Ghosts thought nothing of death or of living enemies.

The shuttle cycled through the lock of his flagship, *Quegsfire*. The giant doors, comfortingly massive and enduring, swung shut behind them. The shuttle pilot plotted a course to the Tandu flagship.

Tandu.

Buoult flexed his ridge crest as a display of confidence. He would lose heat from the sail of nerves and blood vessels in the frigid atmosphere of the Tandu ship, but it was absolutely necessary to maintain appearances.

It might have been slightly less distasteful to make an alliance with the Soro instead. At least the Soro were more Thennaninoid than the arthropod Tandu, and lived at a decent temperature. Also, the Soro's clients were interesting folk, the sort Buoult's people might have liked to uplift themselves.

Better for them if we had, he thought. *For we are kind patrons.*

If the leathern Soro were meddlesome and callous, the spindly Tandu were horrifying beings. Their clients were weird creatures that set off twitches at the base of Buoult's tail when he thought of them.

Buoult grimaced in disgust. Politics made for strange gene transfers. The Soro were now strongest among the survivors. The Thennanin were weakest of the major powers. Although the Tandu philosophy was the most repulsive of those in opposition to the Abdicator Creed, they were now all that stood in the way of a Soro triumph. The Thennanin must ally with them, for now.

Should the Tandu seem about to prevail, there would be another chance to switch sides. It had happened a number of times already, and would happen again.

Buoult steeled himself for the meeting ahead. He was determined not to let show any of his dread of stepping aboard a Tandu ship!

The Tandu didn't seem to care what chances they took with their crazy, poorly understood probability drive. The insane reality manipulations of their Episiarch clients often let them move about more quickly than their opponents. But sometimes the resulting alterations of spacetime swallowed whole groups of ships, impartially snatching the Tandu and their enemies from the universe forever! It was madness!

Just let them not use their perverted drives while I am aboard, Buoult's organs-of-prayer subvocalized. *Let us make our battle plans and be done*.

The Tandu ships came into sight, crazy, stilt-like structures that disdained armor for wild speed and power.

Of course even these unusual ships were mere variations of ancient *Library* designs. The Tandu were daring, but they did not add to their crimes the gaucherie of originality.

Earthlings were in many ways more unconventional than the Tandu. Their sloppy gimmickry was a vulgar habit that came from a poor upbringing.

Buoult wondered what the "dolphins" were doing right now. Pity the poor creatures if the Tandu, or even the Soro got hold of them! Even these primitive sea mammals, clients of a coarse and hairy wolfling race, deserved to be protected, if possible.

Of course there were priorities. They mustn't be allowed to hoard the data they held!

Buoult noticed that his finger-claws had unsheathed in his agitation. He pulled them back and cultivated serenity as the shuttle drew near the Tandu squadron.

Buoult's musing was split by a sudden chill that made his crest tremble . . . a disturbance on a psi band.

"Operator!" he snapped. "Contact the flagship! See if they verify that call!"

"Immediately, General-Protector!"

Buoult controlled his excitement. The psychic energies he felt could be a ruse. Still, they felt right. They bore the image of *Krondorsfire*, which none of them had hoped to see again!

Determination filled him. In the negotiations ahead, he would ask one more favor. The Tandu must provide one added cooperation in exchange for the help of the Thennanin.

"Confirmed, sir. It is battleship *Krondorsfire*," the pilot said, his voice raspy with emotion. Buoult's crest stood erect in acknowledgment. He stared ahead at the looming metal mantis shapes, steeling himself for the confrontation, the negotiations, and the waiting.

Beie Chohooan was listening to whale songs—rare and expensive copies which had cost her a month's pay some time ago—when her detectors picked up the beacon. Reluctantly, she put down her headphones and noted the direction and intensity. There were so many signals...bombs and blasts and traps. It was one of the little wazoon that pointed out to her that this particular beacon emanated from the water-world itself.

Beie groomed her whiskers and considered.

"I believe this will change things, my pretty little ones. Shall we leave this belt of unborn rubble in space and move in a bit closer to the action? Is it time to let the Earthlings know that someone is out here who is a friend?"

The wazoon chittered back that policy was her business. According to union rules, they were spies, not strategists.

Beie approved of their sarcasm. It was very tasty.

"Very well," she said. "Let us try to move closer."

Hikahi hurriedly queried the skiff's battle computer.

"It's a psi weapon of some sort," she announced via hydrophone to the crew working in the alien wreck. Her Anglic was calm and precise, accentuated with the cool overtones of Keneenk. "I detect no other signs of attack, so I believe we're feeling a fringe of the space-battle. We've felt othersss before, if not this intense.

"We're deep underwater, partly shielded from psi-waves. Grit your teeth, *Streakers*. Try to ignore it. Go about your duties in tropic-clear logic."

She switched off the speakers. Hikahi knew Tsh't was even now moving among the workers out there, joking and keeping morale high.

The psi-noise was like a nagging itch, but an itch with a weird rhythm. It pulsed as if in some code she couldn't quite get her jaws around.

She looked at Hannes Suessi, who sat on a wall rail nearby, looking very tired. He had been about to turn in for a few hours' sleep, but the psionic assault apparently affected him even worse than it did the dolphins. He had compared it to fingernails scratching on a blackboard.

"I can think of two possibilities, Hikahi. One would be very good news. The other's about as bad as could be."

She nodded her sleek head. "We've repeatedly rechecked our circuitsss, sent three couriers back with messages, and yet there's only silence from the ship. I must assume the worst."

"That *Streaker*'s been taken," Suessi closed his eyes.

"Yess. This psi havoc comes from somewhere on the surface of the planet. The Galactics may even now be fighting over her—or what's left of her."

Hikahi decided. "I'm returning to *Streaker* in this boat. I'll delay until you've sealed quarters for the work-crew inside the hulk. You need power from the skiff to recharge the Thennanin accumulators."

Suessi nodded. Hikahi was clearly anxious to depart as soon as possible. "I'll go outside and help, then."

"You just got off duty. I cannot permit it."

Suessi shook his head. "Look, Hikahi, when we've got that refuge inside the battleship set up, we can pump in filtered fizzywater for the fen and they'll be able to rest properly. The wreck is well shielded from this psychic screeching, too. And most important, I'll have a room of my own, one that's *dry,* without a crowd of squeaking, practical-joking children goosing me from behind whenever I turn the other way!" His eyes were gently ironic.

Hikahi's jaw made a gentle curve. "Wait a minute, then, Maker of Wonderful Toys. I'll come out and join you. Work will distract usss from the scratching of ET fingernails."

The Soro, Krat, felt no grating tremors. Her ship was girded against psychic annoyances. She first learned of the disturbance from her staff. She took the data scroll from the Pila Cullalberra with mild interest.

They had detected many such signals in the course of the battle. But none yet had emanated from the planet. Only a few skirmishes had taken the war down to Kithrup itself.

Normally she would have simply ordered a homing torpedo dispatched and forgotten the matter. The expected Tandu-Thennanin alliance against the Soro was forming up near the gas-giant world, and she had plans to make. But something about this signal intrigued her.

"Determine the exact origin of this signal on a planetary map," she told the Pila. "Include locations of all known landfalls by enemy ships."

"There would be doz-ens by now, and the pos-itions very vague," the Pil statistician barked. Its voice was high and sharp. Its mouth popped open for each syllable, and hairy cilia waved above its small, black eyes.

Krat did not dignify it with a look. "When the Soro intervened to end Pilan indenture to the Kisa," she hissed, "it was not to make you Grand Elders. Am I to be questioned, like a human who pampers his chimpanzee?"

Cullalberra shivered and bowed quickly. The stocky Pila scuttled away to its data center.

Krat purred happily. Yes, the Pila were *so* close to perfect. Arrogant and domineering with their own clients and neighbors, they scurried to serve the Soro's every whim. How wonderful it was to be a Grand Elder!

She owed the humans something, at that. In a few centuries they had almost replaced the Tymbrimi as the bogeymen to use on recalcitrant clients. They symbolized all that was wrong with Uplift Liberalism. When Terra was finally humbled, and humans were "adopted" into a proper client status, some other bad example would have to serve instead.

Krat opened a private communication line. The display lit up with the image of the Soro Pritil, the young commander of one of the ships in her flotilla.

"Yes, fleet-mother," Pritil bowed slowly and shallowly. "I listen."

Krat's tongues flickered at the young female's insolence. "Ship number sixteen was slow in the last skirmish, Pritil."

"One opinion." Pritil examined her mating claw. She cleaned it in front of the screen, an indelicacy designed to show indifference.

Younger females seldom understood that a real insult should be subtle and require time for the victim to discover it. Krat decided she would teach Pritil this lesson.

"You need a rest for repairs. In the next battle, ship number sixteen would be next to useless. There is, however, a way in which she might win honor, and perhaps the prey, as well."

Pritil looked up, her interest piqued.

"Yes, fleet-mother?"

"We have picked up a call that pretends to be one thing, perhaps an enemy pleading for succor. I suspect it may be something else."

The flavor of intrigue obviously tempted Pritil. "I choose to listen, group-mother."

Krat sighed at the predictability. She knew the younger

captains secretly believed all of the legends about Krat's hunches. She had known Pritil would come around.

You have much yet to learn, she thought, *before you will pull me down and take my place, Pritil. Many learning scars shall have to mar that young hide first. I will enjoy teaching you until that day, my daughter.*

Gillian and Makanee looked up as Takkata-Jim and Dr. Ignacio Metz entered sick bay, accompanied by three stocky, war-harnessed, hard-faced *Stenos*.

Wattaceti squealed an indecipherable indignation and moved to interpose himself. Makanee's assistants chittered behind the ship's surgeon.

Gillian met Makanee's eye. It had come, the confrontation. Now they would see if Makanee was only imagining things. Gillian still held out a hope that Takkata-Jim and Metz had compelling reasons for their actions, and that Creideiki's injury was truly an accident.

Makanee had already made up her mind. Akki, the young midshipfin from Calafia, had still not returned. The doctor glared at Takkata-Jim as she would look at a tiger shark. The expression on the male dolphin's face did little to belie the image.

Gillian had a secret weapon, but she had sworn never to use it except in the direst emergency. *Let them act first,* she thought. *Let them show their cards before we pull that last ace of trumps.*

The first stages might be a little dangerous. She had only had time to make a brief call to the Niss machine from her office before hurrying to sick bay. Her position here might be difficult if she had miscalculated the degree of atavism loose on *Streaker*. Maybe she should have kept Keepiru by her side.

"Dr. Baskin!" Ignacio Metz didn't swim very close before grabbing a wall rail and letting an armed *Stenos* pass before him. "It's good to see you again, but why didn't you announce yourself?"

"A grosss violation of security rules, Doctor," Takkata-Jim added.

So that's the way of it, Gillian thought. And they might try to make that stick long enough to get me into a cell.

"Why, I came for the ship's council meeting, gentlefin

and -mel. I got a message from Dr. Makanee calling me back
for it. Sorry if your bridge crew fouled up my reply. I hear
they're mostly new and inexperienced up there."

Takkata-Jim frowned. It was even possible she *had* sent
such a call, which had been lost in the confusion on the
bridge.

"Makanee's message was also against orderss! And your
return was contrary to my specific instructions."

Gillian put on an expression of bewilderment. "Wasn't
she simply passing on your call for a ship's council? The rules
are clear. You must call a meeting within twenty-four hours of
the death or disability of the captain."

"Preparations were underway! But in an emergency the
acting-captain can dispense with the advice of the council.
When faced with clear disobedience of orders, I am within
rightsss to..."

Gillian tensed herself. Her preparations would do no
good if Takkata-Jim were irrational. She might have to make a
break by vaulting over the row of autodocs to the parapet
above. Her office would be steps away.

"... to order that-t you be detained for a hearing to be
held at some time after the emergency."

Gillian took in the stances of the guard-fen. Would they
really be willing to harm a human being? She read their
expressions and decided they just might be.

Her mouth felt dry, but she didn't let it show. "You
misread your legal status, Lieutenant," she replied carefully.
"I think very few of the fen aboard would be surprised to
learn that..."

The words stopped in her throat. Gillian felt a chill in
her spine as the air itself seemed to waver and throb around
her. Then, as she grabbed a rail for support, a deep, growling
sound began to emanate from *inside* her head.

The others stared at her, confused by her behavior. Then
they began to feel it too.

Takkata-Jim whirled and shouted, "Psi weapon! Makanee,
give me a link to the bridge! We are under attack-k!"

The dolphin physician moved aside, amazed by Takkata-
Jim's quickness as he rushed past. Gillian pressed her hands
over her ears and saw Metz doing the same as the grating
noise grew louder. The security guards were in disarray,
fluting disconsolately with boat-like pupils wide in fear.

Should I make my break now? Gillian tried to think. But

if this *is* an attack we'll have to drop our quarrels and join forces.

"... incompetentsss!" Takkata-Jim shouted at the comm. "What do you mean 'only a thousand miles away'? Pinpoint it-t!... Why *won't* the active sensors work?"

"Wait!" Gillian cried. She clapped her hands together. Through a haze of building emotion she started to laugh. Takkata-Jim continued to bark rapidly at the bridge crew, but everyone else turned to look at her in surprise.

Gillian laughed. She slapped the water, pounded on the nearest autodoc, grabbed Wattaceti around the dolphin's quivering flank. Even Takkata-Jim stopped then, captivated by her apparently psychotic fit of joy. He stared, oblivious to frantic twitters from the bridge.

"Tom!" She cried out loud. "I *told* you you couldn't die! Dammit, I love you, you son of a... Oh, if *I* had gone I would have been *home* by now!"

The fins stared at her, eyes opening still wider as they began to realize what she was talking about.

She laughed, tears running down her face.

"Tom," she said softly. "I *told* you you couldn't die!" And blindly she hugged close whatever was nearest to her.

Sounds came to Creideiki as he drifted in weightlessness.

It was like listening to Beethoven, or like trying actually to *understand* a humpback whale.

Somebody had left the audio link on in case he made any more sounds. No one had considered that the circuit went both ways. Words penetrated the gravity tank from the outer room.

They were tantalizing, like those ghosts of meaning in a great symphony—hinting that the composer had caught a glimpse of something notes could only vaguely convey and words could never even approach.

Takkata-Jim spluttered and mumbled. The threatening tone was clear. So was the cautious clarity of Gillian Baskin's voice. If only he could understand the words! But Anglic was lost to him.

Creideiki knew his ship was in peril, and there was nothing he could do to help. The old gods weren't through with him, and would not let him move. They had much more to show him before he was ready to serve their purposes.

He had become resigned to periodic episodes of terror—

like diving to do battle with a great octopus, then rising for a rest before going back down to the chaos once again. When they came to pull him DOWN he would once more be caught in the maelstrom of idea-glyphs, of throbbing dreams which hammered away at his engineer's mind with insistent impressions of otherness.

The assault never would have been possible without the destruction of his speech centers. Creideiki grieved over the loss of words. He listened to the talk-sounds from the outer world, concentrating as hard as he could on the eerie, musical familiarity.

It wasn't *all* gone, he decided after a while. He could recognize a few words, here and there. Simple ones, mostly the names of objects or people, or simple actions associated with them.

That much his distant ancestors could do.

But he couldn't remember the words more than three or four deep, so it was impossible to follow a conversation. He might laboriously decipher a sentence, only to forget it completely when he worked on the next one. It was agonizingly difficult, and at last he made himself cease the vain effort.

That's not the way, he concluded.

Instead, he should try for the gestalt, he told himself. Use the tricks the old gods had been using on *him*. Encompass. Absorb... like trying to feel what Beethoven felt by submerging into the mystery of the Violin Concerto.

Murmuring sounds of angry sophonts squawked from the speaker. The noises bounced around the chamber and scattered like bitter droplets. After the terrible beauty of DOWN, he felt repelled. He forced himself to listen, to seek a way— some humble way to help *Streaker* and his crew.

Need swelled within him as he concentrated. He sought a center, a focus in the chaotic sounds.

> * *Rancor*
>   *Turbid*
>   *In the rip-tide*
> * *Ignoring*
>   *Sharks!*
>   *Internecine struggle ...*
> * *Inviting*
>   *Sharks!*
>   *Foolish opportunism ...*

Against his will, he felt himself begin to click aloud. He tried to stop, knowing where it would lead, but the clicks emerged involuntarily from his brow, soon joined by a series of low moans.

The sounds of the argument in sick bay drifted away as his own soft singing wove a thicker and thicker web around him. The humming, crackling echoes caused the walls to fade as a new reality took shape all around. A dark presence slowly grew next to him.

Without words, he told it to go away.

: No : We Are Back : You Have More To Learn :

For all I know, you're a delirium of mine! None of you ever make a sound of your own! You always speak in reflections from my own sonar!

: Have Your Echoes Ever Been So Complex? :

Who knows what my unconscious could do? In my memory are more strange sounds than any other living cetacean has heard! I've been where living clouds whistled to tame hurricanes! I've heard the doom-booms of black holes and listened to the songs of stars!

: All The More Reason You Are The One We Want : The One We Need :

I am needed here!

: Indeed.
Come,
Creideiki. :

The old god, K-K-Kph-kree, moved closer. Its sonically translucent form glistened. Its sharp teeth flashed. Figment or not, the great thing began to move, carrying him along, as before, helpless to resist.

: DOWN :

Then, just as resignation washed over Creideiki, he heard a sound. Miraculously, it wasn't one of his own making, diffracted against the insane dream. It came from somewhere else, powerful and urgent!

: Pay No Heed : Come :

Creideiki's mind leaped after it as if it were a school of mullet, even as the noise swelled to deafening volume.

: You Are Sensitized : You Have Psi You Had Not Known Before : You Know Not Yet Its Use : Relinquish Quick Rewards : Come The Hard Way... :

Creideiki laughed, and opened himself to the noise from the outside. It crashed in, dissolving the shining blackness of

the old god into sonic specks that shimmered and then slowly
disappeared.

: **That Way Is Gone For You** :
: **Creideiki . . .** :

Then the great-browed god was gone. Creideiki laughed
at his release from the cruel illusion, grateful for the new
sound that had freed him.

But the noise kept growing. Victory went to panic as it
swelled and became a pressure within his head, pushing
against the walls of his skull, hammering urgently to get out.
The world became a whirling groaning alien cry for help.

Creideiki let out a warbling whistle of despair as he tried
to ride the crashing tide.

50

ᖙᖙᖙᖙᖙᖙᖙᖙᖙᖙᖙᖙᖙᖙᖙᖙᖙᖙᖙᖙᖙᖙ

Streaker

The waves of pseudo-sound were fading at last.

"Creideiki!" Makanee cried and swam to the captain's
tank. The others turned also, just noticing the injured dolphin's
distress.

"What's the matter with him?" Gillian swam up next to
Makanee. She could see the captain struggle feebly, giving off
a slowly diminishing series of low moans.

"I don't know. No one was watching him as the psi-bomb
hit its peak! Just now I saw he was disturbed."

The large, dark gray form within the tank seemed calmer
now. The muscles along Creideiki's back twitched slowly, as
he let out a low, warbling cry.

Ignacio Metz swam up alongside Gillian.

"Ah, Gillian . . ." he began, "I want you to know that I'm
very glad Tom is alive, although this tardiness bodes poorly.
I'd still stake my life that this Trojan Seahorse plan of his is ill
conceived."

"We'll have to discuss that at ship's council, then, won't we, Dr. Metz?" she said coolly.

Metz cleared his throat. "I'm not sure the acting captain will permit . . ." He subsided under her gaze and looked away.

She glanced at Takkata-Jim. If he did anything rash, it could be the last straw that broke *Streaker*'s morale. Gillian had to convince Takkata-Jim that he would lose if he contested with her. And he had to be offered a way out, or there might still be civil war aboard the ship.

Takkata-Jim looked back at her with a mixture of pure hostility and calculation. She saw the sound-sensitive tip of his jaw swing toward each of the fen in turn, gauging their reaction. The news that Thomas Orley still lived would go through the ship like a clarion. Already one of the armed *Stenos* guards, presumably carefully picked by the vice-captain, looked mutinously jubilant and chattered hopefully with Wattaceti.

I've got to act fast, Gillian realized. *He's desperate.*

She swam toward Takkata-Jim, smiling. He backed away, a loyal *Stenos* glaring at her from his side.

Gillian spoke softly, so the others could not hear.

"Don't even think it, Takkata-Jim. The fen aboard this ship have Tom Orley fresh on their minds now. If you thought you could harm me before this, even you know better now."

Takkata-Jim's eyes widened, and Gillian knew she had struck on target, capitalizing on the legend of her psi ability. "Besides, I'm going to stick close to Ignacio Metz. He's gullible, but if he witnesses me being harmed, you'll lose him. You need a token man, don't you? Without at least one, even your *Stenos* will melt away."

Takkata-Jim clapped his jaw loudly.

"Don't try to bully *me*! I don't have to *harm* you. I am the legal authority on this ship. I can have you confined to quarterssss!"

Gillian looked at her fingernails. "Are you so sure?"

"You would incite the crew to disobey the legal ship's master?" Takkata-Jim sounded genuinely shocked. He must know that many, perhaps most of the *Tursiops* would follow her, whatever the law said. But that would be mutiny, and tear the crew apart.

"I have the law on my side!" he hissed.

Gillian sighed. The hand must be played out, for all the

damage this would do if the dolphins of Earth found out. She whispered the two words she had not wanted to utter.

"Secret orders," she said.

Takkata-Jim stared at her, then let out a keening cry. He stood on his tail and did a back flip while his guard blinked in confusion. Gillian turned and saw Metz and Wattaceti staring at them.

"I don't believe you!" Takkata-Jim spluttered, spraying water in all directions. "On Earth we were promisssed! *Streaker* is *our* ship!"

Gillian shrugged. "Ask your bridge crew if the battle controls work," she offered. "Have someone try to leave through the outlock. Try to open the door to the armory."

Takkata-Jim whirled and sped to a comm screen at the far end of the room. His guard stared at Gillian momentarily, then followed. His look conveyed a sense of betrayal.

Not all of the crew would feel that way, Gillian knew. Most would probably be delighted. But deep inside an implication would settle. One of the main purposes of *Streaker*'s mission, to build in the neo-fen a sense of independence and self-confidence, had been compromised.

Did I have any other choice? Is there anything *else I might have tried first?*

She shook her head, wishing Tom were here. Tom might have settled everything with one sarcastic little ditty in Trinary that put everybody to shame.

Oh, Tom, she thought. *I should have gone instead of you.*

"Gillian!"

Makanee's flukes pounded the water and her harness whirred. With one metal arm she pointed up at the wounded dolphin floating in the gravity tank.

Creideiki was looking back at her!

"Joshua H. Bar—but you said his cortex was fried!" Metz stared.

An expression of profound concentration bore down on Creideiki's features. He breathed heavily, then gave voice to a desperate cry.

"*Out!:*"

"It'sss not possible!" Makanee sighed. "His ssspeech centers . . ."

Creideiki frowned in effort.

> * *Out* :
>> *Creideiki!*
> * *Swim* :
>> *Creideiki!*

It was Trinary baby talk, but with a queer tone to it. And the dark eyes burned with intelligence. Gillian's telempathic sense throbbed.

"*Out!:*" He whirled about in the tank and slammed his powerful flukes against the window with a loud boom. He repeated the Anglic word. The falling tone-slope was like a phrase in Primal.

"*Out-t-t!:*"

"Help him out-t!" Makanee commanded her assistants. "Gently! Quickly!"

Takkata-Jim was heading back from his comm screen at high speed, wrath on his face. But he stopped abruptly at the gravity tank, and stared at the bright eye of the captain.

It was the last straw.

He rolled back and forth, as if unable to decide on appropriate body language. Takkata-Jim turned to Gillian.

"What I've done was in what I believed to be the best interest of the ship, crew, and mission. I could make a very good case on Earth."

Gillian shrugged. "Let's hope you get the chance."

Takkata-Jim laughed dryly. "Very well, we'll hold this charade ship'sss council. I'll call it for one hour from now. But let me warn you, don't push too far, Dr. Baskin. I have powers ssstill. We must find a compromise. Try to pillory me and you will divide the ship.

"And then I will fight-t-t you" he added, low.

Gillian nodded. She had achieved what she had to. Even if Takkata-Jim had done the worst things Makanee suspected of him, there was no proof, and it was a matter of compromise or lose the ship to civil war. The first officer had to be offered an out. "I'll remember, Takkata-Jim. In one hour, then. I'll be there."

Takkata-Jim swirled about to leave, followed by his two loyal security guards.

Gillian saw Ignacio Metz staring after the dolphin lieutenant. "You lost control, didn't you?" she asked dryly as she swam past him.

The geneticist's head jerked. "What, Gillian? What do

you mean?" But his face betrayed him. Like many others, Metz tended to overestimate her psychic powers. Now he must be wondering if she had read his mind.

"Never mind," Gillian's smile was narrow. "Let's go and witness this miracle."

She swam to where Makanee waited anxiously for the emerging Creideiki. Metz looked after her uncertainly, before following.

51

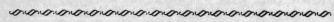

Thomas Orley

With trembling hands, he pulled vines away from the cave entrance. He crept out of his shelter and blinked at the hazy morning.

A thick layer of low clouds had gathered. There were no alien ships, yet, and that was just as well. He had feared they would arrive while he was helpless, struggling against the effects of the psi-bomb.

It hadn't been fun. In the first few minutes the psychic blasts had beaten away at his hypnotic defenses, cresting over them and drenching his brain in alien howling. For two hours—it had felt like eternity—he had wrestled with crazy images, pulsing, nerve-evoked lights and sounds. Tom still shook with reaction.

I sure hope there are still Thennanin out there, and that they fall for it. It had better have been worth it.

According to Gillian, the Niss machine had been confident it had found the right codes in the *Library* taken from the Thennanin wreck. If there were still Thennanin in the system, they should try to answer. The bomb must have been detectable for millions of miles in all directions.

He dragged a handful of muck out of the gap in the

weeds and flung it aside. Scummy sea water welled up almost to the surface of the hole. Another gap probably lay only a few meters beyond the next hummock—the weedscape flexed and breathed incessantly—but Tom wanted a water entrance near at hand.

He scooped away the slime as best he could, then wiped his hands and settled down to scan the sky from his shelter. On his lap he arranged his remaining psi-bombs.

Fortunately, these wouldn't pack the wallop of the Thennanin distress call. They were simply pre-recorded message casts, designed to carry a brief code a few thousand kilometers.

He had only recovered three of the message globes from the glider wreck, so he could only broadcast a narrow range of facts. Depending on which bomb he set off, Gillian and Creideiki would know what kind of aliens had come to investigate the distress call.

Of course, something might happen that didn't fit into any of the scenarios they had discussed. Then he would have to decide whether to broadcast an ambiguous message or do nothing and wait.

Maybe it would have been better to bring a radio, he thought. But a warship in the vicinity could pinpoint a radio transmission almost instantly, and blast his position before he spoke a few words. A message bomb could do its work in a second or so, and would be much harder to locate.

Tom thought about *Streaker*. It seemed like forever since he had last been there. Everything desirable was there—food, sleep, hot showers, his woman.

He smiled at the way the priorities had come out in his thoughts. Ah well, Jill would understand.

Streaker might have to abandon him, if his experiment led to a brief chance to blast away from Kithrup. It would not be a dishonorable way to die.

He wasn't afraid of dying, only of having not done all he could, and not properly spitting in the eye of death when it came for him. That final gesture was important.

Another image came to him, far more unpleasant—*Streaker* already captured, the space battle already over, all of his efforts useless.

Tom shuddered. It was better to imagine a sacrifice being *for* something.

*   *   *

A stiff breeze kept the clouds moving. They merged and separated in thick, wet drifts. Tom shaded his eyes against the glare to the east. About a radian south of the haze-shrouded morning sun, he thought he saw motion in the sky. He huddled deeper into his makeshift cave.

Out of one of the eastern cloud-drifts, a dark object slowly descended. Swirling vapor momentarily obscured its shape and size as it hung high above the sea of weeds.

A faint drumming sound reached Tom. He squinted from his hiding place, wishing for his lost binoculars. Then the mists parted briefly, and he saw the hovering spaceship clearly. It looked like some monstrous dragonfly, sharply tapered and wickedly dangerous.

Few races delved so deeply into the *Library* for weird designs as did the idiosyncratic, ruthless Tandu. Wild protrusions extended from the narrow hull in all directions, a Tandu hallmark.

At one end, however, a blunt, wedge-shaped appendage clashed with the overall impression of careless, cruel delicacy. It didn't seem to fit into the overall design.

Before he could get a better view, the clouds came together, concealing the floating cruiser from sight. The faint hum of powerful engines grew slowly louder, however.

Tom scratched at an itchy five-day growth of beard. The Tandu were bad news. If they were the only ones to show themselves, he would have to set off message bomb number three, to tell *Streaker* to lock up and get ready for a death-fight.

This was an enemy with whom Mankind had never been able to negotiate. In skirmishes on the Galactic marshes, Terran ships seldom conquered Tandu vessels, even with the odds in their favor. And, when there were no witnesses around, the Tandu loved to pick fights. Standing orders were to avoid them at all costs, until such time as Tymbrimi advisors could teach human crews the rare knack of beating these masters of the sneak-and-strike.

If the Tandu were the only ones to appear, it also meant he had likely seen his last sunrise. For in setting off a message bomb he'd almost certainly give away his position. The Tandu had clients who could psi-sniff even a thought, if they once caught the mental scent.

Tell you what, Ifni, he thought. *You send someone else into this confrontation. I won't insist it be Thennanin. A*

Jophur fighting-planetoid will suffice. Mix things up here, and I promise to say five sutras, ten Hail Marys, and Kiddush when I get home. Okay? I'll even dump some credits in a slot machine, if you like.

He envisioned a Tymbrimi-Human-Synthian battle fleet erupting out of the clouds, blasting the Tandu to fragments and sweeping the sky clear of fanatics. It was a lovely image, although he could think of a dozen reasons why it wasn't likely. For one thing, the Synthians, friendly as they were, wouldn't intervene unless it was a sure thing. The Tymbrimi, for that matter, would probably help Earth defend herself, but wouldn't stick their lovely humanoid necks *too* far out for a bunch of lost wolflings.

Okay Ifni, you lady of luck and chance. He fingered bomb number three. *I'll settle for a single, beat-up, old Thennanin cruiser.*

Infinity gave him no immediate answer. He hadn't expected one.

The thrumming seemed to pass right over his head. His hackles rose as the ship's strong-field region swept the area. Its shields screeched at his modest psi sense.

Then the crawling rumble began slowly to recede to his left. Tom looked to the west. The ragged clouds separated just long enough to display the Tandu cruiser—a light destroyer, he now saw, and not really a battleship—only a couple of miles away.

As he watched, the blunt appendage detached from the mother ship and began to drift slowly to the south. Tom frowned. That thing didn't look like the Tandu scout ships he was familiar with. It was a totally different design, stout and stolid, like...

The haze came together again, frustratingly, covering the two ships. Their muttering growl covered the muted grumblings of the nearby volcano.

Suddenly three brilliant streams of green light speared down from the clouds where Tom had last seen the Tandu ship, to hit the sea with flashing incandescence. There came a peal of supersonic thunder.

First he thought the Tandu were blasting the surface below. But a crackling bright explosion in the clouds showed that the destroyer itself was at the receiving end. Something high above the cloud deck was shooting at the Tandu!

He was too busy snatching up his gear to waste time in exultation. He kept his head averted, and so was spared blindness as the destroyer began firing actinic beams of antimatter at its assailant. Waves of heat scorched the back of his head and his left arm, as he stuffed the psi-bombs under his waistband and snapped his breather mask over his head.

The beams of annihilation made streaks of solar heat across the sky. He grabbed up his pack and dove into the hole he had earlier cleared in the thickly woven weeds.

The thunder suddenly muted as he splashed into a jungle of dangling vines. Straight shafts of flickering battle-light speared into the gloom through gaps in the weed.

Tom found he was automatically holding his breath. That didn't make much sense. The breather mask would not allow much oxygen to escape, but it would pass carbon dioxide. He started inhaling and exhaling as he grabbed a strong root for an anchor.

He found he was laboring for breath. With all the vegetation around him, he had expected the oxygen content to be high. But the tiny indicator on the rim of his mask told him that the opposite was true. The water was depleted compared to the normally rich brine of Kithrup's sea. The waving gill fins of the mask were picking up only a third as much oxygen as he would need to maintain himself, even if he stayed perfectly still.

In just a few minutes he would start to get dizzy. Not long thereafter he would pass out.

The battle roar penetrated the weed cover in a series of dull detonations. Shafts of brilliance shot into the gloom through openings in the leafy roof, one right in front of Orley. Even indirectly, the light hurt his eyes. He saw fronds just above the waterline, which had recently survived ashfall from a volcano, curl from the heat, turn brown, and fall away.

So much for the rest of my supplies, he thought.

So much for coming up for air.

He wrapped his legs around the thick root as he shrugged out of his backpack. He started rummaging through the satchel, looking for something to improvise. In the sharp shadows he negotiated the contents mostly by touch.

The inertial tracker Gillian had given him, a pouch of food bars, two canteens of "fresh" water, explosive slivers for his needler, a tool kit.

The air meter was turning an ominous orange. Tom wedged the pack between his knees and tore open the tool kit. He seized a small roll of eight-gauge rubber tubing. Purple blobs flickered on the edge of his field of vision as he used his sheath knife to cut a length of narrow hose.

He crammed one end through the mask's chow-lock. The seal held, but the contents of the tube sprayed at his mouth, making him gag and cough.

There was no time for finesse. He shimmied up the root to a point within reach of the hole in the weeds.

Tom pinched the tube below the other end, but bitter, oily water streamed from the tube as he straightened the coil. He averted his face, but swallowed a little anyway. It tasted foul.

The mask's demon-lock would purge the fluid, *if* too much didn't flood in.

Tom reached out and pushed the tube above the surface of the narrow pool, where the battle flashes sent shafts of light into the depths. He sucked hard at the hose, spitting out slime and a sharp metallic tang, desperately trying to clear it.

One of the searing blasts flashed, scalding his fingers below the waterline. He fought the instinct to shout or pull away from the pain. He felt consciousness begin to slip, and with it the will to hold his left hand into the searing heat.

He drew hard and at last was rewarded with a thin stream of dank air. Tom sucked frantically at the line. The hot, steamy air tasted of smoke, but it nourished. He exhaled into the mask, trusting it to hold the hard-won oxygen.

The aching in his lungs subsided and the agony of his hand took the fore. Just as he thought he couldn't hold it out there any more, the burning heat from above subsided, fading to a dull flickering glow in the sky.

A few meters away was another gap in the weeds, where he might be able to prop the tube between two thick roots without exposing himself. Tom took a few more breaths, then pinched the tube shut. But before he could prepare any further, a sharp blue light suddenly filled the water, brighter than ever, casting stark, blinding shadows everywhere. There was a tremendous detonation, then the sea began tossing him about like a rag doll.

Something huge had struck the ocean and set it bucking. His anchor root came free of its mooring, and he fell into a maelstrom of flailing vines.

The swell tore the backpack from him. He grabbed after it and caught the end of one strap, but something struck him in the back of the head, knocking him dizzy. The pack was snatched away into the noise and flashing shadows.

Tom curled into a ball, his forearms holding the rim of his mask against the whipping vines.

His first thought, on coming around, was a vague surprise that he was still breathing.

He thought the battle-storm was still going on, until he realized that the shaking he felt was his own body. The roar in his ears was only a roar in his ears.

His throbbing left arm was draped over a thick horizontal stump. Scummy green water came up to his chin, lapping against the finned facemask. His lungs ached and the air was stale.

He brought up his trembling right hand, and pulled the mask down to hang around his neck. The filters had kept out the ozone stench, but he inhaled deeply, gratefully.

At the last moment he must have chosen immolation over suffocation and struck out for the surface. Fortunately, the battle ended just before he arrived.

Tom resisted the temptation to rub his itching eyes; the slime on his hands would do them no good. Tears welled, at a biofeedback command, flushing most of the binding mucus away.

He looked up when he could see again.

To the north the volcano fumed on as ever. The cloud cover had parted somewhat, revealing numerous twisted banners of multi-colored smoke. All around Tom, small crawling things were climbing out from the singed weeds, resuming their normal business of eating or being eaten. There were no longer battleships in the sky, blazing away at each other with beams of nova heat.

For the first time, Tom was glad of the monotonous topography of the carpet of vines. He hardly had to rise in the water to see several columns of smoke pouring from slowly settling wrecks.

As he watched, one faraway metal derelict exploded. The

sound arrived seconds later in a series of muted coughs and pops, punctuated unsynchronously by bright flashes. The dim shape sank lower. Tom averted his eyes from the final detonation. When he looked back he could detect nothing but clouds of steam and a faint hissing sound that fell away into silence.

Elsewhere lay other floating fragments. Tom turned a slow circle, somewhat in awe of the destruction. There was more than enough wreckage for a mid-sized skirmish.

He laughed at the irony, although it made his abused lungs hurt. The Galactics had all come to investigate a counterfeit mayday signal, and they had brought their death feuds along to what should have been a mission of mercy. Now they were dead while he still lived. This didn't feel like the random capriciousness of Ifni. It was too like the mysterious, wry work of God himself.

Does this mean I'm all alone again? he wondered. *That would be rich. So much fireworks, and one humble human the only survivor?*

Not for long, perhaps. The battle had caused him to lose almost all of the supplies he had struggled so hard to recover. Tom frowned suddenly. The message bombs! He clutched at his waist, and the world seemed to drop away. Only one of the globes remained! The others must have popped out in the struggle below the clinging vines.

When his right hand stopped shaking, he carefully reached under his waistband and drew out the psi-bomb, his very last link with *Streaker*... with Gillian.

It was the verifier... the one that he was to set off if he thought the Trojan Seahorse should fly. Now he would have to decide whether to set off this one, or none at all. Yes or No were all he could say.

I only wish I knew whose ships those were that fired on the Tandu.

Tucking the bomb away, he resumed his slow turn. One wreck on the northwest horizon looked like a partially crushed eggshell. Smoke still rose from it, but the burning seemed to have stopped. There were no explosions, and it seemed not to be sinking any lower.

All right, Tom thought. *That will do as a goal. It looks intact enough to have possibilities. It may have salvageable gear and food. Certainly it's shelter, if it's not too radioactive.*

It seemed only five kilometers away, or so, though looks

could be deceiving. A destination would give him something to do, at least. He needed more information. The wreck might tell him what he needed to know.

He pondered whether to try to go "by land," trusting his weary legs to negotiate the weedscape, or to attempt the journey underwater, swimming from airhole to airhole, daring the unknown creatures of the deep.

He suddenly heard a warbling whine behind him, turned, and saw a small spacecraft, about a kilometer away, heading slowly northward, wavering bare meters above the ocean. Its shimmering shields flickered. Its drives heaved and faltered.

Tom pulled up his mask and prepared to dive, but the tiny ship wasn't coming his way. It was passing to the west of him, sparks shooting from its stubby stasis flanges. Ugly black streaks stained its hull, and one patch had blistered and boiled away.

Tom caught his breath as it passed. He had never seen a model like this before. But he could think of several races whose style would be compatible with the design.

The scout dipped as its dying drives coughed. The high whine of the gravity generator began to fall.

The boat's crew obviously knew it was done for. It banked to change course for the island. Tom held his breath, unable to help sympathizing with the desperate alien pilot. The boat sputtered along just above the weeds, then passed out of sight behind the mountain's shoulder.

The faint "crump" of its landing carried over the whistling of the tradewinds.

Tom waited. After a few seconds the boat's stasis field released with a loud concussion. Glowing debris flew out over the sea. The fragments quenched in water or burned slowly into the weeds.

He doubted anyone could have gotten away in time.

Tom changed goals. His long-range destination was still the eggshell ship floating a few miles away. But first he wanted to sift through the wreckage of that scout boat. Maybe there would be evidence there to make his decision easier. Maybe there would be food.

He tried to crawl up onto the weeds, but found it too difficult. He was still shaking.

All right, then. We'll go under the sea. It's probably all moot anyway.

I might as well enjoy the scenery.

52

∽∿∽∿∽∿∽∿∽∿∽∿∽∿∽∿∽∿∽∿∽∿∽∿∽∿∽∿

Akki

The son of a blood-gorged lamprey just wouldn't let go!

Akki was exhausted. The metallic tang of the water mixed with the taste of bile from his fore-stomach as he swam hard to the southeast. He wanted desperately to rest, but he knew he couldn't afford to let his pursuer cut away at his lead.

Now and then he caught sight of K'tha-Jon, about two kilometers behind him and closing the gap. The giant, darkly countershaded dolphin seemed tireless. His breath condensed in high vertical spouts, like small rockets of fog, as he plowed ahead through the water.

Akki's breath was ragged, and he felt weak with hunger. He cursed in Anglic and found it unsatisfying. Playing over a resonating, obscene phrase in Primal Delphin helped a little.

He should have been able to outdistance K'tha-Jon, at least over a short stretch. But something in the water was affecting the hydrodynamic properties of his skin. Some substance was causing an allergic reaction. His normally smooth and pliant hide was scratchy and bumpy. He felt like he was plowing through syrup instead of water. Akki wondered why no one else had reported this. Did it only affect dolphins from Calafia?

It was one more unfairness in a series that stretched back to the moment he had left the ship.

Escaping K'tha-Jon hadn't been as easy as he expected. Heading southeast, he should have been able to veer right or left to reach help, either Hikahi and the crew at the Thennanin wreck, or at Toshio's island. But every time he tried to change course, K'tha-Jon moved to cut the corner. Akki couldn't afford to lose any more of his lead.

A wave of focused sonar swept over him from behind. He wanted to curl up into a ball every time it happened. It wasn't natural for a dolphin to flee another for so long. In the deep past a youngster who angered an older male—by trying to copulate with a female in the old bull's harem, for instance— might get thumped or raked. But only rarely was a grudge held. Akki had to stifle an urge to stop and try to reason with K'tha-Jon.

What good would that do? The giant was obviously mad.

His speed advantage was lost to this mysterious skin itch. Diving to get around K'tha-Jon was also out of the question. The *Stenos bredanensis* were pelagic dolphins. K'tha-Jon could probably outdive anyone in the *Streaker's* crew.

When next he glanced back, K'tha-Jon had closed to within about a kilometer. Akki warbled a sigh and redoubled his efforts.

A line of green-topped mounds lay near the horizon, perhaps four or five kilometers away. He had to hold on long enough to reach them!

53

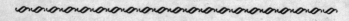

Moki

Moki drove the sled at top speed to the south, blasting its sonar ahead like a bugle.

"...*calling Haoke, calling Moki. This is Heurkah-pete. Come in. Verify p-please!*"

Moki tossed his head in irritation. The ship was trying to reach him again. Moki clicked the sled's transmitter on and tried to talk clearly.

"Yesss! What-t-t you want-t!"

There was a pause, then, *"Moki, let me talk to Haoke."*

Moki barely concealed a laugh. "Haoke . . . dead! K-k-killed by intruder! I'm ch-chasing now. T-t-tell Takkata-Jim I'll get-t 'em!"

Moki's Anglic was almost indecipherable, yet he didn't dare use Trinary. He might slip into Primal in public, and he wasn't ready for that yet.

There was a long silence on the sonar-speak line. Moki hoped that now they'd leave him alone.

When he and Haoke had found the Baskin woman's empty sled, drifting slowly westward at low power, something had finally snapped within him. He had then entered a confused but exalted state, a blur of action, like a violent dream.

Perhaps they were ambushed, or perhaps he merely imagined it. But when it was over Haoke was dead and he, Moki, had no regrets.

After that his sonar had picked up an object heading south. Another sled. Without another thought he had given chase.

The sonar-speak crackled. *"Heurkah again, Moki. You're getting out of saser range, and we still can't use radiosss. You are now given two ordersss. First—relay a sonar-speak message to K'tha-Jon, ordering him back-k! His mission is cancelled!*

"Number two—after that, turn around yourssself! That'sss a direct order!"

The lights and dots meant little to Moki anymore. What mattered were the patterns of sound that the sled's sensors sent him. The expanded hearing sense gave him a god-like feeling, as if he were one of the Great Dreamers himself. He imagined himself a huge *catodon*, a sperm whale, lord of the deep, hunting prey that fled at any hint of his approach.

Not far to the south was the muffled sound of a sled, the one he had been chasing for some time. He could tell that he was catching up to it.

Much farther away, and to the left, were two tiny rhythmic signals, sounds of rapid cetacean swimming. That had to be K'tha-Jon and the upstart Calafian.

Moki would dearly love to steal K'tha-Jon's prey from him, but that could wait. The first enemy was dead ahead.

"Moki, did you copy me? Answer! You have your ordersss! You must . . ."

Moki clapped his jaws in disgust. He shut off the sonar-speak in the middle of Heurkah-pete's complaint. It was getting hard to understand the stuck-up little petty officer anyway. He had never been much of a *Stenos*, always studying Keneenk with the *Tursiops*, and trying to "better himself."

Moki decided he would look the fellow up after he had finished taking care of his enemies *outside* the ship.

54

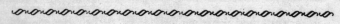

Keepiru

Keepiru knew he was being followed. He had expected that someone might be sent after him to keep him from reaching Hikahi.

But his pursuer was some sort of idiot. He could tell from the distant whine of the engines that the fin's sled was being driven well beyond its rated speed. What did the fellow hope to accomplish? Keepiru had a long enough head start to make it within sonar-speak range of the Thennanin wreck before his pursuer caught up. He only had to push his sled's throttle slightly into the red.

The fin behind him was spraying sonar noise all over the place, as if he wanted to announce to all and sundry that he was coming.

With all his screeching, the imbecile was making it hard for Keepiru to piece together what was going on to the southeast. Keepiru concentrated and tried to block out the noise from behind.

Two dolphins, it seemed, one almost out of breath, the other powerful and still vigorous, were swimming furiously toward a bank of sonar shadows fifty kilometers away.

What was going on? Who was chasing whom?

He listened so hard that Keepiru suddenly had to veer

to avoid colliding with a high seamount. He passed on the west side, banking hard to sweep past by meters. The mountain's bulk momentarily cast him into silence.

> * *'Ware shoals*
>   *Child of Tursiops!* *

He trilled a lesson-rhyme, then switched to Trinary Haiku.

> * *Echoes of the shore*
>   *Are like drifting feathers*
>   *Dropped by pelicans!* *

Keepiru chided himself. Dolphins were supposed to be hot pilots—it was what had won them their first starship berths over a century before—and he was known far and wide as one of the best. So why were forty knots underwater harder to handle than fifty times lightspeed down a wormhole?

His thrumming sled left the shadow of the seamount and came into open water. East of southeast came a faint image-gestalt of racing cetaceans, once again.

Keepiru concentrated. Yes, the one in pursuit was a *Stenos*, a big one. It used a strange pattern of search sonar.

The one in front...

...*It has to be Akki*, he thought. *The kid is in trouble. Bad trouble.*

He was almost deafened as a blast of sound from the sled behind him caught him directly in a focused beam. He chattered a curse-glyph and shook his head to clear it.

He almost turned around to take care of the self-sucking turd swallower behind him, but he knew his duty lay ahead.

Keepiru was tormented by a choice. Strictly speaking, his duty was to get a message to Hikahi. Yet it went against everything inside him to abandon the middie. It sounded like the youngster was exhausted. His pursuer was clearly catching up.

But if he swung to the east he would give his *own* pursuer a chance to catch up...

But he might also distract K'tha-Jon, force him to turn around.

It didn't become a Terragens officer. It didn't reflect Keneenk. But he couldn't decide logically.

He wished some distant, great-great-grandchild of his were here now, a fully mature and logical dolphin who could tell his crude, half-animal ancestor what to do.

Keepiru sighed. *What makes me think they'll let me have great-grandchildren, anyway?*

He chose to be true to himself. He banked the sled to the left and pulled the engine throttle one more notch into the red.

55

Charles Dart

One of the two Earthlings in the room—the human—rummaged through dresser drawers and distractedly tossed things into an open valise on the bed. He listened while the chimpanzee talked.

". . . the probe is down below two kilometers. The radioactivity's rising fast, and the temperature gradient, too. I'm not sure the probe will last more'n another few hundred meters, yet the shaft keeps going!

"Anyway, I'm now *positive* that there's been garbage dumping by a technological race, and recently! Like *hundreds* of years ago!"

"That's very interesting, Dr. Dart. Really, it is." Ignacio Metz tried not to show his exasperation. One had to be patient with chimps, especially Charles Dart. Still, it was hard to pack while the chimp ran on and on, perched on a chair in his stateroom.

Dart went on obliviously. "If anything made me appreciate Toshio, as inefficient as that boy is, it's having to work with that lousy dolphin linguist Sah'ot! Still, I was gettin' good data until Tom Orley's damned bomb went off and Sah'ot started hollering stuff about 'voices' from below! Crazy bloody fin. . . ."

Metz sorted his belongings. *Now where is my blue land-suit? Oh yes, it's already packed. Let's see. Duplicates of all my notes are already loaded aboard the boat. What else is there?*

". . . I said, Dr. Metz!"

"Hmmm?" He looked up quickly. "I'm sorry, Dr. Dart. It's all these sudden changes and all. I'm sure you understand. What were you saying?"

Dart groaned in exasperation. "I said I want to go *with* you! To you this trip may be a form of exile, but to me it'd be an escape! I've *got* to get out to where my work is!" He pounded the wall and showed two rows of large, yellowed teeth.

Metz thought for a moment, shaking his head. Exile? Perhaps Takkata-Jim looked at it that way. Certainly he and Gillian were like oil and water. She was determined to set in motion Orley's and Creideiki's Trojan Seahorse plan. Takkata-Jim was just as adamant resisting it.

Metz agreed with Takkata-Jim, and had been surprised when the lieutenant meekly resigned his acting-captaincy at the ship's council meeting, appointing Gillian in command until Hikahi could be recalled. That meant the Seahorse scheme would go forward after all. *Streaker* was to begin her underwater move in a few hours.

If the ruse was really to be tried, Metz was just as happy to be gone from the ship. The longboat was spacious, and comfortable enough. In it, he and his notes would be safe. The records of his special experiments would get to Earth eventually, even when . . . if *Streaker* was destroyed trying to escape.

Besides, now he could join Dennie Sudman in examining the Kiqui. Metz was more than a little eager to get a look at the pre-sentients.

"You'll have to talk to Gillian about coming with us, Charlie," he shook his head. "She's letting us take your new robot with us to the island. You may have to settle for that."

"But you and Takkata-Jim promised that if I cooperated, if I kept quiet to Toshio earlier, and was willing to give you my proxy on the council . . ."

The chimp lapsed when he saw the expression on Metz's face. Charlie's lips pressed close together and he got up to his feet.

"Thanks for nuthin'!" he growled as he went for the door.

"Now, Charlie . . ."

Dart marched out into the hall. The shutting door cut off Metz's last words.

The chimp walked along the sloping corridor, head bowed in determination.

"I gotta get out there!" He grumbled. "There's *gotta* be a way!"

56

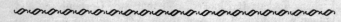

Sah'ot

When Gillian called to ask that he talk to Creideiki, his first thought had been to rebel over the workload.

"I know, I know," her tiny simulacrum had agreed, "but you're the only one I can spare who has the qualifications. Let's rephrase that. You *are* the only one for the job. Creideiki is clearly aware and alert, but he can't talk! We need someone to help him communicate through parts of his brain that weren't damaged. You're our expert."

Sah'ot had never really liked Creideiki. And the type of injury the captain had suffered made Sah'ot feel queasy. Still, the challenge appealed to his vanity.

"What about Charlesss Dart? He's been driving Toshio and me until our flukes droop, and he has top priority on this line."

In the small holo image Gillian looked very tired. "Not any more he doesn't. We're sending out a new probe with Takkata-Jim and Metz, one he'll be able to control himself by commlink. Until then, his project takes last place. *Last* place. Is that understood?"

Sah'ot clapped his jaw loudly in assent. It felt good to hear decisive leadership again. The fact that the voice was that of a human he respected helped, too.

"This bit-t about Metz and Takkata-Jim . . ."

"I've filled in Toshio." Gillian said. "He'll brief you when the chance comes. He is in absolute charge now. You're to obey him with alacrity. Is that clear?"

Gillian never lost her vocabulary under pressure. Sah'ot liked that. "Yesss. Eminently. Now, about these resonances I'm getting from the planet's crust. What shall I do? They are, to my knowledge, totally unprecedented! Can you ssspare someone to do a *Library* search for me?"

Gillian frowned. "You say resonances of apparent intelligent origin are coming from deep in Kithrup's crust?"

"Exactly."

Gillian rolled her eyes. "Ifni! To explore this world in *peace* and *quiet* would demand a decade of work by a dozen survey ships!" She shook her head. "No. My quick guess is that some formation of probability-sensitive rock below the surface is resonating with emanations from the battle overhead. In any event, it comes after the other priorities: security, the Kiqui, and talking to Creideiki. You've got a mouthful to deal with already."

Sah'ot stifled a protest. Complaining would only get Gillian to order him explicitly away from the probe. She hadn't yet, so it would be best to stay quiet.

"Now think about your options," Gillian reminded him. "If *Streaker* makes a break for it, we'll try to get the skiff out to pick up Tom and whoever wants to join us from the island. You can choose to come along, or stay with Metz and Takkata-Jim and wait it out in the longboat. Inform Toshio of your decision."

"I undersstand. I'll think about it." Somehow the issue seemed less urgent than it would have a few days ago. The sounds from below were having an effect on him.

"If I stay, I still wish you all the best of luck," he added.

"You too, mel-fin." Gillian smiled. "You're a strange duck, but if I get home, I'm going to recommend you get lots of grandchildren." Her image vanished as she broke the connection.

Sah'ot stared at the blank screen. The compliment, wholly unexpected, left him momentarily stunned. Then a few Kiqui who were foraging nearby were surprised to see a large dolphin rise up onto his tail and dance about the small pool.

> * To be noticed by—
> A humpback
> * To be credited
> At last
> For being me *

57

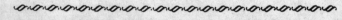

Dennie and Toshio

"I'm afraid."

Almost without a thought, Toshio put his arm around Dennie's shoulder. He gave her a reassuring squeeze. "What for? There's nothing to be scared of."

Dennie looked up from the pounding breakers to see if he was serious. Then she realized she was being teased. She stuck out her tongue at him.

Toshio inhaled deeply and was content. It wasn't clear to him where his new semi-relationship with Dennie was going. It wasn't physical, for one thing. They had slept together last night, but fully clothed. Toshio had thought it would be frustrating, and it was, sort of. But not as much as he had expected.

It would work out, one way or another. Right now Dennie needed someone to be nearby. It was satisfying just filling that need.

Maybe, when all this was over, she would go back to thinking of him as a boy, four years her junior. Somehow he doubted it. She was touching him more now, rather than less, holding his arm and punching him in mock anger, even as shivers from the psi-bomb episode faded.

"When are they supposed to get here with the longboat?" She looked back over the ocean once more. "Late tomorrow, sometime," he answered.

"Takkata-Jim and Metz wanted to negotiate with the

ETs. What's to stop them if they decide to ignore orders and try anyway?"

"Gillian's giving them only enough power to get here. They have a regenerator, so they'll be able to charge up for space-travel in a month or so, but by then *Streaker*'d be gone, one way or another."

Dennie shivered slightly.

Toshio cursed his awkward tongue. "Takkata-Jim won't have a radio. I'm to guard ours until the skiff comes to pick us up. Besides, what could he offer the Galactics? He won't have any of the charts marking the derelict fleet.

"My guess is he and Metz will wait until everybody leaves, then scuttle off to Earth with Metz's tapes and a hold full of gripes."

Dennie looked up at the first stars of the long Kithrup twilight. "Are you going back?" she asked.

"*Streaker*'s my ship. Thank God, Creideiki is still alive. But even if he's not skipper any more, I owe it to him to keep on, as one of his officers should."

Dennie glanced up at him briefly, then nodded and looked back out at the sea.

She's thinking we haven't a chance, Toshio realized. *And maybe we don't. Wearing a Thennanin battlewagon as a disguise, we'll have all the maneuverability of a Calafian mud-gleaner. And even fooling the Galactics might not be so good an idea. They want to capture* Streaker, *but they won't hold back their fire if they see a defeated enemy climbing back up for another round. There still have to be Thennanin around, if the scheme is to work.*

But we can't just sit here waiting, can we? If we do, the Galactics will learn that they can push Earthlings around. We just can't afford to let anyone profit from chasing one of our survey ships.

Dennie seemed worried. Toshio changed the subject. "How's your report coming?"

"Oh, all right, I guess. It's clear the Kiqui are fully pre-sentient. They've been fallow a very long time. In fact, some Darwinist heretics might think they were just getting ripe to bootstrap themselves. They show some signs."

Some iconoclast humans still pushed the idea that a pre-sentient race could make the leap to spacefaring intelligence by evolution alone, without the intervention of a patron. Most Galactics thought the idea absurd and strange, but the failure to find humanity's missing benefactor had gained the theory a few adherents.

"What about the metal-mound?" Toshio asked about Dennie's other research, begun at Charlie Dart's behest when the chimp had been given top priority, but pursued now out of interest.

Dennie shrugged. "Oh, the mound's alive. The professional biologist in me would give her left arm to be able to stay a year on this island, with full laboratory equipment to study it!

"The metal-eating pseudocoral, the drill-tree, the living core of the island, are all symbiots. In effect, they're organs in one giant entity! If I could only write it up at home I'd be famous . . . if anyone believed me."

"They'll believe you," Toshio assured her. "And you'll be famous."

He motioned that they should start heading back to camp. They only had a little time after second supper to walk and talk. Now that he was in command, he had to make sure that timetables were kept.

Dennie held his arm as they turned to return to the encampment. Over the rushing rustle of the wind through the foliage came the intermittent squeaks of the natives, rousing from their siesta to prepare for the evening hunt.

They walked in silence along the narrow trail.

58

Galactics

Krat licked slowly at her mating claw, studiously ignoring the creatures who scurried to clean up the bloody mess in the corner.

There would be trouble over this. The Pilan High Council would protest.

Of course she was within her rights, as grand admiral, to deal with any member of the fleet as she saw fit. But that did not traditionally cover the skewering of a senior Librarian simply because he was the bearer of bad news.

I am getting old, *she realized.* And the daughter I had hoped would soon be strong enough to pull me down is now dead. Who now will do me the honors, before I grow erratic and become a hazard to the clan?

The small, furry body was hauled away, and a sturdy Paha mopped up the bloody mess. The other Pila looked at her.

Let them stare. When we capture the Earthlings it won't matter. I shall be famous, and this incident will be ignored by all, especially the Pila.

If we are the first ones to approach the Progenitors with an offering, the Law won't matter any more. The Pila will not simply be our adult liege-clients. They will be *ours* again, to meddle with, to redesign, to shape once more.

"Back to work! All!" She snapped her mating claw. The twang sent the bridge crew scuttling off to their stations, some to repair the smoking damage from a near miss in the most recent battle with the Tandu.

Think now, Soro mother. Can you spare ships to send once more to the planet? To that hellish volcano where every fleet has already sent a party to fight and die?

There weren't supposed to be any Gubru left here! But a battered Gubru scout had shown up at the place where the distress call came from. It had gone to smoky ruin along with a Tandu destroyer, Pritil's ship number sixteen, and two other vessels even her battle computers could not identify. Perhaps one was a surviving spearship of the Brothers of the Night which had hidden on one of Kithrup's moons.

Meanwhile, out here, the "final" battle with the Tandu's unholy alliance had turned into a bloody draw. The Soro still had a slim advantage, so the remaining Thennanin stayed by their Tandu allies.

Should she risk all in the next encounter? For the Tandu to win would be horrible. They would, if they gained the Power, destroy so many beautiful species that the Soro might someday own.

If it came down to a choice, she guessed the Thennanin would switch sides one more time.

"Strategy section!" *she snapped.*

"Fleet-Mother?" A Paha warrior approached, but stopped just out of arm-reach. It eyed her cautiously.

Given a chance, she would breed respect into the Paha genes so deeply nothing would ever eradicate it.

The Paha stepped back involuntarily as her claw stretched. "Find out which ships are now most expendable. Organize them into a small squadron. We're going to investigate the planet again."

The Paha saluted and returned to its station quickly. Krat settled deeper into the vletoor cushion.

We shall need a distraction, *she thought.* Perhaps another expedition to that volcano would make the Thennanin nervous and let the Tandu think we know something.

Of course, *she reminded herself,* the Tandu themselves may know what we do not.

59

∿∿∿∿∿∿∿∿∿∿∿∿∿∿∿∿∿∿∿∿

Creideiki

Far Away

> *They Call*

> > *The Giants,*
> > > *The Spirits of OCEAN,*
> > > *The Leviathans*

> *Creideiki begins to understand—does, does, begin—*
The old gods are part figment, part racial memory, part ghost . . . and part something else . . . something an engineer could never have allowed his ears to hear, or eyes to see . . .

Far Away

> *They Call*

Leviathans . . .

Not yet. Not yet, not. Creideiki has a duty to perform yet, does have a duty.

No more, no more an engineer—but Creideiki remains a spacer. Not useless, Creideiki will do what he can, can do, can do to help.

Can do to help save his crew, his ship . . .

60

∽∾∽∾∽∾∽∾∽∾∽∾∽∾∽∾∽∾∽∾∽∾∽∾∽∾

Gillian

She wanted to rub her eyes, but the facemask was in the way. Too much remained to be done.

The fins came and went, swooping by her wherever she traveled in the ship, almost toppling her in their hurry to report and then be off again, carrying out orders.

I hope Hikahi gets back soon. I'm not doing badly, I guess, but I'm no starship officer. She has the training to rule a crew.

Hikahi doesn't even know she's captain, Gillian thought. *Much as I pray they get the line open soon, I'll hate having to break that news to her.*

She wrote a brief message to Emerson D'Anite, and the last courier dashed off for the engine room. Wattaceti kept pace alongside her as she turned to swim into the outlock.

There were two small crowds of dolphins in the bay, one at the forward sally hatch and the other clustered about the longboat.

The bow of the small spaceship almost touched the iris of one of the outer hatches. Its stern disappeared into a metal sheath beyond the rear end of the outlock.

When the longboat is gone this place'll look pretty empty, she thought.

A fin in the party at the lock saw her and sped toward Gillian. He halted abruptly before her and hovered in the water at attention.

"Flankers and scoutsss are ready to depart when you give the word, Gillian."

"Thank you, Zaa'pht. It will be soon. Is there still no word from the line-repair party, or from Keepiru?"

"No, ssssir. The courier you sent to follow Keepiru should be near the wreck shortly, though."

It was frustrating. Takkata-Jim had severed the link to the Thennanin wreck, and now it seemed impossible to find the break. For once she cursed the fact that monofilaments could be hidden so well.

For all they knew, some terrible disaster might have struck the work party, at the very site she was planning on moving *Streaker* to.

At least the detectors indicated the space battle was still going on, almost as fierce as ever.

But what was keeping Tom? He was supposed to set off a message bomb when ETs showed up to investigate his ruse. But since the faked distress call there had been nothing.

In addition to everything else, the damned Niss machine wanted to talk to her. It had not set off the hidden alarm in her office to indicate that it was an emergency, but every time she used a comm unit she heard a faint click that signaled the thing's desire to talk.

It was enough to make a fem just want to climb into bed and stay there.

A sudden commotion broke out near the lock. The wall speaker let out a brief, sloppy squeal of Trinary, followed by a longer report in loose, high-pitched Anglic.

"Sssir!" Zaa'pht turned excitedly. "They report . . ."

"I heard." She nodded. "The line's been repaired. Congratulate the repair team for me, and get them inside for a couple of hours' rest. Then please ask Heurkah-pete to contact Hikahi right away. He's to ascertain her situation and tell her we begin moving the ship at 2100 hours unless she objects. I'll be calling her shortly."

"Aye, sssir!" Zaa'pht whirled and sped off.

Wattaceti watched her silently, waiting.

"All right," she said. "Let's see Takkata-Jim and Metz off. You've made certain the crew has offloaded everything that wasn't on our checklist, and inspected everything the exiles took aboard?"

"Yesss. They haven't even got a flaregun. No radio and no more fuel than the minimum needed to reach the island."

Gillian had gone on her own inspection of the boat a few hours back, while Metz and Takkata-Jim were still packing. She had taken a few additional precautions that nobody else knew about.

"Who's going with them?"

"Three volunteers, all of them 'strange' *Stenos*. All males. We searched them down to their penile sheathsss. They're clean. They're all in the longboat now, ready to go."

Gillian nodded. "Then, for better or worse, let's get them out of here so we can get on with other things."

Mentally she had already begun rehearsing what she had to tell Hikahi.

61

∽∾∾∾∾∾∾∾∾∾∾∾∾∾∾∾∾∾∾∾∾∾∽

Hikahi & Suessi

"Remember," she told Tsh't and Suessi, "maintain radio silence at all cossst. And try to keep those crazy fen in the wreck from eating up all the supplies in the first few days, hmmm?"

Tsh't signaled assent with a jaw clap, although her eyes were heavy with reservation. Suessi said, "Are you sure you won't let one of us come with you?"

"I'm sure. If I encounter disaster I want no more lives lost. If I find survivors, I might need every bit of room. In any event, the skiff runs itself, essentially. All I have to do is watch it."

"You can't fight while piloting," Hannes pointed out.

"If I had a gunner along I might be *tempted* to fight. This way I *have* to run away. If *Streaker* is dead or captured, I must be able to return the skiff to you here, or you'll all be doomed."

Suessi frowned, but found he had to agree with her reasoning. He was thankful Hikahi had stayed as long as she had, letting them use the skiff's power to finish preparing a habitat inside the wreck.

We're all worried about Streaker *and the captain,* he thought. *But Hikahi must be in agony.*

"All right, then. Good-bye and good luck, Hikahi. May Ifni's boss watch over you."

"The sssame to both of you," Hikahi took Suessi's hand gently between her jaws, then did the same with Tsh't's left pectoral fin.

Tsh't and Suessi left through the skiff's small airlock. They backed their sled toward the yawning opening in the sunken alien battleship.

A low whine spread from the skiff as power came on. The sound echoed back to them from the mammoth sea-cliff that towered over the crash site.

The tiny space vessel began to move slowly eastward, picking up speed underwater. Hikahi had chosen a roundabout route, taking her far out before swinging back in an arc to *Streaker's* hiding place. This would keep her out of touch for as long as a couple of days, but it would also mean that her point of origin could not be traced, if an enemy lay in wait where *Streaker* had been.

They watched until the boat disappeared into the gloom. Long after Suessi ceased hearing anything. Tsh't waved her jaw slowly back and forth, following the diminishing sound.

Two hours later, as Hannes was lying down for his first nap in his new dry-quarters, the makeshift intercom by his pallet squawked.

Not more *bad news.* He sighed.

Lying in the darkness with one arm over his eyes, he touched the comm. "What?" he said simply.

It was Lucky Kaa, the young electronics tech and junior pilot. His voice fizzed with excitement. "Sir! Tsh't says you should come quickly! It'sss the ship!"

Suessi rolled over onto one elbow.

"*Streaker?*"

"Yesss! The line just re-opened! They want to talk to Hikahi right away!"

All of the strength went out of Suessi's arms. He slumped back and groaned. *Oh, frabjous day! By now she's well out of sonar-speak range!*

It's at times like these that I wish I could talk dolphin jabber like Tom Orley can. Maybe in Trinary I could express something properly ironic and vulgar about the way the universe works.

62

Exiles

The longboat slid smoothly through the port and out into the twilight blue of Kithrup's ocean.

"You're going the wrong way," Ignacio Metz said, after the iris had closed behind them. Instead of turning east, the boat spiraled upward.

"Just a small detour, Dr. Metz," Takkata-Jim soothed. "Sneekah-jo, tell *Streaker* I'm adjusting the trim."

The dolphin on the co-pilot's ramp began whistling to his counterpart on the ship. The sonar-speak squawked back angrily. *Streaker*, also, had noticed the change in course.

Metz's seat was above and behind Takkata-Jim's. The water level came up to his waist. "What are you *doing*?" he asked.

"Jusst getting used to the controls..."

"Well, watch out! You're headed straight for the detection buoys!"

Metz watched, amazed, as the craft sped toward the crew of dolphins dismantling the listening devices. The workfen scattered out of the way, cursing shrilly as the boat crashed into the tethered buoys. Metal smithereens clattered along its prow and fell into the blackness.

Takkata-Jim seemed oblivious. He calmly turned the small ship around and piloted it at a sedate pace eastward, toward their island destination.

The sonar-speak squawked. Dr. Metz blushed. Good fin-persons shouldn't use language like that!

"Tell them it was an accident-t," Takkata-Jim told his co-pilot. "The trim was out of line, but now we've got it under control. We're proceeding underwater to the island, as ordered."

The longboat drove down a narrow canyon, leaving the brightly lit subsea vale and *Streaker* behind it.

"*Accident, my hairy uncle Fred's scrotum!*"

The words were followed by a sniggering laugh from the back of the control room. "You know, I kinda *figured* you wouldn't leave without destroying the incriminatin' evidence first, Takkata-Jim."

Dr. Metz struggled with his straps to turn around. He stared. "Charles Dart! What are you doing here?"

Perched on a shelf in a storage locker—whose door was now open—a spacesuited chimpanzee grinned back at him. "Why, exercisin' a teeny tiny bit of *initiative*, Dr. Metz! Now you be sure and note that in your records. I wanna be given credit for it." He broke into a shrieking giggle, amplified by his suit speaker.

Takkata-Jim twisted about on his ramp to regard the chimp for a moment. He snorted and turned back to his piloting.

Charlie visibly screwed up his nerve to slide out of the cabinet into the water, even though none of it could touch him through the spacesuit. He floundered in the liquid up to his helmet-ring.

"But how . . . ?" Metz started to ask.

Charlie hefted a large, heavy waterproof sack from the locker to a man-seat next to Metz. "I used deductive reasoning," he said as he climbed up. "I figured Gillian's boys'd only be watching out for misbehavin' by a few grumbling *Stenos*. So, thought I, why not get to the longboat by a route they wouldn't even *think* of watching?"

Metz's eyes widened. "The sleeve! You crawled into one of the sealed maintenance ways that the builders used on Earth, and made your way to the boat's access panels, down by the thrust motors. . . ."

"Righto!" Charlie beamed as he buckled his seatbelt.

"You probably had to remove some plates in the sleeve wall, using a jack-pry. No dolphin could manage such a thing in an enclosed space, so they didn't think of it."

"No, they didn't."

Metz looked Charlie up and down. "You passed pretty close to the thrusters. Did you get cooked?"

"Hmmm. My suit rad-meter says raw to medium rare." Charlie mocked blowing on his fingertips.

Metz grinned. "I shall, indeed, take note of this rare display of ingenuity, Dr. Dart! And welcome aboard. I'll be too busy anyway, inspecting the Kiqui, to take proper care of that robot of yours. Now you can do it right."

Dart nodded eagerly. "That's why I'm here."

"Excellent. Perhaps we can have a few games of chess, as well."

"I'd like that."

They sat back and watched as the ocean ridges passed by. Every few minutes one would look at the other, and would burst out laughing. The *Stenos* were silent.

"What's in the sack?" Metz pointed to the large satchel on Dart's lap.

Charlie shrugged. "Personal effects, instruments. Only the barest, most minuscule, most Spartan necessities."

Metz nodded and settled back again. It would, indeed, be nice to have the chimpanzee along on the trip. Dolphins were fine people, of course. But Mankind's older client race had always struck him as better conversationalists. And dolphins didn't play chess worth a damn.

It was an hour later that Metz recalled Charlie's first words, on announcing his presence aboard. Just what did the chimp mean when he accused Takkata-Jim of "destroying evidence"? That was a very strange thing to say.

He put the question to Dart. "Ask the lieutenant," Charlie suggested. "He seemed to know what I meant. We're not exactly on speaking terms," he grumbled.

Metz nodded earnestly. "I *will* ask him. As soon as we get settled on the island, I will certainly do that."

63

Tom Orley

In the tangled shadows below the weed carpet, he made his way cautiously from airhole to airhole. The facemask helped him stretch a deep breath a long way, especially when he got near the island and had to search for an opening to the shore.

Tom finally crawled out onto land just as the orange sun Kthsemenee slipped behind a large bank of clouds to the west. The long Kithrup day would last for a while yet, but he missed the direct warming of the sun's rays. Evaporation-chill made him shiver as he pulled himself through a gap in the weeds, and up the rocky shoreline. He climbed on his hands and knees to a hummock a few meters above the sea, and sat back heavily against the rough basalt. Then he pulled the breathing mask down around his neck.

The island seemed to rock slowly, as if it were a cork bobbing in the sea. It would take a while to grow used to solid ground again—just long enough, he realized ironically, for him to finish what he had to do here and get back into the water again.

He pulled clumps of green slime from his shoulders, and shivered as the damp slowly evaporated.

Hunger. Ah, there was that, too.

It took his mind off the damp and chill, at least. He thought about pulling out his last foodbar, but decided it could wait. It was all within a thousand kilometers that he could eat, barring what he might find in alien wreckage.

Smoke still rose where the small ET scout had crashed, just over the shoulder of the mountain. The thin stream climbed to merge high above with sooty drifts from the volcano's crater. Once in a while, Tom heard the mountain itself growl.

Okay. Let's move.

He gathered his feet beneath him and pushed off.

The world wavered about him unsteadily. Still, he was pleasantly surprised to find himself standing without too much trouble.

Maybe Jill's right, he thought. *Maybe I have reserves I'd never touched before.*

He turned to his right, took a step, and almost tripped. He recovered, then stumbled along the rocky slope, thankful for his webbed gloves when it came to climbing over jagged rocks, serrated like chipped flint. One step after another, he drew near the source of the smoke.

Topping a small rise, he came into view of the wreck.

The scout had broken into three pieces. The stern section lay submerged, only its torn front end protruding from the charred weeds in the shallows. Tom checked the radiation meter at the rim of his facemask. He could stand the dose for a few days, if necessary.

The forward half of the wreck had split longitudinally, spilling the contents of the cockpit along a stony strand. Loose banners of fine wire wafted above metal bulkheads which had been pulled and twisted apart like taffy.

He thought about drawing his needler, but decided it would be better to have both hands free in case he fell.

Looks easy enough, Tom thought. *I just go down and inspect the damned thing. One step at a time.*

He moved carefully down the slope, and made it without catastrophe.

There wasn't much left.

Tom poked through the scattered small pieces, recognizing bits of various machines. But nothing told him what he wanted to know.

And there was no food.

Large bent sheets of metal lay everywhere. Tom approached one that seemed to have cooled off, and tried to lift it. It was too heavy to budge more than a few inches before he had to let it drop.

Tom panted with his hands on his knees for a moment, breathing heavily.

A few meters away was a great pile of driftwood. He went over and pulled out a few of the thicker stumps of dried seaweed. They were tough, but too springy to use as pry-bars.

Tom scratched his stubble and thought. He looked at the sea, covered all the way to the horizon with vile, slimy vines. Finally he started gathering dried vines together into two piles.

After dark he sat by a driftwood fire, weaving tough strands of vine into a pair of large flat fans, somewhat like tennis rackets with loops on one side. He wasn't sure they would work as desired, but tomorrow he would find out.

He sang softly in Trinary, to distract himself from his hunger. The whistled nursery rhyme echoed softly from the nearby cliffside.

> * *Hands and fire?*
> *Hands and fire!*
> * *Use them, use them*
> *To leap higher!*
>
> * *Dreams and song?*
> *Dreams and song!*
> * *Use them, use them*
> *To leap-long!* *

Tom stopped suddenly, and cocked his head. After a silent moment he slid his needler out of its holster.

Had he heard a sound? Or was it his imagination?

He rolled quietly out of the firelight and crouched in the shadows. He looked into the darkness, and like a dolphin, tried to listen to the shape of things. In a stalker's crouch, from cover to cover, he made a slow circuit of the wreckage-strewn beach.

"*Barkeemkleph Annatan P'Klenno. V'hoominph?*"

Tom dove behind a hull-sherd and rolled over. Breathing open-mouthed to keep silent, he listened.

"*V'hoomin Kent'thoon ph?*"

The voice resonated, as if from a metal cavity . . . from under one of the large pieces of wreckage? A survivor? Who would have imagined?

Tom called out. "*Birkech'kleph. V'human ides'k. V'Thennan' kleph ph?*"

He waited. When the voice in the darkness answered, Tom was up and running.

"*Idatess. V'Thennan'kleeph* . . ."

He dove once again and fetched up against another shard of metal. He crawled on his elbows and took a quick look around the side of the bulkhead.

And aimed his weapon directly into the eyes of a large, reptiloid face, only a meter away. The face grimaced in the dim starlight.

He had only met Thennanin once, and studied them at the school on Cathrhennlin for one week. The creature was half-squashed under a massive, warped metal plate. Tom could guess its expression was one of agony. The scout's arms and back had been broken under the piece of hull.

"*V'hoomin t'barrchit pa* . . ."

Tom adjusted to the dialect the other spoke. The Thennanin used a version of Galactic Six.

". . . would not kill you, human, had I even the means. I wish only to persuade you to talk to me and distract me for a time."

Tom holstered the needler and moved to sit cross-legged in front of the pilot. It would only be polite to listen to the creature—and be ready to put him out of his misery if he asked the favor.

"I grieve that I am unable to succor you," Tom answered in Galactic Six. "Though you are an enemy, I have never been one to call Thennanin wholly evil."

The creature grimaced again. His ridge-crest bumped intermittently against the metal roof and he winced each time.

"Nor do we think of *hooman'vlech* as totally without promise, though recalcitrant, wild, and irreverent."

Tom bowed, accepting as whole the partial compliment.

"I am prepared to do the service of termination, should you wish it," he offered.

"You are kind, but that is not our way. I will wait as my pain balances my life. The Great Ghosts shall judge me brave."

Tom lowered his gaze. "May they judge you brave."

The Thennanin breathed raggedly, eyes closed. Tom's hand drifted to his waistband. He touched the bulge that was the message bomb. *Are they still waiting, back at* Streaker? He wondered. *What will Creideiki decide to do if he doesn't hear from me?*

I must know what's been happening in the battle above Kithrup.

"For conversation and distraction," he offered, "shall we exchange questions?"

The Thennanin opened his eyes. They actually seemed to hold a hint of gratitude. "Nice. A nice idea. As elder, I shall begin. I will ask simple questions, so as not to strain you."

Tom shrugged. *Almost three hundred years we've had the* Library. *We have had six thousand years of intricate civilization. And still nobody believes humans could be anything but ignorant savages.*

"Why did you not, from Morgran, flee to a safer haven?" the scout asked. "Earth could not protect you, nor even those scoundrel Tymbrimi who lead you into evil ways. But the Abdicators are strong. You would have found safety with us. Why did you not come into our arms?"

He made it all sound so simple! If only it were so. If only there had been a truly powerful alignment to flee to, one that would not have charged, in return, more than *Streaker's* crew or Earth could afford to pay. How to tell the Thennanin that his Abdicators were only slightly less unpalatable than most of the other fanatics.

"It is our policy never to surrender to bullying threats," Tom said. "Never. Our history tells us the value of this tradition, more than those brought up on the *Library* annals could imagine. Our discovery will be given only to the Galactic Institutes, and only by our Terragens Council leaders themselves."

At mention of *Streaker's* "discovery" the Thennanin's face showed unmistakable interest. But he waited his turn, allowing Tom the next question.

"Are the Thennanin victorious overhead?" Tom asked anxiously. "I saw Tandu. Who prevails in the sky?"

Air whistled through the pilot's breathing vents. "The Glorious fail. The killer Tandu thrive, and Soro pagans abound. We harass where we can, but the Glorious have failed. Heretics shall gain the prize."

It was a bit of a tactless way to put it, with one of the "prizes" sitting in front of him. Tom cursed softly. What was he going to do? Some of the Thennanin survived, but could he tell Creideiki to go ahead and take off on that basis?

Should they try a ruse which, even if successful, would gain them allies too weak to do any good?

The Thennanin breathed raggedly.

Although it was not his turn, Tom asked the next question. "Are you cold? I will move my fire here. Also, there is work I must do, as we talk. Forgive this junior patron if I offend."

The Thennanin looked at him with purple, cat-irised eyes. "Politely spoken. We are told you humans are without manners. Perhaps you are merely unlearned, yet well-meaning..."

The scout wheezed and blew sand grains from his breathing slits, while Tom quickly moved his camp. By the flickering flame-light, the Thennanin sighed. "It is appropriate that, trapped and dying on a primitive world, I shall be warmed by the crafty fire-making skills of a wolfling. I shall ask you to tell a death-bound being about your discovery. No secrets, just a story...a story about the miracle of the Great Return..."

Tom drew forth a memory, one that still gave him chills.

"Consider ships," he began. "Think of starships—ancient, pitted, and great as moons..."

When he awakened next to the warm coals of his fire, the dawn was barely breaking, casting long dim shadows along the beach.

Tom felt much better. His stomach had become resigned to a fast, and sleep had done him a lot of good. He was still weak, but he felt ready to try a dash for the next possible haven.

He got up, brushed off the multi-colored sand, and peered to the north. Yes the floating derelict was still there. Hope on the horizon.

To his left, under the massive bulkhead, the Thennanin scout breathed softly, slowly dying. It had fallen asleep listening to Tom's story of the Shallow Cluster, of the shining giant ships, and the mysterious symbols on their sides. Tom doubted the creature would ever reawaken.

He was about to turn and pick up the shoes he had woven the night before, when he frowned and peered under a shading hand toward the eastern horizon.

If only the binoculars had been saved!

He squinted, and at last he made out a line of shadows

moving slowly against the brightening horizon, spindly-legged figures, and one smaller, shambling thing. A column of tiny silhouettes moved slowly northward.

Tom shivered. They were headed toward the eggshell wreck. Unless he acted quickly, they would cut him off from his only chance at survival.

And he could tell already that they were Tandu.

PART SIX

Scatter

"*The moot point is, whether Leviathan can long endure so wide a chase, and so remorseless a havoc...and the last whale, like the last man, smoke his last pipe, and then himself evaporate in the final puff.*"

—MELVILLE

64

Creideiki/Sah'ot

Creideiki stared at the holo display and concentrated. It was easier to talk than to listen. He could call up the words one or two at a time, speak them slowly, shuttling them like pearls on a string.

". . . neural link . . . repaired . . . by . . . Gillian and Maka-nee . . . but . . . but . . . speech . . . still . . . still . . ."

"Still gone," Sah'ot's image nodded. "You can use tools now, though?"

Creideiki concentrated on Sah'ot's simple question. You-can-use- . . . Each word was clear, its meaning obvious. But in a row they meant nothing. It was frustrating!

Sah'ot switched to Trinary.

> * Tools to prod?
> The balls
> The starships—
> * Is your jaw?
> The player
> The pilot— *

Creideiki nodded. That was much better, though even Trinary came to him like a foreign tongue, with difficulty.

> * Spider walkers, walkers, walkers
> * Holocomm talkers, talkers, talkers
> Are my playthings, are— *

Creideiki averted his eyes. He knew there were elements of Primal in that simple phrase, in the repetition and high whistling. It was humiliating to still have an active, able mind, and know that to the outside world you sounded retarded.

At the same time, he wondered if Sah'ot noticed a trace of the language of his dreams—the voices of the old gods.

Listening to the captain, Sah'ot was relieved. Their first conversation had started off well, but toward the end Creideiki's attention had begun to wander, especially when Sah'ot had started running him through a battery of linguistic tests.

Now, after Makanee's last operation, he seemed much more attentive.

He decided to test Creideiki's listening ability by telling him about his discovery. He carefully and slowly explained in Trinary about the "singing" he had heard while linked to the robot in the drill-tree funnel.

Creideiki looked confused for a long moment as he concentrated on Sah'ot's slow, simplified explanation, then he seemed to understand. In fact, from his expression, it seemed he thought it the most natural thing in the world that a planet should sing.

"Link...link me...pl—please....I...I will...listen... listen..."

Sah'ot clapped his jaw in assent, pleased. Not that Creideiki, with his language centers burned, would be able to make out anything but static. It took all of Sah'ot's subtle training and experience to trace the refrain. Except for that one time, when the voices from below had shouted in apparent anger, the sounds had been almost amorphous.

He still shuddered, remembering that one episode of lucidity.

"Okay, Creideiki," he said as he made the connection. "Listen closely!"

Creideiki's eyes recessed in concentration as the static crackled and popped over the line.

65

Gillian

"Triple damn! Well, we can't wait for her to get here to start the move. It might take Hikahi two days to circle around in the skiff. I want to have *Streaker* safely inside the Seahorse by then."

Suessi's simulacrum shrugged. "Well, you could leave her a note."

Gillian rubbed her eyes. "That's just what we'll do. We'll drop a monofilament relay link at *Streaker's* present position, so we can stay in touch with the party on the island. I'll stick a message to the relay telling her where we've gone."

"What about Toshio and Dennie?"

Gillian shrugged. "I'd hoped to send the skiff after them and Sah'ot . . . and maybe after Tom. But as things are, I'd better have Dennie and Sah'ot head toward your site by sled. I hate doing it. It's dangerous and I need Toshio there watching Takkata-Jim until just before we take off."

She didn't mention the other reason for wanting Toshio to stay as long as possible. They both knew that Tom Orley, if he flew the glider home, would return to the island. He ought to have someone waiting for him.

"Are we really going to abandon Metz and Takkata-Jim?" Suessi looked perplexed.

"And Charlie Dart, apparently. He stowed away on the longboat. Yes, it's their choice. They hope to make it home after the Galactics blow us to kingdom come. For all I know they may be right. Anyway, the final decision's Hikahi's, when she finally shows up and finds out she's in command."

Gillian shook her head. "Ifni sure seems to have gone out of her way to throw us curves, hasn't she, Hannes?"

The elderly engineer smiled. "Luck's always been fickle. That's why she's a lady."

"Hmmph!" But Gillian didn't have the energy to give him much of a dirty look. A light winked on the console next to the holo display.

"Here it is, Hannes. The engine room is ready. I've got to go, now. We're getting under way."

"Good luck, Gillian." Suessi held up an "O" sign, then broke the connection.

Gillian flicked a switch cutting into the comm line from *Streaker* to the island. "Sah'ot, this is Gillian. Sorry to break in, but would you please tell the captain we're about to move." It was a courtesy to let Creideiki know. *Streaker* had been his, once.

"Yesss, Gillian." There was a series of high, repetitious whistles in very Primal-like Trinary. Much of it crested over the upper range of even Gillian's gene-enhanced hearing.

"The captain wantss to go outside to watch," Sah'ot said. "He promises not to get in the way."

Gillian couldn't see any real reason to refuse. "All right. But tell him to check with Wattaceti first, to use a sled, and to be careful! We won't be able to spare anyone to go chasing him if he wanders off!"

There was another high series of whistles that Gillian could barely follow. Creideiki signaled that he understood.

"Oh, by the way, Sah'ot," Gillian added. "Please ask Toshio to call me as soon as the longboat arrives."

"Yes!"

Gillian cut the connection and got up to dress. There were so many things to juggle simultaneously!

I wonder if I did the right thing, letting Charlie Dart sneak away, she thought. *If he or Takkata-Jim behave in a way I don't expect, what'll I do?*

A tiny light shone at the corner of her console. The Niss machine still wanted to talk to her. The light didn't flash urgent. Gillian decided to ignore it as she hurried out to supervise the move.

66

⸙⸙⸙⸙⸙⸙⸙⸙⸙⸙⸙⸙⸙⸙⸙⸙⸙⸙⸙⸙⸙⸙⸙⸙

Akki

With aching muscles, Akki swam slowly out of the notch in which he had rested until dawn.

He took several deep breaths and dove, scattering a school of brightly scaled fish-like creatures through shafts of morning light. Without thinking, he speared through the school and snapped up a large fish, relishing its frantic struggle between his jaws. But the metal taste was bitter. He flipped the creature away, spitting.

Red clouds spread a pink glow across the east as he surfaced again. Hunger growled in his compound stomachs. He wondered if the sound was loud enough to be picked up by his hunter.

It's unfair. When K'tha-Jon finds me, he, *at least, will have something to eat!*

Akki shook himself. What a bizarre thought! "You're falling apart, middie. K'tha-Jon is no cannibal. He's a...a..."

A what? Akki remembered the final stretch, yesterday at sunset, when he had somehow made it to the chain of metal-mounds just meters ahead of his pursuer. The chase amidst the tiny islands had been a confusion of bubbles and surf and hunting cries. For hours after he had finally found a hiding place, he listened to staccato bursts of sonar that proved K'tha-Jon had not gone far.

Thought of the bosun sent chills down Akki's spine. What kind of creature *was* he? It wasn't just the irrationality of this death-chase; there was something else as well, something in the *way* K'tha-Jon hunted. The giant's sonar sweeps contained something malevolent that made Akki want to curl up in a ball.

Of course, *Stenos* gene-grafts might account for some of his size and irritability. But in K'tha-Jon there was more. Something very different must have gone into the bosun's gene splice. Something terrifying. Something Akki, raised on Calafia, had never encountered.

Akki swam close to the edge of the coral mound and stuck his jaw out beyond the northern verge. There were only the natural sounds of the Kithrup sea.

He hopped up on his tail and scanned visually. To go west, or north? To Hikahi, or Toshio?

Better north. This chain of mounds might extend to the one where the encampment lay. It might provide cover.

He dashed across the quarter-kilometer gap to the next island, then listened quietly. There was no change. Breathing a little more easily, he crossed the next channel, then the next, swimming quick bursts, then listening, then resuming his cautious passage.

Once he heard a strange, complex chatter to his right. He lay motionless until he realized that it couldn't be K'tha-Jon. He detoured slightly to take a look.

It was an underwater skirmish line of balloon-like creatures, with distended air bladders and lively blue faces. They carried crude implements and nets filled with thrashing prey. Except for a few holos sent back by Dennie Sudman and Sah'ot, this was Akki's first glimpse of the Kithrup natives, the Kiqui. He watched, fascinated, then swam toward them. He had thought himself still far south of Toshio, but if this group was the same . . .

As soon as they caught sight of him the hunters squeaked in panic. Dropping their nets, they scrambled up the vine-covered face of a nearby island. Akki realized that he must have encountered a different tribe, one which had never seen dolphins before.

Still, seeing them was something. He watched the last one climb out of sight. Then he turned northward once more.

But when he passed the northern shore of the next mound, a sharp beam of sound passed over him.

Akki quailed. How! Had K'tha-Jon duplicated his logic about an island chain? Or had some demon instinct told him where to hunt his prey?

The eerie call passed over him once more. It had mutated

further during the night into a piercing, falling cry that set
Akki shivering.

The cry pealed again, nearer, and Akki knew he couldn't
hide. That cry would seek him out in any cleft or cranny,
until the panic took hold. He had to make a break for it,
while he still had control over his mind!

67

∽∾∽∾∽∾∽∾∽∾∽∾∽∾∽∾∽∾∽∾∽∾∽∾∽∾∽∾∽∾∽

Keepiru

The fight had begun in the predawn darkness.

A few hours ago Keepiru realized that his pursuer's sled
was showing no sign of failing. The engine screamed, but it
would not die. Keepiru notched his own upward well beyond
the red line, but it was too late. A short time later, he heard
the whine of a torpedo homing in on him from behind. He
zigged leftward and down, blowing ballast to leave a cloud of
noisy bubbles in his wake.

The torpedo streaked past him and into the gloom
beyond. An amplified squawk of disappointment and indignation echoed amongst the rills and seamounts. Keepiru was
used to hearing Primal obscenities from his pursuer.

He had almost reached the line of metal-mounds behind
which the two swimming dolphins had disappeared a few
hours back. As he had drawn nearer, Keepiru had listened to
the distant hunt cries, and been chilled by a gnawing associa-
tion that he couldn't bring himself yet to believe. It made
him dread for Akki.

Now Keepiru had his own problems. He wished Akki luck
holding out until he could get rid of this idiot on his own tail.

It was growing light overhead. Keepiru dove his sled
behind a lumpy ridge, then throttled the engine back and
waited.

Moki cursed as the tiny torpedo failed to detonate.

> # Teeth, teeth are—are—
> Better, better than—
> # Things! #

He swung his jaw left and right. He had abandoned the sled's sensors, and was controlling the machine purely by habit.

Where *was* the smart-aleck! Let him come out and get it over with!

Moki was tired and cranky and unutterably bored. He had never imagined that being a Great Bull could be so tedious. Moki wanted the hot, almost orgasmic rage back. He tried to call up the bloodlust again, but kept thinking about killing fish, not dolphins.

If only he could emulate the savagery he had heard in K'tha-Jon's hunt-cry! Moki no longer hated the frightening bosun. He had begun to think of the giant as a spirit creature of pure and evil nature. He would kill this smart-aleck *Tursiops* and bring its head to K'tha-Jon as proof of his worthiness as a disciple. Then he, too, would become elemental, a terror that none would ever dare thwart.

Moki brought the machine about in a circle, keeping close to the seafloor to take advantage of shadows of sound. The *Tursiops* had turned left at high speed. His turn *had* to be wider than Moki's, so all Moki had to do was hunt in the correct arc.

Moki had been on guard duty when this chase began, so his sled had torpedoes. He was sure the smartass didn't have any. He whistled in eager anticipation of an end to the tedious chase.

A sound! He turned so quickly he banged his snout against the plastic bubble-dome. Moki gunned the sled forward, readying another torpedo. *This* one would finish his enemy off.

A sheer drop opened into a broad ocean canyon. Moki took ballast and fell, hugging the wall. He throttled back and stopped.

Minutes passed as the sound of muffled engines grew louder from his left. The oncoming sled was staying close to the cliff face, at a greater depth.

Suddenly, it was below him! Moki chose not to fire right away. This was too easy! Let the smart-aleck hear death suddenly fall upon him from behind, too close to evade. Let him writhe in panic before Moki's torpedo tore his body into pieces!

His sled growled, then dropped in pursuit. His victim could never turn in time! Moki crowed,

> # A herd bull is! -is!
> # A Great Bull ... #

Moki interrupted his chant. Why wasn't the smart-aleck fleeing?

He had been relying entirely upon sound. Only now did he turn his eye on his intended victim.

The other sled was empty! It drove along slowly, unpiloted. But then where ... ?

> * Hunting ears
>   Can make a bull—
> * But eyes
>   And brains
>   Make spacefen— *

The voice was above him! Moki cried out, trying to turn the sled and fire a torpedo at the same time. With a despairing wail the engines screamed and then died. His neural link went dead just as he came about into sight of a sleek, gray *Tursiops* dolphin, two meters above him, white teeth shining in the light from the surface.

> * And fools
>   Make only
>   Corpses— *

Moki screamed as the cutting torch on the pilot's harness exploded into laser-blue brilliance.

68

∽◠∽

Tom Orley

Where did they all come from?

Tom Orley hid behind a low weed mound and looked about at the various alien parties on the horizon. He counted at least three groups, all converging from different directions on the floating eggshell-shaped wreck.

About a mile behind him, the volcano still rumbled. He had left the crashed Thennanin scoutship at dawn, leaving a pan of precious fresh water under the dying pilot's mouth, within reach if he should ever awaken.

He had set out soon after sighting the party of Tandu, testing his newly woven "weed-shoes" on the uneven slimy surface. The splayed, snowshoe-like devices helped him walk cautiously across the slick carpet of vines.

At first he moved much faster than the others. But soon the Tandu developed a new technique. They stopped floundering in the mire, and came on at a brisk walk. Tom kept low and worried about what would happen if they caught sight of him.

And now there were other parties as well, one approaching from the southwest and one from the west. He couldn't make them out clearly yet, just dots bobbing slowly and with difficulty on a low, serrated horizon. But where the hell had they all come from?

The Tandu were closest. There were at least eight or nine of them, approaching in a column. Each creature splayed its six spindly legs wide apart to spread its weight. In their arms they cradled long, glistening instruments that could only be weapons. They marched forward rapidly.

Tom wondered what their new tactic was. Then he noticed that the lead Tandu did not carry a weapon. Instead, it held the leash of a shaggy, shambling creature. The keeper leaned forward over its charge, as if coaxing it to keep at a given task.

Tom risked raising his head a couple of feet above the mound.

"Well, I'll be damned."

The hairy creature was *creating* land—or at least solidity—in a narrow causeway in front of the party! Just before and on both sides of the trail, there was a faint shimmering where reality seemed to struggle against a noxious intrusion.

An Episiarch! Momentarily, Tom forgot his predicament, grateful for this rare sight.

As he watched, the causeway failed in one spot. The luminous band around the edges of the trail snapped together with a loud bang. The Tandu warrior standing there flailed and thrashed as it fell into the weeds. By fighting it merely tore the carpet and opened the hole wider until, finally, it sank like a stone into the sea.

None of the other Tandu seemed to take notice. The two behind the gap leaped across to the temporarily solid "ground" beyond. The party, diminished by one, continued to advance.

Tom shook his head. He *had* to reach the wreck first! He couldn't afford to let the Tandu pass him.

Yet if he did anything, even resumed his own march, they'd certainly spot him. He didn't doubt their efficiency with those weapons they carried. No human warrior ever underestimated the Tandu for long.

Reluctantly, he knelt and untied the fastenings on his weed-shoes. Discarding them, he crawled carefully to the edge of an open pool.

He counted slowly, waiting until he could hear the column of Galactics approaching. He rehearsed his moves in his mind.

Taking several deep breaths, he pulled his diving mask over his face, making certain it was snug and the collecting fins were clear. Then he pulled his needler from its holster, holding it in two hands.

Tom set his feet on two firm roots and checked his balance. The pool was just in front of him.

He closed his eyes.

> * Listen—
> > For the swishing tail
> > > Of the tiger shark— *

His empathy sense pinpointed the powerful psi emissions of the mad ET adept, now only some eighty meters away.

"Gillian...," he sighed. Then, in one sudden fluid motion, he stood up and extended his weapon. His eyes opened and he fired.

69

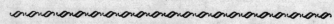

Toshio

Against Toshio's objections, they had used the last of the longboat's energy to lift it to a landing site on top of the island. He had offered to blast a wider opening into the chamber below the metal-mound, but Takkata-Jim had turned his suggestion down cold.

That meant two hours of backbreaking work, heaping chopped foliage over the small ship to camouflage it. Toshio wasn't sure even that would do any good if the Galactics finished their battle and turned their full attention to the planet's surface.

Metz and Dart were supposed to help him. Toshio had set them to work cutting brush, but found that he had to tell them to do each and every thing. Dart was sullen and angry at being commanded by a middie he had ordered around only days before. He obviously wanted to get to the supplies he had excitedly dropped by the drill-tree pool before being drafted into the work crew. Metz had been willing enough, but was so anxious to be off talking to Dennie that he was distracted and worse than useless.

Toshio finally sent them both away and finished the job by himself.

At last the boat was covered. He slumped to the ground and rested against the bole of an oli-nut tree.

Damn Takkata-Jim! Toshio and Dennie were supposed to

see the encampment secure, report their findings on the
Kiqui to Metz, and then climb on their sleds and get *out* of
here! Gillian expected them to set out in a few hours, and yet
almost nothing was accomplished!

To top it all off, *Streaker* had only warned him an hour or
so in advance that he could probably expect a stowaway.
Gillian decided not to have Charlie arrested for violation of
orders, even though it appeared he had stolen equipment
from at least a dozen labs aboard the ship. Toshio was glad to
be spared the added chore. There wasn't much of anything
hereabouts to use as a jail, anyway.

Foliage rustled to Toshio's left. A series of mechanical
whirrings accompanied the sound of crushing vegetation.
Then four "spiders" pushed through the brush to enter his
tiny clearing. A *Stenos* dolphin lay on the flotation pad of
each armored mechanical, controlling the four high-jointed
legs with neural-link commands. Toshio stood up as they
approached.

Takkata-Jim passed by, eyeing him coolly, silently. The
other three spiders followed him across the clearing and back
into the forest. The *Stenos* piped to each other in gutter-Trinary.

Toshio stared after them. He discovered that he had
been holding his breath.

"I don't know about Takkata-Jim, but those fen *with* him
are crazier than Atlast pier-nesters," he said to himself,
shaking his head. He had met few so-called *Stenos* on Calafia.
Some had displayed quirks, positive and negative, like Sah'ot.
But none had ever had the look that the former vice-captain's
followers had in their eyes.

The sound of the procession faded away. Toshio got up to
his feet.

He wondered why Gillian had let Takkata-Jim go at all.
Why not just throw him and his cohorts in the brig and have
done with it?

Granted, it was a good idea to leave a party with the
longboat, to try to sneak back to Earth if *Streaker* was lost
trying to escape. Gillian probably couldn't spare any of the
reliable members of the crew. But . . .

He turned toward the village of the Kiqui, thinking as
he walked.

Of course, the longboat was stripped. Theoretically, Takkata-
Jim couldn't contact the Galactics even if he wanted to. And
Toshio couldn't imagine a reason he'd want to.

But what if he *had* a reason? And what if he found a way?

Toshio almost bumped into a tree in his worried concentration. He looked up and corrected his path.

I'll just have to make sure, he decided. Tonight I'll have to find out if he can cause trouble.

Tonight.

The tribe's adults squatted around a circle in a clearing in the center of the village. Ignacio Metz and Dennie Sudman sat to one side. The Nest-Mother squatted across from them, her bright green-and-red-striped puffer sacks fully inflated. The elders on either side of her billowed and chuffed like a chain of gaily painted balloons in the forest-filtered sunshine.

Toshio stopped at the edge of the village clearing. The sunshine filtered through the trees, revealing a conclave of races.

The Kiqui Nest-Mother chattered, waving her paws in a queer up-and-down pattern that Dennie had said connoted happy emphasis. If the oldest female had been angry, her gestures would have been crosswise. It was a blissfully simple expression pattern. The rest of the tribe repeated her sounds, sometimes anticipating her in a rising and falling chant of consensus.

Ignacio Metz nodded excitedly, cupping one hand over an earphone as he listened to the translation computer. When the chant died down he spoke a few words into a microphone. A long series of high-pitched repetitive squeaks came out of the machine's speaker.

Dennie's expression was one of relief. She had dreaded the uplift specialist's first meeting with the Kiqui. But Metz had not, apparently, muffed her long and careful negotiations with the pre-sentients. The meeting seemed to be coming to a satisfactory conclusion.

Dennie caught sight of Toshio, and smiled brilliantly. Without ceremony she stood up and left the circle. She hurried over to where he waited at the edge of the village clearing.

"How's it going?" he asked.

"Wonderfully! It turns out he's read every word I sent back! He understands their pack protocol, their physical manifestations of sex and age, and he thought my behavioral analysis was 'exemplary'! Exemplary!"

Toshio smiled, sharing her pleasure.

"He's talking about getting me an appointment as a fellow at the Uplift Center! Can you imagine that?" Dennie couldn't help bouncing up and down excitedly.

"What about the treaty?"

"Oh they're ready any time. If Hikahi makes it here in the skiff we'll take a dozen Kiqui back to *Streaker* with us. Otherwise a few will go back to Earth with Metz in the longboat. It's all settled."

Toshio looked back at the happy villagers and tried not to show his misgivings.

Of course, it was for the good of the Kiqui as a species. They would fare far better under the patronage of Mankind than under almost any other starfaring race. And Earth geneticists had to have living beings to examine before any sort of adoption claim could be made.

Every attempt would be made to keep the first group of aboriginals healthy. Half of Dennie's job had been to analyze their bodily requirements, including needed trace elements. But it was still unlikely any of the first group would survive. Even if they did, Toshio doubted the Kiqui had a notion of the strangeness they were about to embark upon.

They're not sentients yet, he reminded himself. By Galactic law they're still animals. And, unlike anyone else in the Five Galaxies, we'll at least try to explain to their limited understanding, and ask permission.

But he remembered a stormy night, with driving rain and flashing lightning, when the little amphibians had huddled around him and an injured dolphin who was his friend, keeping them warm and warding off despair with their company.

He turned away from the sun-washed clearing.

"Then there's nothing keeping you here any longer?" He asked Dennie.

She shook her head. "I'd rather stay a while longer, of course. Now that I'm finished with the Kiqui I can really work on the problem of the metal-mound. That's why I was so grouchy a couple of days ago. Besides being so tired trying to do two major jobs, I was also frustrated. But now we're a step closer to solving that problem. And did you know the core of the metal-mound is still alive? It's . . ."

Toshio had to interrupt to stop the flow of words. "Dennie! Stop it for a minute, please. Answer my question. Are you ready to leave now?"

Dennie blinked. She changed tracks, frowning. "Is it *Streaker?* Has something gone wrong?"

"They began the move a few hours ago. I want you to gather all of your notes and samples and secure them to your sled. You and Sah'ot are leaving in the morning."

She looked at him, his words slowly sinking in. "You mean *you*, me, and Sah'ot, don't you?"

"No. I'm staying for another day. I have to."

"But why?"

"Look, Dennie, I can't talk about it now. Just do as I ask, please."

As he turned to walk back toward the drill-tree pool she grabbed his arm. Holding on, she was forced to follow.

"But we were going to go together! If you have things to do here, I'll wait for you!"

He walked along without answering. He couldn't think of anything to say. It was bitter to win her respect and affection at last, only to lose her within hours.

If this is what being grown up means, they can have it, he thought. *It sucks*.

As they approached the pool, sounds of loud argument came from that direction. Toshio hurried. Dennie trotted alongside until they burst into the clearing.

Charles Dart screamed and clutched at a slender cylinder that was gripped at the other end by the manipulator arm of Takkata-Jim's spider. Charlie strained against the pull of the waldo-machine. Takkata-Jim grinned open-mouthed.

The tug of war lasted for a few seconds as the neochimp's powerful muscles strained, then the cylinder popped out of his hands. He fell back to the dust and barely stopped before rolling into the pool. He hopped up and shrieked his anger.

Toshio saw three other *Stenos*-controlled spiders trooping off toward the longboat. Each carried another of the thin cylinders. Toshio stopped in his tracks when he got a good look at the one Takkata-Jim had taken. His eyes went wide.

"There is no longer any danger," Takkata-Jim told him. His voice carried insouciance. "I have confissscated these. They'll be kept safe aboard my boat, and there will be no harm."

"They're mine, you thief!" Charles Dart hopped angrily, and his hands fluttered. "You criminal!" he growled. "You think I don't know you tried to m-murder Creideiki? We all know you did! You wrecked the buoys to destroy the evidence! And n-now you steal the tools of m-my trade!"

"Which you stole from *Streaker*'s armory, no doubt. Or do you wish to call Dr. Baskin for confirmation that they truly are yoursss?"

Dart growled and showed an impressive display of teeth. He whirled away from the neo-dolphin and sat down in the dust in front of a complex diving robot, freshly unpacked on the verge of the pool.

Takkata-Jim's spider started to turn, but the fin noticed Toshio looking at him. For just a moment, Takkata-Jim's cool reserve broke under the youth's fierce gaze. He looked away, and then back at Toshio.

"Don't-t believe everything you hear, boy-human," he said. "Much I have done, and will do, and I'm convinced I am right. But it wasss not I who hurt Creideiki."

"Did you destroy the buoys?" Toshio could sense Dennie standing close behind him, watching the large dolphin silently over his shoulder.

"Yesss. But it was not I who ssset the trap. Like King Henry with Beckett-t, I only found out about it after. Tell this, on Earth, if by some strange chance you should escape and I don't. Another took the initiative."

"Who did it, then?" Toshio's fists were tight balls.

A long sigh escaped Takkata-Jim's blowmouth.

"Our Dr. Metz wrung from the Survey Board berths for some who shouldn't have been on this voyage. He was impatient. A few of his *Stenos* had . . . *unusual* family trees."

"The *Stenos* . . ."

"A *few Stenos*! I am not one of Metz's experiments! I am a starship officer. I earned my place!" The dolphin's voice was defiant.

"When the pressure built to the breaking point, some of them turned to me. I thought I could control them. But there was one who turned out to be more than even I could manage. Tell them if you get home, Toshio Iwashika. Tell them on Earth that it'sss possible to turn a dolphin into a monster. They should be warned."

Takkata-Jim gave him one long, intent look, then his spider turned away and followed his crew back to the longboat.

"He's a liar!" Dennie whispered after he had gone. "He sounds so reasonable and logical, but I shiver when I listen to him!"

Toshio watched the spider disappear down the trail.

"No," he said. "He is ambitious, and maybe crazy too. He's probably a traitor, as well. But for some reason I think everything he said was explicitly true. Maybe a surface honesty is what he clings to now, for pride's sake."

He turned, shaking his head. "Not that that makes him any less dangerous."

He approached Charles Dart, who looked up with a friendly smile. Toshio squatted near the chimp planetologist.

"Dr. Dart, how big were they?"

"Were what, Toshio? Say! Have you *seen* this new robot? I made it up special. It can dive to the base of the shaft, then dig laterally to those big magma tunnels we detected . . ."

"How big *were* they, Charlie?" Toshio demanded. He was tense, and ready to throttle the chimpanzee. "*Tell* me!"

Dart glanced briefly, guiltily, at Toshio, then looked down at the pool wistfully.

"Only about a kiloton each," he sighed. "Hardly big enough to set off decent crust waves, really." He looked up with large, innocent brown eyes. "They were really only teeny little A-bombs, honest!"

70

Hikahi

The need to run quietly kept her speed to little more than it might have been with a sled. It was frustrating.

Cut off from contact with anyone for more than a day, Hikahi studied the seascape around her to avoid thinking about the possible fate of Creideiki and *Streaker*. She would find out what had happened sooner or later. Until then worry would only wear her out.

The morning light filtered down to the canyon bottoms as she swung east and then northward. Clots of dangle-weed drifted overhead, and copper-backed fish darted briefly alongside, until the driving skiff left them behind.

Once she caught sight of something long and sinuous that quickly slithered into a sea-cave as she approached. There was no time to stop and explore, but she did take the monster's picture as she passed.

What will I do if I find Streaker *destroyed?* The thought came unwanted.

I'll go back to the Thennanin wreck as an intermediate step. They'd need me there. But I'd be commander, then. And hiding at the bottom of the ocean wouldn't be a long-term solution. Not on this deadly world.

Can I bring myself to negotiate a surrender?

If she did, she wouldn't let the Galactics take her personally. She was one of the few who, with the right notes, could plot an accurate course back to the derelict fleet.

Maybe I'd see the crew safely interned and then make a break for it in the skiff, she thought. *Not that the skiff could ever make it all the way home, even if it could run a Galactic blockade. But someone had to try to get word back to Earth. Perhaps there would be a way to punish the fanatics . . . make their behavior so costly to them that they'd think twice before bullying Earthlings again.*

Hikahi knew she was dreaming. In a few thousand years humans and their clients might have that kind of power, maybe.

Hikahi listened. There was a sound . . .

She turned up the gain on the ship's hydrophones. Filters removed the background growl of the engines and the tide. She heard the soft scurrying sounds of the ocean creatures.

"Computer! Filter for cetacean output!"

The patterns of sound changed. The sea became quiet. Still, there was a trace of something.

"Increase gain!" The noise level rose. Above the static hiss she heard the faint but distinguishable cries of swimming dolphins! They were desperate sounds of combat.

Was she picking up the echoes of straggling survivors of a disaster? What to do? She wanted to rush to the aid of the distressed fen. But who was pursuing them?

"Machine soundsss!" She commanded. But the detector winked a red light, indicating that there were none within range. So, the dolphins were sledless.

If she attempted a rescue, she risked the only hope of

the crew back at the Seahorse. Should she make a detour around the refugees, and hurry toward *Streaker* as planned? It was an agonizing choice.

Hikahi cut her speed to run still quieter, and sent the skiff due north, toward the dim cries.

71

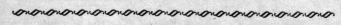

Charles Dart

He waited until everyone had left before he unscrewed the back of the new robot and checked its contents.

Yes, it was still there. Safely concealed.

Ah, well, he thought. *I'd hoped to repeat the experiment. But one bomb should be enough.*

72

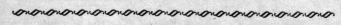

Streaker

FROM THE JOURNAL OF GILLIAN BASKIN

We're on our way. Everyone aboard seems relieved to be moving at last.

Streaker lifted off the ocean floor late last night, impellers barely ticking over. I was on the bridge, monitoring reports by the fen outside, and watching the strain gauges until we were sure Streaker was okay. In fact, she sounded positively eager to be off.

Emerson and the crew in the engine room should be proud of the job they've done, though, of course, it's the coils Tom and Tsh't found, that made it possible. Streaker *hums like a starship once again.*

Our course is due south. We dropped a monofilament relay behind to keep us in touch with the party on the island, and left a message for Hikahi when she shows up.

I hope she hurries. Being a commander is more complicated than I'd ever imagined. I have to make sure everything is done in the right order and correctly, and all as unobtrusively as possible, without making the fen feel "the old lady" is hovering over them. It makes me wish I had some of the military training Tom got while I was away in medical school.

Less than thirty hours and we'll reach the Thennanin shell. Suessi says they'll be ready for us. Meanwhile, we have scouts out, and Wattaceti paces us overhead in a detection sled. His instruments show very little leakage, so we should be safe for now.

I'd give a year's wages for Hikahi or Tsh't, or even Keepiru right now. I'd never understood, before, why a captain treasures a good executive officer so much.

Speaking of captains. Ours is a wonder.

Creideiki seemed to be in a daze for a long time, after getting out of sick bay. But his long conversation with Sah'ot appears to have roused him. I don't know what Sah'ot did, but I would never have believed a person so severely damaged as Creideiki could be so vigorous, or make himself so useful.

When we lifted off he asked to be allowed to supervise the scouts and flankers. I was desperate for a reliable fin to put in charge out there, and thought that having him visible could help morale. Even the Stenos were excited to have him about. Their last bitterness over my "coup"—and Takkata-Jim's exile—seems to have dissipated.

Creideiki is limited to the simplest calls in Trinary, but that seems to be enough. He's out there now, zipping about in his sled, keeping things orderly by pointing, nudging, and setting an example. In only a few hours Tsh't should rendezvous with the scouts we sent ahead, and then Creideiki can come back aboard.

There's a tiny light on my comm that's been flashing since I returned. It's that crazy Tymbrimi Niss machine. I've been keeping the damned thing waiting.

Tom wouldn't approve, I guess. But a fem has only so much strength, and I've got to take a nap. If the matter were urgent it would have broken in and spoken by now.

Oh, Tom, we could use your endurance now. Are you on your way back? Is your little glider even now winging home to Toshio's island?

Who am I fooling? Since the first psi-bomb we've detected nothing, only noise from the space battle, some of it indicating fighting over his last known position. He's set off none of the message globes. So either he's decided not to send an ambiguous message or worse.

Without word from Tom, how can we decide what to do, once we enter the Seahorse? Do we take off and try our luck, or hide within the hulk as long as we can?

It will be Hikahi's decision when the time comes.

Gillian closed the journal and applied her thumbprint to the fail-safe self-destruct. She got up and turned off the light.

On her way out of the lab, she passed the stasis-bier of the ancient cadaver they had reclaimed at such cost from the Shallow Cluster. Herbie just lay there grinning under a tiny spotlight, an ancient enigma. A mystery.

A troublemaker.

Battered, battle-scarred, *Streaker* moved slowly along the valley floor, her engines turning over with gentle, suppressed power. A dark, foamy mist rose below her where impellers kicked up the surface ooze.

The nubby cylinder slid over gloomy black rills and abysses, skirting the edges of seamounts and valley walls. Tiny sleds paced alongside, guiding the ship by sonar-speak.

Creideiki watched his ship in motion once again. He listened to the clipped reports of the scouts and sentries, and the replies of the bridge staff. He couldn't follow the messages in detail; the sophisticated technical argot was as out of reach to him as last year's wine. But he could sense the under-meaning; the crew had things well in hand.

Streaker couldn't really shine in this light, dim and blue, fifty meters down, but he could listen—his own sonar clicked softly in accompaniment as he savored the deep rumble of her engines, and he imagined he could be with her when she flew again.

: Never Again Creideiki : You Shall Never Fly With Her Again :

The spectre, K-K-Kph-kree, came into being gradually alongside him, a ghostly figure of silver and sonic shadows. The presence of the god did not surprise, or even bother Creideiki. He had been expecting It to come. It swam lazily, easily keeping pace alongside the sled.

: You Escaped Us : Yet Now You Purposely Sculpt Me Out Of Song : Because Of The Old Voices You Heard? : The Voices From Below? :

: Yes :
Creideiki thought not in Anglic or Trinary, but in the new language he had been learning.
: There is ancient anger within this world : I have heard its song :
The dream-god's great brow sparkled starlight. Its small jaw opened. Teeth shone.

: And What Do You Plan To Do? :

Creideiki sensed that It already knew the answer.
: My Duty : He replied in Its own speech.
: What Else Can I Ever Do? :
From the depths of the Whale Dream, It sighed approval.

Creideiki turned up the gain on his hydrophones. There were faraway excited echoes from up ahead—joyous sounds of greeting.
Creideiki looked at his sled's sonar display. At the far edge of its range was a small cluster of dots coming inward. They joined the specks that were *Streaker*'s scouts. The first group had to be Tsh't's party from the Seahorse.
Making sure no one was nearby to take note, he turned his sled aside into a small side canyon. He slipped behind the shadows of a rock outcrop and turned off his engine. He

waited then, watching *Streaker* pass below his aerie, until she vanished, along with the last of her flankers, around a curve in the long canyon.

"Good-bye..." He concentrated on the Anglic words, one at a time. "Good-bye...and...good luck..."

When it was safe, he turned on his sled and rose out of the little niche. He swung about and headed northward, toward the place they had left twenty hours before.

: You Can Come Along If You Like : he told the god—part figment of his mind, part something else. The ghostly figure answered in un-words made up from Creideiki's own sonar sounds.

: I Accompany You : I Would Not Miss This For The Song of the World :

PART SEVEN

∽∾∽∾∽∾∽∾∽∾∽∾∽∾∽∾∽∾∽∾∽∾∽∾∽∾∽∾

The Food Chain

"Master, I marvel how the fishes live in the sea."
"Why, as men do aland—the great ones eat up the little ones."
—WILLIAM SHAKESPEARE
King Richard the Second

73

∽∾∽∾∽∾∽∾∽∾∽∾∽∾∽∾∽∾∽∾∽∾∽∾∽∾∽∾∽

Akki

It was a scream that curdled his marrow. Only a monster could make a sound like that. He fled *it* almost as hard as he fled the creature that voiced it.

By noontime Akki realized it was nearly over.

His exhaustion showed in a laboring heart and heavy breathing, but also in a painful sloughing of the outer layers of his skin. His allergic reaction to the water seemed to be aggravated by fatigue. It had grown worse as he frantically dodged in and out amongst tiny islets. His once-smooth, dynamically supple hide was now a rough mass of sores. His mind felt little more agile than his body.

Several times he had escaped traps that should have left him meat. Once he had fled a sonar reflection almost into K'tha-Jon's jaws. The giant had grinned and flourished his laser rifle as Akki turned away frantically. It hadn't been by speed or cleverness that Akki escaped. He realized that his enemy was just toying with him.

He had hoped to flee northward, toward Toshio's island, but now he was all turned around, and north was lost to him. Perhaps if he could wait until sunset . . .

No. I won't last that long. It's time to end it.

The chilling hunt-scream pealed out again. The ululation seemed to coagulate the water around him.

A large part of Akki's fatigue had come from the involuntary terror that cry sent through him. What devil *was* it, that chased him?

A little while ago he thought he had distantly heard

333

another cry. It sounded like a *Tursiops* search call. But he was probably imagining things. Whatever was going on back at *Streaker*, they couldn't have spared anyone to look for him. Even if they had, how could anyone ever find him in this wide ocean?

He had done *Streaker* one service, in distracting the monster K'tha-Jon, in leading him away from where he could do worse harm.

I hope Gillian and Hikahi got back and straightened things out, he thought. *I'm sure they did.*

He took quiet breaths in the shadow of a rock cleft. K'tha-Jon knew where he was, of course. It was only a matter of time until he grew bored with the chase and came to collect his prey.

I'm fading, Akki thought. *I've got to finish this while there's a chance to win something from it—even if it's just the honor of choosing my own time to die.*

He checked the charge on his harness cells. There was only enough for two good shots from his cutter torch. Those would have to be from very short range, and no doubt K'tha-Jon's rifle was almost fully charged.

With his harness-hands Akki plugged his breather back over his blowmouth. Ten minutes of oxygen remained. More than enough.

The high scream echoed again, chilling, taunting.

All right, monster. He clenched his jaw to keep from shivering again. *Hold your horses. I'm coming.*

74

Keepiru

Keepiru raced to the northeast, toward the battle sounds he had heard during the night. He swam hard and fast at the surface, arching and thrusting to drive through the water. He cursed at the drag of his harness, but to drop it was unthinkable.

Once again he cursed the damnable luck. Both his and Moki's sleds were used up, worthless, and had to be left behind.

As he entered the maze of tiny islands, he heard the hunt-scream clearly for the first time.

Until now he could tell himself he was imagining things—that distance or some strange refraction in the water had tricked him into hearing what could not be.

The screeching cry pealed out, reflecting from the metal-mounds. Keepiru whirled, and it momentarily seemed a pack of hunters was all around him.

Then came another sound, a brave and very faint skirr of distant Trinary. Keepiru swung his jaw about, chose a direction, and swam for all he was worth.

His muscles flexed powerfully as he streaked through the maze. When a rasping buzz told him his breather was near empty, he cursed as he popped the thing loose, and continued his dash along the surface, puffing and blowing with each driving arch.

He came to a narrow meeting of channels and swung about in confusion.

Which way! He swiveled about until the hunt cry echoed once more. Then there was a terrible crashing sound. He heard a squeal of outrage and pain, and the soft whine of a harness in operation. Another faint Trinary challenge was answered by a shivering scream and another crash.

Keepiru sprinted. It couldn't be far! He dashed, sparing none of his reserves, just as there came a final call of exhausted defiance.

> * *For the honor*
> *Of Calafia . . .* *

The voice disappeared under a scream of savage triumph. Then there was silence.

It took him another five minutes, frantically casting about the narrow passages, to find the battleground. The taste of the water, when Keepiru sped into the quiet strait, told him he was too late.

He caught up short and stopped just short of entering a

small vale between three metal-mounds. Coppery strands of dangle-weed floated overhead.

Pink froth spread from the center of the tiny valley, with streamers of red in the direction of the prevailing currents. At the center, enmeshed in a tangle of wrecked harness parts, the body of a young *amicus* neo-fin, already partly dismembered, drifted belly up, teased and tugged at by the red jaws of a giant dolphin.

A giant dolphin? How, in all the time since they had left Earth, had he not noticed this before? He desperately re-attached a fresh breather from his harness, and took gasping breaths while he watched and listened to the killer.

Look at the deep countershading, he told himself. *Look at the short jaw, the great teeth, the short, sharp dorsal fin. Listen to him!*

K'tha-Jon grunted contentedly as he ripped a piece from Akki's side. The giant didn't even appear to notice the long burn along his left flank, or the bruise slowly spreading from the point where Akki's last desperate ramming had come home.

Keepiru knew the monster was aware of him. K'tha-Jon lazily swallowed, then rose to the surface for air. When he descended he looked right at Keepiru.

"Well, Pilot?" he murmured happily.

Keepiru used Anglic, though the breather muffled the words.

"I've just dealt with one monster, K'tha-Jon, but *your* devolution fouls our entire race."

K'tha-Jon's derision was a series of high snorts.

"You think I have reverted, like that pathetic *Stenosss* Moki, don't you, Pilot?"

Keepiru could only shake his head, unable to bring himself to say what he thought the bosun had become.

"Can a devolved dolphin speak Anglic as well as I?" K'tha-Jon sneered. "Or use logic thisss way? Would a reverted *Tursiops*, or even a pure *Stenosss*, have pursued an air-breathing prey with such determination . . . and satisssfaction?

"True, the crisis of the last few weeks allowed something deep within me to burssst free. But can you truly listen to me and then call me a *devolved dolphin*?"

Keepiru looked at the pink froth around the giant's stubby, powerful jaws. Akki's corpse drifted away slowly with the tide.

"I know what you are, K'tha-Jon." Keepiru switched to Trinary.

> * Cold water boils
>   When you scream
> * Red-jawed hunger
>   Fills your dream.
> * Harpoons slew
>   The whales,
> * The nets of Iki
>   Caught us,
> * Yet you, alone
>   We feared at night
> * You alone—
>   ...Orca.

K'tha-Jon's jaw gaped in satisfaction, as if he were accepting an accolade. He rose for air and returned a few meters closer to Keepiru, grinning.

"I guessssed the truth some time ago. I am one of the prized experiments of our beloved human-patron Ignacio Metz. That-t fool did one great thing, for all of his ssstupidity. Some of the others he snuck into berths on *Streaker* did revert or go mad. But *I* am a successs. . . ."

"You are a calamity!" Keepiru spluttered, prevented by the breather from using other words more to the point.

K'tha-Jon drifted a few meters closer, causing Keepiru to back away involuntarily. The giant stopped again; a satisfied clicking emanated from his brow.

"Am I, Pilot? Can you, a simple fish-eater, understand your betters? Are you worthy to judge one whose forebears were at the top-p of the ocean food-chain? And dealt as judges of the sssea with all your kind?"

Keepiru was hardly listening, uncomfortably aware of the vanishing distance between himself and the monster.

"You arrogate t-too much. You have only a few gene splices from . . ."

"I am ORCA!" K'tha-Jon screamed. The cry echoed like a high paean of bugles. "The superficial body is *nothing*! It is the brain and *blood* that matter. *Listen* to me, and dare deny what I am!"

K'tha-Jon's jaw-clap was like a gunshot. The hunt cry pealed forth and Keepiru, under its direct focus, felt a deep instinct well up, a desire to tuck himself inward, to hide or die.

Keepiru resisted. He forced himself to assume an assertive body stance and bite out words of defiance.

"You *are* devolved, K'tha-Jon! Worse, you are a mutant thing, with no heritage at all. Metz's grafts went bad. Do you think-k a true Orca would do what you've done? They do hunt fallow dolphins on Earth, but never when sssated! The true killer whale does not kill out of spite!"

Keepiru defecated and flicked it in the giant's direction with his flukes.

"You are a failed experiment, K'tha-Jon! You say you're still logical, but now you have no home. And when my report gets back to Earth your gene-plasm will be poured into the sewers! Your line will end the way monsters end."

K'tha-Jon's eyes gleamed. He swept Keepiru with sonar, as if to memorize every curve of an intended prey.

"What gave you the idea you were ever going to report-t-t?" he hissed.

Keepiru grinned open-mouthed. "Why, the simple fact that you are a crippled, insane monster whose blunt snout couldn't stave in cardboard, whose maleness satisfies only pool-gratings, bringing forth nothing but stale water...."

The giant screamed again, this time in rage. As K'tha-Jon charged, Keepiru whirled and darted into a side channel, fleeing just ahead of the powerful jaws.

Tearing through a thick hedge of dangle-weed, Keepiru congratulated himself. By taunting K'tha-Jon into a personal vendetta he had made the creature forget entirely about his harness... and the laser rifle. K'tha-Jon obviously intended to kill Keepiru the way he had finished off Akki.

Keepiru fled a bare body length ahead of the mutant.

So far so good, he thought as the sparkling metal hillsides rushed past.

But it proved hard to shake his pursuer. And the menacing jaws made Keepiru wonder if his strategy had been so wise, after all. The chase went on and on, while the afternoon waned. As the sun set they were at it, still.

In the darkness, it became purely a battle of wits and of sound.

The nocturnal denizens of the archipelago fled in dismay as two swift foreign monsters streaked in and out of the interisland channels, swerving and darting in streaming clouds of bubbles. As they swept by, they sprayed the depths and shallows with complex and confusing patterns of sound—compounded images and vivid illusions of echoes. Local fishes, even the giants, fled the area, leaving it to the battling aliens.

It was an eerie game of image and shadow, of deception and sudden ambush.

Keepiru slid out of a narrow, silted channel and listened. It had been an hour since he last heard the hunt-scream, but that didn't mean K'tha-Jon was being silent. Keepiru built a mental map of the surrounding area from the reflections that came to him, and knew that some of those images were subtly crafted constructs. The giant was nearby, using his immensely talented sonic organs to place an overlay of untruth over the echoes of this place.

Keepiru wished he could see. But the midnight clouds cast everything into darkness. Only faintly phosphorescent plants illuminated the seascape.

He rose to the surface for breath, and looked at the faint, silvery underlining of the clouds. In a dismal, gloomy drizzle, the vegetation on the hulking metal-mounds swished and swayed.

Keepiru took seven breaths then descended again. Down below was where the battle would be settled.

Phantoms swam through the open channels. A false echo seemed to present an opening directly to the north, the direction Keepiru had been trying to lead the chase, but on careful examination he concluded it was an illusion.

Another such fake passage earlier had fooled him until, at the last moment, he had swerved away, too late to keep from slamming into the vine-covered verge of a metal-mound. Battered, he had fought free of the tangle just in time to escape a ramming. K'tha-Jon's giant muzzle missed him by inches. As he fled, Keepiru was struck by a grazing bolt from the laser rifle. It had seared a hot burn into his left side. It hurt like bloody hell.

Only his greater maneuverability had enabled him to escape that time, to find a refuge to ride out waves of pain.

He could probably elude the pseudo-Orca in time. But time was not on his side. K'tha-Jon had dedicated himself to a ritual hunt and spared no thought for anything beyond it.

He did not plan to return to civilization. All he had to do was prevent Keepiru from reporting back, and trust Ignacio Metz to protect his birthright back on Earth.

Keepiru, though, had responsibilities. And *Streaker* wouldn't wait for him if she got a chance to flee.

Still, he thought. *Am I really trying all that hard to get away?*

He frowned and shook his head. Two hours ago he had been almost sure he had lost K'tha-Jon. Instead of making good his escape, he had turned around, under some rationalization he couldn't even remember now, until he picked up the giant's sound-scent again. His enemy felt him, too. In moments the hunt-scream pealed forth, and the mutant was after him again.

Why did I do that?

An idea glimmered for a moment... the truth... But Keepiru thrust it aside. K'tha-Jon was coming. He barely noticed the thrill of adrenalin that overcame the pain of his bruises and burns.

The illusions vanished like an unraveling bank of fog, dissolving into constituent clicks and whispers. In a swirl of powerful fluke strokes, the giant entered the channel below Keepiru. The white countershading of the sport's belly showed against the gloom as K'tha-Jon rose for air, then swam past Keepiru's niche, casting pulse-beams of search sonar in front of him.

Keepiru waited until the monster had passed, then rose to the surface himself. He blew softly five times, then sank without moving a fin.

The monster was ten meters away. Keepiru made no sound as K'tha-Jon ascended and blew again. But as the *Stenos* descended, Keepiru aimed a tight burst of clicks to carom off two metal-mounds across the channel.

The semi-Orca swerved quickly and dashed to Keepiru's left, passing almost beneath him, chasing the illusion.

Like a diving missile, Keepiru dropped, nose first, toward his enemy.

The hunter's senses were incredible, for all of Keepiru's unnatural quiet. K'tha-Jon heard something behind him and swiveled like a dervish to come upright in the water, half facing Keepiru.

The angle was suddenly wrong for a ramming or raking.

The laser rifle swung toward him, and the giant jaws. To abort and flee would invite a sure laser blast!

Keepiru had a sudden flash of memory. He remembered his tactics instructor at the academy, lecturing about the benefits of surprise.

"...It's the one unique weapon in our arsenal, as sentient Earthlings, that others cannot duplicate...."

Keepiru accelerated, and pulled up in front of K'tha-Jon, coming belly to belly with the astonished creature. He grinned.

> * Who can deny
>   An attentive suitor—
> * Let's dance ! *

Keepiru's harness whined, and the three waldo-arms snapped out to grab K'tha-Jon's and lock them into place.

The stunned ex-bosun screamed in rage and snapped his jaws at Keepiru, but he couldn't bend far enough. He tried to lash out with his massive flukes, but Keepiru's tail flexed back and forth with his adversary's in perfect rhythm.

Keepiru felt an erection begin, and encouraged it. In adolescent erotic play between young male dolphins the dominant one usually took the male role. He prodded K'tha-Jon, and elicited a howl of dismay.

The giant writhed and shook. He bucked and kicked, then sped off in a random direction, filling the waters with his ululation. Keepiru held on tightly, knowing what K'tha-Jon's next tactic would be.

The semi-Orca sped slantwise toward a steep-sided metal-mound. Keepiru held still until K'tha-Jon was just about to slam into the wall, with him in between. Suddenly he arched, and swung his weight to one side in a savage jerk.

A giant he might be, but K'tha-Jon was no true Orca. Keepiru weighed enough to swing them about just before the collision. K'tha-Jon's right flank hit the wall of rugged metal coral, and bloody streaks of blubber were left behind.

K'tha-Jon swam on, shaking his head dizzily and leaving behind a bloody cloud. For the moment the monster seemed to lose interest in anything except air as he rose to the surface and blew.

I'll be needing air very shortly, Keepiru realized. *But now's the time to strike!*

He tried to pull back to bring his short-range cutting torch into play.

It was caught! Locked into K'tha-Jon's harness rack! Keepiru tugged but it wouldn't come loose.

K'tha-Jon eyed him.

"Your t-turn now, little-porp," he grinned. "You ssset me off there. But now all I have to do is keep you under water. It will be interessssting to lisssten to you beg for air!"

Keepiru wanted to curse, but he needed to save his strength. He struggled to force K'tha-Jon over onto his back so he could reach the surface, a bare meter away, but the half-Orca was ready and stopped his every move.

Think, Keepiru told himself. *I've got to think. If only I knew Keneenk better! If only . . .*

His lungs burned. Almost, he gave vent to a Primal distress call.

He recalled the last time he had been tempted by Primal. He replayed Toshio's voice, patron-chiding, then patron-soothing. He remembered his private vow to die before sinking to the animal level ever again.

Of course! I am an idiotic, overrated fish! Why didn't I think!

First he sent a neural command jettisoning the torch. It was useless anyway. Then he set his harness arms in motion.

> * *Those who choose*
> *Reversion's patterns*
> * *Need not space,*
> *Nor a spacer's tools* *

With one claw he seized the neural link in the side of K'tha-Jon's head. The monster's eyes widened, but before he could do a thing, Keepiru wrenched the plug free, making sure to cause the maximum amount of pain and damage. While his enemy screamed, he ripped the cable out of its housing, rendering the harness permanently useless.

K'tha-Jon's harness arms, which had been pulsing under his, went dead. The tiny whine of the laser rifle was silenced. K'tha-Jon howled and thrashed.

Keepiru gasped for breath as the mutant's bucking brought them both briefly out of the water in a great leap. They crashed back underwater as he transferred his grip on K'tha-Jon's harness. He held on with two waldo-arms. "*Kootchie-*

Koo," he crooned as he brought the other into play, ready to
tear into his enemy.

But in a writhing body twist, K'tha-Jon managed to fling
him away. Keepiru sailed through the air, to land with a great
splash on the other side of a narrow mudbank.

Puffing, they eyed each other across the tiny shoals.
Then K'tha-Jon clapped his jaws and moved to find a way
around the barrier. The chase was on again.

All subtlety went out of the fight with the coming of
dawn. There were no more delicate sonic deceptions, no
tasteful taunts. K'tha-Jon chased Keepiru with awesome single-mindedness. Exhaustion seemed to hold no meaning
to the monster. Blood loss only seemed to feed his rage.

Keepiru dodged through the narrow channels, some as
shallow as twelve inches, trying to run the wounded pseudo-
Orca ragged before he himself collapsed. Keepiru no longer
thought of getting away. This was a battle that could only end
in victory or death.

But there seemed no limit to K'tha-Jon's stamina.

The hunt-scream echoed through the shallows. The monster was casting about, a few channels over.

"Pilot-t-t! Why do you fight-t-t? You know I have the
food chain on my sssside!"

Keepiru blinked. How could K'tha-Jon bring *religion*
into this?

Prior to uplift, the concept of the food chain as a
mystical hierarchy had been central to cetacean morality—to
the temporal portion of the Whale Dream.

Keepiru broadcast omnidirectionally.

"K'tha-Jon, you're insane. Jussst because Metz stuffed
your zygote with a few mini-Orca genes, that doesn't give you
the right to eat anybody!"

In the old days humans used to wonder why dolphins
and many whales remained friendly to man after experiencing
wholesale slaughter at his hands. Humans began to understand,
a little, when they first tried to house Orcas and dolphins next
to each other at ocean parks, and discovered, to their
amazement, that the dolphins would leap over barriers to be
with the killer whales . . . so long as the Orcas weren't hungry.

In Primal, a cetacean did not blame a member of another
race for killing him, not when that other race was higher on
the food-chain. For centuries cetaceans simply assumed that

man was at the topmost rung, and begrudged only the *most* senseless of his killing sprees.

It was a code of honor which, when humans learned about it, made most of them more, not less ashamed of what had been done.

Keepiru slid out into the open channel to change his location, certain that K'tha-Jon had taken a fix from that last exchange.

There was something familiar about this area. Keepiru couldn't pin it down, but there was something to the taste of the water. It had the flavor of stale dolphin death.

> * Eating—eaten
>   Biting—bitten
> * Repay the sea . . .
>   Come and feed me! *

Too close. K'tha-Jon's voice was much too near, chanting religious blasphemies. Keepiru headed for a crevice to take cover, and stopped suddenly as the death-taste became suddenly overpowering.

He nosed in slowly, and halted when he saw the skeleton suspended in the weeds.

"Hist-t!" he sighed.

The dolphin spacer had been missing since that first day, when the wave had stranded Hikahi and he had behaved like such a fool. The body had been picked clean by scavengers. The cause of death was not apparent.

I know where I am . . . Keepiru thought. At that moment the hunt-scream pealed again. Close! Very close!

He whirled and darted back into the channel, saw a flash of movement, and dove out of the way even as a monstrous form plunged past him. He was knocked spinning by a whack from the giant's flukes.

Keepiru arched and darted away, though his side hurt as if a rib was broken. He called out.

> * After me—reverted scoundrel
> * I know—now it's time to feed you *

K'tha-Jon roared in answer, and charged after him.

A body length ahead, now two, now a half, Keepiru

knew he only had moments. The gaping jaws were right behind him. *It's near here,* he thought. *It's got to be!*

Then he saw another crevice and knew.

K'tha-Jon roared when he saw that Keepiru was trapped against the island.

> # Slow, slow
>   or fast, fast—
> # Time to feed me—feed me! #

"I'll feed you," Keepiru gasped as he dove into the narrow-walled canyon. On all sides a dangling-weed bobbed, as if tugged by the tide.

> # Trapped! Trapped!
>   I have you . . . #

K'tha-Jon squawked in surprise. Keepiru shot to the surface of the crevice, struggling to reach the top before vines closed in around him. He surfaced and blew, inhaling heavily and clinging close to the wall.

Nearby the water churned and frothed. Keepiru watched and listened in awe, as K'tha-Jon struggled alone, without harness or any aid, tearing great ropes of the killer weed with his jaws, thrashing as strand after strand fell over his great body.

Keepiru was busy as well. He forced himself to remain calm and use his harness. The strong claws of his waldo-arms snapped the strands that grabbed at him. He recited his multiplication tables in order to stay in Anglic thought-patterns, dealing with the vines one at a time.

The half-Orca's struggle sent geysers of seawater and torn vegetation into the sky. The surface of the water soon became a beaten green-and-pink froth. The hunt-scream filled the cavern with defiance.

But the minutes passed. The ropes that attempted to seize Keepiru grew fewer and fewer. More and more descended to fall upon the struggling giant. The hunt-scream came again, weaker—still defiant, but desperate, now.

Keepiru watched and listened as the battle began to subside. A strange sadness filled him, as if he almost regretted the end.

              * *I told you—I would feed you* *

He sang softly to the dying creature below.

               * *But I did not say who—*
                   I would feed you to . . . *

75

∽ᴗ∽ᴗ∽ᴗ∽ᴗ∽ᴗ∽ᴗ∽ᴗ∽ᴗ∽ᴗ∽ᴗ∽ᴗ∽ᴗ∽ᴗ∽ᴗ∽ᴗ∽

Hikahi

Since nightfall she had hunted for the refugees, first slowly
and cautiously, then with growing desperation. There came a
point when she threw caution away and began broadcasting a
sonar beacon for them to home in on.

Nothing! There were fen out there, but they ignored her
totally!

Only after entering the maze did she get a good fix on
the sound. Then she realized that one of the fen was desperately
crazy, and that both were engaged in ritual combat, closing
out all the universe until the battle was over.

Of all the things that could have happened, this stunned
Hikahi most of all. Ritual combat? Here? What did this have
to do with the silence from *Streaker*?

She had an uneasy feeling that *this* ritual battle was to
the death.

She set the sonar on automatic and let the skiff guide
itself. She napped, letting one hemisphere and then the
other go into alpha state as the little ship slid through the
narrow channels, always headed northeastward.

She snapped out of a snooze to the sound of a loud
buzzer. The skiff was stopped. Her instruments showed traces
of cetacean movement just beyond a sheer shelf of metallic
rock, heading slowly westward.

Hikahi activated the hydrophones.

"Whoever you are," her voice boomed through the water. "Come out at once!"

There was a faint query sound, a weary, confused whistle.

"*This* way, idiot-t! Follow my voice!"

Something moved out from a broad channel between islands. She snapped on the skiff's spotlights. A gray dolphin blinked back in the sharp glare.

"Keepiru!" Hikahi gasped.

The pilot's body was a mass of bruises, and one side bore a savage burn, but he smiled nevertheless.

> * *Ah, the gentle rains—*
> *Dear lady, for you to come here*
> *And rescue me.... **

The smile faded like a quenched fire and his eyes rolled. Then, on pure instinct, his half-unconscious body rose to the surface, to drift until she came for him.

PART EIGHT

The "Trojan Seahorse"

Ebony half-moons that soar
From pools where the half light begins
To set when, on what far shore,
Dolphins? Dolphins?
—HAMISH MACLAREN

76

Galactics

Beie Chohooan cursed the parsimony of her superiors.

If the Synthian High Command had sent a mothership to observe the battle of the fanatics, she might have been able to approach the war zone in a flitter—a vessel too small to be detected. As it was, she had been compelled to use a starship large enough to travel through transfer points and hyperspace, too small to defend itself adequately, and too large to sneak past the combatants.

She almost fired upon the tiny globe that nosed around the asteroid that sheltered her ship. Just in time she recognized the little wazoon-piloted probe. She pressed a stud to open a docking port, but the wazoon hung back, sending a frantic series of tight laser pulses.

Your position discovered, *it flashed.* Enemy missiles closing...

Beie uttered her vilest damnations. Every time she almost got close enough to 'cast a message through the jamming to the Earthlings, she had to flee from some random, paranoid tentacle of battle.

Come in quickly and dock! *She tapped out a command to the wazoon.* Too many of the loyal little clients had died for her already.

Negative. Flee, Beie. Wazoo-two will distract...

Beie snarled at the disobedience. The three wazoon who remained on the shelf to her left cringed and blinked their large eyes at her.

The scout globe sped off into the night.

351

Beie closed the port and fired up her engines. Carefully, she weaved her way through the lanes between chunks of primordial stone, away from the area of danger.

Too late, she thought as she glanced at the threat board. The missiles were closing too fast.

A sudden glare from behind told of the fate of the little wazoon. Beie's whiskered upper lip curled as she contemplated a suitable way to get even with the fanatics, if she ever got a chance.

Then the missiles arrived, and she was suddenly too busy even for nasty, pleasant thoughts.

She blasted two missiles to vapor with her particle gun. Two others fired back; their beams were barely refracted by her shields.

Ah, Earthlings, *she contemplated.* You'll not even know I was ever here. For all you know, you have been forsaken by all the universe.

But don't let that stop you, wolflings. Fight on! Snarl at your pursuers! And when all your weapons fail, *bite* them!

Beie destroyed four more missiles before one managed to explode close by, sending her broken ship spinning, burning, into the dusty Galactic dark.

77

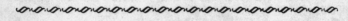

Toshio

The night blew wet with scattered blustery sheets of rain. The glossy broadleaf plants waved uncertainly under contrary gusts from a wind that seemed unable to decide on a direction. The dripping foliage glistened when two of Kithrup's nearby tiny moons shone briefly through the clouds.

At the far southern end of the island, a crude thatch covering allowed rain to seep through in slow trickles. It dripped onto the finely pitted hull of a small spaceship. The water formed small meniscus pools atop the gently curving metal surface, then ran off in little rivulets. The tappity-tap of the heavy raindrops hitting the thatch was joined by a steady patter as streams of runoff poured onto the smashed mud and vegetation beneath the cylindrical flying machine.

The trickles sluiced over the stubby stasis flanges. They sent jagged trails over the forward viewports, dark and clear in the intermittent moonlight.

Trails penetrated the narrow cracks around the aft airlock, using the straight channels to pour dribbling streams out onto the muddy ground.

There came a tiny mechanical hiss, barely louder than the rainfall. The cracks around the airlock widened almost imperceptibly. Neighboring streams merged to fill the new crevices. A pool began to form in a dirt basin below the hatch.

The doorway cracked open a little farther. More streams merged to pour in, as if seeking to enter the ship. All at once a gurgling stream poured from the bottom of the crack. The flow became a gushing waterfall that splashed into a puddle below. Then, just as abruptly, the torrent subsided.

The armored hatch slid open with a muted sigh. The rain sent a flurry of slanting droplets pelting into the opening.

A dark, helmeted figure stood in the threshold, ignoring the onslaught. It turned to look left and right, then stepped out and splashed in the puddle. The hatch shut again with a whine and a small click.

The figure bent into the wind, searching in the darkness for a trail.

Dennie sat up suddenly at the sound of wet footsteps. With her hand at her breast she whispered.

"Toshio?"

The tent's fly was pushed aside and the flap zipped open. For a moment a dark shape loomed. Then a quiet voice whispered. "Yeah, it's me."

Dennie's rapid pulse subsided. "I was afraid it was somebody else."

"Who'd you expect, Dennie? Charlie Dart? Come out of his tent to ravish you? Or, better yet, one of the Kiqui?" He teased her gently, but could not hide the tension in his voice.

He shrugged out of his drysuit and helmet, which he hung on
a peg by the opening. In his underwear, Toshio crawled over
to his own sleeping bag and slid in.

"Where have you been?"

"Nowhere. Go back to sleep, Dennie."

The rain pattered on the fly in an uneven tattoo. She
remained sitting up, looking at him in the faint light from the
opening. She could see little more than the whites of his
eyes, staring straight up at nothing.

"Please Tosh, tell me. When I woke up and you weren't
in your sleeping bag..." Her voice trailed off as he turned to
look back at her. The difference that had grown in Toshio
Iwashika the last week or so was never more manifest than in
his narrowed expression, than in this slitted intensity in his
eyes.

She heard him sigh finally. "All right, Dennie. I was just
over at the longboat. I snuck inside and had a look around."

Dennie's pulse sped again. She started to speak, stopped,
then finally said, "Wasn't that dangerous? I mean there's no
telling how Takkata-Jim might react! Especially if he really is
a traitor."

Toshio shrugged. "There was something I had to find out."

"But how could you get in and out without being caught?"

Toshio rolled over onto one elbow. She saw a brief flash
of white as he smiled slightly. "A middie sometimes knows
things even the engineering officers never find out, Dennie.
Especially when it comes to hiding places aboard ship. When
off-duty time comes, there's always a pilot or a lieutenant
around thinking up homework for idle hands and fins... always
just a *little* more astrogation or protocol to study, for instance.
Akki and I used to grab sack time in the hold of the longboat.
We learned how to open the locks without it flashing on the
control room."

Dennie shook her head. "I'm glad you didn't tell me you
were going, after all. I would have died of worry."

Toshio frowned. Now Dennie was beginning to sound
like his mother again. Dennie still wasn't happy about having
to leave while he stayed behind. Toshio hoped she wouldn't
take this opportunity to bring up the subject again.

She lay down and faced him, using her arm as a pillow.
She thought for a moment, then whispered. "What did you
find out?"

Toshio closed his eyes. "You might as well know," he said. "I'll want you to tell Gillian in case I can't get through to her in the morning. I found out what Takkata-Jim is doing with those bombs he took from Charlie."

"He's converting them to fuel for the longboat."

Dennie blinked. "But . . . but what can we do about it?"

"I don't know! I'm not even sure we *have* to do anything about it. After all, in a couple weeks his accumulators would be recharged enough to lift him off, anyway. Maybe Gillian doesn't care.

"On the other hand, it might be darned important. I still haven't figured it all out yet. I may have to do something pretty drastic."

He had seen the partially dismantled bombs through the thick window of the security door to the longboat's specimen lab. Getting to them would be considerably more difficult than simply sneaking back aboard.

"Whatever happens," he tried to reassure her, "I'm sure it will all be all right. You just make certain your notes are all packed properly in the morning. That data on the Kiqui is the second most important thing to come out of this crazy odyssey, and it's got to get back. Okay?"

"Sure, Tosh."

He let gravity pull him over onto his back. He closed his eyes and breathed slowly to feign sleep.

"Toshio?"

The young man sighed. "Yes, Denn . . ."

"Um, it's about Sah'ot. He's only leaving to escort me. Otherwise I think you'd have a mutiny on your hands."

"I know. He wants to stay and listen to those underground 'voices' of his." Toshio rubbed his eyes, wondering why Dennie was keeping him awake with all this. He already had listened to Sah'ot's importunities.

"Don't shrug them off like that, Tosh. He says Creideiki listened to them, too, and that he had to cut the channel to break the captain out of a listening trance, the sounds were so fascinating."

"The captain is a brain-damaged cripple." The words were bitter. "And Sah'ot is an egocentric, unstable . . ."

"I used to think so too," Dennie interrupted. "He used to scare me until I learned he was really quite sweet and harmless. But even if we could suppose the two fen were having hallucinations, there's the stuff I've been finding out about the metal-mounds."

"Mmmph," Toshio commented sleepily. "What is it? More about the metal-mounds being alive?"

Dennie winced a little at his mild disparagement. "Yes, and the weird eco-niche of the drill-trees. Toshio, I did an analysis on my pocketcomp, and there's only one possible solution! The drill-tree shafts are part of the life cycle of one organism—an organism that lives part of its life cycle above the surface as a superficially simple coral colony, and later falls into the pit prepared for it..."

"All that clever adaptation and energy expended to dig a grave for itself?" Toshio cut in.

"No! Not a grave! A channel! The metal-mound is only the *beginning* of this creature's life cycle... the *larval* stage. Its destiny as an adult form lies below, below the shallow crust of the planet, where convective veins of magma can provide all the energy a metallo-organic life form might ever need!"

Toshio tried earnestly to pay attention, but his thoughts kept drifting—to bombs, to traitors, to worry over Akki, his missing comrade, and to a man somewhere far to the north, who deserved to have someone waiting for him if—*when* he finally returned to his island launching point.

"... only thing wrong is there's no way I see that such a life form could have evolved! There's no sign of intermediate forms, no mention of any possible precursors in the old *Library* records on Kithrup... and this is certainly unique enough a life form to merit mention!"

"Mmm-hmmm."

Dennie looked over at Toshio. His arm was over his eyes and he breathed slowly as if drifting off into slumber. But she saw a fine vein on his temple pulse rapidly, and his other fist clenched at even intervals.

She lay there watching him in the dimness. She wanted to shake him and *make* him listen to her!

Why am I pestering him like this. She suddenly asked herself. *Sure, the stuff's important, but it's all intellectual, and Toshio's got our corner of the world on his shoulders. He's so young, yet he's carrying a fighting man's load now.*

How do I feel about that?

A queasy stomach told her. *I'm pestering him because I want attention.*

I want his attention, she corrected. *In my clumsy way I've been trying to give him opportunities to . . .*

Nervously, she faced her own foolishness.

If I, the older one, can get my signals this crossed, I can hardly expect him to figure out the cues, she realized at last.

Her hand reached out. It stopped just short of the glossy black hair that lay in long, wet strands over his temples. Trembling, she looked again at her feelings, and saw only fear of rejection holding her back.

As if on a will of its own, her hand moved to touch the soft stubble on Toshio's cheek. The youth started and turned to look at her, wide-eyed.

"Toshio," she swallowed. "I'm cold."

78

Tom Orley

When there came a moment of relative calm, Tom made a mental note. *Remind me next time*, he told himself, *not to go around kicking hornets' nests*.

He sucked on one end of the makeshift breathing tube. The other end protruded from the surface of a tiny opening in the weedscape. Fortunately, he didn't have to pull in quite so much air this time, to supplement what his mask provided. There was more dissolved oxygen in this area.

Battle beams sizzled overhead again, and weak cries carried to him from the miniature war going on above. Twice, the water trembled from nearby explosions.

At least this time I don't have to worry about being baked by the near misses, he consoled himself. *All these stragglers have are hand weapons*.

Tom smiled at that irony. *All* they had were hand weapons.

He had picked off two of the Tandu in that first ambush, before they could snap up their particle guns to fire back.

More importantly, he managed to wing the shaggy Episiarch before diving head-first into a hole in the weeds.

He had cut it close. One near-miss had left second-degree burns on the sole of his bare left foot. In that last instant he glimpsed the Episiarch rearing in outrage, a nimbus of unreality coruscating like a fiery halo around its head. Tom thought he momentarily saw stars through that wavering brilliance.

The Tandu flailed to stay upon their wildly bucking causeway. That probably was what spoiled their much vaunted aim, and accounted for his still being alive.

As he had expected, the Tandu's vengeance hunt had led them westward. He popped up, from time to time, to keep their interest keen with brief enfilades of needles.

Then, as he swam between openings in the weedscape, the battle seemed to take off without him. He heard sounds of combat and knew his pursuers had come into contact with another party of ET stragglers.

Tom had left then, underwater, in search of other mischief to do.

The battle noise drifted away from his present position. From his brief glimpse an hour ago, this particular skirmish seemed to involve a half-dozen Gubru and three battered, balloon-tired rover machines of some type. Tom hadn't been able to tell if they were robots or crewed, but they had seemed unable to adapt to the tricky surface, for all of their firepower.

He listened for a minute, then coiled his tube and put it away in his waistband. He rose quietly to the surface of the tiny pool and risked lifting his eyes to the level of the interwoven loops of weed.

In his mosquito raids, he had moved toward the egg-shell wreck. Now he saw that it was only a few hundred meters away. Two smoking ruins told of the fate of the wheeled machines. As he watched, first one, then the other slowly sank out of sight. Three slime-covered Gubru, apparently the last of their party, struggled over the morass toward the floating ship. Their feathers were plastered against their slender, hawk-beaked bodies. They looked desperately unhappy.

Tom rose up and saw flashes of more fighting to the south.

Three hours before, a small Soro scoutship had come diving in, strafing all in sight, until a delta-winged Tandu atmospheric fighter swooped out of the clouds to intercept it. They blasted away at each other, harassed by small arms fire from below, until they finally collided in a fiery explosion, falling to the sea in a tangled heap.

About an hour later the story repeated itself. This time the participants were a lumbering Pthaca rescue-tender and a battered spearship of the Brothers of the Night. Their wreckage joined the smoky ruins which slowly subsided in every direction.

No food, no place to hide, and the only race of fanatics I really want to see is the one not represented out here in this dribble-drabble charnel house.

The message bomb pressed under his waistband. Again, he wished he knew whether or not to use it.

Gillian has to be worried by now, he thought. *Thank God, at least she's safe.*

And the battle's still going on. That means there's still time. We've still got a chance.

Yes. And dolphins like to go for long walks along the beach.

Ah, well. Let's see if there's some more trouble I can cause.

79

∽∽∽∽∽∽∽∽∽∽∽∽∽∽∽∽∽∽∽∽∽∽∽∽

Galactics

The Soro, Krat, cursed at the strategy schematic. Her clients took the precaution of backing away while she vented her anger by tearing great rips out of the vletoor cushion.

Four ships lost! To only one by the Tandu! The recent battle had been a disaster!

And meanwhile, the sideshow down at the planet's surface was bleeding away her small support craft in ones and twos!

It seemed that tiny remnants of all of the defeated fleets, stragglers that had hidden out on moons or planetoids, must have decided the Earthlings were hiding near that volcano down in Kithrup's mid-northern latitudes. Why did they think that?

Because surely nobody would be fighting over nothing at all, would they? The skirmish had a momentum all its own by now. Who would have thought that the defeated alliances would have hidden away so much firepower for one last desperate attempt at the prize?

Krat's mating claw flexed in wrath. She couldn't afford to ignore the possibility that they were right. What if the distress call had, indeed, emanated from the Earthlings' ship? No doubt this was some sort of fiendish human distraction, but she could not risk the chance that the fugitives actually were there.

"Have the Thennanin called yet?" she snapped.

A Pil from the communications section bowed quickly and answered. "Not yet, Fleet-Mother, though they have pulled away from their Tandu allies. We expect to hear from Buoult soon."

Krat nodded curtly. "Let me know the very instant!" The Pil assented hurriedly and backed away.

Krat went back to considering her options. Finally, it came down to deciding which damaged and nearly useless vessel she could spare from the coming battle for one more foray to the planet's surface.

Briefly, she toyed with the idea of sending a Thennanin ship, once the upcoming alliance against the now-pre-eminent Tandu was consummated. But then she decided that would be unwise. Best to keep the priggish, sanctimonious Thennanin up here where she could keep her eyes on them. She would choose one of her own small cripples to go.

Krat contemplated a mental image of the Earthlings— dough-skinned, spindly, shaggy-maned humans, who were sneakiness embodied—and their weird, squawking, handless dolphin clients.

When they are finally mine, *she thought*, I will make them regret the trouble they are causing me.

80

The Journal of Gillian Baskin

We've arrived.

For the last four hours I've been the matriarch of a madhouse. Thank heaven for Hannes and Tsh't and Lucky Kaa and all the beautiful, competent fen we've missed for so long. I hadn't realized until we arrived just how many of the best had been sent ahead to prepare our new home.

There was an ecstatic reunion. Fen dashed about bumping each other and making a racket that I kept telling myself the Galactics couldn't really hear. . . . The only real pall came when we thought about the absent members of our crew, the six missing fen, including Hikahi, Akki, and Keepiru. And Tom, of course.

It wasn't until later that we discovered that Creideiki was missing, also.

After a brief celebration, we got to work. Lucky Kaa took the helm, almost as sure and steady as Keepiru would have been, and piloted Streaker along a set of guide rails into the cavity in the Thennanin wreck. Giant clamps came down and girdled Streaker, almost making her part of the outer shell. It's a snug fit. Techs immediately started integrating the sensors and tuning the impedances of the stasis flanges. The thrusters are already aligned. Carefully disguised weapons ports have been opened, in case we have to fight.

What an undertaking! I never would have thought it possible. I can't believe the Galactics will expect anything like this. Tom's imagination is astounding.

If only we would hear his signal. . . .

*   *   *

I've asked Toshio to send Dennie and Sah'ot here by sled. If they take a direct route at top speed they should arrive in a little over a day. It'll take that long, at least, to finish setting up here.

It really is vital we get Dennie's notes and plasma samples. If Hikahi reports in, I'll ask her to stop at the island for the Kiqui emissaries. Second only to our need to escape with our data is our duty to the little amphibians, to save them from indenture to some crazy race of Galactic patrons.

Toshio chose to stay to keep an eye on Takkata-Jim and Metz, and to meet Tom, should he show up. I think he added that last part knowing it would make it impossible for me to refuse. . . . Of course, I knew he'd make the offer. I was counting on it.

It only makes me feel worse, using him to keep Takkata-Jim in check. Even if our ex-vice-captain disappoints me, and behaves himself, I don't know how Toshio's to get back here in time, especially if we have to take off in a hurry.

I'm learning what they mean by the "agony of command."

I had to pretend shocked surprise when Toshio told me about the mini-bombs Charlie Dart stole out of the armory. Toshio offered to try to get them back from Takkata-Jim, but I've forbidden it. I told him we'd take our chances.

I couldn't take him into my confidence. Toshio is a bright young man, but he has no poker face.

I think I have things timed right. If only I were certain.

The damned Niss is calling me again. This time I'll go see what it wants.

Oh, Tom. Would you, if you were here, have misplaced an entire ship's captain? How can I forgive myself for letting Creideiki go out there alone?

He seemed to be doing so well, though. What in Ifni's crap-shoot went wrong?

81

Charles Dart

Early in the morning, he was at his console at the water's edge, happily conversing with his new robot. It was already down a kilometer, planting tiny detectors in the drill-tree shaft wall along the way.

Charles Dart mumbled cheerfully. In a few hours he would have it down as deep as the old one, the next-to-worthless probe he had abandoned. Then, after a few more tests to verify his theories about local crustal formations, he could start finding out about bigger questions, like what Kithrup the *planet* was like.

Nobody, but *nobody*, could stop him now!

He remembered the years he had spent in California, in Chile, in Italy, studying earthquakes as they happened, working with some of the greatest minds in geophysical science. It had been exciting. Still, after a few years he had begun to realize that something was wrong.

He had been admitted into all the right professional societies, his papers were greeted with both high praise and occasional vehement rejection—both reactions far preferred by any decent scientist over yawns. There was no lack of prestigious job offers.

But there came a time when he suddenly wondered where the *students* were.

Why didn't graduate students seek him out as an advisor? He saw his colleagues besieged by eager applicants for research assistantships, yet, in spite of his list of publications, his widely known and controversial theories, only the second-raters came to him, the students searching more for grant support than a mentor. None of the bright young mels and fems sought him out as an academic patron.

Of course, there had been a couple of minor cases in which his temper had gotten the better of him, and one or two of his students had departed acrimoniously, but that couldn't account for the doldrums in the pedagogical side of his career, could it?

Slowly, he came to think that it must be something else. Something... racial.

Dart had always held himself aloof from the uplift obsession of many chimps—either the fastidious respectfulness of the majority toward humans, or the sulking resentfulness of a small but vocal minority. A couple of years ago he began paying attention, however. Soon he had a theory. The students were avoiding him because he was a chimpanzee!

It had stunned him. For three solid months he dropped everything to study the problem. He read the protocols governing humanity's patronhood over his race, and grew outraged over the ultimate authority Mankind held over his species—until, that is, he read about uplift practice in the galaxy at large. Then he learned that no other patron gave a four-hundred-year-old client race seats on its high councils, as Mankind did.

Charles Dart was confused. But then he thought about that word "gave."

He read about humanity's age-old racial struggles. Had it really been less than half a millennium since humans contrived gigantic, fatuous lies about each other simply because of pigment shades, and killed millions because they believed their own lies?

He learned a new word, "tokenism," and felt a burning shame. That was when he volunteered for a deep space mission, determined not to return without *proof* of his academic prowess—his skill as a scientist on a par with any human!

Alas that he had been assigned to *Streaker*, a ship filled with squeaking dolphins, and *water*. To top it off, that smugpot Ignacio Metz immediately started treating him like another of his unfinished experimental half-breeds!

He'd learned to live with that. He cosied up with Metz. He would bear anything until the results from Kithrup were announced.

Then they'll stand up as Charles Dart enters rooms! The bright young human students will come to him. They'll all see that *he*, at least, was no token!

Charlie's deep thoughts were interrupted by sounds from the forest nearby. He hurriedly slapped the cover plate over a set of controls in a lower corner of his console. He was taking no chances with anyone finding out about the *secret* part of his experiment.

Dennie Sudman and Toshio Iwashika emerged from the village trail, talking in low voices, carrying small bundles. Charlie busied himself with detailed commands to the robot, but cast a surreptitious eye toward the humans, wondering if they suspected anything.

But no. They were too much into each other, touching, caressing, murmuring. Charlie snorted under his breath at the human preoccupation with sex, day in, day out; but he grinned and waved when they glanced his way.

They don't suspect a thing, he congratulated himself, as they waved back, then turned to their own concerns. How lucky for me they're in love.

"I still want to stay. What if Gillian's wrong? What if Takkata-Jim finishes converting the bombs early?"

Toshio shrugged. "I still have something he needs." He glanced down at the second of two sleds in the pool, the one that had belonged to Tom Orley. "Takkata-Jim won't take off without it."

"Exactly!" Dennie was emphatic. "He'd need that radio, or the ETs would blast him to bits before he could negotiate. But you'll be all alone! That fin is dangerous!"

"That's just one of many reasons I'm sending you away right now."

"Is this the big, macho mel talking?" Dennie tried sarcasm, but was unable to put much bite into it.

"No." Toshio shook his head. "This is your military commander talking. And that's that. Now let's get these last samples loaded. I'll escort you and Sah'ot a few miles before we say good-bye."

He bent over to pick up one of the parcels, but before he touched it he felt a hand in the small of his back. A sharp push threw him off balance, flailing.

"Denneee!" He caught a glimpse of her, grinning devilishly. At the last moment his left hand darted out and caught hers. Her laughter turned into a shriek as he dragged her after him into the water.

They came up, spluttering, between the sleds. Dennie

cried out in triumph as she grabbed the top of his head with
both hands and dunked him. Then she leapt half out of the
water as something goosed her from behind.

"Toshio!" she accused.

"That wasn't me." He caught his breath and backed out
of arms' reach. "It must have been your other lover."

"My . . . Oh, no! Sah'ot!" Dennie whirled around searching and kicking, then whooped as something got her from
behind again. "Do you scrotum-brained males ever think of
anything *else*?"

A mottled gray dolphin's head broached the surface
nearby. The breather wrapped over his blowmouth only
muted his chattering laughter slightly.

> * Long before humans
>   Rowed out on logs—
> * We made an invention
>
> * Care to
>   Manage a try—
> * At
>   Ménage à trois? *

He leered, and Toshio had to laugh as Dennie blushed.
That only set her splashing water at him until he swam over
and pinned her arms against one of the sleds. To stop her
imprecations he kissed her.

Her lips bore the desperate tang of Kithrup as she kissed
him back. Sah'ot sidled up alongside them, and nibbled their
legs softly with jagged, sharp teeth.

"You know we're not supposed to expose ourselves to
this stuff if we can help it," Toshio told her as they held each
other. "You shouldn't have done that."

Dennie shook her head, then buried her face in his
shoulder to hide it.

"Who are we fooling, Tosh?" she mumbled. "Why worry
about slow metal poisoning? We'll be dead long before our
gums start to turn blue."

"Aw, Dennie. That's nuts . . ." He tried to find words to
comfort her, but found that all he could do was hold her close
as the dolphin wrapped himself around them both.

A comm buzzed. Sah'ot went over to switch on the unit on Orley's sled. It was the one connected by monofilament cable to *Streaker*'s old position.

He listened to a brief burst of primitive clicks, then squawked quickly in reply. He rose high in the water, popping his breather loose.

"It's for you, Toshio!"

Toshio didn't bother asking if it was important. Over that line it had to be. Gently, he disengaged from Dennie. "You finish packing. I'll be back right away to help."

She nodded, rubbing her eyes.

"Stay with her for a while, will you, Sah'ot?" he asked as he swam over to the comm unit. The *Stenos* shook his head.

"I would gladly, Toshio. It'sss my turn to amuse the lady, anyway. Unfortunately, you need me here to translate."

Toshio looked at him uncomprehendingly.

"It is the captain," Sah'ot informed him. "Creideiki wants to talk to both of usss. Then he wants us to help him get in touch with the techno-inhabitants of this world."

"Creideiki? Calling here? But Gillian said he was missing!" Toshio's brow furrowed as Sah'ot's sentence sunk in. "Techno . . . He wants to talk to the *Kiqui*?"

Sah'ot grinned.

"No, sir; they hardly qualify, fearless military leader. Our captain wants to talk with my 'voices.' He wants to talk to those who dwell below."

82

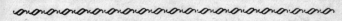

Tom Orley

The Brother of Twelve Shadows piped softly. His pleasure spread through the waters around him, below the carpet of weeds. He swam away from the site of the ambush, the faint thrashing sounds of the victims dying down behind him.

The darkness beneath the weeds didn't bother him. Never would absence of light displease a Brother of the Night.

"Brother of the Dim Gloom," he hissed. "Do you rejoice as I do?"

From somewhere to his left, amongst the dangling sea vines, came a joyful reply.

"I rejoice, Senior Brother. That group of Paha warriors shall never again kneel before perverted Soro females. Thank the ancient warlords."

"We shall thank them in person," Brother of Twelve Shadows answered, "when we learn the location of their returning fleet from the half-sentient Earthers. For now, thank our long-deceased Nighthunter patrons, who made us such formidable fighters."

"I thank their spirits, Senior Brother."

They swam on, separated by the three score body lengths demanded by underwater skirmish doctrine. The pattern was inconvenient with all these weeds about, and the water echoed strangely, but doctrine was doctrine, as unquestionable as instinct.

Senior Brother listened until the last weak struggles of the drowning Paha ceased. Now he and his fellow would swim toward one of the floating wrecks, where more victims surely awaited.

It was like picking fruits from a tree. Even powerful warriors such as the Tandu were reduced to floundering dolts on this carpet of noxious weeds, but not the Brothers of the Night! Adaptable, mutable, they swam *below*, wreaking havoc where it could be wrought.

His gill-slits pulsed, sucking the metal-tangy water through. The Brother of Twelve Shadows detected a patch of slightly higher oxygen content and took a slight detour to pass through it. Keeping to doctrine was important, surely, but here, underwater, what could harm them?

There was suddenly a flurry of crashing sounds to his left, a brief cry, and then silence.

"Lesser Brother, what was that disturbance?" he called in the direction his surviving partner had been. But speech carried poorly underwater. He waited with growing anxiety.

"Brother of the Dim Gloom!"

He dove beneath a cluster of hanging tendrils, holding a flechette gun in each of his four tool-hands.

What, down here, could have overcome so formidable a fighter as his lesser brother? Surely none of the patrons or clients he knew of could do such a thing. A robot should have caused his metal detectors to go off.

It suddenly occurred to him that the half-sentient "dolphins" they sought might be dangerous in the water.

But no. Dolphins were air-breathers. And they were large. He swept the area around him and heard no reflections.

The Eldest Brother—who commanded the remnants of their flotilla from a cave on a small moon—had concluded that the Earthlings were not here in this northern sea, but he had sent a small vessel to harass and observe. The two brothers in the water were all that had survived. Everything they had seen suggested the quarry wasn't here.

The Brother of Twelve Shadows quickly skirted the edge of an open pool. Had his younger brother strayed into the open and been blasted by a walker above?

He swam toward a faint sound, weapons ready.

In the darkness he sensed a bulky body up ahead. He chirped out, and concentrated on the complex echoes.

The returning sounds showed only one large creature in the vicinity, still and silent.

He swam forward and took hold of it, and mourned. Water pulsed through his gill-slits and he cried out.

"*I am going to avenge you, Brother!*
"*I am going to slay all in this sea who think!*
"*I am going to bring darkness upon all who hope!*
"*I am going to . . .*"

There came a loud splash. He let out a small "urk" sound as something heavy fell from *above* onto his right side and wrapped long legs and arms around him.

As the Brother of Twelve Shadows struggled, he realized in stupefaction that his enemy was a human! A half-sentient, frail-skinned, wolfling *human*!

"*Before you do all those other things, there's one thing you'll do first,*" the voice rasped in Galactic Ten, just behind his hearing organs.

The Brother wailed. Something fiery sharp pierced his throat near the dorsal nerve-chord.

He heard his enemy say, almost sympathetically, *"You are going to die."*

83

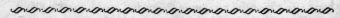

Gillian

"All I can tell you, Gillian Baskin, is that he knew how to find me. He came here aboard a 'walker,' and spoke to me from the hallway."

"Creideiki was *here*? Tom and I figured he'd deduce we had a private high-level computer, but the location should have been impossible . . ."

"I was not terribly surprised, Dr. Baskin," the Niss machine interrupted, covering the impoliteness with a soothing pattern of abstract images. "The captain clearly knows his ship. I had expected him to guess my location."

Gillian sat by the door and shook her head. "I should have come when you first signaled for me. I might have been able to stop him from leaving."

"It is not your fault," the machine answered with uncharacteristic sensitivity. "I would have made the request more demanding if I thought the situation urgent."

"Oh sure," Gillian was sarcastic. "It's not urgent when a valuable fleet officer succumbs to pressure atavism and subsequently gets lost out in a deadly alien wilderness!"

The patterns danced. "You are mistaken. Captain Creideiki has not fallen prey to reversion schizophrenia."

"How would you know?" Gillian said hotly. "Over a third of the crew of this vessel have shown signs since the ambush at Morgran, including all but a few of the *Stenos*-grafted fen. How can you say Creideiki hasn't reverted after all he's suffered? How can he practice Keneenk when he can't even talk!"

The Niss answered calmly. "He came here seeking specific information. He knew I had access not only to *Streaker's* micro-branch *Library,* but the more complete one taken from the Thennanin wreck. He could not tell me what it was he wanted to know, but we found a way to get across the speech barrier."

"How?" Gillian was fascinated in spite of her anger and guilt.

"By pictograms, visual and sound pictures of alternate choices which I presented to him quite rapidly. He made quick yes or no sounds to tell when I was getting—as you humans say—hotter or colder. Before long he was leading *me,* making associations I had not even begun to consider."

"Like what?"

The light-motes sparkled. "Like the way many of the mysteries regarding this unique world seem to come together, the strangely long time this planet has lain fallow since its last tenants became degenerate and settled here to die, the unnatural ecological niche of the so-called drill-tree mounds, Sah'ot's strange 'voices from the depths'..."

"Dolphins of Sah'ot's temperament are *always* hearing 'voices.'" Gillian sighed. "And don't forget he's another of those experimental *Stenos.* I'm sure some of them were passed into this crew without the normal stress tests."

After a short pause, the machine answered matter-of-factly.

"There is evidence, Dr. Baskin. Apparently Dr. Ignacio Metz is a representative of an impatient faction at the Center for Uplift...."

Gillian stood up. "Uplift! Dammit! I *know* what Metz did! You think I'm blind? I've lost several dear friends and irreplaceable crewmates because of his crazy scheme. Oh, he 'hot-tested' his sports, all right. And some of the new models failed under pressure!

"But all that's finished! What does uplift have to do with voices from below, or drill-tree mounds, or the history of Kithrup, or our friendly cadaver Herbie, for that matter? What does *any* of it have to do with rescuing our lost people and getting away from here!"

Her heart raced, and Gillian found that her fists were clenched.

"Doctor Baskin," the Niss replied smoothly. "That was exactly what I asked your Captain Creideiki. When he put the pieces together for me I, too, realized that uplift is not an irrelevant question here. It is the only question. Here at Kithrup all that is good and evil about this several-billion-year-old system is represented. It is almost as if the very basis of Galactic society has been placed on trial."

Gillian blinked at the abstract images.

"How ironic," the disembodied voice went on, "that the question rests with you humans, the first sophont race in aeons to claim 'evolved' intelligence.

"Your discovery in the so-called Shallow Cluster may result in a war that fills the Five Galaxies, or it may fade away like so many other chimerical crises. But what is done here on Kithrup will become a legend. All of the elements are there.

"And legends have a tendency to affect events long after wars are forgotten."

Gillian stared at the hologram for a long moment. Then she shook her head.

"Will you please tell me what the bloody damn *hell* you are *talking* about?"

84

Hikahi/Keepiru

"We mussst hurry!" the pilot insisted.

Keepiru lay strapped to a porta-doc. Catheters and tubes ran from the webbing that kept him suspended above the water's surface. The sound of the skiff's engines filled the tiny chamber.

"*You* must relax," Hikahi soothed. "The autopilot is in charge now. We're going as fast as we can underwater. We should be there very soon."

Hikahi was still somewhat numbed by the news about Creideiki, and shaken by Takkata-Jim's treachery. But over it all she could not bring herself to accept Keepiru's frantic urgency. He was obviously driven by his devotion to Gillian Baskin, and wanted to return to her aid instantly, if possible. Hikahi looked at things from another perspective. She knew Gillian probably already had things well under control back at the ship. Compared with the disasters she had been fantasizing the last few days, the news was almost buoyant. Even Creideiki's injury could not suppress Hikahi's relief that *Streaker* survived intact.

Her harness whined. With one waldo-hand she touched a control to give Keepiru a mild soporific.

"Now I want you to sssleep," she told him. "You must regain your strength. Consider that an order, if, as you say, I am now acting captain."

Keepiru's eye began to recess; the lids drooped together slowly. "I'm shorry, sir. I . . . I guesss I'm not much-ch more logical than Moki. I'm alwaysss causssing t-trouble . . ."

His speech slurred as the drug took hold. Hikahi swam almost underneath the drowsy pilot and sighed a brief, soft lullaby.

> * *Dream, defender—*
>   *Dream of those who love you*
>   *And bless your courage—* *

85

Gillian

"You're saying these . . . Karrank% . . . were the last sophonts to have a license to the planet Kithrup, a hundred million years ago?"

"Correct," the Niss machine replied. "They were savagely abused by their patrons, mutated far beyond the degree allowed by the codes. According to the Thennanin battleship's

Library, it caused quite a scandal at the time. In compensation, the Karrank% were released from their indenture as clients and granted a world suited to their needs, one with low potential for developing pre-sentience. Water worlds make good retirement homes for that reason. Few pre-sophonts ever arise on such planets. The Kiqui seem to be an exception."

Gillian paced the sloping ceiling of the lopsided room. An occasional clanking, transmitted by the metal walls, told of the final fittings being made to secure *Streaker* into the Trojan Seahorse.

"You aren't saying the Kiqui have anything to do with these ancient..."

"No. They appear to be a genuine find, and a major reason why you should endeavor to escape this trap and return to Earth with what you have learned."

Gillian smiled ironically. "Thanks. We'll do our best.

"So, what was done to the Karr... the Karrank%," she did her best with the double glottal stop, "to make them want to hide away on Kithrup, never to associate with Galactic culture again?"

The Niss explained. "In their pre-sentient form, they were mole-like creatures on a metal-rich world like this one. They had carbon-oxygen metabolisms, such as yours, but they were excellent diggers."

"Let me guess. They were bred as miners, to extract ores on metal-poor worlds. It would be cheaper to import and breed Karrank% miners than to ship large quantities of metals across interstellar space."

"A very good guess, Dr. Baskin. The client-Karrank% were indeed transformed into miners, and in the process converted to a metabolism extracting energy directly from radioactives. Their patrons thought it would help serve as an *incentive*."

Gillian whistled. "Such a drastic shift in their structure couldn't have been very successful! *Ifni,* they must have suffered!"

"It was a perversion," the Niss agreed. "When it was discovered, the Karrank% were freed and offered recompense. But after a few millennia trying to adapt to standard starfaring life, they chose to retire to Kithrup. This planet was ceded them for the duration of their race. No one expected them to survive for long.

"Instead of dying out, however, they seem to have

continued to modify themselves, on their own. They appear to have adopted a life style unique in known space."

Gillian brought together the threads of the earlier part of the conversation, and made an inference. Her eyes widened. "You mean to tell me the *metal-mounds* . . .?"

"Are larvae of an intelligent life form which dwells in the crust of this planet. Yes. I might have surmised this from the latest data sent by Dr. Dennie Sudman, but Creideiki had leapt to the conclusion before we had even heard from her. That is why he came to see me, to get confirmation of his hypothesis."

"Sah'ot's *voices*," Gillian whispered. "They're Karrank%!"

"An acceptable tentative deduction," the Niss approved. "It would have been the discovery of the century, were it not for the *other* things you've already turned up on this expedition. I believe you humans have an old expression in English—'It doesn't rain but it pours'—it's quaint, but apropos."

Gillian wasn't listening. "The bombs!" She slapped her forehead.

"I beg your pardon?"

"I let Charlie Dart steal some low-yield bombs from our armory. I knew Takkata-Jim would confiscate them and begin transforming them into fuel. It was part of a plan I had cooked up. But . . ."

"You assumed Takkata-Jim would confiscate all of the bombs?"

"Yes! I was going to call him and tip him off if he overlooked them, but he was quite efficient and discovered them right away. I had to lie to Toshio about it, but that couldn't be helped."

"If all went according to plan, I do not see the problem."

"The problem is that Takkata-Jim may not have seized *all* of the bombs! It never occurred to me that Charlie could harm living sophonts if he still had one! *Now*, though . . . I've got to get in touch with Toshio, at once!"

"Can it wait a few minutes? Takkata-Jim probably was thorough, and there is another matter I wish to discuss with you."

"No! You don't understand. Toshio's about to sabotage his comm set! It's part of my plan! If there's even a *chance* Charlie's got a bomb we have to find out quickly!"

The holo patterns were agitated.

"I'll make the connection at once," the Niss announced.

"It will take me a few moments to worm through *Streaker*'s comm system without being detected. Stand by."

Gillian paced the sloping floor, hoping they would be in time.

86

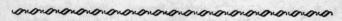

Toshio

Toshio finished the re-wiring, slapped the cover over the transmitter on Thomas Orley's sled, and spread a light smear of mud on the plate to make it seem long unopened.

Then he unhitched the monofilament line from the unit, tied a small red marker ribbon to the end, and let the almost invisible fiber drift down into the depths.

Now he was out of touch with *Streaker*. It made him feel more alone than ever—even lonelier than when Dennie and Sah'ot had departed early in the morning.

He hoped Takkata-Jim would follow orders and wait here until *Streaker* left. If he did, Gillian would call down as they blasted away, and warn him of the modifications that had been made to the longboat and this transmitter.

But what if Takkata-Jim were, indeed, a traitor? What if he took off early?

Charles Dart would probably be aboard then, as well as Ignacio Metz, three *Stenos*, and perhaps three or four Kiqui. Toshio wished none of them harm. It was an agonizing choice.

He looked up and saw Charles Dart happily muttering to himself as he played with his new robot.

Toshio shook his head, glad that the chimp, at least, was happy.

He slid into the water and swam over to his own sled. He had jettisoned *its* tiny radio an hour ago. He strapped himself in and turned on the motors.

He still had to make one more splice below the island. The old robot, the damaged probe Charles Dart had abandoned down near the bottom of the drill-tree shaft, had one last customer. Creideiki, hanging around *Streaker*'s old site, still wanted to talk to Sah'ot's "voices." Toshio figured he owed the captain the favor, even if it did feel like he was humoring a delusion.

As the sled sank, Toshio thought about the rest of his job here . . . the things he might have to do before he could leave.

Let Tom Orley be waiting for me when I come back up, he wished fervently. *That would solve everything. Let Mr. Orley be finished with his job up in the north, and land up there while I'm below.*

Toshio smiled ironically. *And while you're at it, Ifni, why not throw in a giant fleet of good guys to clear the skies of baddies, hmmm?*

He descended down the narrow shaft, into the gloom.

87

∽∾∽∾∽∾∽∾∽∾∽∾∽∾∽∾∽∾∽∾∽∾∽∾

Gillian

"Drat! Triple hell! The line's dead. Toshio's already cut it."

"Don't be overly alarmed." The Niss spoke reassuringly. "It is quite likely that Takkata-Jim confiscated all of the bombs. Did not Midshipman Iwashika report that he saw several being dismantled for fuel, as you expected?"

"Yes, and I told him not to worry about it. But it never occurred to me to ask him to *count* them. I was caught up in the minutiae of moving the ship, and I didn't think Charlie would do any real harm even if, by some chance, he managed to keep one!"

"Now, of course, we know better."

Gillian looked up, wondering if the Tymbrimi machine was being tactful or obliquely sarcastic.

"Well," she said, "what's done is done. Whatever happens can't affect us here. I just hope we don't add a crime against a sentient race to our dubious record on this voyage."

She sighed. "Now, will you tell me again how all this is going to become some sort of legend?"

88

Toshio

The connection was made. Now Creideiki could listen to the underground sounds to his heart's content. Toshio let the monofilament drop into the mud. He emptied ballast, and the sled rose in a spiral toward the drill-tree shaft.

When he surfaced, Toshio knew at once that something had changed. The second sled, the one belonging to Tom Orley, had been dragged up the steep embankment and lay on the sward to the south of the pool. Wires dangled from an open section in the control panel.

Charles Dart squatted by the water's edge. The chimp leaned forward with his finger to his lips.

Toshio cut the motors and loosened his straps. He sat up and looked about the clearing, but saw only the waving forest fronds.

Charlie said in a guttural whisper, "I think Takkata-Jim and Metz are planning to take off soon, Toshio, with or without me." Dart looked confused, as if dazed by the foolishness of the idea.

Toshio kept his expression guarded. "What makes you think that, Dr. Dart?"

"As soon as you went down, two of Takkata-Jim's *Stenos* came to take that sled's radio. Also, when you were below, they tested the engines. They sounded kinda ragged at first, but they're working on 'em now. I think now they don't even care if you report back anymore."

Toshio heard a soft growling sound to the south—a low whine that rose and fell unevenly.

A rustle of movement to the north caught his eye. He saw Ignacio Metz hurrying southward down the forest trail, carrying bundles of records. Behind him trooped four sturdy Kiqui volunteers from the village. Their air-sacks were puffed up proudly, but they obviously did not like approaching the rough engine noises. They carried crude bundles in front of them.

From the foliage, several dozen pairs of wide eyes watched the procession nervously.

Toshio listened to the sound of the engines, and wondered how much time was left. Takkata-Jim had finished recycling the bombs sooner than expected. Perhaps they had underestimated the dolphin lieutenant. How much else had he jury-rigged to make the longboat serviceable ahead of schedule?

Should I try to delay their takeoff? If I stay any longer it's unlikely I'd ever reach Streaker *in time.*

"What about you, Dr. Dart? Are you ready to finish up and hop aboard when Takkata-Jim calls?"

Dart glanced to his console. He shook his head. "I need another six hours," he grumbled. "Maybe we've got a common interest in delaying th' longboat takin' off. You got any ideas?"

Toshio considered.

Well, this is it, isn't it? This is where you decide. Leave now, if you plan to go at all.

Toshio exhaled deeply. *Ah, well.*

"If I think of a way to delay them for a while, Dr. Dart, will you help me? It may be a little risky."

Dart shrugged. "All I'm doin' right now is waiting for my 'bot to dig into the crust to bury a . . . an instrument. I'm free until then. What do I have to do?"

Toshio unhooked the monofilament feeder coil from his sled and cut the free end. "Well, for starters I think we'll need someone to climb some trees."

Charlie grimaced. "Stereotypes," he muttered to himself. "Allatime gettin' trapped by stereotypes."

89

❀❀❀❀❀❀❀❀❀❀❀❀❀❀❀❀❀❀❀❀❀❀❀❀

Gillian

She shook her head slowly. Maybe it was her tiredness, but she couldn't understand more than a fraction of the Niss machine's explanation. Every time she tried to get it to simplify some subtle point of Galactic tradition, it insisted on bringing in examples that only muddied things further.

She felt like a Cro-Magnon trying to understand the intrigues in the court of Louis XIV. The Niss seemed to be saying that *Streaker*'s discoveries would have consequences that reached beyond the immediate crisis over the derelict fleet. But the subtleties eluded her.

"Dr. Baskin." The machine tried again. "Every epoch has its turning point. Sometimes it occurs on the battlefield. Sometimes it takes the form of a technological advance. On occasion, the pivotal event is philosophical and so obscure that the species in existence at the time are hardly aware that anything has changed before their world-view is turned topsy-turvy around them.

"But often, very often, these upheavals are preceded by a legend. I know of no other Anglic word to use for it . . . a *story* whose images will stand out in the minds of almost all sophonts . . . a *true* story of prodigious deeds and powerful archetypal symbols, which presages the change to come."

"You're saying *we* may become one of these legends?"

"That is what I am saying."

Gillian could not remember ever feeling so small. She couldn't lift the weight of what the Niss was implying. Her duty to Earth and the lives of one hundred and fifty friends and crewmates were burdens enough.

"Archetype symbols, you say..."

"What could be more symbolic, Dr. Baskin, than *Streaker* and her discoveries? Just one, the derelict fleet, has turned the Five Galaxies upside down. Now add the fact that the discovery was made by the newest of all client races, whose patrons are wolflings, claiming no patrons at all. Here on Kithrup, where no pre-sentient life was supposed to be able to arise, they *find* a ripe pre-sentient race, and take great risks to protect the innocents from a Galactic civilization grown rigid and calcified...."

"Now just a..."

"Now add the Karrank%. In all of the recent epochs, no sapient race has been treated so foully, so abused by the system which was supposed to protect them.

"So what were the chances that *this* ship would happen to flee to the very planet that was *their* last refuge? Can you not see the overlying images, Dr. Baskin? From the Progenitors down to the very newest race, what one sees is a powerful sermon about the Uplift System.

"Whatever the outcome of your attempt to escape Kithrup, whether you succeed or fail, the stars cannot help but make a great song of your adventure. This song, I believe, will change more than you can imagine." The voice of Niss finished, with a hushed, almost reverent tone. It's implication was left spinning in the silence.

Gillian stood on the sloping ceiling of the dark, lopsided room, blinking in the sparkling light cast by the swirling motes. The silence hung. Finally, she shook her head.

"Another damned Tymbrimi practical joke," she sighed. "A goddamn shaggy dog story. You've been pulling my leg."

The motes spun silently for a long moment. "Would it make you feel any better if I said I were, Dr. Baskin? And would it change what you have to do one bit if I said I weren't?"

She shrugged. "I guess not. At least you pulled me back from my own troubles for a little while. I feel a bit light-headed from all that philosophical crap, and maybe even ready to get some sleep."

"I am always ready to be of service."

Gillian smirked. "Sure you are." She climbed up on a packing crate to reach the door-plate, but before opening the door she looked back up at the machine.

"Tell me one thing, Niss. Did you give Creideiki any of this bullshit you were feeding me just now?"

"Not in Anglic words, no. But we did cover most of the same themes."

"And he believed you?"

"Yes. I believe he did. Frankly, I was a bit surprised. It was almost as if he had heard it all before, from another source."

That explained part of the mystery of the captain's disappearance, then. And there was nothing that could be done about it now.

"Assuming he did believe you, just what does Creideiki think he's going to accomplish out there?"

The motes spun for a few seconds.

"I suppose, Dr. Baskin, he is first off looking for *allies*. On an entirely different level, I think he is out there trying to add a few choice stanzas to the legend."

90

Creideiki

They moaned. They had always been in pain. For aeons life had hurt them.

　　:Listen:

He called out in the language of the ancient gods, coaxing the Karrank% to answer him.

　　:Listen: You Deep, Hidden Ones—You Sad, Abused Ones : I Call From The Outside : I Crave an Audience :

The doleful singing paused. He felt a hint of irritation. It came in both sound and psi, a shrug to shake a bothersome flea away.

The song of lamentation resumed.

Creideiki kept at it, pushing, probing. He floated at the

relay link *Streaker* had left behind, breathing from his sled's airdome, trying to get the attention of the ancient misanthropes, using the electrical buzz of a distant robot to amplify his faint message.

: I Call From The Outside : Seeking Aid : Your Ancient Tormentors Are Our Enemies Too :

That stretched the truth slightly, but not in essence. He hurried on, sculpting sound images as he felt their attention finally swing his way.

: We Are Your Brothers: Will You Help Us? :

The growling drone suddenly erupted. The psi portion felt angry and *alien*. The part that was sound grated like static. Without his apprenticeship in the Sea of Dreams, Creideiki felt certain he would have found it unfathomable.

+ DO NOT BOTHER US −
− DO NOT STAY ! WE +
+ HAVE NO BROTHERS −
− WE   REJECT +
+ THE   UNIVERSE −
− GO   AWAY! +

Creideiki's head rang with the powerful dimissal. Still, the potency of the psi was encouraging.

What *Streaker*'s crew had needed all along was an ally, *any* ally. They had to have some help, at least a distraction, if Thomas Orley's clever plan of deception and disguise stood a chance of success. As alien and bitter as these underground creatures were, they had once been starfarers. Perhaps they would take some satisfaction in helping other victims of Galactic civilization.

He persisted.

: Look! : Listen! : Your World Is Surrounded By Gene-Meddlers : They Seek Us : And Small Ones Who Share This Planet With You : They Wish To Warp Us : As They Did You : They Will Invade Your Private Agony :

He crafted a sonic image of great fleets of ships, embellished with gaping jaws. He painted over them an impression of malicious intent.

His picture was shattered by a thundering response.

+ WE ARE NOT INVOLVED! −

Creideiki shook his head and concentrated.
: They May Seek You Out, As Well :

+ THEY HAVE NO USE FOR US! −
− IT IS YOU THEY SEEK! +
+ NOT   US! −

The reply dazed him. Creideiki only had strength for one
more question. He tried to ask what the Karrank% would do
if they *were* attacked.

Before he finished, he was answered by a gnashing that
could not be parsed even in the sense-glyphs of the ancient
gods. It was more a roar of defiance than anything decipherable.
Then, in an instant, the sound and mental echoes cut off. He
was left there, drifting with his head ringing from their anger.

He had done his best. Now what?

With nothing better to do, he closed his eyes and
meditated. He clicked out sonar spirals and wove the echoes
of the surrounding ridges into patterns. His disappointment
subsided as he sensed Nukapai take shape alongside him, her
body a complex matting of his own sounds and those of the
sea. She seemed to rub along his side and Creideiki thought
he could *almost* feel her. He felt a brief sexual thrill.

: Not Nice People : she commented.

Creideiki smiled sadly.

: No, Not Nice : But They Hurt : I Would Not
Bother Such Hermits But For The Need :

He sighed.

: The World-Song Seems To Say They Will Not Help :

Nukapai grinned at his pessimism. She changed tempo
and whistled softly in an amused tone.

> * *Go below*
> *And hear tomorrow's weather*
> * *Go below*
> *Prescience, prescience....* *

Creideiki concentrated to understand her. Why did she
speak Trinary, a language almost as difficult for him now as
Anglic? There was another speech, subtle and powerful, that
they could share now. Why did she remind him of his
disability?

He shook his head, confused. Nukapai was a figment of

his own mind . . . or at least she was limited to whatever sounds his own voice could create. So *how* was it she could talk in Trinary at all?

There were mysteries still. The deeper he went the more mysteries there seemed to be.

> * *Go below*
>   *Deep night-diver*
> * *Go below*
>   *Prescience, prescience—* *

He repeated the message to himself. Did she mean that something could be read from the future? That something inevitable was fated to bring the Karrank% out of their isolation?

He was still trying to puzzle out the riddle when he heard the sound of engines. Creideiki listened for a few moments. But he didn't need to turn on the sled's hydrophones to recognize the pattern of those motors.

Cautiously, tentatively, a tiny spacecraft nosed into the canyon. Sonar swept slowly from one end to another. A searchlight took in the scars in the sea-bed that the departing *Streaker* had left behind. They scanned bits and pieces of abandoned equipment, and finally came to rest on the little boxy relay, and his sled.

Creideiki blinked in the bright beam. He opened his jaws wide in a smile of greeting. But his voice froze. For the first time in several days he felt bashful, unable to speak for fear of choking over even the simplest words and seeming a fool.

The ship's speakers amplified a single happy sigh, elegantly simple.

> * *Creideiki!* *

With a warm pleasure he recognized that voice. He turned on the sled's motors and cast loose from the relay. As he sped toward the skiff's opening hatch he called out careful words in Anglic, one at a time.

"Hikahi . . . Nice . . . to hear . . . your . . . voice . . . again . . ."

91

Tom Orley

Fog swirled over the sea of weeds. That was good, up to a point. It made stealth easier. But it also made it hard to look for traps.

Tom searched carefully as he crawled across the last stretch of weeds before the open end of the wrecked cruiser. This patch couldn't be taken underwater, and he didn't doubt those who had taken shelter within the hulk had set upward.

He found the device only a few meters from the gaping opening. Thin wires were strung from one small hump of vines to the next. Tom inspected the arrangement, then carefully dug below the tripwire and slithered underneath. When he was clear, he scrambled quietly to the edge of the floating ship and rested against the pitted hull.

The weed beasties had taken cover during the fighting. They were out again, now that almost all of the combatants were dead. Their frog-like croaks refracted eerily in the noisome vapor. Distantly, Tom heard the rumble of the volcano. His empty stomach growled. It sounded loud enough to rouse the Progenitors.

He checked his weapon. The needler had only a few shots left. He had better be right about the number of ETs that had taken shelter aboard this vessel.

I'd better be right about a number of things, he reminded himself. *I've staked a lot on there being food here, as well as the information I need.*

He closed his eyes in brief meditation, then turned to crouch below the opening. He peeked one eye just past the ragged edge.

386

Three bird-like Gubru huddled around a motley array of equipment on the smoke-stained, canted deck. A tiny, inadequate heater held the attention of two, who warmed slender-boned arms over it. The third sat before a battered portable console and squeaked in Galactic Four, a language popular among many avian species.

"No sign of humans or their clients," the creature peeped. "We have lost our deep-search equipment, so we cannot be certain. But we find no sign of Earthlings. We cannot achieve anything more. Come for us!"

The radio sputtered. "Impossible to come out of hiding. Impossible to squander last resources at this time. You must maintain. You must lie low. You must wait."

"Wait? We shelter in a hull whose food supply is radioactive. We shelter in a hull whose equipment is ruined. Yet this hull we shelter in is the best still afloat! You must come for us!"

Tom cursed silently at the news. So much for eating!

The radio operator maintained its protests. The other two Gubru listened, shifting their weight impatiently. One of them stamped its clawed feet and turned around suddenly as if to interrupt the radio operator. Its gaze swept past the gap in the hull. Before Tom could duck back, the creature's eyes went wide. It began to point.

"A human! *Quickly . . .*"

Tom shot it in the thorax. Without bothering to watch it fall, he dove through the opening and rolled behind a tilted console. He scuttled to the other end and snapped off two quick shots just as the second standing Gubru tried to fire. A thin flame spat out of a small handgun, searing the already scarred ceiling as the alien shrieked and toppled backward.

The Galactic at the radio stared at Tom. It glanced at the radio beside it.

"Don't even think it," Tom squawked in heavily accented Galactic Four. The alien's crest riffled in surprise. It lowered its hands and kept still.

Tom rose carefully, never drawing bead away from the surviving Gubru. "Drop your weapons belt and stand away from the transmitter. Slowly. Remember, we humans are wolflings. We are feral, carnivorous, and extremely fast! Do not make me eat you." He grinned his broadest grin to display a maximum of teeth.

The creature shuddered and moved to obey. Tom rein-

forced obedience with a growl. Sometimes a reputation as a
primitive had its uses.

"All right," he said as the alien moved to where he
gestured, by the gaping hole. Tom kept his gun trained and
sat by the radio. The receiver gave out excited twitters.

He recognized the model, thank Ifni, and switched it off.
"Were you transmitting when your friend here spotted me?"
he asked his captive. He wondered if the commander of the
hidden Gubru forces had heard the word "human."

The Galactic's comb fluttered. Its answer was so irrelevant that Tom momentarily wondered if he had totally mis-
phrased the question.

"You must surrender pride," it chanted, puffing its feathers.
"All young ones must surrender pride. Pride leads to error.
Hubris leads to error. Only orthodoxy can save. We can
save..."

"That's enough!" Tom snapped.

"...save you from heretics. Lead us to the returning
Progenitors. Lead us to the ancient masters. Lead us to the
rule-givers. Lead us to them. They expect to return to the
Paradise they decreed when they long ago departed. They
expect Paradise and would be helpless before such as the
Soro or the Tandu or the Thennanin or..."

"Thennanin! That's what I want to know! Are the Thennanin
still fighting? Are they powers in the battle?" Tom swayed
with the intensity of his need to know.

"...or the Dark Brothers. They will need protection
until they are made to understand what terrible things are
being done in their name, orthodoxies broken, heresies
abounding. Lead us to them, help us cleanse the universe.
Your rewards will be great. Your modifications small. Your
indenture short..."

"Stop it!" Tom felt the strain and exhaustion of the last
few days rise in a boiling rage. Next to the Soro and Tandu,
the Gubru had been among humanity's worst persecutors.
He had had all he was about to take from this one.

"Stop it and answer my questions!" He fired at the floor
near the alien's feet. It hopped in surprise, wide-eyed. Tom
fired twice more. The first time the Gubru danced away from
a ricochet. The second time it winced as the needler misfired
and jammed.

The Galactic peered at him, then squawked joyfully. It
spread its feathered arms wide and unsheathed long talons.

For the first time it said something direct and intelligible.

"Now *you* shall talk, impertinent, half-formed, masterless upstart!"

It charged, screaming.

Tom dove to one side as the shrieking avian screeched past him. Slowed by hunger and exhaustion, he couldn't prevent one razor-sharp claw from passing through his wet-suit and ripping his side along one rib. He gasped and stumbled against a blood-stained wall as the Gubru turned around to renew the attack.

Neither of them even considered the handguns that lay on the floor. Depleted and slippery, the weapons weren't worth the gamble to stoop to retrieve them.

"Where are the dolphinnnns?" the Gubru squawked as it danced back and forth. "Tell me or I shall teach you respect for your elders the hard way."

Tom nodded. "Learn to swim, bird-brain, and I'll take you to them."

The Gubru's talons spread again. It shrieked and charged.

Tom summoned his reserves. He leapt into the air and met the creature's throat with a savage kick. The shriek was cut off abruptly, and he felt its vertebrae snap as it went down, sliding along the damp deck to fetch up at the wall in a heap.

Tom landed stumbling beside it. His eyes swam. Breathing heavily with hands on his knees, he looked down at his enemy.

"I told... told you we were... wolflings," he muttered.

When he could, he walked unsteadily to the ragged tear in the side of the ship and leaned on the curled and blackened lower edge, staring out at the drifting fog.

All he had left were his mask, his freshwater still, his clothes, and... oh yes, the nearly worthless hand weapons of the Gubru.

And the message-bomb, of course. The weight pressed against his midriff.

I've put off a decision long enough, he decided. While the battle lasted he could pretend he was searching for answers. Maybe he had been procrastinating, though.

I wanted to be sure. I wanted to know the trick had a maximum chance of working. For that to happen there had to be Thennanin.

I met that scout. The Gubru mentioned Thennanin. Do I

have to see their fleet to guess there are still some in the battle above?

He realized there was another reason he had been putting the decision off.

Once I set it off, Creideiki and Gillian are gone. There's no way they'll be able to stop for me. I was to get back to the ship on my own, if at all.

While fighting on the weeds, he had kept hoping to find a working vessel. Anything that could fly him home. But there were only wrecks.

He sat down heavily with his back to the cool metal and drew out the message-bomb.

Do I set it off?

The Seahorse was his plan. Why was he out here, far from Gillian and home, but to find out if it would work?

Across the blood-smeared deck of the alien cruiser, his gaze fell on the Gubru radio.

You know, he told himself, *there is one more thing I can do. Even if it means I'll be putting myself right in the middle of a bull's-eye, at least it'll give Jill and the others all I know.*

And maybe it'll accomplish more than that.

Tom summoned the strength to stand up one more time. *Ah, well,* he thought as he staggered to his feet. *There's no food anyway. I might as well go out in style.*

PART NINE

Ascent

"Sunset and evening star,
And one clear call for me!
And may there be no moaning of the bar
When I put out to sea."

—A. TENNYSON

∾∾∾∾∾∾∾∾∾∾∾∾∾∾∾∾∾∾∾∾∾∾∾∾∾∾

92

Dennie & Sah'ot

"It'sss the longer way, Dennie. Are you sure we shouldn't just cut southwest?"

Sah'ot swam alongside the sled, keeping pace fairly easily. Every few strokes he glided smoothly to the surface to blow, then rejoined his companion without breaking stride.

"I know it would be faster, Sah'ot." Dennie answered without looking up from her sonar display. She was careful to skirt far from any metal-mounds. It was in this area that the killer-weed grew. Toshio's story about his encounter with the deadly plant had terrified her, and she was determined to give the unfamiliar mounds a wide berth.

"Then why are we returning to *Streaker*'s old site before heading sssouth?"

"For several reasons," Dennie answered. "First of all, we *know* this part of the route, having been over it before. And the path from the old site to the Seahorse is straight south, so there's less chance of getting lost."

Sah'ot snickered, unconvinced. "And?"

"And this way we'll stand a chance of finding Hikahi. My guess is she may be nosing around the old site about now."

"Did Gillian ask you to look for her?"

"Yeah," Dennie lied. Actually, she had her own reasons for wanting to find Hikahi.

Dennie was afraid of what Toshio intended to do. It was possible that he meant to delay leaving the island until *Streaker*'s preparations were finished and it was too late for

Takkata-Jim to interfere. Of course, by then it would be too late for him to rejoin the ship via sled.

In that case the skiff would be Toshio's only chance. She had to find Hikahi before Gillian did. Gillian might decide to send the skiff after Tom Orley instead of Toshio.

She knew she wasn't thinking things out, and felt a little guilty about her decision. But if she could lie to one dolphin, she could lie to another.

93

❦❦❦❦❦❦❦❦❦❦❦❦❦❦❦❦❦❦❦❦❦❦

Takkata-Jim & Metz

The former vice-captain tossed his head and gnashed his teeth as he contemplated the latest sabotage.

"I will string their entrails from the foressst branches!" he hissed. The heavy waldo-arms of his armored spider whined.

Ignacio Metz stared up at the thin, almost invisible wires that formed a tight tracery over the longboat, holding it to the ground. He blinked, trying to follow the trail of fibers into the forest.

Metz shook his head. "Are you sure you're not over-reacting, vice-captain? It seems to me the boy was only trying to make sure we didn't take off before we agreed to."

Takkata-Jim whirled to glare down on the human. "And have you sssuddenly changed your mind, *Doctor* Metz? Do you now think we should let the lunatic woman who now controls *Streaker* send our crewmates out to certain death?"

"N-no, of course not!" Metz shrank back from the dolphin officer's rancor. "We should persevere, I agree. We must try to make our offer of compromise to the Galactics, but . . ."

"But what?"

Metz shrugged uncertainly. "I just don't think you should blame Toshio for doing his job. . . ."

Takkata-Jim's jaws clapped together like a gunshot, and he caused the spider to advance upon Metz, stopping less than a meter from the nervous man.

"You *think*! You THINK! Of all comedies, that one topsss all! *You*, who had the arrogance to suppose his wisdom exceded the councils of Earth—who brought pet monsters amongst an already fragile crew—who deceived himself into thinking all was well, and ignored danger signs when his wisdom was needed by his desperate clients—*yes*, Ignacio Metz. Tell me how you think-k!" Takkata-Jim snorted in derision.

"B-but we . . . you and I agreed on nearly everything! My gene-graft *Stenos* were your most loyal supporters! They're the only ones who stood by you!"

"*Your Stenos* were not *Stenos*! They were benighted, erratic creatures who did not belong on thisss mission! I *used* them, as I've used *you*. But don't class me with your monsters, Metz!"

Stunned, Metz sagged back against the hull of the longboat.

From nearby came the sounds of returning machines. With a withering glance, Takkata-Jim warned the human to be silent. Sreekah-pol's spider pushed through the foliage.

"The fibersss lead to the p-pool," the fin announced. His Anglic was almost too high-pitched for Metz to follow. "They go below and wrap around the drill-tree shshaft-t."

"You've cut them?"

"Yesss!" The neo-fin tossed its head.

Takkata-Jim nodded. "Dr. Metz, please prepare the Kiqui. They are our second greatest trade item, and musst be ready for inspection by whichever race we contact-t."

"Where are you going?" Metz asked.

"You don't want to know."

Metz saw Takkata-Jim's determined expression. Then he noted the three *Stenos*. Their eyes gleamed with an eager madness.

"You've been goading them in Primal!" he gasped. "I can tell! You've taken these fen over the edge! You're going to make them homicidals!"

Takkata-Jim sighed. "I will wrestle with my conscience later, Dr. Metz. In the meantime I will do what I must to save the ship and our mission. Since a sane dolphin cannot kill human beings, I needed insane dolphins."

The three *Stenos* grinned at Metz. He looked at their eyes in terror, and listened to their feral clickings.

"You're mad!" he whispered.

"No, Dr. Metz," Takkata-Jim shook his head pityingly. "*You* are mad. These fen are mad. But I am only acting as a desperate and dedicated human being might act. Criminal or patriot, that's a matter of opinion, but I am sentient."

Metz's eyes were wide. "You can't take back to Earth anyone who knows..." He paled, and turned to run for the airlock.

Takkata-Jim did not even have to give the order. From Sreekah-pol's spider a burst of actinic blue light lanced out. Ignacio Metz sighed and fell to the muddy ground just outside the longboat's hatch. He stared up at Sreekah-pol, like a father betrayed by a son he had doted on.

Takkata-Jim turned to his crew, hiding the nauseated feeling that churned within him.

> \# *Find, Find,*
> > *Find and Kill,*
> \# *Kill*
> > *Soft-skin human*
> > *Hairy ape*
>
> \# *I wait, wait*
> > *Here*
> \# *Wait Here—* \#

The fen gave out a shrill assent in unison, and turned as one to go crashing back into the forest, heavy manipulator arms brushing aside saplings like twigs.

The man groaned. Takkata-Jim looked down at him and considered putting him out of his misery. He wanted to. But he couldn't bring himself to do direct violence against a human being.

Just as well, he thought. There are still repairs to do. I must be ready when my monsters return.

Takkata-Jim stepped daintily over the supine human and climbed into the airlock.

"Dr. Metz!" Toshio pulled the wounded man to one side and lifted his head. He whispered urgently as he applied a spray ampule of pain killer to the geneticist's neck. "Dr. Metz, can you hear me?"

Metz blearily looked up at the young man. "Toshio? My boy, you've got to get away! Takkata-Jim has sent . . ."

"I know, Dr. Metz. I was hiding in the bushes when they shot you."

"Then you heard," he sighed.

"Yes, sir."

"And you know what a fool I've been . . ."

"Now's not the time for that, Dr. Metz. We've got to get you away. Charlie Dart's hiding nearby. I'll go get him now, while the *Stenos* are searching another part of the island."

Metz clutched Toshio's arm. "They're hunting for him, too."

"I know. And you've never seen a more stunned chimp. He honestly believed they'd never think he helped me! Let me go get him, and we'll move you away from here."

Metz coughed, and red foam appeared on his lips. He shook his head.

"No. Like Victor Frankenstein, it seems I am murdered by my own hubris. Leave me. You must go to your sled and depart."

Toshio grimaced. "Their first stop was the pool, Dr. Metz. I followed and saw them sink my sled.

"I ran ahead then to chase the Kiqui off the island. Dennie taught me their panic signal, and they split like crazed lemmings when I called it out, so at least they're safe from the *Stenos* . . ."

"Not *Stenos*," Metz corrected. "*Demenso cetus metzii*, I should think. 'Metz's mad dolphins' . . . you know, I think I'm the first dolphin-perpetrated homicide in . . ." He brought his fist to his mouth and coughed again.

Metz looked at the red spittle in his hand, then up at Toshio. "We were going to give the Kiqui to the Galactics, you know. I wasn't too happy about it, but he convinced me . . ."

"Takkata-Jim?"

"Yes. He didn't think offering the ETs the location of the derelict fleet would be enough . . ."

"He's got *tapes*?" Toshio felt stunned. "But how . . . ?"

Metz wasn't listening. He seemed to be fading fast. ". . . He didn't think that would be enough to win *Streaker's* freedom, so . . . decided we'd give them the aboriginals, as well."

The man grabbed feebly at Toshio's arm. "You must set them free, Toshio. Don't let the fanatics have them. They are so promising. They must have kind patrons. Maybe the Linten, or the Synthians . . . but we're not suited for the job . . . we'd . . . we'd make them into caricatures of ourselves. We'd . . ."

The geneticist sagged.

Toshio waited with him. It was all he could do for the man. His tiny aid kit could do nothing but ease the pain.

Metz roused once more, a minute later. He stared up without seeing.

"Takkata-Jim . . ." he gasped. "I never thought of it before. Why, he's exactly what we've been looking for! I never realized, but he's not a dolphin. He's a *man* . . . . Who in the world would have thought . . ."

His voice faded into a rattle. His eyes rolled upward.

Toshio found no pulse. He lowered the corpse to the ground and slipped back into the forest.

"Metz is dead," he told Charles Dart. The chimp looked out from the bushes. The whites of his eyes shone.

"B-b-but th-that's . . ."

"That's homicide, I know." Toshio nodded, sympathizing with Charles Dart. The one standard technique of uplift humans had taken unmodified from the Galactics was to ingrain a revulsion of patron-murder in their clients. Few thought it particularly hypocritical, considering man's liberal record in other areas. Still . . .

"Then they w-won't think twice about shooting you and me!"

Toshio shrugged.

"What're we gonna do?" Charlie had dropped all professorial mannerisms. He looked to Toshio for guidance.

He's the adult and I'm the kid, Toshio thought bitterly. *It should be the other way around.*

No, that's foolish. Age or patron-client status has nothing to do with it. I'm military. Keeping us alive is my job.

He kept his nervousness hidden. "We'll do as we have done, Dr. Dart. We've got to harass them, and keep them from taking off as long as possible."

Dart blinked a few times, then protested. "But we'll

have no way *off*, then! Can't you get *Streaker* to come for us?"

"If it turns out to be at all possible, I'm sure Gillian will try to make arrangements. But you and I are expendable now. Try to understand that, Dr. Dart. We're soldiers. They say there's a kind of satisfaction in sacrificing oneself for others. I guess it's true; otherwise there wouldn't ever be legends."

The chimp tried to believe. His hands fluttered. "If they get b-back to Earth, they'll tell about what we did, won't they?"

Toshio smiled. "You bet."

Charlie looked at the ground for a moment. In the distance they could hear the *Stenos* crashing through the forest.

"Uh, Toshio, there's something you oughta know."

"What is it, Dr. Dart?"

"Uh, you remember that thing I wanted to make them wait a few hours for, before taking off?"

"Your experiment. Yes, I remember."

"Well the instruments I left aboard *Streaker* will take the data, so the info will get home even if I don't."

"Hey, that's great, Dr. Dart! I'm happy for you." Toshio knew what that meant to the chimp scientist.

Charlie smiled weakly. "Yeah, well, it's too late to stop it from happening, so I figure you oughta know so it doesn't surprise you."

Something about the way he said it made Toshio feel uneasy. "Tell me," he said.

Charlie looked at his watch. "The robot will be where I want it in eighty minutes." He glanced up at Toshio a little nervously. "Then my bomb goes off."

Toshio fell back against the bole of a tree. "Oh, great, that's all we need . . ."

"I was *gonna* tell Takkata-Jim just before, so we could hover when it exploded," Charlie explained sheepishly. "I wouldn't worry too much, though. I looked over Dennie's map of the cavern below the island. I'd say there's at least even money the mound won't fall in, but, you know . . ." He spread his hands.

Toshio sighed. They were going to die anyway. Fortunately, this latest twist didn't seem to have any cosmic implications.

94

Streaker

"We're ready." He made the announcement quite matter-of-factly.

Gillian looked up from the holo display. Hannes Suessi gave Gillian a two-fingered salute from the door jamb. Light from the bright hallway cast a stark trapezoid onto the floor of the dimly lit room.

"The impedance matchings...?" she asked.

"All darn near perfect. In fact, when we get back to Earth I'm going to suggest we buy a bunch of old hulls from the Thennanin to refit all Snarks with. We'll be slow, doubly so because of all the water in the central bay, but *Streaker* will lift, fly, and warp. And it'll take a hell of a punch to pound through the outer shell."

Gillian put one foot on the desk. "There's still a lot of punch out there, Hannes."

"She'll fly. As for the rest..." The engineer shrugged. "The only constraint I'd suggest is that you let the engineering staff get an hour or so under sleep machines if you don't want us sagging on takeoff. Other than that, it's up to you now, Madame Captain."

He stopped her before she could speak. "And don't go looking to *us* for any advice, either, Gillian. You've been doing too good a job so far, and neither Tsh't nor I are going to say anything but aye aye, sir, and jump when you say so."

Gillian closed her eyes and nodded. "All right," she said softly.

Hannes looked through the open door from her office to Gillian's laboratory. He knew about the ancient cadaver. He had been there to help Tom Orley bring it back into the ship.

400

He saw a glimpse of a silhouette suspended within a glass case. He shivered and turned away.

Gillian's holo display showed a small, Ping-Pong-ball-sized representation of Kithrup, and a scattering of small BBs as the planet's moons. Two clusters of blue and red dots were accompanied by tiny computer-code letters suspended in space.

"Don't seem like too many of the nasty buggers are left," Suessi commented.

"Those are just the ships in nearby space. The expanded view, about a cubic astron, shows two still substantial Galactic squadrons. We can't actually identify the fleets, of course, but the battle computer assigns colors on the basis of movement. They're still changing alliances out there.

"Also, there's a plethora of survivors hiding out on the moons."

Suessi pursed his lips. Almost he asked the question that was on everyone's mind, but he bit it back. Gillian answered anyway.

"There's still been no word from Tom." She looked at her hands. "Until now we didn't really have any use for the information, but now . . ." She paused.

"But now we've got to know whether taking off would be suicide." Suessi finished her thought. He noticed Gillian was studying the display again.

"You're trying to figure it out for yourself, aren't you?"

Gillian shrugged. "Go get that hour, Hannes, or three, or ten. Tell your fen to take their naps at their stations, and toggle their sleep machines to the bridge."

She frowned as she looked at the drifting dots. "I may be wrong. We may wind up choosing the lesser evil—hiding down here until our gums start turning blue from metal poisoning or we starve. But I have a feeling, a hunch, we may have to act soon." She shook her head.

"What about Toshio and Hikahi and the others?"

Gillian did not answer. No answer was necessary. After a moment Suessi turned and left. He closed the door behind him.

Dots. No more could be resolved by *Streaker*'s passive sensors than drifting dots that occasionally came together in sparkling swarms and separated smaller in number. The battle computer went over the patterns and drew tentative conclusions. But the answer she needed was never there. "Would the surviving fleets be indifferent to the sudden reappearance of a long-lost Thennanin cruiser, or would they join forces to swat it out of the sky?" The decision lay with her. Never had Gillian felt so alone.

"Where are you, boy? You live, I know. I can feel your distant breath. What are you doing right now?"

To her left a green light started flashing. "Yes," she told the comm link.

"Dr. Bassskin!" It was the voice of Wattaceti, calling from the bridge. "Hikahi callsss! She is at-t the relay! And she has Creideiki!"

"Put her through!"

There was a hiss as the operator raised the gain on the attenuated signal.

"Gillian? Is that-t you?"

"Yes, Hikahi. Thank God! Are you all right? And Creideiki's still at the relay?"

"We are both quite well, Life-Cleaner. From what the fen on the bridge tell usss, you don't seem to need us there at all!"

"They're damned patron-sucking liars! And I wouldn't trade a one of them away for my left arm. Listen, we're missing five crewfen. You should be warned, two are atavistic and highly dangerous."

The line hissed for a long moment. Then, "All are accounted for, Gillian," came the reply at last. "Four of them are dead."

Gillian covered her eyes. "Dear Lord . . ."

"Keepiru is with usss," Hikahi answered her unasked question.

"Poor Akki," Gillian sighed.

"Send word to Calafia that he did his duty. Keepiru says he was defiant and sentient till the end."

Gillian did not like the implication of Hikahi's message. "Hikahi, you're in command now. We need you back here *now*. I am this instant officially handing over . . ."

"Don't, Gillian," the fluting voice interrupted. "Please. Not yet-t. There are still things to be done with the skiffff. Those on the island must be recovered, and the Kiqui volunteers."

"I'm not sure we'll have time, Hikahi." The words were

bitter as she spoke them. She thought of bright, ever self-deprecating Dennie Sudman, of the erudite Sah'ot, and Toshio, so very young and noble.

"Has T-Tom called? Is there an emergency?"

"Neither, yet. But..."

"Then what-t?"

She couldn't explain. She tried in Trinary.

> * *What a piercing sound I hear—*
> * *The peal of bugles, engines rising—*
> * *The tears of love abandoned—*
>   * *Soon, so very soon—* *

There was a long silence from the skiff. Then, it was not Hikahi's voice, but Creideiki's, that answered. In his repetitious, simply-phrased Trinary, there was something Gillian could only catch a hint of, something deep and a little eerie.

> * *Sounds, All Sounds*
>   *Answer Something*
>   *Answer Something :*

> * *Acts, All Acts*
>   *Make Sounds*
>   *Make Sounds :*

> * *But Duty, All Duty*
>   *Calls Silently*
>   *Calls Silently :*

Gillian didn't breathe as she listened to Creideiki's last note fall away. Her spine was chilled.

"'Bye, Gillian," Hikahi said. "You do what you have to. We'll be back as quick-kly as we can. But don't wait for usss."

"Hikahi!" Gillian reached for the comm link, but the carrier wave cut off before she could say another word.

95

Toshio

"Both airlocks are bolted from the inside," Toshio panted when he returned to the hiding place. "Looks like we try it your way."

Charles Dart nodded, and led him to the impulse thrusters at the stern of the small spacecraft.

Twice they had hidden themselves by climbing tall trees as the patrolling *Stenos* passed below. It seemed not to occur to the mad fen to look above for their quarry. But Toshio knew they'd be deadly if they ever caught him and Charlie in the open.

Charlie removed the rear cover to the maintenance bay between the engines. "I got in by crawling between the feedlines, over there, until I reached the access plate in that bulkhead." He pointed. Toshio peered into the maze of pipes.

He looked back at Dart, amazed. "No wonder nobody expected a stowaway. Is this how you got into the armory, as well? By climbing through ducts where no human could fit?"

The planetologist nodded. "I guess you can't go in with me. That means I gotta get the little critters out by myself, right?"

Toshio nodded. "I think they're in the aft hold. Here's the voder."

He handed over the translator. It looked like a large medallion hanging from a neck-chain. All neo-chimps knew about voders, since they generally had trouble talking until the age of three. Charlie slipped it over his head. He started to climb into the small opening, but stopped and looked sidelong at the middie.

"Say, Toshio. Imagine this was one of those 20th-century

404

'zoo' ships, and those are a bunch of pre-sentient chimps in the hold of a clipper ship—or whatever they used back then—on their way from Africa to some laboratory or circus. Would *you* have snuck in to rescue *them*?"

Toshio shrugged. "I don't honestly know, Charlie. I'd like to think I would've. But I really don't know what I'd've done."

The neo-chimp met the human's eyes for a long instant, then he grunted. "Okay, you guard the rear."

He took a boost from Toshio and squirmed into the mechanical maze. Toshio squatted beneath the thruster tubes and listened to the forest. While Charlie struggled to get the inner access plate off, he made what felt like a terrible racket. Then it stopped.

Toshio slid into the forest to make a cautious circuit of the immediate area.

From crashing sounds up in the direction of the Kiqui village, he guessed the *Stenos* were amusing themselves with a destructive spree. He hoped none of the little natives had come back yet to witness, or worse, be caught in the violence.

He returned to the longboat and looked at his watch. Seventeen minutes until the bomb went off. They were cutting it close.

He reached into the maintenance area and spent a few minutes twiddling with some of the valves, spoiling their settings. Of course, Takkata-Jim didn't need the thrusters at all. If he was, indeed, refueled, he could take off on gravitics. Leaving the access panel loose would decrease the boat's aerodynamic stability, but even that effect would be slight. Longboats like these were built rugged.

He stopped and listened. The rampage through the forest was heading this way again. The fen were on their way back.

"Hurry up, Charlie!" He fingered the grip of his holstered needler, not certain he could aim well enough to hit the vulnerable patches where the dolphins were unprotected by the metal-sided spiders.

"Come on!"

There came a series of small, wet, slapping sounds from within the cavity. Intermittent squeaks echoed from the narrow confines, and then he saw a pair of widely splayed, green-finned hands.

They were followed by the head of a rather distressed-looking Kiqui. The aboriginal scuttled through the inner panel and crept through the maze of pipes until it leapt into Toshio's arms.

Toshio had to peel the frightened creature loose and put it down in order to reach for the next one. The little Kiqui were making a fearful racket, squeaking dolefully.

Finally all four were out. Toshio peered inside and saw Charles Dart trying to replace the inner panel.

"Never mind that!" Toshio hissed.

"I gotta! Takkata-Jim'll notice the change in air pressure on his panel! It's only luck he hasn't yet!"

"Come on! They're..." He heard the whine of waldo motors and crushed vegetation. "They're here! I'm going to draw them away from you. Good luck, Charlie!"

"Wait!"

Toshio crawled a few meters into the shrubbery so they would not guess where he came from. Then, from a crouch start, he ran.

> # *There! There!*
> # *Whaler!*
> # *Iki-netman!*
> # *Tuna-follower!*
> # *There! Kill! There! #*

The *Stenos* squawked from very close nearby. Toshio dove behind an oli-nut tree as bolts of blue death sizzled overhead. The Kiqui screamed and scattered into the forest.

Toshio rolled to his feet and ran, trying to keep the tree between him and his pursuers.

He heard sounds to the left and right as the fen moved quickly to surround him. His drysuit slowed him down as he tried to reach the shore cliffs before the circle was closed.

96

∿∿∿∿∿∿∿∿∿∿∿∿∿∿∿∿∿∿∿∿∿∿∿

Tom Orley

He spent a while listening to the radio, but, although he recognized a few species-types in the voices, so much of the traffic was inter-computer that there was little to be learned that way.

All right, he told himself. *Let's work out the proper phrasing. This had better be good.*

97

∿∿∿∿∿∿∿∿∿∿∿∿∿∿∿∿∿∿∿∿∿∿∿

The Skiff

Dennie stumbled over the words she had so carefully prepared. She tried to rephrase her arguments, but Hikahi stopped her.

"Dr. Sudman. You needn't persissst! Our next stop is the island anyway. We'll pick up Toshio if he hasn't left already. And perhaps we'll deal with Takkata-Jim, as well. We'll be on our way as soon as Creideiki finishes."

Dennie exhaled all of her remaining tension. It was out of her hands, then. The professionals would take care of things. She might as well relax.

"How long . . . ?"

Hikahi tossed her head. "Creideiki doesn't expect to do
any better this time than lassst. It shouldn't take long. Why
don't you and Sah'ot go and rest in the meantime?"

Dennie nodded and turned to find some space to stretch
out in the tiny hold.

Sah'ot swam alongside.

"Say, Dennie, as long as we're going to try to relax, want
to trade backrubs?"

Dennie laughed. "Sure, Sah'ot. Just don't get carried
away, okay?"

Creideiki tried to reason with them one more time.

  :We Are Desperate : As You Once Were : We Offer
Hope To Little Unfinished Ones On This Very World : *Hope*
To Grow Unbent :

    : Our Enemies Will Harm You, As Well, In Time :
    : Help Us :

The static pulsed and throbbed in response. It carried a
partly psychic feeling of closedness, of pressure and molten
heat. It was a claustrophilic song, in praise of rough hard
stone and flowing metal.

   + CEASE −
   − PEACE +
   + RELEASE!! −

   − ISOLATION +

Silence fell suddenly with a squeal of tortured machinery.
The old robot which had so long hung two kilometers down
the narrow drill-tree shaft had been destroyed.

Creideiki clicked a familiar phrase in Trinary.

     * It is, that is— *

He was tempted to enter the Dream again. But there
was, on this level of reality, no time for such things.

This level of reality was where duty lay, for the moment.
Later, perhaps. Later he would visit Nukapai again. Perhaps
she would show him the untellable things that she heard
through the vague avenues of prescience.

He headed back to the airlock of the tiny spaceship. Hikahi, seeing him approach, started warming up the engines.

98

∽∾∽∾∽∾∽∾∽∾∽∾∽∾∽∾∽∾∽∾∽∾∽∾∽∾∽∾∽

Tom Orley

". . . a small group of dolphins spotted a few hundred paktaars north of this location! They were moving north quite rapidly. They may have come this way to see what all the fighting was about. Hurry! Now is the time to strike!"

Tom clicked off the receiver. His head hurt from the concentration it took to speak Galactic Ten rapidly. Not that he expected the Brothers of the Night to believe his was the voice of one of their missing scouts. That didn't matter to his plan. All he wanted to do was stir up their interest before the final jab.

He switched frequency and pursed his lips in preparation to speaking Galactic Twelve.

Actually, this was fun! It distracted him from his exhaustion and hunger and satisfied his aesthetic sense, even if it did mean everyone and his client would be down here shortly, all looking for him.

". . . Paha warriors! Paha-ab-Kleppko -ab-puber ab-Soro ab-Hul! Inform the Soro fleet-mistress we have news!"

Tom chuckled as he thought of a pun that could only be phrased in Galactic Twelve and which, nevertheless, he was sure the Soro would never get.

99

Gillian

Something was making the fleets shift all of a sudden. Small squadrons raveled off the battered fleets and joined tiny groups from Kithrup's moons, all heading toward the planet. As they merged, the groups swirled about and tiny explosions took the place of individual lights.

What in the world was going on? Whatever it was, Gillian felt a glimmer of opportunity.

"Dr. Bassskin! Gillian!" Tsh't's voice came over the comm-speaker. "We're getting radio traffic from the planet's surface again. It'sss from a single transmitter, but it keeps putting out stuff in different Galactic languages! Yet I ssswear they all sound like one voice!"

She leaned forward and touched a switch. "I'm on my way up, Tsh't. Please call half of the off-duty shift to stations. We'll let the others rest a while longer." She switched off the unit.

Oh, Tom, she thought as she hurried out the door. *Why this? Couldn't you have come up with anything more elegant? Anything less desperate?*

Of course he couldn't, she chided herself as she ran down the hallway. *Come on, Jill. The least you can do is not be a nag.*

In moments she was on the bridge, listening for herself.

࿇࿇࿇࿇࿇࿇࿇࿇࿇࿇࿇࿇࿇࿇࿇࿇࿇࿇࿇࿇

Toshio

Cornered, Toshio couldn't even climb a tree. They were too close, and would be on him the instant they heard him move.

He could hear them as they spiraled closer, tightening the noose. Toshio clutched his needler and decided he had better attack first, before they were close enough to support each other. It would be a small handgun against armored machines and high-powered lasers, and he was no marksman like Tom Orley. In fact, he had never fired at a sentient being before. But it beat waiting here.

He crouched and began to crawl to his right, toward the shoreline. He tried not to snap any twigs, but a minute after leaving his hiding place he flushed some small animal, which fled noisily through the bushes.

Immediately he heard the noise of approaching mechanicals. Toshio slithered quickly under a thick bush, only to emerge facing the broad footpad of a spider.

Gotcha! Gotcha!

There was a squeal of triumph. He looked up to meet the mad eye of Sreekah-pol. The fin leered as he commanded the spider to lift its leg.

Toshio rolled aside as the foot crashed down where his head had been. He reversed direction, avoiding a kick. The mechanical reared back, bringing both front legs into play. Toshio saw no place to turn. He fired his small pistol against the armored belly of the machine, and tiny needles ricocheted harmlessly into the forest.

The triumphant whistle was pure Primal.

Gotcha!

Then the island began to shake.

The ground heaved up and down. Toshio was jounced right and left and his head hit the loam rhythmically. The spider teetered, then crashed backward into the forest.

The shaking accelerated. Toshio somehow rolled over onto his stomach. he fought the oscillations to rise to his knees.

There was a crunching sound as two spider-riders stumbled into the clearing. One crashed past Toshio in panic. The other, though, saw him and squawked in wrath.

Toshio tried to hold out his needler, but the island's trembling began to turn into a list. It became a race between him and the mad dolphin to see who could aim and fire first.

Then both of them were staggered by a scream that echoed within their heads.

> +   *BAD!*   –
> – *BAD ONES!* +
> +   *LEAVE*   –
> –   *US*   +
> +   *ALONE!*   –

It was a roar of rejection that made Toshio moan and grab at his temples. The needler slipped out of his grasp and fell to the rapidly tilting ground.

The dolphin whistled shrilly as its spider collapsed in convulsions. It wailed in a foxhole lamentation.

> # *Sorry! Sorry!*
> # *Patron forgive!*
> # *Forgive!* #

Toshio stumbled forward. "Forgiven," he managed to say as he hurried past. He couldn't deal with the fin's schizoid conversion. "Come this way if you can!" he called back, as he tried to make it to the shore. The noise in his head was like an earthquake. Somehow Toshio managed to stay on his feet and stumble through the forest.

When he reached the edge of the mound the sea was a froth below. Toshio looked right and left and saw no place that looked any better.

At that moment, a scream of engines pealed forth. He looked back to see a tornado of broken vegetation fly up from a spot only a hundred meters away. The gun-metal gray longboat rose above the rapidly tilting forest. It was surrounded by a glowing nimbus of ionization. Toshio's hackles rose as the island was swept by the throbbing antigravity field. The boat turned slowly and seemed to hesitate. Then, with a thunderclap, it speared into the eastern sky.

Toshio crouched as the boom whipped at him, tugging at his clothes.

There was no time to delay. Either Charles Dart had got away or he hadn't. Toshio pulled his mask up over his face, held it with one hand, and leapt.

"Ifni's boss . . ." he prayed. And he fell into the stormy waters.

101

∾∽∾∽∾∽∾∽∾∽∾∽∾∽∾∽∾∽∾∽∾∽∾∽∾∽∾

Galactics

Above the planet small flotillas of battered warships paused suddenly in their multi-sided butchery.

They had left hiding places on Kithrup's tiny moons, gambling all on the chance that the strange radio broadcasts from the planet's northern hemisphere were, indeed, of human origin. On their way down to Kithrup, the tiny alliances sniped at each other with their waning strength, until a sudden wave of psychic noise hit the entire motley ensemble. It rose from the planet with a power none could have expected, overwhelming psi-shields and striking the crews temporarily motionless.

The ships continued to plunge toward the planet, but their living crews blinked limply, unable to fire their weapons or guide their vessels.

If it had been a weapon, the psychic shout would have cleansed half of the ships of their crews. As it was, the mental scream of anger and rejection reverberated within their brains, driving a few of the least flexible completely mad.

For long moments the cruisers drifted out of formation, uncontrolled, downward into the upper fringes of the atmosphere.

Finally, the psi-scream began to fade. The grating anger growled and diminished, leaving burning after-images as the numb crews slowly came to their senses.

The Xatinni and their clients, having drifted away from the others, looked about and discovered that they had lost their appetite for further fighting. They decided to accept the pointed invitation to depart. Their four ragged ships left Kthsemenee's system as quickly as their laboring engines could manage.

The J'8lek were slow coming around. After succumbing to the numbing mind-scream, they drifted in amongst the ships of the Brothers of the Night. The Brothers awakened sooner, and used the J'8lek for target practice.

Sophisticated autopilots brought two Jophur warships to land on the slope of a steaming mountain, far to the south of their original destination. Automatic weapons kept watch for enemies while the Jophur struggled with their confusion. Finally, as the stunning psychic noise subsided, the crews began to revive and retake control of their grounded ships.

The Jophur were almost ready to lift off again, and head north to rejoin the fray, when the entire top of their mountain blew away in a column of superheated steam.

102

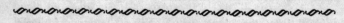

Streaker

Gillian stared, slack-jawed, until the grating "sounds" finally began to fade. She swallowed. Her ears popped, and she shook her head to clear away the numb feeling. Then she saw that the dolphins were staring at her.

"That was awful!" she stated. "Is everybody all right?"

Tsh't looked relieved. "We're all fine, Gillian. We detected an extremely powerful psi-explosion a few moments ago. It easily pierced our shields, and seems to have dazed you for a few minutes. But except for some momentary discomfort, we hardly felt it!"

Gillian rubbed her temples. "It must be my esper sensitivity that made me susceptible. Let's just hope the Eatees don't follow that attack up with another even closer. . . ." She stopped. Tsh't was shaking her head.

"Gillian, I don't think it was the Eatees. Or if it was, they weren't aiming for us. Instruments indicate that that burst came from very close nearby, and was almost perfectly tuned *not* to be received by cetaceans! Your brain is similar to ours, so you only felt it a little. Suessi reports hardly feeling a thing.

"But I imagine some of the Galactics had a rough t-time weathering that psi-storm!"

Gillian shook her head a second time. "I don't understand."

"That makes two of usss. But I don't suppose we *have* to understand. All I can tell you is thisss—at almost the same time that psi-burst went off, there was an intense ground tremor not two hundred klicks from here. The crustal waves are only now starting to arrive."

Gillian swam over to Tsh't's station in the glassy sphere of *Streaker*'s bridge. The dolphin lieutenant pointed with her jaw toward a globe model of the planet.

Not far from *Streaker*'s position on the globe, a small cluster of flashing red symbols was displayed.

"That's Toshio's island!" Gillian said. "Then Charlie *did* have a spare bomb after all!"

"Beg p-pardon?" Tsh't looked confused. "But I thought Takkata-Jim had confiscated . . ."

"*Ship rising!*" A detection officer announced. "*Anti-g and stasis—from the same site as the crust tremors, one hundred and fifffty klicks from here. Tracking . . . tracking . . . Ship is now heading off at Mach two, due east!*"

Gillian looked at Tsh't. They shared the same thought. *Takkata-Jim.*

Gillian saw the question in the dolphin officer's eye. "We may face a decision shortly. Have his blip followed to see where he's headed. And we'd better start awakening the rest of the off-duty crew."

"Aye, sir. Those that managed to remain asleep through

the last few minutes." Tsh't turned and relayed the command.

A few minutes later the battle computer began to chatter.

"What *now*?" Gillian asked.

Bright yellow pinpoints began to glow up and down a long jagged streak on the globe of Kithrup, starting from the site of Toshio's island.

"Detonations of some sort," Tsh't commented. "The computer's interpreting them as bombings, but we've detected no missiles! And why this scattered pattern? The detonations are only occurring along thisss narrow stripe of longitude!"

"*More psi disturbances!*" an operator announced. "*Strong! And from numerous sources, all on the planet!*"

Gillian frowned. "Those detonations aren't bombings. I remember seeing that pattern before. That's the boundary of this planetary crustal plate. Those disturbances may be volcanoes.

"I'd say it's the locals' way of showing they're unhappy."

"?" Tsh't queried confusedly.

Gillian's expression was thoughtful, as if she was looking at something very far away. "I think I'm starting to understand what's been going on. We can thank Creideiki for the fact that the psi-disturbances don't affect dolphins, for instance."

The dolphins stared at her. Gillian smiled and patted Tsh't's flank.

"Not to worry, fem-fin. It's a long story, but I'll explain if we have time. I expect the biggest effect all this will have on us is crustquakes. We should be getting some shortly. Will we be able to ride them out down here?"

The dolphin lieutenant frowned. The way humans could change mental tracks midstride was beyond her comprehension.

"Yesss, I think so, Gillian. That is, so long as *that-t* remains stable." She gestured through a port, toward the seacliff that loomed over their hybrid ship.

Gillian looked up at the hulking mass of rock, visible through cracks in the Thennanin armor. "I'd forgotten about that. We'd better keep an eye on it."

She turned back to the holo display, watching the spreading pattern of disturbances.

Come on, Hikahi! she urged silently. *Pick up Toshio and the others and get back here! I have to make a decision soon, and you might get back too late!*

The minutes passed. Several times the water seemed to tremble as a low rumble passed through the seafloor.

Gillian watched the blue globe of Kithrup. A string of flickering yellow pinponts spread gradually northward, like an angry wound in the planet's side. Finally, the yellow dots merged with a small group of tiny islands in the northeast quadrant.

That's where Tom is, she remembered.

Suddenly the comm operator thrashed at his station. "Commander! I'm gett-ting a transmission! And it'sss in Anglic!"

103

Tom Orley

He held the microphone awkwardly. It had been designed for alien hands. Tom ran his tongue over his cracked lips. He didn't have time to go over his speech once more. Company would be arriving any moment now.

He pressed the transmit lever.

"Creideiki!" He spoke carefully. "Listen carefully! Record and replay for Gillian! She'll interpret!"

He knew every ship in near-space was listening to this transmitter by now. Probably a large number of them were already on their way here. If he composed his new lies properly, he could make sure even more of them came.

"My direct wire to the ship is broken," he said. "And a hundred kilometers is a long way to have to carry a message, so I'll risk this new coder, hoping it's not been broken in all the fighting here."

That last was a tissue of fantasies for Galactic consumption. Now for the real message. Hidden in context, he had to tell *Streaker* what he knew.

"Jill? Our egg hatched, hon. And a zoo spilled out. A zoo of fierce critters!

"But I came across only one bedraggled sample of the brand we're shopping for. I've heard clues it's still for sale, on higher shelves, but those have been just clues. You and H and C are going to have to decide on that basis.

"Remember when old Jake Demwa took us along with him on that mission to the central *Library* on Tanith? Remember what he said about hunches? Tell Creideiki about it. It's his decision, but my gut feeling is, follow Jake's advice!"

He felt a thickening in his throat. He should cut this off. No sense in letting the Eatees zero in *too* closely.

"Jill." He coughed. "Hon, I'm out of the game now. Get Herbie and the rest of the data to the Council. And those abos, too. I've got to believe all this has been worth it."

He closed his eyes and gripped the mike. "When you see old Jake, hoist a glass with him for me, will you?"

He wanted to say more, but realized that he was already getting a little too unambiguous. He couldn't afford to let the Galactics' language computers figure out what he was talking about.

He pursed his lips. And bid adieu in a language designed for such things.

> *   Petals floating by,*
> * Drift through my woman's hand,*
> *   As she remembers me— *

The carrier wave hissed until he cut the circuit.

He rose and carried the radio outside. Carefully approaching the edge of an open pool, he dropped the transmitter in. If anyone had locked into a resonance with the crystals in the set, that Eatee would have to dive for it.

He stood there, by the pool, and watched the low clouds roll past, dark and heavy with unspent rain.

They'd be arriving any moment. His weapons were at his belt, and his breathing tube, and a full canteen. He was ready for them.

He was standing that way, watching and waiting, when the steaming volcano on the horizon began to growl, then cough, then angrily spout bright fireworks into the sky.

The bridge was a blur. Gillian's eyes swam, but when she blinked the tears would not bead and drop away. Her eyes clung to them, like precious things.

"Shall we answer?" Tsh't spoke softly from next to her. Gillian shook her head. *No*, she tried to say. But she could only mouth the word. Telempathically, she sensed the sympathy of those around her.

How can I mourn, she wondered, *when I can still feel him faintly? He is still alive out there, somewhere.*

How can I mourn?

She felt a swirl of movement as a fin approached cautiously and tried to report to Tsh't without disturbing her.

Gillian pressed her burning eyelids together. The tears flowed at last, in narrow trails down her cheeks. She couldn't reach under her mask to brush them away, so she let them lie. When she opened her eyes, her vision had cleared.

"I heard that, Wattaceti. Which way is Takkata-Jim headed?"

"Toward the Galactic flotillas, Commander. Though the fleets seem to be in chaosss! They are boiling every which way, after the confusion caused by that psi-burst. A major free-for-all is shaping up above...above Mr. Orley's position."

Gillian nodded. "We'll wait a little while longer. Go to condition yellow and keep me informed."

Off-duty personnel were called to their posts. Suessi and D'Anite reported that the engines were warm.

Last chance, Hikahi, Gillian thought. *Are you coming?*

"Gillian!" Lucky Kaa called. With his harness arm he pointed out one of the ports. "The cliff!"

Gillian hurried over and looked where the pilot indicated. The entire mass of rock was trembling. Cracks began to appear in the great wall that towered over *Streaker.*

"Lift stations!" Gillian commanded. "Tsh't, take us out of here!"

104

Galactics

Cullcullabra bowed low before the Soro Krat.

"Have you interpreted the human's broadcast?" She snapped.

The stocky Pil bowed again, backing away slightly. "No, Fleet-Mother, not completely. The human spoke in their two doggerel languages called 'Anglic' and 'Trinary.' We have translation programs for both, of course, but they are so chaotic and contextual—unlike any civilized language . . ."

The Librarian flinched as Krat hissed at him. "Have you nothing?"

"Mistress, we think the last part of his message, in the dolphin-speech, may be the important part. It might have been a command to his clients, or . . ."

The Librarian piped dismay and dodged back into his station as a ling-plum missed him by inches.

"Hypotheses! Tentative conjectures!" Krat stormed. "Even the Tandu boil with excitement and send expedition after futile piddling expedition to the site on the planet's surface from which the message emanated. And we must, perforce, follow, no?"

She stared about. Her crew avoided her gaze.

"Has anyone even a hypothesis to explain that psi-assault which struck a short time ago, and seems to have disoriented every sophont in the system? Was that, also, a chimera of the Earthlings? Are the volcanoes that fill our instruments with static mere trickery?"

The crew tried to look simultaneously busy and attentive. No one wanted to risk the ire of the fleet mother.

A Paha warrior strode from the office of detection.

"Mistress," it announced. "We did not notice before because of the volcanoes, but there has been a launching from the planet's surface."

Krat felt a turn of glee. This was what she had been waiting for! Though she had sent ships of her own to the site of the radio messages, she had kept the core of her fleet together.

"Diversions! They were all diversions! The radio calls, the psi attacks, even the volcanoes!"

A part of her was curious about how the Earthlings had managed the last two. But that question would be solved when the humans and their clients were captured and interrogated.

"The Earthlings waited until much of the battle had moved near the planet," she muttered. "And now they make their attempt to escape! Now we must . . ."

Cullcullabra came up to her side and bowed. "Mistress, I've done a deep search of the Library, and I think I know the source of the psi and the . . ."

The Pil's eyes bugged out as Krat stabbed him in the abdomen with her mating claw. Krat stood up, carrying the Librarian in the air, then flung his lifeless body over to the wall.

She stood over the body breathing deeply of the death odors. No trouble would come over this killing, at least. The idiotic Pil had actually interrupted her! No one would deny that she had been within her rights this time.

She sheathed her claw. It had felt good. Not quite like mating with a male of her own race, who could fight back in kind, but good.

"Tell me about the Earthling ship," she crooned to the Paha.

She noticed it waited a full second after she finished speaking to begin. "Mistress," it said. "It is not their main vessel. It appears to be a scout ship, of some sort."

Krat nodded. "An emissary. I wondered why they did not try to work out a surrender agreement before this. Move the fleet to intercept this vessel. We must act before the Tandu notice it!

"Have our new Thennanin allies take the rear. I want them to understand that they are junior partners in this enterprise."

"Mistress, the Thennanin have already begun prepara-

tions to leave us. They appear to be eager to join the chaos at
the planet's surface."

Krat grunted. "Let them. We are even with the Tandu
again. And the Thennanin are almost used up anyway. Let
them depart. Then we proceed after the scout ship!"

She settled back onto the vletoor cushion and hummed to
herself.

Soon. Soon.

The masters demanded too much. How could they expect
the Acceptor to report specifically when so much was happening!

It was beautiful! Everything was going on at once!
Sparkling little battles over the planet's surface . . . bright hot
volcanoes . . . and that great psychic roar of anger that had
poured out of the planet itself only a little while ago!

The anger still steamed and spumed. Why were the
masters so uninterested in something so unique? Psi from
below a planet's surface? The Acceptor could tell the Tandu
so much about that angry voice, but they were only interested
in shutting it out. It distracted them and made them feel
vulnerable.

The Acceptor witnessed it all in bliss, until the punishment came again. The masters applied a neural whip. Its legs
jerked at the unpleasant sensation that coursed through its
brain.

Should it let the "punishment" alter its behavior this
time? The Acceptor considered.

It decided to ignore the "pain." Let them cajole and
shout. The Acceptor was enthralled by the angry voices that
churned below, and listened with all its might.

105

The Skiff

"What the devil...?"

Dennie was rolled off the dry-shelf to splash into the water below. Sah'ot squawked in confusion as the tiny ship's hold tipped.

Then, in addition to the physical tossing, a rolling wave and psychic discomfort began to fill their heads. Dennie coughed water and grabbed a wall stanchion. She wanted to cover her ears.

"Not again," she moaned. She tried to use the techniques Toshio had taught her...focusing on her heartbeat to drive out the grinding static in her head. She hardly even noticed when Sah'ot shouted, "It'sss them!"

The fin pressed the hatch button with his beak and sped out into the hallway. He streaked into the tiny control room.

"Creideiki!" he began, forgetting for a moment that the captain could not understand him. "It's *them*. The voices from below!"

Creideiki looked back at him, and Sah'ot realized that the captain already knew. In fact, he seemed hardly surprised. Creideiki crooned a soft melody of acceptance. He appeared content.

From the pilot's station, Keepiru announced, "I'm getting neutrinos and anti-g flux! They're coming from dead ahead. A small ship taking off."

Hikahi nodded. "Probably Takkata-Jim. I hope Gillian's right that he's been taken care of."

They continued to drive underwater toward the east. About a half-hour later, Keepiru shouted again. "More anti-g! A big ship! Taking off from near to the southwest!"

Creideiki's flukes struck the surface of the water.

> * *Up, up!*
>   *Up and Look!*
> * *Look!* :

Hikahi nodded to Keepiru. "Take her up."

The skiff surfaced. Seawater slid in sheets off the ports.

They clustered around a southern port and watched as a distant wedge-shaped object erupted from the horizon, and lumbered into the sky, slowly gathering speed. They watched as it flew south, passing the speed of sound, finally disappearing into the high clouds.

They watched even after *Streaker*'s contrail began to drift and slowly come apart under Kithrup's contrary winds.

PART TEN

∿∿∿∿∿∿∿∿∿∿∿∿∿∿∿∿∿∿∿∿∿∿∿∿∿∿∿∿

Rapture

*"They are the lads that always
live before the wind."*
—HERMAN MELVILLE

106

$\infty\infty\infty\infty\infty\infty\infty\infty\infty\infty\infty\infty\infty\infty\infty\infty\infty$

Toshio

Toshio swam hard as the swell tried to drag him backward. He fought the current and strove for the open sea. Finally, just as he felt his aching arms and legs could do no more, he reached calmer waters. With burning lungs he turned and watched as the metal-mound, now almost two kilometers away, sank slowly into its pit.

The sinking couldn't go on. The drill-tree had not completed its excavations when he and Dennie had blown it apart. The island would probably settle until the shaft was plugged.

Dull detonations groaned on all sides of him. Toshio treaded water and looked around. On islands in all directions trees swayed, and not from the wind. In the distance he saw at least three roiling clouds of steam and smoke rise from boiling patches in the sea. There was a growling of subsea quakes.

All this because of one little bomb? In spite of all he had been through, Toshio calmly wondered about the cause of it all. There was nothing left to do but choose the manner of his dying. He felt queerly liberated.

What if the bomb released a vein of magma, Toshio wondered. If a volcano appeared anywhere, I'd think it would be in that drill-tree shaft. But I guess the island's plugging it.

The metal-mound that had been his home for two weeks seemed to have stopped sinking. A few treetops waved above the water.

Toshio wondered about the fate of Charles Dart. He

couldn't imagine the chimpanzee swimming very far. Perhaps it was just as well. At least Charlie had had a clean exit.

Toshio felt a bit better having rested. He began swimming again, for the open sea.

About twenty minutes later there came another low rumbling. He turned around just in time to see the distant mound rocked by a terrific explosion. Dirt and vegetation flew in all directions. The mound itself heaved upward, almost out of the water, split apart, then fell back into a cloud of steam.

107

∾∾∾∾∾∾∾∾∾∾∾∾∾∾∾∾∾∾∾∾∾∾∾∾∾

Takkata-Jim

"Calling battle fleet! Calling the battle fleet ahead! This is Lieutenant Takkata-Jim of the Terragens Survey Service. I wish to negotiate! Please ressspond!"

The receiver was silent. Takkata-Jim cursed. The radio *must* work. He had taken it from Thomas Orley's sled, and that human *always* maintained his equipment! Why weren't the Galactics answering?

The longboat was designed to be run by more than one person. The sudden and unexpected disaster at the island had forced him to abandon his *Stenos*. Now he had no one to help him. He had to juggle two or three jobs at once.

He watched the tactics display. A cluster of yellow lights were heading his way from Galactic north. It was a paltry flotilla compared with the great armadas that had come sweeping into the system only weeks ago. But it was still an awesome array of firepower. They were heading right for him.

Elsewhere, all was chaos. The planet was pockmarked with energy releases—boiling steam tornadoes where volcanoes emptied into the sea. And above the planet's northern hemisphere a free-for-all battle was going on.

Takkata-Jim increased the scale on his display and saw another fleet. It, too, had just started turning toward him.

The ether was filled with a roar of voices. AM, FM, PCM—every spot on the dial took part in the confusion. Could that explain why nobody seemed to hear him?

No. The Galactics had sophisticated computers. It had to be his own equipment. There had been no time to check it all before taking off!

Takkata-Jim nervously watched the map.

He was flying into a pod of tiger sharks, hoping to negotiate *Streaker's* protection and eventual release. But he remembered the look on Gillian Baskin's face, a week before, when he had suggested giving the ETs everything they wanted. Metz had supported him then, but the expression on the woman's face came to mind now. She had looked at him pityingly and told him that fanatics never worked that way.

"They'll take all we have, thank us politely, and *then* boil us in oil," she had commented.

Takkata-Jim tossed his head. *I don't believe it. Besides, anything is better than what she plans!*

He watched the tactics holo. The first fleet was only a hundred thousand klicks away, now. The computer gave him data on the ships, at last. They were Soro battlecruisers.

Soro! Takkata-Jim tasted bile from his first stomach. All the stories he had heard about them came to mind.

What if they shoot first? What if they're not even interested in prisoners? He looked at his own battle controls. The armament of the longboat was pitiful, but...

A claw of his harness reached over to flick on the arming switch... just for the small comfort it gave.

108

Streaker

"Now both of the larger fleets turn toward Takkata-Jim!"

Gillian nodded. "Keep me informed, Wattaceti." She turned. "Tsh't, how long can we stay hidden by these tectonic disturbances?"

"Our anti-g's been detectable for five minutess, Gillian. I don't think we can put off energy detection much longer by flying over volcanoes. If we're to make a break for it we've *got* to gain altitude."

"We're being scanned at long range!" the detector operator snapped. "A couple of ships from that battle over Orley's position are curiousss!"

"That's it, then," Tsh't commented. "We go for it."

Gillian shook her head.

"Buy me five more minutes, Tsh't. I don't care about the stragglers up north. Keep me hidden from the main fleets just a little while longer!"

Tsh't whirled through the oxywater, leaving a trail of bubbles. "Lucky Kaa! Steer south by southwest, toward that new volcano!"

Gillian stared intently at the display. A tiny blue speck showed the longboat, flying toward a mass of over thirty *much* larger dots.

"Come on, Takkata-Jim," Gillian murmured to herself. "I thought I had you figured out. Prove me right!"

There hadn't been a sound on the radio from the renegade lieutenant. Toshio must have done his job, and sabotaged the sets on the island.

The blue speck drew within one hundred thousand kilometers of the enemy.

430

"Telemetry! Takkata-Jim's armed his weaponsss!" Wattaceti announced.

Gillian nodded. *I knew it. The fellow's almost human. He'd have to have a stronger personality than I'd ever expected, not to do that, just for the security-blanket effect. As pointless as it seemed, who would go to face an enemy with his safeties on?*

Now, just a little closer...

"Gillian!" The detector officer cried. "I don't believe it-t! Takkata-Jim hasss..."

Gillian smiled, a little sadly.

"Let me guess. Our brave vice-captain is firing on the entire battle fleet."

Tsh't and Wattaceti turned to look at her, wide-eyed. She shrugged. "Come now. For all his faults, no one ever said Takkata-Jim wasn't brave."

She grinned to hide her own nervousness. "Get ready, everybody."

109

~~~~~~~~~~~~~~~~~~~~~~~~~~~~~

Takkata-Jim

Takkata-Jim shrieked and grabbed at the toggle switch. It didn't work! The fire controls were activating without his orders!

Every few seconds a shudder passed through the little ship as a small seeker missile launched from the single torpedo tube. Small bursts of antimatter erupted from the longboat's nose, automatically aimed at the nearest alien vessel.

In a lucky shot, the lead Soro ship blossomed open like a fiery flower unfolding. The sheer surprise of the attack had overcome defenses designed to withstand nova heat.

He cursed and tried the override. It, too, had no effect.

As the Soro fleet began firing in return, Takkata-Jim
wailed and swerved the little scout into a wild series of
evasive maneuvers. With a dolphin's natural three-dimensional
sense, he whirled off in a high-g gyration, threading salvos
that passed chillingly close.

There was only one thing to do, only one possible source
of succor. Takkata-Jim sent the scout streaking toward the
second battle fleet. They must have witnessed his attack.
They would think him an ally, if he survived long enough to
reach them.

He sped out into space, chased by a herd of behemoths
that turned and lumbered after him.

110

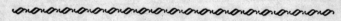

Streaker

"Now, Gillian?"

"Almost, dear. Another minute."

"Those shipsss from the north seem to have decided.
Several of them are turning this way. . . . Correction, the whole
skirmish is heading southward, toward usss!"

Gillian couldn't make herself feel too bad about drawing
fire away from Tom's position. It was only returning his favor,
after all.

"All right. You choose a trajectory. I want to head out
east on the ecliptic, just as soon as that second fleet finishes
turning toward the longboat."

Tsh't warbled an impatient sigh. "Aye, sir." She swam to
the pilot's position and confered with Lucky Kaa.

111

Tom

He raised his head above the surface of the pool where he had taken refuge.

Where had everybody gone, all of a sudden?

Minutes ago the sky had been ablaze with pyrotechnics. Burning ships were falling out of the sky, right and left. Now he caught sight of a few stragglers, high in the distant sky, speeding southward.

It took him a moment to come up with a guess.

Thanks, Jill, he thought. *Now give 'em hell for me.*

112

Takkata-Jim

Takkata-Jim spluttered in frustration. He was so busy there wasn't time to work on the fire controls. Desperate, he sent impulses shutting down whole blocks of computer memory. Finally, something worked. The weapons system turned off.

Frantically, he made the ship roll left and applied full thrust to escape a spread of torpedos.

The two fleets were coming together quickly, with him in between.

Takkata-Jim intended to dive into the second fleet and stop behind it, conveying by his actions what he couldn't say by radio, that he was seeking protection.

But the controls wouldn't respond! He couldn't correct from his last evasive maneuver! He must have shut down too much memory!

The longboat streaked outward at right angles to the converging fleets, away from both of them.

Both fleets turned to follow.

113

∽∾∽∾∽∾∽∾∽∾∽∾∽∾∽∾∽∾∽∾∽∾∽∾∽∾∽∾∽∾

Streaker

"Now!" she said.

The pilot needed no urging. He had already been adding momentum. Now he applied full power. *Streaker's* engines roared and she left the atmosphere on a crackling trail of ionization. The acceleration could be felt even through stasis, even inside the fluid-filled bridge.

The gray sea disappeared under a white blanket of clouds. The horizon became a curve, then an arc. *Streaker* fell outward into an ocean of stars.

"They're following us. The skirmishers from up north."

"How many?"

"About twenty." Tsh't listened to her neural link for a moment. "They're strung out. Except for a fairly big group at the rear, hardly any two of them seem to be of the same race. I hear shooting. They're fighting each other even as they chase us."

How many in that final bunch?"

"Um . . . sssssix, I think."

"Well, let's see what we can do when we stretch our legs."

The planet fell behind them as Lucky Kaa sent *Streaker* accelerating in the direction Gillian had chosen.

Beyond Kithrup's horizon, a great battle had begun. Her path kept her hidden by the planet's bulk for several minutes. Then they came into view of the conflagration.

A million kilometers away, space was filled with bright explosions and hackle-raising shrieks that feebly penetrated the psi-screens.

Tsh't commented. "The big boys are fighting over Takkata-Jim. We might even make it out of the system before the major fleets could catch up with usss."

Gillian nodded. Toshio's sacrifice had not been in vain.

"Then our problem is these little guys on our tail. Somehow we've got to shake them off. Maybe we can do a dodge behind the gas giant planet. How long until we can get to it?"

"It's hard to judge, Gillian. Maybe an hour. We can't use overdrive in system, and we're carrying a lot of excess mass."

Tsh't listened to her link, concentrating. "The ones on our tail have mostly stopped beating on each other. They may be damaged, but I think at least two of the lead ships will catch up with us about the time we reach the gasss giant."

Gillian looked at the holo tank. Kithrup had shrunk into a tiny ball in one corner, a sparkle of battle beyond it. On this side a chain of small dots showed *Streaker*'s pursuers.

In the forward tank a shining pastel-striped globe began to grow. A huge world of frigid gas, looking much like Jupiter, swelled slowly but perceptibly.

Gillian pursed her lips and whistled softly. "Well, if we can't outrun them I guess we'll have to try an ambush."

Tsh't stared at her. "Gillian, those are battleships! We're only an overweight Snark-class survey ship!"

Gillian grinned. "This snark has become a boojum, girl. The Thennanin shell will do more than just slow us down. And we may be able to try something they'll never expect."

She didn't mention that, given a chance, she wanted to hang around this system a while, in case of a miracle.

"Have all loose objects been secured?"

"Sstandard procedure. It's been done."

"Good. Please order all crew out of the central bay. They're to strap themselves in wherever they can."

Tsh't gave the order, then turned back with a question-ing look.

Gillian explained. "We're slow because we're overweight, right? They'll be shooting at us before we reach the cover of the gas giant, let alone overdrive range. Tell me, Tsh't, what's making us overweight?"

"The Thennanin shell!"

"And? What else?"

Tsh't looked puzzled.

Gillian hinted with a riddle.

> * *Living touch*
>   *The substance of motion—*
> * *Like air, forgotten*
>   *Until it's gone!* *

Tsh't stared blankly. Then she got it. Her eyes widened.

"Pretty tricky, yesss. It just might work, at that. Still, I'm glad you told me. The crew are going to want to wear the right apparel."

Gillian tried to snap her fingers in the water, and failed. "Spacesuits! You're right! Tsh't, what would I do without you!"

114

∞∞∞∞∞∞∞∞∞∞∞∞∞∞∞∞∞∞∞∞∞

Galactics

"The side battle amongst all the remnant forces seems to have moved away from the planet," a Paha warrior reported. "They are streaming away from Kithrup, chasing a rather large vessel."

The Soro, Krat, finished paring a ling-plum. She fought to hide the nervous tremor in her left arm.

"*Can you identify the one they pursue?*"

"*It does not appear to be the quarry.*"

The Paha tastefully ignored the fleet-mistress's obvious wave of relief on hearing this. "*It is too large to be the Earth ship. We have tentatively identified it as a crippled Thennanin, although . . .*"

"*Yes?*" Krat asked archly.

The Paha hesitated. "*It behaves strangely. It is inordinately massive, and its motors seem to have a quasi-Tymbrimi tone. It is already too far to read clearly.*"

Krat grunted. "*What is our status?*"

"*The Tandu parallel us, sniping at our flanks as we do theirs. We both chase the Earth scout. Both of us have ceased firing at the boat except when it gets too close to the other side.*"

Krat growled. "*This vessel leads us farther and farther from the planet—from the true quarry. Have you contemplated a scoutship whose very purpose may have been to accomplish this?*" she snapped.

The Paha considered, then nodded. "*Yes, Fleet-Mother. It would be just like a Tymbrimi or wolfling trick. What do you suggest?*"

Krat was filled with frustration. It had to be a trick! Yet she couldn't abandon the chase, or the Tandu would capture the scoutship. And the longer the chase went on, the worse the attrition on both sides!

She threw the plum across the room. It splattered dead center on the rayed spiral glyph of the Library. A startled Pil jumped and squeaked in dismay, then glared at her insolently.

"*Transmit Standard Truce Call Three,*" Krat commanded with distaste. "*Contact the Tandu Stalker. We must put an end to this farce and get back to the planet at once!*"

The Tandu Stalker asked the Trainer one more time. "*Can you arouse the Acceptor?*"

The Trainer knelt before the Stalker, offering its own head. "*I cannot. It has entered an orgasmic state. It is over-stimulated. Operant manipulation does not achieve success.*"

"*Then we have no meta-physical way to investigate the strange chase behind us?*"

"*We do not. We can only use physical means.*"

The Stalker's legs ratchetted. "*Go and remove your*

head. With your last volition, place it in my trophy rack."

The Trainer rasped assent.

"May the new one I grow serve you better."

"Indeed. But first," the Stalker suggested, "arrange to open a talk-line with the Soro. I shall sever the leg I use to talk with them, of course. But talk to them we now must."

Buoult bit at his elbow spikes, then used them to preen his ridgecrest. He had guessed correctly! He had taken the last six Thennanin ships out of the battle between the Tandu and Soro, and arrived at the planet in time to join a long chase. Ten ragged ships were ahead of him, chasing an object that could only dimly be made out.

"More speed," he urged. "The others are uncoordinated. While the Tandu and Soro chase a ruse, we are the only fair-sized squadron in the vicinity! We must chase!"

Far ahead of the Thennanin, a Gubru captain ruffled its feathers and cackled.

"We catch up! We catch up with the lumbering thing! And look! Now that we are near, look and see that its emanations are human! They fly inside a shell, but now we are near and can look and see and catch that which is inside that shell!

"Now we are near, and will catch them!"

Failure was still possible, of course. But total *defeat* would be unpermissible.

"If we cannot catch them," it reminded itself, "then we must make certain to destroy them."

115

Streaker

The gas giant loomed ahead. The heavily laden *Streaker* lumbered toward it.

"They'll expect us to dive in close for a tight hyperbolic," Tsh't commented. "It's generally a good tactic when being chased in a planetary system. A quick thrusst while we're swinging near the planet can translate into a major shift in direction."

Gillian nodded. "That's what they'll expect, but that's not what we'll do."

They watched the screens as three large blips grew and then took form as solid figures—ships with ugly battle-scars and uglier weapons.

The great bulk of the planet began to intrude even as the pursuing ships grew larger.

"Are all fen secured?"

"Yesss!"

"Then you choose the time, Lieutenant. You have a better feel for space battles than I. You know what we want to do."

Tsh't clapped her jaws together. "I do, Gillian."

They dove toward the planet.

"Sssoon. Soon they'll be committed...." Tsh't's eyes narrowed. She concentrated on sound images, transmitted by her neural link. The bridge was silent except for the nervous clicking of dolphin sonar. Gillian was reminded of tense situations on human ships, when half the crew would be whistling through their teeth without ever being aware of it.

"Get-t ready," Tsh't told the engineering crew by intercom.

The pursuing ships disappeared briefly behind the planet's limb.

"Now!" she cried for Suessi to hear. "Open the rear locks! Activate all pumps!" She swung to the pilot. "Launch that decoy probe! Hard lateral acceleration! Apply stasis to compensate all but one g rearward! Repeat, allow one gravity rearward in the ship!"

Half the control boards in the bridge sprouted red lights. Forewarned, the crew overrode safeguards as the contents of *Streaker's* central bay flew out behind her into the vacuum of open space.

The Gubru captain was concerned with a Pthaca ship encroaching on its lead. The commander contemplated maneuvers to destroy the Pthaca, but the master computer suddenly squawked frantically for attention.

"They have not done that!" the captain chanted as it stared in disbelief at the display. "They cannot have done such a thing. They cannot have found such a devilish trap. They cannot have . . ."

It watched the Pthaca ship collide at a large fraction of lightspeed with a barrier that had not been there minutes before.

It was only a diffuse stream of gas particles, drifting in their path. But, unexpected, it met the Pthaca warship's screens like a solid wall. At a fair fraction of light speed, any barrier was deadly.

"Veer off!" the Gubru commanded. "Fire all weapons on the quarry!"

Fiery energy lanced out, but the beams stuck an intangible wall between the Gubru and the rapidly turning Earth ship.

"Water!" it shrieked as it read the spectral report. "A barrier of water vapor! A civilized race could not have found such a trick in the Library! *A civilized race could not have stooped so low! A civilized race would not have . . ."*

It screamed as the Gubru ship hit a cloud of drifting snowflakes.

Lightened by megatonnes, *Streaker* screamed about in an arc far tighter than she could have managed minutes before. Her locks closed, and the ship slowly refilled with air. Internal anti-gravity was reapplied. Her spacesuited crewfen flew back to their duty stations from the hull rooms where they had taken refuge.

In the still water-filled bridge, Gillian watched the annihilation of the first two pursuing vessels. The crew cheered as the third battered cruiser swerved desperately, then suffered a malfunction at the last moment, and collided disastrously with the diffuse cloud. It dissolved into a flat ball of plasma.

"The rest of them are still out of sight beyond the gas giant," Gillian said. "After the chase from Kithrup, they'll think they know our dynamic, and never guess we could turn around like this!"

Tsh't looked less certain. "Perhapsss. We did fire off a decoy probe along our old flight path, mimicking our radiation. They *may* chase it.

"At least I'd be willing to bet they'll come in on a tight and fast hyperbolic-c."

"And we'll pick 'em off as they come!" Gillian felt a little giddy. There was just a chance they might be able to do it cleanly, so cleanly that they might be able to lie low, to wait a little longer for Hikahi and Creideiki. For another miracle.

Streaker groaned as she fought to change direction.

"Suessi says the wall braces are under stresss," Lucky Kaa reported. "He asks if you're going to be turning off stasis again, or pulling any other . . . uh, he calls them 'wild, crazy, female maneuvers.' His words, sssir!"

Gillian gave no answer. Suessi certainly didn't expect one.

Streaker completed her sharp turn and sped back the way she had come, just as two more battle cruisers came into view around the limb of the gas giant.

"Get 'em, Tsh't," Gillian told the dolphin officer. An outrage she had not allowed to show in weeks of frustration came out in her voice. "Use your own tactics. But *get* them!"

"Yesss!" Tsh't noted Gillian's balled fists. She felt it too. "Now!"

She whirled and called to the crew.

> * Patiently,
>   We took the insults—
> * Patiently,
>   Evil intent—
>
> * Now we stop,
>   Patient no longer—

> * *Dream and logic,*
> *Join in combat !!* *

The bridge crew cheered. *Streaker* dove toward the surprised foe.

116

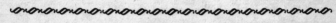

Galactics

The voice of the Soro matriarch growled out of the communications web. "Then we are in agreement to stop this chase and join our forces?"

The Tandu Stalker promised itself it would remove two legs, not one, for the shame of making this agreement.

"Yes," *it replied.* "If we continue in the present manner, we will only erode ourselves down to nothing. You Soro fight well, for vermin. Let us unite and end it."

Krat made it explicit. "We swear by Pact Number One, the oldest and most binding to be found in the Library, to capture the Earthlings together, to extract the information together, and to seek out together the emissaries of our ancestors, to let them be the judges of our dispute."

"Agreed," *the Tandu assented.* "Now let us finish here and turn about together to seize the prize."

117

∽∾∽∾∽∾∽∾∽∾∽∾∽∾∽∾∽∾∽∾∽∾∽∾∽∾∽

Takkata-Jim

He now understood what humans meant by a "Nantucket sleighride."

Takkata-Jim was tired. He had fled for what seemed like hours. Every time he tried to make the boat drift to one side, so he could surrender to one party, the other side fired salvos between him and his goal, forcing him back.

Then, some time ago, he detected a long chain of ships leaving Kithrup in the other direction. It didn't take much to figure out that *Streaker* was making her move.

It's over, then, he thought. *I tried to do my duty as I saw it, and save my own life at the same time. Now the die is cast. My plan is lost.*

I'm lost. There's nothing I can do except, maybe, buy Streaker *a few minutes.*

Some time ago the two fleets had stopped tearing at each other as they chased him. Takkata-Jim realized they were coming to an agreement.

Suddenly his receiver buzzed with a basic contact code in Galactic One. The message was simple . . . stop and surrender to the combined Tandu-Soro fleet.

Takkata-Jim clapped his jaws together. He hadn't a transmitter, so he couldn't respond. But if he stopped dead in space they would probably take that as a surrender.

He delayed until the message had been repeated three times. Then he began decreasing speed . . . but slowly. Very slowly, drawing out the time.

When the Galactics had drawn close, and their threats began to sound final, Takkata-Jim sighed and turned the longboat's fire-control computers back on.

443

The boat bucked as small missiles leaped away. He applied full thrust again.

When both flotillas simultaneously fired volleys of missiles at him, he tried to evade, of course. It would be unsporting to give up.

But he didn't have the heart for a major effort. Instead, while he waited, he worked on a poem.

> * *The saddest of things*
> *To a dolphin—even me—*
> *Is to die alone....* *

118

~~~~~~~~~~~~~~~~~~~~~~~~~~~~~~~~~~

Streaker

The ambush at the gas giant was unexpected. The enemy came in close, using the great planet's gravity to swing about in a tight hyperbolic turn. They were unprepared for an attack on their flanks.

Compared with their breakneck dive, *Streaker* was almost motionless. She fell upon the pair of cruisers as they passed, lacing a web-like tracery of antimatter in their paths.

One of the battleships blossomed into a fireball before *Streaker*'s computers could even identify it. Its screens were probably already damaged after weeks of battle.

The other cruiser was in better shape. Its screens flashed an ominous violet, and thin lines of exploding metal brightened its hull. But it passed through the trap and began decelerating furiously.

"It'll misss our mines, worse luck," Tsh't announced. "There wasn't time to lay a perfect pattern."

"We can't have everything," Gillian replied. "You handled that brilliantly. He'll be some time getting back to us."

Tsh't peered at the screen and listened to her neural link. "He may be *very* tardy, if his engines keep missssing. He's on a collision spiral with the planet!"

"Goody. Let's leave him and see about the others."

Streaker's motion was taking her away from the giant planet, toward another group of five onrushing cruisers. Having witnessed part of the ambush, these were all adjusting course furiously.

"Now we see how well the Trojan Seahorse works," Gillian said. "The first bunch was close enough to read our engines and know we're Earth-made. But these guys were too far back. Has Suessi altered our power output along Thennanin lines, as planned?"

Wattaceti whistled confirmation. "It's done. Suesssi says it'll cut efficiency, though. He reminds you that our engines aren't Thennanin."

"Thank him for me. Now, for all our lives, what happens next depends on whether they're an unimaginative lot, as Tom guessed they'd be.

"Full power to the psi shields!"

"Aye, sssir!"

Energy detectors lit up as the oncoming ships swept them with probe-beams. The motley assortment of approaching ET vessels seemed to hesitate, then diverged.

"Numbers one, four, and five are accelerating to pass us by!" Tsh't announced. The bridge was filled with chattering dolphin applause.

"What about the others?"

Tsh't's manipulator arm pointed to two dots in the holotank. "Decelerating and preparing for battle! We're picking up a beam-cast in Galactic Ten! It's a ritual challenge!"

Tsh't shook her head. "They *do* think we're Thennanin! But they want to stop and finish us off!"

"Who are they?"

"Brothers of the Night!"

The magnification screens showed the two approaching battlewagons, dark and deadly and growing nearer.

What to do? Gillian kept her face impassive. She knew the fen were watching her.

We can't outrun them, especially not while we're faking Thennanin engines or wearing this heavy Thennanin shell.

But only a fool would try to take them in a straight battle.

A fighting fool like Tom, she thought ironically. *Or Creideiki. If either of them were in command I'd be preparing condolence wreaths for the Brothers of the Night right now.*

"Gillian?" Tsh't asked nervously.

Gillian shook herself. *Now. Decide now!*

She looked at the approaching death machines.

"Down their throats," she said. "Head toward Kithrup."

119

Galactics

"We shall leave half of our joint fleet above the planet. None of the others will dare return, now that we have consolidated. We shall also send squadrons to clean the moons of hiding enemies, and to investigate the happenings out beyond the gas giant."

The Tandu Stalker had only four legs now, instead of the former six. The Soro, Krat, wondered what accident had befallen the leader of her unpleasant allies.

Not that it really mattered. Krat dreamt of the day when she could personally detach the Stalker's remaining limbs, and then all its head buds.

"Is it possible that that out-planet chaos may be caused by the quarry?" she asked.

The Tandu's expression was unreadable on the display screen. "All things are possible, even the impossible." It sounded like a Tandu truism. "But the quarry could not escape even the stragglers' small might. If they are captured by them, the remnants will fight over the spoils. When our task force arrives, we will take over. It is simple."

Krat nodded. It did sound elegant.

Soon, she told herself. Soon we will wring the information out of the Earthlings, or sift it out of their wreckage. And soon thereafter we will be before our ancestors themselves.

I must try to make certain some few of the humans and dolphins are left alive, after they tell us where the Progenitor Fleet is located. My clients do not appreciate it when I use them for entertainment. It would save trouble if I found amusements outside the family.

Wistfully, she longed for a scrappy male of her own species, as a joint Tandu-Soro detachment of thirteen ships blasted at full thrust toward the gas-giant planet.

120

Streaker

"Damage to the stasis flanges on the port ssside!" Wattaceti announced. "All missile slots in that sector are out!"

"Any harm to the inner hull?" Gillian asked anxiously.

The fin looked blank as he sounded out the damage control computer. "Nope. The Thennanin shell's taken it all, ssso far. But Suessi says the bracings are weakening!"

"They'll try to concentrate fire on the port side now that it'ss damaged," Tsh't said. "And they'll expect us to turn away. Starboard missile batteries! Fire mines at forty degrees azimuth by one hundred south! Slow thrust and lurk fuses!"

"But-t no one's there!"

"They *will* be! Fire! Helm, roll ship left two radians per minute, pitch up one per minute!"

Streaker shuddered and groaned as she turned slowly in space. Her screens flickered dangerously under powerful battle beams she could never hope to match. Not a blow had been struck on her opponents. They kept up easily with her lumbering attempts at evasion.

From *Streaker's* shadowed quarter six small missiles puffed lazily outward, then cut thrust. *Streaker* turned to try to protect her weakened side, a little more slowly than she was really capable of turning.

Sensing a fatal weakness, the enemy battleships followed the turn. Beams stabbed out to blast at *Streaker*'s damaged side, at what the Brothers of the Night thought was their supine enemy's real hull.

Streaker shook as the beams penetrated her shields and struck the Thennanin armor. Stasis flickered, giving them all eerily vivid feelings of déjà vu. Even in the water-filled bridge the blasts nearly threw the crew from their stations. Damage control spotters screamed reports of smoke and fire, of melting armor and buckling walls.

The cruisers drifted confidently into the mined region, and the missiles exploded.

Gillian clutched a handrail whitely. On those sensors that had not been blasted to vapor, the enemy was hidden by a cloud of roiling gas.

"Hard thrussst, twenty degrees by two seventy!" Tsh't called. "Stop roll and pitch!"

The abused engines struggled. The bracings holding *Streaker* to her armored shell groaned as she accelerated in a new direction.

"Blessings on that damned Thennanin armor!" One of the fins sighed. "Those beams would've sliced *Streaker* like toasssst!"

Gillian peered into one of the few operational holotanks, straining to see through the space-smoke and debris. Finally, she saw the enemy.

"A hit! A palpable hit!" she exulted.

One of the battlewagons bore a gaping hole in its side, burning metal still curled away from the cavity, and secondary explosions shook the cruiser.

The other one appeared undamaged, but more wary than before.

Oh, keep hesitating, she urged them silently. *Let us get a head start!*

"Anybody else around?" she asked Tsh't. If these two ships were the only ones left, she'd be willing to turn the engines back on full power, and let even the devil know they were an Earth ship!

The lieutenant blinked. "Yes, Gillian. Six more. Approaching rapidly." Tsh't shook her head. "There's no way we'll get away from this new bunch. They're coming too fasst. Sorry, Gillian."

"The Brothers have made up their minds," Wattaceti announced. "They're coming after uss!"

Tsh't rolled her eyes. Gillian silently agreed. *We won't fool them again.*

"Suessi calls. He wants to know ifff. . ."

Gillian sighed. "Tell Hannes there don't seem to be any more 'female tricks' forthcoming. I'm fresh out of ideas."

The two battleships drew nearer, chasing *Streaker's* stern. They held their fire, saving it for a total assault.

Gillian thought about Tom. She couldn't help feeling that she had failed him.

It really was a good plan, hon. I only wish I'd executed it competently for you.

The enemy bore down on them, looming ominously.

Then Lucky Kaa shouted. "Vector change!" The pilot's tail thrashed. "They're veering offff! Fleeing like mullet-t!"

Gillian blinked in confusion. "But they had us!"

"It's the newcomers, Gillian! Those six oncoming shipsss!" Tsh't shouted joyfully.

"What? What *about* them?"

Tsh't grinned as broadly as a neo-fin could manage. "They're *Thennanin*! They're coming in blassting! And it'sss not *us* they're shooting at!"

The screens showed the pair of cruisers that had been chasing them, now in full flight, firing Parthian style at the approaching mini-flotilla.

Gillian laughed. "Wattaceti! Tell Suessi to shut down! Put everything on idle and pour out smoke. We want to play the gravely wounded soldier!"

After a moment came the engineer's reply.

"Suessi says that that-t will be no problem. No problem at all."

∾∾∾∾∾∾∾∾∾∾∾∾∾∾∾∾∾∾∾∾∾∾∾∾∾

121

Galactics

Buoult's crest riffled with waves of emotion. Krondorsfire lay ahead of them, battered but proud. He had thought the old battlewagon lost since the first day of the battle, and Baron Ebremsev, its commander. Buoult longed to see his old comrade again.

"Is there still no response?" he asked the communicator.

"No, Commander. The ship is silent. It is possible they just now sustained a fatal blow that…Wait! there is something! A flashing-light signal in uncoded open-talk! They are sending from one of the viewing ports!"

Buoult edged forward eagerly. "What do they say? Do they require help?"

The communications officer huddled before his monitor, watching the winking lights, jotting notes.

"All weapons and communications destroyed," he recited, "life support and auxiliary drives still serviceable…Earthlings ahead, chased by a few dregs … We shall withdraw … happy hunting … Krondorsfire out."

Buoult thought the message a little odd. Why would Ebremsev want to pull out if he could still follow and at least draw fire from the enemy?

Perhaps he was making a brave show in order not to hold them back. Buoult was about to insist on sending aid anyway when the communications officer spoke again.

"Commander! A squadron is outbound from the water planet! At least ten vessels! I read signs of both Tandu and Soro!"

Buoult's crest momentarily collapsed. It had come to pass, the very last alliance of heretics.

"We have one chance! After the fugitives at once! We can overpower the remnants even as they overpower the Earthlings, and be off before the Tandu and Soro arrive!"

As his ship leapt outward, he had a message sent back to Krondorsfire. "*May the Great Ghosts dwell with you. . . .*"

122

∞∞∞∞∞∞∞∞∞∞∞∞∞∞∞∞∞

Streaker

"That's a pretty sophisticated little computer you've kept hidden away all this time," Tsh't commented.

Gillian smiled. "It's actually Tom's."

The fins nodded wisely. That was explanation enough.

Gillian thanked the Niss machine for its hurry-up Thennanin translation. The disembodied voice whispered from a cluster of sparkles that floated near her, dancing and whirling amidst the fizzing oxywater bubbles.

"I could do nothing else, Gillian Baskin," it replied. "You few lost Earthlings have accumulated, in the course of heaping disasters upon yourselves, more data than my masters have gathered in the last thousand years. The lessons about uplift alone will profit the Tymbrimi, who are always willing to learn—even from wolflings."

The voice faded, and the sparkles vanished before Gillian could reply.

"The signal party's returned from the viewport, Gillian," Tsh't said. "The Thennanin have gone off chasing our shadows, but they'll be back. What-t do we do now?"

Gillian felt tremors of adrenalin reaction. She had not planned beyond this point. There was only one thing she wanted desperately to do now. Only one destination in the universe she wanted to go.

"Kithrup," she whispered.

Gillian shook herself. "Kithrup?" She looked at Tsh't,

knowing what the answer would be, but wishing it weren't so.

Tsh't shook her sleek head. "There'sss a flotilla orbiting Kithrup now, Gillian. No fighting. There must've been a winner in the big battle.

"Another squadron's heading this way fassst. A big one. We don't want 'em to get close enough to see through our disguise."

Gillian nodded. Her voice didn't want to function, but she made the words come.

"North," she said.

"Take us out along Galactic north, Tsh't . . . to the transfer point. Full speed. When we get close enough, we'll dump the Seahorse, and get the Ifni-damned hell out of here with . . . with the ashes we've won."

The dolphins returned to their posts. The rumble of the engines gathered strength.

Gillian swam to one dark corner of the crystal dome, to a place where there was a chink in the Thennanin armor, where she could look at the stars directly.

Streaker picked up speed.

123

Galactics

The Tandu-Soro detachment was gaining on the strung-out fugitives.

"Mistress, a crippled Thennanin is approaching the transfer point on an escape trajectory."

Krat squirmed on her cushion and snarled. "So? Casualties have left the battle area before. All sides try to evacuate their wounded. Why do you bother me when we are even now closing in!"

The little Pila detector officer scuttled back into its cubbyhole. Krat bent to watch her forward screens.

A small squadron of Thennanin struggled to keep ahead. Further on, at the edge of detection, sparks of desultory battle showed that the leaders were still bickering, even as they closed on the quarry.

What if they're mistaken, Krat wondered. *We chase the Thennanin, who chase the remnants, who chase what? Those fools might even be chasing each other!*

It didn't matter. Half the Tandu-Soro fleet orbited Kithrup, so the Earthlings were trapped, one way or another.

We'll deal with the Tandu in good time, she thought, and meet the ancient ones alone.

"Mistress!" the Pila shouted shrilly. "There is a transmission from the transfer point!"

"*Bother me one more time with inconsequentials...*" she rumbled, flexing her mating claw threateningly. But the client interrupted her! The Pil dared to interrupt!

"Mistress. It is the Earth ship! They taunt us! They defy us! They..."

"Show me!" Krat hissed. "It must be a trick! Show me at once!"

The Pil ducked back into its section. On Krat's main screen appeared the holo image of a man, and several dolphins. From the man's shape, Krat could tell it was a female, probably their leader.

"*...stupid creatures unworthy of the name 'sophonts.' Foolish, pre-sentient upspring of errant masters. We slip away from all your armed might, laughing at your clumsiness! We slip away as we always will, you pathetic creatures. And now that we have a real head start, you'll never catch us! What better proof that the Progenitors favor not you, but us! What better proof...*"

The taunt went on. Krat listened, enraged, yet at the same time savoring the artistry of it. *These men are better than I'd thought. Their insults are wordy and overblown, but they have talent. They deserve honorable, slow deaths.*

"Mistress! The Tandu with us are changing course! Their other ships are leaving Kithrup for the transfer point!"

Krat hissed in despair. "After them! After them at once! We followed them through space this far. The chase only goes on!"

The crew bent to their tasks resignedly. The Earth ship was in a good position to escape. Even at best this would be a long chase.

Krat realized that she would never make it home in time for mating. She would die out here.

On her screen, the man continued to taunt them.

"Librarian!" she called. "I do not understand some of the man's words. Find out what that phrase—Nyaahh nyaaah—means in their beastly wolfling tongue!"

124

Tom Orley

Crosslegged on a woven mat of reeds, shaded by a floating wreck, he listened as a muttering volcano slowly sputtered into silence. Contemplating starvation, he listened to the soft, wet sounds of the endless weedscape, and found in them a homely beauty. The squishy, random rhythms blended into a backdrop for his meditation.

On the mat in front of him, like a focus mandala, lay the message bomb he had never set off. The container glistened in the sunlight of north Kithrup's first fine day in weeks. Highlights shone in dimpled places where the metal had been battered, as he had been. The dented surface gleamed still.

Where are you now?

The subsurface sea-waves made his platform undulate gently. He floated in a trance through levels of awareness, like an old man poking idly through his attic, like an old-time hobo looking with mild curiosity through the slats of a moving boxcar.

Where are you now, my love?

He recalled a Japanese haiku from the eighteenth century, by the great poet Yosa Buson.

As the spring rains fall,
Soaking in them, on the roof,
Is a child's rag ball.

Watching blank images in the dents on the psi-globe, he listened to the creaking of the flat jungle—its skittering little animal sounds—the wind riffling through the wet, flat leaves.

Where is that part of me that has departed?

He listened to the slow pulse of a world ocean, watched patterns in the metal, and after a while, in the reflections in the dents and creases, an image came to him.

A blunt, bulky, wedge shape approached a place that was a *not-place*, a shining blackness in space. As he watched, the bulky thing cracked open. The thick carapace slowly split apart, like a hatching egg. The shards fell away, and there remained a slender nubbed cylinder, looking a bit like a caterpillar. Around it glowed a nimbus, a thickening shell of probability that hardened even as he watched.

No illusion, he decided. It cannot be an illusion.

He opened himself to the image, accepting it. And from the caterpillar a thought winged to him.

Blossoms on the pear
and a woman in the moonlight
reads a letter there....

His slowly healing lips hurt as he smiled. It was another haiku by Buson. Her message was as unambiguous as could be, under the circumstances. She had somehow picked up his trance-poem, and responded in kind.

"*Jill...*" he cast as hard as he could.

The caterpillar shape, sheathed in a cocoon of stasis, approached the great hole in space. It dropped forward toward the *not-place*, grew transparent as it fell, then vanished.

For a long time Tom sat very still, watching the highlights on the metal globe slowly shift as the morning passed.

Finally, he decided it wouldn't do him or the universe any harm if he started doing something about survival.

125

The Skiff

"Between you two crazy males, have you come any closer to figuring out what he'sss talking about?"

Keepiru and Sah'ot just stared back at Hikahi. They turned back to their discussion without answering her, huddling with Creideiki, trying to interpret the captain's convoluted instructions.

Hikahi rolled her eyes and turned to Toshio. "You'd think they'd include me in these seances of theirs. After all, Creideiki and I are mates!"

Toshio shrugged. "Creideiki needs Sah'ot's language skill and Keepiru's ability as a pilot. But you saw their faces. They're halfway into the Whale Dream right now. We can't afford to have you that way while you're in command."

"Hmmmph." Hikahi spumed, only slightly mollified. "I suppose you've finished the inventory, Toshio?"

"Yes, sir." He nodded. "I have a written list ready. We're well enough stocked in consumables to last to the first transfer point, and at least one beyond that. Of course, we're in the middle of nowhere, so we'll need at least *five* transfer jumps to get anywhere near civilization. Our charts are pitifully inadequate, our drives will probably fail over the long haul, and few ships our size have even taken transfer points successfully. Aside from all that, and the cramped living quarters, I think we're all right."

Hikahi sighed. "We can't lose anything by trying. At leasst the Galactics are gone."

"Yeah," he agreed. "It was a nice stroke, Gillian taunting the Eatees from the transfer point. It let us know they got away, and got the Eatees off our backs."

"Don't say 'Eatees,' Toshio. It'ss not polite. You may offend some nice Kanten or Linten one day if you get into the habit."

Toshio swallowed and ducked his head. No matter where or when, no lieutenant had ever been known to slacken off on a middie. "Yes, sir," he said.

Hikahi grinned and flicked a small splash of water on the youth with her lower jaw.

> * *Duty, duty*
> > *Brave shark-biter*
> * *What reward*
> > *Could taste better?* *

Toshio blushed and nodded.

The skiff started to move again. Keepiru was back in the pilot's saddle. Creideiki and Sah'ot chattered excitedly in a semi-Primal rhythm which still sent shivers down Hikahi's spine. And Sah'ot had said that Creideiki was toning it down on purpose!

She was still getting used to the idea that Creideiki's injury might have been a door opening, rather than a closing.

The skiff lifted from the sea and began to speed eastward, following Creideiki's hunch.

"What about passenger morale?" Hikahi asked Toshio.

"Well, I guess it's all right. That pair of Kiqui are happy so long as they're with Dennie. And Dennie's happy . . . well, she's happy enough for now."

Hikahi was amused. Why should the youth be embarrassed about Dennie's other preoccupation? She was glad the two young humans had each other, as she had Creideiki.

In spite of his new, eerie side, Creideiki was the same dolphin. The newness was something he used, something he seemed only to have begun exploring. He could hardly speak, but he conveyed his great intellect—and his caring—in other ways.

"What about Charlie?" she asked Toshio.

Toshio sighed. "He's still embarrassed."

They had found the chimp a day after the great earthquakes, clinging to a floating tree-trunk, sopping wet. He had been unable to speak for ten hours, and had kept climbing the walls in the skiff's tiny hold until he finally calmed down.

Charlie finally admitted that he had scrambled to the top of a tall tree just before the island blew. It had saved his life, but the stereotype mortified him.

Toshio and Hikahi crowded in behind Keepiru's station and watched as the ocean rolled swiftly beneath the skiff. For minutes at a time the sea turned a brilliant green as they passed over great swatches of vine. The little boat sped toward the sun.

They had been searching for almost a week, ever since *Streaker* had departed.

First found had been Toshio, swimming purposefully westward, never giving up. Then Dennie had led them to another island where there was a tribe of Kiqui. While she negotiated another treaty, they searched for and found Charles Dart.

Takkata-Jim's *Stenos* were all missing or dead.

After that had come one last, and apparently forlorn, search. They had been at this last phase for several days now.

Hikahi was about to give up. They couldn't go on wasting time and consumables like this. Not with the journey they had ahead of them.

Not that they really had much of a chance. No one had ever heard of a voyage like they planned. A cross-Galactic journey in the skiff would make Captain Bligh's epic crossing of the Pacific in the *Bounty*'s longboat seem like an afternoon jaunt.

She kept her appraisal to herself, though. Creideiki and Keepiru probably understood what lay ahead of them. Toshio seemed to have guessed part of it already. There was no reason to inform the others until they had to cut the rations for the fourth time.

She sighed.

> * *Of what else*
>   *Are heroes made*
> * *Than men and women*
>   *Who, like us,*
> * *Try—* *

Keepiru's fluting call of triumph was like a shrill trumpet. He squawled and tossed on his platform. The skiff rolled left and right in a wiggle-waggle, then went into a screaming climb.

"What the f—!!" Toshio stopped himself. "Holy jumping turtle-fish, Keepiru! What *is* it?"

Hikahi used a harness arm to grab a wall stanchion, and looked out a port. She sighed for a third time, long and deep.

The smoke from his fire momentarily hid the boat from sight. The first he knew of it was the sonic boom that rolled over him, nearly knocking over his drying racks.

The human standing on the woven reed mat almost dove for cover, but a hunch made him stop and look up instead.

His eyes were sun-squinted. Crow's-feet that had not been there a few weeks before lay at the corners. His beard was black with thin gray flecks. It had grown out and nearly stopped itching. It almost covered a ragged scar that ran down one cheek.

Shading his eyes, he recognized the wild maneuvers before he did the outlines of the tiny ship. It streaked high into the sky and looped about, coming back to screech past him again.

He reached out to steady the drying racks against the thunder. No sense in letting the meat go to waste. It had taken a lot of work to harvest it, strip it, and prepare it. They might need it for the voyage ahead.

He wasn't sure how the fen would take to the stuff, but it was nourishing . . . the only food on the planet that an Earthling could eat.

Gubru jerky, Tandu strips, and flayed Episiarch would never make it into haute cuisine, of course. But perhaps they were an acquired taste.

He grinned and waved as Keepiru finally calmed down enough to bring the skiff to a halt nearby.

How could I ever have doubted he'd still be alive? Hikahi wondered, joyfully. *Gillian said he had to live. None of the Galactics could ever touch him. How* could *they?*

And why, in the wide universe, was I ever worried about getting home?

Epilog

: Rest : Rest And Listen :
: Rest And Listen And Learn, Creideiki :
: For The Startide Rises :
: In The Currents Of The Dark :
: And We Have Waited Long, For What Must Be :

Postscript

෴෴෴෴෴෴෴෴෴෴෴෴෴

Dolphin names often sound as if they are Polynesian or Japanese. In some cases this is true. In general, however, the neo-fin chooses for a name a sound he likes, usually a polysyllabic word with strong alternating vowels and consonants.

In Anglic, the words "man," "men," and "mankind" apply to humans without reference to gender. On those occasions when gender is important, a female human is refered to as a "fem," and a male human as a "mel."

Dolphin languages are the author's invention, and are not meant to represent the communication of natural dolphins and whales today. We are only beginning to understand the place of the cetaceans in the world, as we are just beginning to understand our own.

The author wishes to thank all those who helped with this work, with their advice and criticism and encouragement, especially Mark Grygier, Anita Everson, Patrick Maher, Rick and Pattie Harper, Ray Feist, Richard Spahl, Tim LaSelle, Ethan Munson, and, as always, Dan Brin. Lou Aronica and Tappan King of Bantam Books were most helpful with encouragement when morale was lowest.

The translated haiku by Yosa Buson were from *An Anthology of Japanese Literature*, compiled and edited by Donald Keene, published by Grove Press.

The world's many paths diverge, in both reality and imagination. The creatures of this novel are all fanciful. But it may happen that some of our fellow mammals will one day be our partners. We owe it to that possible future to let their potential survive.

—DAVID BRIN

August 1982

ABOUT THE AUTHOR

DAVID BRIN was born in 1950 in southern California. He has been an engineer with Hughes Aircraft Co., and attended Caltech and the University of California at San Diego, where he completed doctoral studies on comets and asteroids. He is presently a consultant with the California Space Institute, a unit of the University of California, San Diego, doing advanced studies concerning the space shuttle and space science. He also teaches university physics and occasionally creative writing.

Twice nominated for the Hugo and John W. Campbell awards, Brin won the Hugo and Nebula awards for best novel for *Startide Rising*. He is the author of two other novels, *Sundiver* and *The Practice Effect*. He is presently at work on several novels, including a collaboration with Nebula Award-winning author Gregory Benford.

The long-awaited new novel from
Hugo and Nebula Award-Winning Author

DAVID BRIN
THE POSTMAN

Here is the powerful story of a post-holocaust
United States, a shattered country slipping into a
new dark age—until one man, Gordon Krantz,
offers new hope for the future . . . using a symbol
from the vanished past.

THE POSTMAN—available November 1985 in
hardcover wherever Bantam Spectra Books are
sold.

SPECIAL
MONEY SAVING
OFFER

Now you can have an up-to-date listing of Bantam's hundreds of titles plus take advantage of our unique and exciting bonus book offer. A special offer which gives you the opportunity to purchase a Bantam book for only 50¢. Here's how!

By ordering any five books at the regular price per order, you can also choose any other single book listed (up to a $4.95 value) for just 50¢. Some restrictions do apply, but for further details why not send for Bantam's listing of titles today!

Just send us your name and address plus 50¢ to defray the postage and handling costs.

SAMUEL R. DELANY

Hailed by *The New York Times* as "the most interesting writer of science fiction writing in English today," this Hugo and four-time Nebula Award-winning author is one of SF's most insightful and dazzling talents.